THE
DARK
WEB

CHRISTOPHER LOWERY

URBANE

urbanepublications.com

THE
DARK
WEB

**Book 3 in the
African Diamonds Trilogy**

A NOVEL BY

CHRISTOPHER LOWERY

First published in Great Britain in 2018
by Urbane Publications Ltd
Suite 3, Brown Europe House,
33/34 Gleaming Wood Drive,
Chatham,
Kent ME5 8RZ

A CIP catalogue record for this book is
available from the BritishLibrary.

ISBN 978-1-911583-22-6
EPUB 978-1-911583-23-3
MOBI 978-1-911583-24-0

Design and Typeset by
Chandler Book Design

Cover by Julie Martin

Printed and bound by 4edge UK

URBANE
urbanepublications.com

Dedicated to my amazing wife, Marjorie

and our beautiful daughter,
Kerry-Jane.

Timeo Danaos et dona ferentes –
I fear the Greeks, even when they bear gifts.

Virgil; The Aeneid, 29 – 19 BC

THE DARK WEB
GLOSSARY OF TERMS

BIP	Banque International de Paris,
BPE	Bishop Private Equity
Lee-Win	Lee-Win Micro-Technology, Shanghai
XPC	XPlus Circuits, its Dubai subsidiary
UNSC	United Nations Security Council
IGIS	Institute for Global Internet Security
PE	Private Equity Investment
Botulism	A neurotoxin, poison formed by the *Clostridium Botulinum* organism
CPU	Central Processing Unit, a mini-computer managing a piece of equipment
Processor/Micro-Processor	A tiny silicon card containing hundreds of millions of CPU instruction cells
Firmware	Software programmes/instructions built into a processor
Flash Drive	Memory stick for copying data from a computer
ACRE	Automatic Constant Recurring Encryption
MARK VII	Lee-Win's latest micro-processor
A2	A malicious cell inserted onto a silicone card to provide a hacking entry point
Upgrade	New version of previous software technology
Upload	Distribution of software technology over the Internet
Download	Reception of software over the Internet and implementation by users

Web Network	Pieces of equipment linked by any kind of wireless connectivity
M2M - IoT	Internet of Things – Remote and Machine to Machine communication
The Cloud	Remote computing equipment made available to users over the Internet
Connectivity Module	Unit in a micro-processor which permits wireless connectivity
Hub	A powerful wireless transmitter capable of distributing information over the Internet
CAD, CAM	Computer aided design, Computer aided machines
Time Differences	London GMT: Dubai +3, USEC – 5, USWC -8, Hong Kong/Shanghai +7, Europe, SA +1, Moscow +2

INTRODUCTION

The list of names in the Internet Hall of Fame is long: Licklider, Kleinrock, MIT, Defence Advanced Research Projects Agency, Kahn, Cerf, UCLA, Santa Barbara and Utah Universities, Roberts, Stanford Research Institute, Tomlinson, Kirstein, Crocker, Mockapetris, Metcalfe, Dalal, Sunshine, Berners Lee, Wales, Zenndström, Frijs, Zuckerberg. Just a few of the thousands who contributed to its creation, development and global commercialisation.

These brilliant visionaries, scientists, engineers and governments worked with one common and praiseworthy objective: to give the world a valuable and useful tool to facilitate global communication and learning and to create unity. That is the reason for the name, *Internet Protocol*, the etiquette of connecting to a global communications network.

Then, as in the case of every discovery or invention introduced for the benefit of mankind, evil minds exploited their creation, with totally different and less altruistic motives. Thus was born the Internet of today, with its litany of examples of the worst of mankind's inventions, corruption, perversion, fraud, terrorism, hatred, pornography and worse, unfettered and uncontrolled. A Dark Web of depravity hidden in a Cloud behind an anonymous, invisible façade, ready to be unleashed on the naive and unsuspecting world at the press of a button.

As Virgil wrote, two millennia before the birth of Christ, describing the treachery of the Greeks who infiltrated their soldiers into Troy, hidden in a massive wooden horse presented as a gift: 'I fear the Greeks, even when they bear gifts'.

But Virgil was writing about a wooden horse, not the Internet.

PROLOGUE

Shanghai, People's Republic of China
Monday, 9 July 2012

'That man from the syndicate called again, that's the fifth time since we turned them away.' Madame Xiu Lee-Win poured a glass of green tea for her husband.

'What did you say?'

'The same as every time they came and every time they've called, "The company is not for sale, please stop pestering us".'

'I don't understand their obsession with our business,' Chongkun Lee-Win sipped his tea. 'There's dozens of microprocessor companies around just as good as ours. If they've got the kind of money they say, they can take their pick. Just keep refusing, dearest, and they'll finally realise we won't change our minds.'

'I suppose so, but I'm tired of answering the phone and hearing that man's voice. And he said a peculiar thing before he rang off this time.'

'And that was?'

'He said, "I think it's time to convince you to sell".'

'I don't know how they'd do that. They've already offered a fair price. Don't worry about it, just ignore them and they'll go away.'

'You're right, I'll stop answering the phone. I'll get the Filipino girl to answer in Spanish, that'll put them off. Anyway, how was your day?'

'Excellent. We just got the second quarter results and they're very good, we're ten per cent ahead of revenue forecasts with two per cent gross margin improvement. We can afford to continue to invest in our development programmes without worrying about cash flow.'

'You're talking about the ACRE project, aren't you? How's it coming along?'

'We're making good progress; Han and I were reviewing the latest test results this afternoon. I think we're still a year or two from perfecting it, but you know how long it takes to transform a concept into a working solution.'

She wagged a finger fondly at him. 'You'd better deliver it soon or you'll be embarrassed in front of the world. Remember? I told you not to authorise those press releases last year. "Announcing ACRE, The Ultimate Level of Encrypted Transmission from Lee-Win Micro-Technology". You could be prosecuted under the Trade Descriptions Act.'

Her husband laughed and kissed her cheek. 'Nonsense. It was a smart move, it brought us lots of publicity and new customers. They're all waiting for ACRE and we'll get there in the end. It's just a matter of time and money and the breakthrough will come, you'll see.'

'Yes, it certainly is. According to the cost summary I saw on your desk, we've invested over $40 million since you came up with the concept two years ago. And you were sixty years old last month, are you going to follow that dream into retirement?'

'It's not just a dream, Xiu. ACRE is much more than that. Do you remember how we pioneered the change in the concept of CPUs and microprocessors back in the eighties? Now we're going to do the same thing for encrypted transmission. I forecast that five years from now, Automatic Constant Recurring Encryption will be the de facto system of protecting and transmitting data all over the world.'

'If you say so, darling. You can keep up the project, just don't stress about it constantly, or it will be the death of you.'

Thursday, 26 July 2012

It was six-thirty on a dark, rainy morning when Chongkun climbed into his white 2009 Volkswagen Golf. Although he had a chauffeur and several other cars, including a 1999 Rolls Royce Silver Spirit Mark IV, he preferred to weave through the traffic in the little saloon and drop it in the employees' parking lot behind the Lee-Win building in Pudong, leaving the luxury travel for his wife. The sky was black with heavy rainclouds, and he strained to see through the windscreen wipers as he drove slowly along the street lit up by the headlights of the passing cars. Their colonial-style town house in the Jing'an area was about fifteen kilometres from the office, on the other side of the Huangpu River. Chongkun would meet their two sons, Junjie and Jiang, for a coffee before work and chat over the day's programme. Both were married and worked with him in the microprocessor business, as heads of finance and marketing respectively. Although the family owned several other companies involved in manufacturing and commerce, he loved the challenge of the continual innovations in the world of the Internet, often led by Lee-Win under his stewardship.

Chongkun always took the same route to work. Experience had taught him it involved the fewest hold-ups, and the trip took less than thirty minutes at that time in the morning. He made his way to the Fuxing East Road to cross the river by the tunnel and then come down Century Avenue to the business park. At the roundabout near the Xiao Taoyuan Qingzhensi Mosque, the cars were bunched up, nervous drivers waiting for a gap to enter the traffic. As Chongkun inched his car forward, a massive black Hummer pulled alongside him on the right and a green Ford saloon came up on his left side, moving to the inside lane of the roundabout. The Hummer also moved ahead and he drove slowly out with it, protected by the saloon on his left. Suddenly he felt a soft impact from behind and the Golf was pushed several metres forward, onto the roundabout. He jammed his foot on the brake and looked in the rear-view mirror. An old red Land Rover had run into the back of his car. The Ford on his left had stopped, and he looked past it to see a Tsingtao Beer truck bearing directly down on him. The Hummer had also stopped on his right, and he pushed the throttle flat to the floor to try to get past it and over the roundabout.

The fully loaded lorry smashed into the Golf, pushing it into the Hummer. The little car was crushed to half its size, with Chongkun inside. It took the firemen three hours to extricate his dead body from the wreckage. The Land Rover had disappeared from the scene. In the dark, pouring rain no one was sure what had happened and why he had driven into the path of the truck.

The verdict of the inquest was accidental death, but his heartbroken widow didn't believe it. In October, she sold Lee-Win Micro-Technology to the syndicate for twenty per cent less than their original offer, and the Lee-Win family left Shanghai and settled in Macau.

Xiu Lee-Win's prophesy had proved to be accurate, but not for the reasons she supposed.

ONE

Dubai, United Arab Emirates
March 2017

'Decider! Two clear points. My serve.'

'Hang on. I need a minute.' 'Scotty' Fitzgerald opened the door of the squash court and grabbed his bottle of water. He took a swig and wiped his face with his towel. 'Shit! It must be a hundred degrees in here.' It was seven in the evening, but the court was like an oven.

'It's hot. Even I'm feeling it.' His colleague, Sharif Kayani, took a swallow from his bottle and poured the rest over his shaved head, drying off with his T-shirt. They went back onto the court and he took up his serving position. 'Right. Time to show you who's in charge.'

Sharif served from the right box; a sliced forehand, coming off the left side of the front wall so the ball spun down towards the floor of the left quarter. Scotty took it on the volley with a swipe towards the right wall, ricocheting off the front and coming back to the left, behind him. The other man stepped quickly across and smashed it against the back wall, so it rebounded directly onto the service area. Scotty sliced it softly back against the front wall and it died onto the floor before Sharif could retrieve it.

'Who did you say was in charge?' Scotty gave a condescending smile as he took up his serving position on the left. 'Winning point coming up.'

Fifteen minutes later, the men were towelling off in the shower room of the enormous underground sports facility below the XPlus Circuits building in the Dubai Investments Park. The Park was home to many high-tech businesses with a presence in the fast-growing industrial centre of the Emirates, and the facilities available to employees were legendary. Each floor of the four-storey edifice had an area of 1,000 square metres, with two basement levels housing not only the computer network centre and test labs, but squash and badminton courts, snooker, swimming pool, a cycling track and a fabulously well-equipped gymnasium.

Scotty was actually a Welshman, born in Cardiff, previously a software development manager for a US telecoms company. His parents had moved to the US when he was a child, and after obtaining his degree in Computer Sciences at Princeton he'd joined Verizon's IoT, Internet of Things, development team in Silicon Valley. He was an acknowledged leader in encryption technology and was headhunted by Lee-Win Micro-Technology, one of China's largest manufacturers of microprocessors, routers and microchips, when they allocated a billion dollars to create a new design centre to support their Shanghai manufacturing unit.

The new centre was set up in a separate entity, XPC, in Dubai. The owners of Lee-Win were smart enough to know they could attract the very best industry talent to Dubai more easily than to Shanghai. XPC had opened two and a half years previously, having been built in just eighteen months while an intensive recruitment programme was initiated to poach these experienced professionals from around the world. Not only in traditional fixed machine technology, where Lee-Win had several billions of products installed throughout the world, but also in the booming mobile IoT sector, where they enjoyed a fast-growing share. Sharif had been brought from Lahore, Pakistan, with his entire team of programmers and Daniel Oberhart, Senior VP of Operations and Support, was bribed from Zurich, Switzerland, where he had been Director of Operations for MicroCentral SA, a fast-growing competitor in the global processor industry.

Scotty and Sharif were both VPs of Product Software Development in the corporate hierarchy, although the Welshman wasn't impressed by the title. He disliked the American habit of calling just about everyone a vice president, making middle-range jobs sound more important than they were. His team developed new and improved firmware, the software which was embedded in all Lee-Win processors, and Sharif's Asian colleagues designed the physical hardware itself, the tiny silicon cards that contained the printed circuits. Lee-Win had been in the processor business for forty years and had earned an international reputation for their products, specifically designed for huge industrial conglomerates, government departments and essential service providers.

At the moment, Scotty and Sharif were both under pressure to deliver their upgrades for Lee-Win's Mark VII line of products by the end of July, to meet the 1 September launch date in Shanghai; less than six months from now. The launch would feature a new version of ACRE, an innovation that had first been incorporated in the Mark VI models the previous year. The invention had been conceived in Shanghai and developed by a separate team at XPC, managed by Scotty.

The full name of ACRE was Automatic Constant Random Encryption, a revolutionary technology whereby data was automatically and continuously encrypted in a random fashion, while it was stored in computer files, in databases or on smart cards and, vitally, while it was being transmitted, since the programme also took over the data transmission management through the network. ACRE made data hacking valueless unless the culprits had access to the algorithms produced during the encryption process. Even if they succeeded in capturing data, it would be meaningless and impossible to reconfigure into coherent information, because unlike conventional systems, there was no key available to de-encrypt it.

After many years of increasingly addictive and pervasive social media, Internet commerce, online banking, mobile apps and all their apparent advantages, the true cost of sending personal information across the ether was becoming more and more apparent. Hardly a day went by without another high-profile hacking or data theft occurrence making headlines. Global deployment of ACRE would revolutionise the way data was stored and transmitted, creating the security needed by Internet users around the globe and making the world a safer and more secure place. And the financial rewards to Lee-Win would be beyond measure.

Although the software that Scotty's team had written to control the encryption algorithms was not yet in its perfected stage, many Lee-Win customers had agreed to live-test the new technology when the Mark VI devices were released, and the reception had been overwhelmingly positive. The uproar in the marketplace was such that sales of Mark VI products had exploded, and especially to the large private and public service institutions where Lee-Win's processor units handled billions of pieces of ultra-confidential information every minute of every day. Governments, banks, energy companies, institutions of every kind, were finding, once and for all, the protection they had long sought against invasions of their valuable data.

Now the market was waiting impatiently to see if they could keep it up with Mark VII, and the pressure to meet their deadline was weighing heavily on the two men. The stakes Lee-Win was playing for were enormous, and Scotty and Sharif were key players in this poker game. With the responsibility of delivering the next level of ACRE technology, Scotty especially knew his head was on the block.

The Welshman pulled on his light cotton slacks and combed his tangled hair. 'Winner's choice. Let's go to the Crystal Lagoon for a Thai salad, it's too hot for anything else.'

'Cool. The meal's on me and the beer's on you.' Sharif sat on the bench to tie up his canvas shoes and his sports bag fell to the floor. A small object clattered from the bag as it landed upside down.

'What's that?' Scotty picked up the tube-like device. 'It's a memory stick.' He gave the Pakistani a look. 'You know we're not allowed to take them off the premises,' he said, exercising his seniority over the other man.

'Oh, that. It's not really mine. Just some family photos and music my brother sent me from Lahore the other day. We can't get music like that here. Come round to my place sometime and I'll play it for you, you'll love it. Thanks.' He went to take the device from Scotty's hand, ignoring his querulous look.

He held on to the stick. 'I'm not comfortable with this, Sharif. Nothing personal, but we're doing billion-dollar development work, we've got rules and we all have to obey them. I think I'd better look after this until Tom or Shen get back. If they're OK with it, I'll give it back and we'll forget the whole thing. I won't look at it, so if it's family stuff, no harm done. OK?'

'No problem, Scotty, we'll talk to Shen next week. Right, let's take my car and I'll run you back later to get yours. Come on.'

Driving over to the restaurant, Scotty was turning the matter over in his mind. *Why would Sharif have a memory stick containing family material in his sports bag?* They had come down to the squash courts directly from the office, there would be no reason to have that stick at work. *He said it was sent to him 'the other day', so why would he have it with him at all?* Their boss, Shen Fu Liáng, who had been parachuted in from Shanghai as Executive VP of Operations, was in San Francisco for an industry trade show all week. Scotty could have called him, but he had little respect for the Chinaman. He habitually sided with Sharif on matters which were in the Welshman's domain, ignoring his knowledge and experience, sometimes with costly consequences. There was also no point in talking to Daniel Oberhart, since he was involved in operations and not the development group.

He decided to let the matter drop for the moment, their working relationship was too important to be jeopardised by what was probably a trivial event. He would wait to talk with Tom Connor, the company CEO, when he returned from holiday that weekend, and leave him to sort it out with Liáng and Sharif. Tom habitually left the development division pretty much alone, concentrating on his commercial responsibilities in marketing, operations and finance. It was a compliment to the standard of his and Sharif's work, but now he figured he needed to talk to the big boss on Sunday. He had to keep reminding himself that in the Middle East, the weekend consisted of Friday and Saturday, although many of the staff worked on Saturday. In the meantime, he tried to put it out of his mind; it wasn't his area of concern after all.

TWO

Dubai, United Arab Emirates
March 2017

'Hi, guys. You're in early.' Daniel Oberhart and Sharif were on their second coffee when the Welshman joined them in the canteen at seven the next morning. They were deep in conversation, talking quietly with their heads close together.

Sharif looked up with a start, 'Oh, hi, Scotty. We've got a full programme of tests today, just making sure Daniel can fit it all in.' He shifted nervously on his chair and checked the time on his mobile. 'I'd better get up there and make sure everything's ready. I'll catch you later. Don't forget our revenge match tonight.' He walked quickly past him and out the door.

The Swiss man said, 'I was up at five o'clock, it's too hot to sleep. In Zurich in March, you still need a duvet. That's what I call normal.'

Scotty wasn't very keen on Oberhart. He seemed to find something to complain about in everything concerning Dubai and XPC. 'You won't be bitching when you go to the beach at the weekend. Sitting on the sand and swimming in the warm sea in March, you can't do that in Zurich.'

'I never go to public beaches,' he replied. 'See you later.' He got up and left Scotty sitting alone with his coffee.

What the hell was that all about? he asked himself. *Are the Swiss Germans really so hard to get along with?*

Sharif won their game that evening hands down. Scotty was still a little preoccupied by the incident with the flash drive, but was waiting until his CEO returned on Sunday.

'What's on the menu tonight?' he asked.

'It's a lot cooler and I need my curry. We're going to the Karachi House. OK?'

It was just after eleven when Scotty got back to his apartment near Jumeirah Beach. XPC had rented several upmarket residences for their senior people and, although a single man, he was fortunate enough to have one of them. He'd had several beers during and after dinner and was ready to crash out. Throwing his clothes onto the sofa, he fell into bed and was out to the world five minutes later.

At two a.m. he awoke with a headache and stomach cramps. Sitting up, he felt nauseous, dizzy and had difficulty focusing his eyes. *Too many beers*, he said to himself. He switched on the bedside lamp and unsteadily got out of bed to go to the toilet, where he threw up violently. *Shit. I've caught something.* He stirred an Alka Seltzer and an aspirin into a glass of water, swigged it back, then staggered to bed and fell into a deep sleep.

At five-thirty, Scotty awoke again feeling terrible. He was aching in his shoulders and back, as if he'd been carrying a huge weight, and his muscles were sore and tired. The lamp was still on, but he had to force his eyes open, then could hardly see across the room. His vision was blurred and when he tried to concentrate he saw double. He still felt nauseous and wanted to get up again to go to the toilet, but his body wouldn't respond. His mouth and throat were dry and his head was throbbing. He tried to swallow but for some reason his throat wouldn't work, and he realised he couldn't move his lips. Just trying to raise his right hand to his mouth he was unable to lift his arm up from the bed.

Scotty had a vision of himself lying helpless on the bed, as if he was looking down on the scene from above. With a rising sense of panic, he attempted to move every part of his body; his arms, his head, his shoulders, his legs, but nothing would work. His left arm was lying across his chest with his hand in front of his face and he tried to move the fingers. Nothing. His mind filled with terror when he realised that he couldn't even feel the hand, it could have belonged to someone else, so detached from him did it seem. Now he noticed his breath was coming in short gasps. His brain was still trying to process his condition; he knew he had to breathe to stay alive. He tried to force it to tell his body to take a deep breath, but his lungs wouldn't respond. His breathing became shallower and shallower until he felt he would asphyxiate. Now he knew he would die if he didn't get help. He made a desperate last attempt to open his mouth to scream for help, but all that came out was a mumbled gurgle. Scotty was in an almost complete state of paralysis.

At ten the next morning, Friday, the Filipino cleaning lady employed by XPC entered his apartment for the twice-weekly service. Mr Fitzgerald was a particularly tidy person and she was surprised to find some of his clothes on the living room sofa. She collected them and went through to the bedroom, where she found Scotty lying motionless on the bed. After trying unsuccessfully to wake him, she panicked and ran out of the apartment to find the building manager. When he saw Scotty's condition his first reaction was to think about the effect it would have on the other tenants and his reputation. He sent the crying woman away and tried to resuscitate him, in vain. Finally, he called the emergency service for an ambulance. Scotty was pronounced dead on arrival at the hospital, and the next morning his corpse was transferred to the police mortuary in Al Twar.

The autopsy was carried out that morning, Saturday, at eight o'clock. Shen Fu Liáng, his immediate boss, was stuck in San Francisco, but Tom Connor, the CEO, had learned the news when he returned on Friday evening. He'd immediately contacted Scotty's parents in Fort Lauderdale, where they were now living in retirement. The distraught couple couldn't get to Dubai until Monday and he agreed to attend the autopsy on their behalf. He was now sitting with Dr Alzahabi, a young, voluble pathologist who was explaining the cause of death to him.

'I'm still awaiting some analysis of food and tissue samples, but I can already inform you that Mr Fitzgerald died from an abnormally aggressive form of botulism. It's a neurotoxin, a very virulent type of food poisoning. Analysis of his stomach contents shows that he ate a meal of curried lamb the previous evening, and that could be the source of the attack.'

'That's right. He had a curry supper with a colleague, after a game of squash.' Tom had already quizzed Sharif on their Thursday evening activity. 'But I've never heard of anyone dying from food poisoning. I've had it myself and you feel like you're dying, but you don't. At least not that I've ever heard.'

'There are several types of food poisoning. Botulism is by far the most dangerous, but I agree it's seldom fatal. His blood alcohol level was also high, he must have had a lot to drink.'

'I didn't know that. Maybe the alcohol increased the likelihood of his death by poison?'

'Well, it wouldn't have helped. Alcohol always exacerbates any other harmful condition.'

'Would it be very painful?' Tom grimaced. He had personally hired Scotty away from San Francisco, and now he would have to explain to his parents what had happened to their only son. *What a way to die*, he said to himself. *How am I going to tell them?* He wasn't looking forward to it.

'It would be disagreeable and distressing for the first few hours, but then he would gradually lose all feeling until he was unable to breathe. Botulinum toxin causes flaccid paralysis by blocking motor nerve terminals. It's used a lot in medicine to temporarily paralyse muscles, so they don't cause damage. That's why Botox is very effective in creating temporary improvements in the facial appearance. It's the same basic material, just a tiny dose that paralyses the facial muscles so that you look more relaxed and youthful.'

'But this dose was so large that the paralysis spread through his body?'

'I believe so. The paralysis usually starts with the eyes and face then progresses downward, to the throat, chest and extremities. When the diaphragm and chest muscles become affected, respiration is inhibited and death from asphyxia can result. I think that's what happened.'

'You mean he suffocated? But why didn't he call for help? He's got all the emergency numbers in his mobile: ambulance, police, hospital, everything. We've all got the contact details, it's company procedure.'

'If he fell into an alcohol-induced sleep, he may have slept through the first symptoms until it was too late for him to react. But that wouldn't explain why the attack was so virulent, Mr Connor. I'll call you as soon as I get the final results from the lab. Now, I have a lot of further work to perform, so I have to leave you.'

When Tom got back to XPC, Nora, his PA, was waiting in reception for him. He had called her to come in and help out with the crisis. She took him to one side. 'The police are waiting in your office,' she whispered, eyes wide with concern.

'What do they want?'

'They just said it was in connection with Scotty's death.'

Tom's face turned pale. 'Shit, that's all we need. As if we haven't got enough to do, sorting things out here. And his parents arrive on Monday.' He sighed. 'Call Hatim and tell him what's happened so he's up to speed.' Hatim Ackerman was the local attorney for the company. 'If it's like everything else here, we're bound to need a lawyer.'

'Right. Time to face the music, I'm going up. There's nothing I can tell them that'll change anything, but they've got to conduct a proper enquiry – for everybody's sake, especially poor Scotty's.'

The two police officers had just left his office when Tom received the call from Dr Alzahabi. 'Good afternoon, Doctor, I hope you've got some good news for me.' He listened for a few minutes. 'So what does that mean exactly?'

Tom put the phone down and called Nora into his office. 'Tell Hatim to drop everything and get over here asap. Apparently the amount of toxin in Scotty's stomach couldn't have occurred naturally. It was enough to paralyse a horse. There's going to be a full police enquiry and I want us to be ready for whatever happens.'

By now, the whole building was awash with rumours and counter-rumours. Tom called a staff meeting in the gym to officially announce that Scotty had succumbed to a severe bout of food poisoning and the matter was being investigated. 'He was a brilliant guy and a great team leader, we're going to miss him a lot, as both a friend and a colleague.' He asked everyone to join him in one minute of silence, then finished by saying, 'I want everyone to cooperate fully with the police investigation. It's vital that we find out how Scotty was exposed to the poison, so if you know anything that could help in any way, please talk to me or to Shen. He'll be taking over Scotty's functions until other arrangements can be made. In the meanwhile, I'll keep everyone informed whenever there's any information to share.'

He fielded the various questions as best he could, then exhorted everyone to get back to work. 'Sales of the Mark VI range are going through the roof, and the marketing people are already screaming for Mark VII and the new ACRE upgrade. We need to keep focused. Thank you, guys. Let's get it done for Scotty. That's what he would have wanted.'

At midday, the Karachi House restaurant was closed down and cordoned off. Under Dr Alzahabi's watchful eye, two laboratory workers were taking samples of all the food in the kitchen for analysis. The police were back in the office, interviewing everyone who had worked with Scotty, and especially those who had been with him on Friday.

Sharif was subjected to a thirty-minute interrogation, emerging in a state of panic. 'They think I killed him, I know they do,' he said, fighting back tears. 'He wasn't just a colleague, he was my friend as well.'

'Don't worry. They're just doing their job, you were the last person to see him. The staff from the restaurant are being questioned as well. They have to talk to everyone until they find out what happened.' Hatim, the lawyer, had been present during the interview.

Tom added, 'We'll have to wait for the food analysis. I'm sure that'll be conclusive, it's the only possible explanation. There must be something that's been contaminated.' He was quietly praying that there would be a breakthrough before Scotty's parents arrived on Monday morning. He didn't want to face them without some kind of explanation.

He went back to his office to think about the situation. Whatever the outcome of the investigation, one thing was clear: he needed to find a new team leader to replace Scotty. And, he realised, maybe a replacement for Sharif. He started looking at competitors' websites.

Zurich, Switzerland

'*Scheisse*, shit! I thought things were going too well. How did it happen?' The caller was speaking *Schwyzerdütsch*, the Swiss German dialect.

Daniel Oberhart replied, 'Seems like he died of food poisoning, but a mega-dose, so the police are involved. There'll be an inquest in a couple of days and we'll find out for sure.'

'Have they got anything to go on?'

'Not that I've heard, but I don't want to ask too many questions, it might look suspicious. As far as I know, there's no evidence at all, so I guess it'll be filed away as death by misadventure or whatever they call it here.'

'You realise this could kill the whole plan? If it holds up the launch, or the publicity affects XPC's reputation in the industry, the Chinese might get cold feet and then we're screwed.'

'If the verdict is accidental death there'll be no publicity, accidents happen all the time and it's in no one's interests to make a big noise about it. And Tom Connor told us he's going out next week to look for a replacement for Scotty. In the meantime, Shen's taken charge. God help us all!'

'Can you do anything to speed things up?'

'I don't want to get involved until the inquest's over, it wouldn't look right. Then I'll talk with Tom to see where his head's at. Do you have anyone in mind?'

'Let me think about it and do some research. I'll have to call Julius at Hai-Sat, they're bound to find out soon. They'll be worried about meeting the delivery date, and the possible bad publicity. We can't let this mess things up. Call me when you know the result of the inquest and we'll talk about our options.'

THREE

Marbella, Spain
March 2017

'So what exactly do you do? You explained it to me once before, but I don't remember.' Jenny Bishop put aside her monthly business reports and looked across at her nephew, Leo Stewart.

Leo gave an imperceptible smile. People often said 'remember' when they really meant 'understand'. Although he was used to having to explain what he did, it was never easy. He turned away from his laptop. 'The simple answer is that I manage a team of computer programmers for a US company called M2M Microtech Corp. We develop CPUs and microprocessors for conventional machines and for the Internet of Things.' He waited for the inevitable reaction.

'If that's the simple answer, I'd hate to hear the complicated one,' she laughed. 'Come on, you can do better than that. I understand the commercial aspects of the Internet; most of the companies I'm involved with depend on it for marketing, distribution and customer services, but I have no idea how it actually works. So, assume I'm dumb and split the question into two parts. What is a microprocessor, and what is the Internet of Things?'

Jenny, in her late thirties, was his mother Emma's younger sister, and they had become close after she organised his escape from a gang of kidnappers in South Africa. She always insisted that they never talk about it, but he knew she had probably saved his life and it had cost her a lot of money. Besides that, the truth couldn't be shared with anyone. It might be dangerous for him and the others concerned. It would always be a well-guarded secret between them and their friend Pedro Espinoza, the Spanish private detective. Even now, seven years after the traumatic events, there could be a possibility that a careless word might alert the UK authorities that he had been brought into the country illegally. Considering the wave of self-serving and unfounded lawsuits that was sweeping the country, his mother could face criminal charges. *Let sleeping dogs lie* had been their decision, and it would always remain so.

But his mother was a crime writer and the events had spawned a fictional account called *My Son, the Hostage,* which had become a bestseller, reinvigorating Emma's career. The book's success had funded his college education at the University of California, Berkeley, where he had emerged with a degree in Applied Computer Sciences, graduating Summa Cum Laude after four years of study.

Leo had been approached by M2M during his final year. They regularly poached the best computer scientists from the top universities and rewarded them with long, exhausting days and nights and more money than they had time to spend. The company manufactured microprocessors and designed software and firmware for applications in modems, smart cards, SIMs and embedded chips in all types of equipment. Leo had been with them in San Francisco for eighteen months, plus the six months' part-time work experience he had been enlisted to after the job offer.

Working and studying that last year of college had almost killed him, but the experience got him off to a flying start in the company. Then, three months into the internship, he had the luckiest break he could have hoped for when he stumbled across the solution to a problem facing their encryption team. Someone leaked the story to the Silicon Valley press, and suddenly he became the most celebrated intern in history. On the first day of his full-time employment, he was immediately promoted to Programme Development Manager, leading the encryption development team. He was happy with M2M and they were excited about him. The future was bright.

Presently, Leo was on a week's vacation in Europe and had chosen to spend a few days with his aunt at York House, the magnificent property in Marbella she had inherited from her father-in-law, successful businessman Charlie Bishop.

Now, he gave Jenny a sheepish grin. 'Sorry, I wasn't trying to impress. M2M is a big US technology company. We make the tiny brains that are in all kinds of machines to carry out lots of complicated instructions. They're called Central Processing Units – CPUs, semiconductors and microprocessors, and we design, build and sell them all over the world.'

'So they're really miniature computers?'

'Dead right. Computers so miniscule you can hardly see them, but that have more memory and computing power than a room full of massive IBM machines used to have. Each unit has hundreds of millions or billions of components, connected together in a network on a tiny piece of silicon. Every one of those components is less than a thousandth of the width of a human hair, so you can't really get your head around how small they are. But just about every machine that's produced nowadays has at least one microprocessor in it, like your fridge or iron, all the machines you've got in this house. Cameras, TVs, phones, cars and so on can have a number of them, all linked together to provide different parts of the management process. You don't think about it, you just press a button and they work out what to do. It's a really cool business. There's hundreds of billions of these tiny computers in machines all over the world, and we're inventing new solutions and ways to reduce their size and increase power and memory all the time.'

Jenny was thinking quietly. 'So these are machines that everyone has in their homes all over the world?'

'Not just in homes; in businesses, government departments, energy and water companies, hospitals, cinemas, every place where intelligent machines are used. And there's also billions of remote devices around the world that communicate via a mobile network. That's what we call IoT, the Internet of Things. It's fairly recent technology and one of the fastest-growing industries in the world.'

'I don't understand that bit. What kind of devices?'

'They're machines that have a connectivity module in them linked to a mobile data network, instead of being cabled to a fixed network. It could be a SIM, a WiFi, Bluetooth or some other type of low power radio transceiver. They're managed over the Internet, just like a mobile phone. You use this technology with a tablet or a smartphone in the street, or to make a credit card payment from a cordless swipe machine, or find your destination on the satnav in your car. There's so many new applications coming out it's hard to keep track of them. Things like mobile parking meters, automated meter reading, 'Tap & Pay' mobile phone payment systems, connected cars, remote home alarm systems.'

'Then I'll repeat my first question. What exactly do you do?'

This time he laughed out loud. 'Fair enough. My job at M2M is to make sure that our encryption team keeps pace with the improvements in our designs. That means finding better ways of protecting people's data in these devices, wherever they are in the world.'

'So, there are billions and billions of machines out there, with even more billions of computer chips in them? Does anybody know where they all are?'

'I never really thought about that. I suppose every manufacturer or distributor has some kind of a record of where their stuff is, but I don't think there's any kind of overall control.'

'Hmm. Does M2M have a large percentage of them?'

'We've got about three per cent of the fixed market and about seven percent of the IoT market, so it's a few billions. But there's some huge players around. ARM is the biggest by far and they're English, which is great, then there's Intel, Qualcomm and AMD in the US and Samsung in Korea. Lee-Win out of Shanghai is very strong in the institutional arena, governments, banks, public services, and the word is they've just perfected an incredible new encryption technology. But the market's growing like crazy so there's plenty room for everyone, and M2M is growing fast. Now do you get the picture?'

'I think so.' She paused, assembling her thoughts. 'There are hundreds of billions of machines, both fixed and mobile, all over the world, inside and outside of homes, businesses and public organisations, being managed over the Internet by mini computers designed and manufactured by companies like M2M. And no one knows where they all are.'

'That's a pretty fair summary of the industry, Aunt Jenny. So what do you think?'

'I think it's the most terrifying thing I've ever heard in my life.'

FOUR

**Dubai International Airport
March 2017**

'Goodbye, Arthur. Goodbye Thelma.' Tom Connor shook hands with Mr and Mrs Fitzgerald, Scotty's parents, who thanked him tearfully then joined the check-in line for their Qatar Airways flight from DXB to Miami. The refrigerated casket containing their son's body was already on the plane, and the funeral had been arranged in three days' time at a crematorium in Fort Lauderdale. The complicated paperwork for the death certificate, registration and repatriation had all been handled by Nora and Hatim.

Tom had spent most of the last few days with them, doing his best to assuage the sadness and despair that would engulf them sooner or later. It also helped a little to alleviate the sense of guilt that he couldn't help feeling, for having convinced their son to leave his home to seek success and fortune, but instead to suffer a horrible and painful death. *There's nothing left for them to do in Dubai,* thought Tom. *All they face is returning home to bury their son. Shit! Why did that have to happen to them?* He walked back to his car, cursing the bad luck that had brought death and distress to all of them.

His mind shifted to the problems Scotty's death had caused at XPC. Shen Fu Liáng had returned from San Francisco on Monday, but he had been of little help. His attitude to Scotty's death seemed to be one of disinterest. Tom's relationship with the Chinaman was complex, and often made him feel uncomfortable. Shen had been with Lee-Win for five years and was a member of the holding company main board. He had been sent down from Shanghai as their representative to work with Tom, which sometimes led to disagreements, or misunderstandings. He understood that his Chinese masters needed some 'eyes on the ground' and they'd sent Liáng, but it was sometimes difficult to know who was in charge. Tom found him a dispassionate and reserved man, whose most extreme expression, appropriately, seemed to be inscrutability. Despite living in the US for several years and speaking perfect English, he often seemed to have difficulty reconciling himself with the subtleties of the workings of the western mind. But now Tom observed a cold, uncaring side of the Chinaman that he'd never shown before, and he had kept him away from Scotty's distraught parents.

Liáng was also totally convinced that Sharif had nothing to answer for. 'You can discount him from being involved in the poisoning,' he asserted forcefully. 'I've known him for five years and he's one of the nicest guys you could find.' Tom was aware that when he was in Shanghai, Liáng had outsourced work to Sharif's software services company in Pakistan and they had worked on projects together, although he didn't consider that it qualified him to judge anyone in such desperate circumstances. But he didn't have time to discuss the matter, he had too many other problems to worry about. It was now Thursday, the whole week had been lost, and he knew the next months would be filled with challenges. Not the normal, or even abnormal, business challenges that he faced every day and relished because he could do something about them, but worries about people and outside events over which he had no control and which gave him a deep sense of foreboding.

Tom Connor was a common-sense man from south Boston who had come up the hard way, and didn't care who knew it. His parents, third generation Irish, could just about feed and clothe their four children and there was no money for costly education. He worked his way through school, then college, obtaining an MBA in Finance at the Boston University Questrom School of Business when he was twenty-four. He went to work as a management trainee with T-Mobile US in 2002, a year after Deutsche Telekom, the German telecoms giant, purchased VoiceStream and Powertel, creating T-Mobile, one of the largest US wireless telecoms businesses. His timing was good, they needed management talent to sort out their 60-billion-dollar acquisitions and he benefited from a crash course in wireless technology.

Tom was a Senior VP of T-Mobile's new product development division when Lee-Win approached him to head up their soon-to-be-opened XPC subsidiary in Dubai. Within two months he'd moved his family to the Emirates State, and a few months later he watched a member of the ruling family cut the ribbon at the official opening. Tom was not a specialist, either in telecoms or micro-technology. He was a business developer and a people manager, who succeeded by hiring people with the right skills and creating the appropriate creative and cultural environment. He knew this disaster had to be managed well or it would spiral out of control and cause irreparable damage to the business. *Thank God I've got three key people I can count on,* he reflected. *Shen can hold things together with Daniel and Sharif until I can find a replacement for Scotty.*

He summoned up in his mind what information had been discovered to date. The forensic examination of the food from his stomach had shown that the lamb eaten by Scotty was highly infected by the toxin, abnormally so. There was no doubt of the origin of the poisoning, but how it got there was a mystery. The wholesalers who supplied all the restaurant's meat products welcomed the technicians who arrived to inspect the premises, but there was no trace of contamination of any kind on their products. The same applied to their refrigerated vehicles and to the various pieces of equipment used during the preparation and delivery procedure.

'Miraculously, no one else in the restaurant who ordered the lamb curry suffered any ill-effects,' Dr Alzahabi had told him. He was still helping the police with their enquiries and was fully informed of their progress, or lack of. 'Apparently, they had a special three-course dinner on, a popular chicken speciality, and most customers chose that. Only five people ordered the lamb, but we don't know who they were and we've had no reports of illness. The restaurant's not open on a Friday, so there were no other customers before the police closed them up on Saturday morning.'

'Thank God for small mercies.' Tom had been so preoccupied with the aftermath of Scotty's death and looking after his parents that he hadn't considered the possibility of other deaths. He thought of the implications for a moment. 'I suppose they pre-prepare their curries in large batches and keep them frozen, then heat them up in servings when they're ordered. That means the toxin must have been in the container that they took the portion from?'

'That was my expectation, but it wasn't. There is no trace of the toxin anywhere in the kitchen, the container, the pans or the oven, nothing. The plates have been through a very efficient washing machine, so there's no trace there either, but that's the only place it can have been. It can only have been on the portion that was served to Scotty, there's no other possible explanation.'

'But that means…'

'Exactly. It means that somehow, that dish of curry was contaminated somewhere between the kitchen and Scotty's table. The police are questioning the restaurant staff again, but they're getting nowhere. It's a big place, about one hundred and fifty seats, and there are forty employees. Thursday night is always busy, there were over a hundred customers, many of whom they can't identify. They had a lot bookings and regular clients, but there's just as many casual diners who come in without reserving. So if the toxin was administered deliberately, there are seventy or eighty suspects, most of whom cannot be traced.'

'I know the place, it's fairly upmarket, I've been there quite a few times. If I remember, they bring the dishes of food out on trays and place them at a serving station until the waiter comes and serves them to the customer. So anyone going by could poison the food. What does it look like?'

'A fatal dose could be contained in a few drops of water. Just about anyone in the restaurant could have done it.'

'A needle in a haystack. Unless the police find a motive, they're never going to solve it.'

'They've given permission for the restaurant to open again tomorrow, but it's bound to suffer enormously from the bad publicity. Most of these independent businesses don't have much capital in reserve and it could go under. Another unfortunate result of the incident.'

'That could be a motive for a competitor, I suppose. But a bit drastic to poison someone to put your competition out of business.'

'The police followed that line of enquiry too. There's a lot of competition with the owners of the Taj Mahal, just along the street, but there again there's no proof of anything untoward. It looks like a dead end.'

The inquest had been held the next day, where the only witnesses were the police chief in charge of the short enquiry and Dr Alzahabi. Tom had attended on behalf of Scotty's parents, who were too distressed to cope with the formal procedure. There had been no pre-inquest review hearing and it was clear to him that the police had given up on the investigation. They had no more time to spend on the death of a foreigner, but wanted to get the case filed away as soon as possible. Despite the obvious implication that the toxin had been deliberately administered by someone in the restaurant, the coroner returned a verdict of 'accidental death by poisoning'. Tom conveyed the verdict to the Fitzgeralds as gently as he could, and they received the news stoically.

'There's nothing we can do,' Scotty's father said. 'We're in a foreign country where we don't understand the procedure. And the sad fact is, our son's gone and nothing will bring him back.

Whatever happened, it's too late to change it. We just have to try to put it behind us and go back to our life in Florida.'

Driving back to the XPC building, Tom forced himself to put the poisoning problem out of his thoughts. He reflected again on Shen's recent attitude. Not only had he shown little sympathy for Scotty's death, but he immediately suggested that it wasn't really necessary to replace him. In his opinion, Sharif could run both teams, he was more capable than the Welshman and could fulfil both roles. Daniel Oberhart could help him reorganise the work programme to compensate for Scotty's absence. He, Shen, would work closer with the teams to ensure that Scotty wasn't missed. He could also assist Sharif in managing the ACRE upgrade programme. 'Problem solved,' he told Tom confidently.

The American immediately saw the motivation behind this suggestion, and the dangers of accepting it. Shen was a good administrative manager and his overall grasp of the programme requirements was adequate, but he wasn't up to the complexities of the security algorithms created by Scotty, and was even less able to manage the long-term projects. In Tom's opinion he was also lazy, preferring to attend sales and industry events and conferences rather than running his department. Although Scotty had never said anything, he was aware that several of Shen's interventions had caused more problems than they'd resolved. And for some reason he'd always supported Sharif, even when he was wrong, and any criticism he had was reserved for Scotty. But although Sharif was good, he was only as good as the combination of him and Scotty. He was also wary of giving the Swiss SVP any increased responsibilities. He was effectively holding down three jobs and seemed to only just be coping, his recent attitude had been almost unpleasant, he was not a man who engendered affection in his employees. In his areas of responsibility, network management and support services, this was less of a problem, but programmers could be prickly and touchy and needed a lot of stroking. Oberhart was not the guy to provide that.

No, Tom decided, *I need a new team leader strong enough to resist Shen's ambition to sidestep the structure. Or maybe we need to change our current structure altogether.* He wasn't looking forward to the future discussions, but he knew he had to be flexible. The main — only — objective, was to get the right person to replace Scotty as soon as possible. It would be nigh on impossible to find someone as good as the Welshman, but whatever transpired, he couldn't afford to lose or alienate any other key people in the process.

He called Nora into his office and started on his reports. The next few weeks were going to test his mettle, but he was confident he was up to the task.

Zurich, Switzerland

'The official verdict was accidental death, so don't worry about bad publicity,' Daniel Oberhart was speaking on the phone in Swiss German. 'XPC won't want to make a big thing of it and the police are obviously disinterested, so I would just forget about that problem.'

'Have you talked to Connor about a replacement?'

'I spoke to him this morning. He's already looking. We're ninety per cent away from finishing and the delivery date is end July. That's more than four months, so if he finds someone quickly, we should be OK.'

'I'll send you files on a couple of names I've dug up. You might be able to point Connor in their direction.'

'OK, I'll see what I can do and get back as soon as I know anything definite.'

'I'll call Julius and try to calm him down. He's been a bit highly strung for the last few days. Have a good evening, Daniel.'

FIVE

London, England
April 2017

'Oh yes, that's good! Oh yes, darling, don't stop!'

Jenny Bishop was in an unusual situation. After nine years of celibacy since the death of her husband Ron, she was having wonderful sex. But that was not the most unusual aspect of the event. Jenny didn't trust bankers or divorced men, and Bill Redman, the man she was in bed with, was both.

Jenny was in London for a meeting with one of her business partners, and Bill had a flat in Gloucester Place, near the Hyatt Regency Churchill Hotel, and had managed to get a table for dinner at Locanda Locatelli, the hotel's Michelin-starred Italian restaurant. She was not a regular drinker, and after sharing a fine bottle of Vino Nobile de Montepulciano, from Tuscany, Jenny accepted his invitation to go back to his flat for a nightcap and one thing had led to another.

She was not at all unhappy at the turn of events. She hadn't been affected by the wine as much as it seemed, and used it as an excuse to let down her guard and see what happened. And what happened was better than she had hoped for, much better.

Bill was an ardent but considerate lover, more concerned with her pleasure than his own. After so many years, Jenny had forgotten what it was to drop her defences and enjoy the moment. Several moments, in fact. It seemed she was determined to make up for lost time, and the night had been one long delightful journey of discovering each other's desires and fulfilling them. Jenny was sated, replete and happier than she could remember being for a very long time.

She had known Bill for three years, since Patrice de Moncrieff had introduced her to Fletcher, Rice & Co, the UK subsidiary of BIP, Banque Internationale de Paris, a global financial institution. Jenny had severed her relations with their Swiss bank, Klein, Fellay, several years ago but still banked with their Spanish arm, Banco de Iberia in Marbella, where Patrice, the husband of her friend Leticia, was now branch manager. Bill Redman was a senior UK partner, and because of her long-standing relationship with BIP, he decided to give her his personal attention. Jenny was an attractive and intelligent woman and he continued as her personal advisor. The substantial funds to be handled justified his decision to the other partners. She'd since learned that he'd previously lived with his family in Bury St Edmonds, just twenty miles from her home in Ipswich. He was now involved in prolonged divorce proceedings, so he spent most of his time at his London flat. By coincidence, like many UK businessmen, he also had a house near Marbella, and they started to meet from time to time for a meal in London or Spain.

Bill was good company, and she gradually became fond of him. He was thoughtful and funny, unlike some bankers she had met in the past, notably in Switzerland. Also, from the little he mentioned about his divorce she was convinced that he hadn't and didn't intend to act badly. He was principally concerned about the effect on his two children, and that was the reason the split-up was quite protracted. Jenny was wary of entering into a complicated liaison, and until last night their relationship had been totally platonic. Now, she was glad she'd changed that. *What's the worst thing that can happen?* she asked herself. *I'm not getting any younger. I'll make the most of it as long as it lasts.*

They both had meetings in London the next morning, so after a shower and coffee, Jenny kissed him goodbye. 'I hope that's the start of something and not the end,' he said.

'I hope so too,' she replied. 'I'll call you when I get to Marbella. Let me know your plans.' She went out to find a taxi, feeling quite radiant. In the cab, she felt a pang of guilt, having planned the event so carefully. But she didn't regret it, not for a moment.

Dubai, United Arab Emirates

'Good morning, Tom. Mind if I join you, unless you're busy?' Daniel Oberhart put his coffee cup on the table and plonked his backside on the chair across from his CEO in the canteen.

'Oh, hi Daniel. No problem, I'm just catching up on last night's emails.' He finished flicking through the messages on his mobile. 'Most of them are hardly worth reading, mostly people just reminding me they exist and they'd be happy to see me sometime. I guess I haven't had much time to socialise these last few weeks, too many problems to sort. Anything special you wanted to talk about?' Connor looked tired, dark shadows under his eyes. He sipped his coffee, looking expectantly at the Swiss man.

'I was wondering about Scotty's replacement. No progress on the headhunting I suppose?'

'Nothing worth reporting.' He frowned. 'Between you and me, it's a lot more difficult than I expected. Seems like I've looked at a thousand job search sites and CVs and had a hundred phone interviews and I've got nothing to show for it. Scotty was an outstanding encryption programmer, but I didn't think it'd be impossible to replace him. Any suggestions?'

Oberhart shrugged. 'I've had a few thoughts, but it's not really my field.'

'At this juncture, any help would be welcome. What were you thinking?'

'I suppose you've been looking mainly in Europe?'

'Seemed logical. Given our time frame, I figured that was my best option.'

'I got a tip about someone who might be available quickly. Encryption specialist, like Scotty, great reputation. He's young, very young actually, but he's already made quite a name for himself in the industry, knows a lot about the IoT.'

'But he's not in Europe, I suppose?'

'He's English, but working in California, that's probably why you haven't come across him. And he's not actively looking for a change, but I know his contract's coming up for renewal and he's the kind of kid who'd be attracted by a challenge like ACRE.'

'You have a file on him?'

'I'll bring it up for you after I finish my coffee.'

Tom got up to go. 'Great, thanks Daniel, I appreciate it.'

The CEO left him, and he called a Zurich number. 'I've put Tom Connor onto your suggestion. I hope you're right about him. We need to get this sorted fast.'

London, England

'How do you like the circulation numbers for March?' It was eleven o'clock and Jenny was in the office of Josephine Greenwell, the founder and editor of *Thinking Woman Magazine*, a business in which she owned a thirty per cent share.

'I think a glass of champers is called for. One hundred thousand has a nice ring to it, doesn't it?'

'When I consider how long it took to get to ten thousand, it certainly does.'

Jenny's company, BPE, had first invested in Jo's business two years ago, and it had been a tough struggle, requiring several additional funding rounds to get to this point. Now, not only had the January circulation finally broken through the 100,000 mark, the magazine had made an operating profit for the first time since Jo had started it four years before. There was a lot to celebrate.

The two women had met in 2015 at a cocktail party at Bill Redman's bank, Fletcher, Rice & Co. After inheriting a substantial fortune in 2008, due to the deaths of her husband Ron and his father Charlie Bishop at the hands of the psychopathic killer Ray d'Almeida, Jenny had led a very quiet life for the next two years. Apart from travelling occasionally between her home in the UK and the house she had inherited from Charlie in Spain, she had done nothing useful. Then, in 2010, the abduction in South Africa of her only sister Emma Stewart's son, Leo, had galvanised her into a period of frenetic activity until he was safely returned to his mother. As harrowing as the experience had been, it had served to reunite the three remaining members of the Stewart family and strengthen the bonds between them. And in a strange way, Jenny had enjoyed the experience; being instrumental in bringing her nephew safely back from Africa had made her feel useful and needed again.

Jenny was single and only thirty-six years old. Since Ron's death she hadn't had a serious relationship, and she missed having someone to share her life with. The reconciliation with her sister and nephew had helped to ease that feeling of loneliness, but it didn't replace the pleasure of mutual companionship. *I have to find something to keep myself busy, get out and meet new people,* she told herself. *I'm still able to make a contribution to society.*

She thought about it for a long while, considering possible options that might be available to her, trying to assess her personal qualities and defects. *Strong-minded, pragmatic, not good at taking orders, creative thinker. (All useful when dealing with pathological murderers)* she remembered. *Numerically competent with a good education. (She had taught children with learning difficulties, and then managed her husband's garage business.) Financially independent with no family ties. (Is that a quality or a defect?)* she wondered.

On her next trip to Marbella, Jenny confided in Leticia de Moncrieff, her close friend, co-beneficiary of Charlie Bishop's will and mother of his son Emilio. As usual, she was impressed with the Angolan woman's ability to lecture her in one of her adopted languages.

'It's about time you decided to do something, Jenny. You're far too clever to spend your time travelling all over the place for no special reason. Why don't you talk about it with Patrice when you come for dinner tonight? He's very good at advising people about all kinds of things. I think that's why he got promoted to manager.'

Although she still had an apartment there, Leticia had moved out of the house she co-owned with Jenny when she married Patrice. They now lived with Emilio and their second son Joachim in a villa in Puente Romano, a luxurious urbanisation on the beachfront a few kilometres away. Jenny had never been keen on Patrice and they had a rather prickly relationship, but he had obviously been prompted by his wife before her arrival that evening and was bent on fulfilling his task to her satisfaction.

Knowing she hated prevarication, he came straight to the point. 'One of my jobs at the bank is to examine investment opportunities for our clients. We get a lot of would-be entrepreneurs with bright ideas, or businesses in early stages who are looking for funding to develop. A few years ago, we allocated some of Leticia's funds into some of these opportunities and they're doing really well.

'Because of the Internet, there are more and more of these start-ups coming along. Many of them are specialised hi-tech businesses which I don't understand, so I leave them alone. But there's a lot of non-technical opportunities too that would have been difficult to introduce before the Internet, now they're much easier. They use the Web to commercialise and manage them, but you don't need to be a technical genius to analyse and assess their potential. They're regular businesses, like online stores for retail distribution, specialised products, travel services, real estate or insurance brokerage, the kinds of goods and services that can be sold over the Internet without reinventing the wheel.

'I turn away most of the requests I get because I don't have the time to look at them, and some I just don't want to get involved. That's why we've done only eight deals in almost two years. But in France and the UK the demand is so great our banks have set up separate private equity divisions. Same thing in Hong Kong. I went over there to help them set up an Asian operation and it's growing exponentially. My point is, there's a lot of opportunity for clever people who have funds available to invest.

'If you want to find a new activity and make money in the process, then think about this avenue. It's something you can do yourself, trusting your own instincts and knowledge. You're a smart person, Jenny, and you could do well in any kind of business, but in this way you can be involved in several businesses as an investor, with oversight, but without committing yourself full-time to any of them. I'd be happy to help you to identify opportunities and vet them before introducing you, to reduce your exposure.' He paused, wondering what her reaction would be.

Before she could respond, Leticia interrupted, 'Jenny, that's exactly what you should do, and you know it is.'

That conversation sparked the creation, in 2014, of Bishop Private Equity Plc; BPE, a UK company that she formed when Patrice sent her a financial dossier from Accessibiliti, a struggling online business selling holiday packages: flights, hotels and rental cars. She immediately saw their problem came from poor cash management, and made them a funding proposal which they desperately needed. Patrice then introduced her to Fletcher, Rice & Co, where she met Bill Redman, who assisted her in setting up BPE and organising relations with her other banks in Marbella and Geneva. With a modest investment and some hands-on involvement, she acquired twenty-five per cent of the business and helped them to turn the corner to profitability. Since then, BPE had funded six businesses, each in a different area of activity. One of them had gone bust, due to a crooked manager who embezzled every penny he could lay his hands on, but the other five were doing well. Her most audacious choice was Lady Knick Knack, an online store selling erotic clothing and sex toys. Its headquarters were in Sunderland, which brought back fond memories, since Jenny had worked there as a teacher. Since her involvement, the company had outperformed all forecasts, and on the way won a government award for overseas sales.

Jo Greenwell's magazine business was Jenny's fourth investment, and it had not been an easy road to success. Jo was a highly successful model who, at twenty-five, had called time out on that phase of her life to launch her own fashion/social women's magazine. She had been dedicated full-time to the project for two years when Jenny met her, with very little success. Sadly, she had also just lost her mother to cancer and was close to calling it a day.

Jenny had taken an immediate liking to the young woman. She was beautiful, clever and devoted to her business, and all she needed was some help and direction to turn it around. Her other participations in BPE had given Jenny a crash course in Internet marketing and social media techniques, both essential to developing new businesses. *Thinking Woman Magazine*, she reasoned, was perfectly suited to this approach, and she was right. Her first investment provided money for the company to steal a media expert from the competition. Then her funds were ploughed into targeted marketing campaigns, supported by celebrity endorsements, blogging sites, et cetera. Jo was still a stunningly beautiful young woman, and she encouraged her to appear in a limited number of modelling shoots to represent the face of the magazine. Another of Jenny's ideas was to ask her sister Emma Stewart, a successful novelist, to write a monthly blog on creative writing, a sure-fire winner with women who had ambitions to write. Slowly but surely, they saw a steady rise in advertising space, media recognition and above all, circulation and revenues.

She and Jo went to celebrate that evening at Club Gaston, a popular French restaurant near Smithfield Market, and toasted their success with a glass of Moët & Chandon. They didn't order a whole bottle. Jenny was very careful with her money.

At that time of night, the taxi to Heathrow took only forty minutes. Jenny had booked into the Marriott on Bath Road, just off the airport property. Her BA economy flight to Malaga was at nine the next morning. Travelling with only a carry-on bag, she should be at her house in Marbella in time for lunch. Sitting back in the darkened cab, she reviewed her new-found status with satisfaction. She had investments in five successful businesses and a new man in her life. Patrice and Leticia had been right: Jenny was smart, and she was enjoying her new vocation.

SIX

San Diego, California, USA
April 2017

Leo Stewart was sitting in the Pacific Ballroom of the Hilton
Garden Inn, Mission Valley, San Diego, with one hundred and
thirty other attendees. The ballroom had been organised as a
conference room, and the title on the screen in front of them read:

SECURITY THREATS IN INTERNET AND
CLOUD COMPUTING.

The room was full of senior executives and high-ranking
technicians from telecoms and Internet providers, or equipment and
microcircuit manufacturers and software design companies. The
man standing by the screen, Four-Star General William R. 'Billy'
Chillicott, an ex-US Air Force officer and NATO ambassador, was
now a low-profile senior officer with the US Homeland Security
Agency. He was dressed in casual clothes, a large, barrel-chested man
with an abrasive voice and manner. He was also the acting chairman
of the UN Group of Governmental Experts on Developments in
the Field of Information and Telecommunications in the Context
of International Security, or GGE Cyber Security by its snappier
abbreviation.

There was a smaller TV screen on the platform, which showed a portly, bespectacled man in a Savile Row pinstriped suit sitting waiting. Chillicott had introduced him as, 'Dr Hugh Middleton, Director of Research at the Institute for Global Internet Security in London, who's joining us on our video link. We've been collaborating with them for a couple of years now. They're pretty savvy folk.'

Chillicott's first admonition was to keep all questions for a two-way session at the end, ''Cos answering questions during the presentation defeats its own object. No one can remember where the hell they were up to. Second, please switch off your cell phones, and I mean completely off, no cheating. And lastly, I'm well aware that most of what I have to say you already know, but I want you to listen anyways, because knowing about something and fully understanding its potential consequences are two quite different matters.' He looked around, waiting for an argument. No one dared speak. 'Right, let's get started.' He tapped the screen to bring up the first slide.

'First off, I want you to look at a few statistics on the increase in Internet crime:

'*Global cyber-attacks* – For six years, *Red October* collected billions of pieces of information from governments, research firms, military installations, energy providers, nuclear and critical infrastructures around the world. And they did it through Microsoft Internet programmes.

'*Intellectual Property* – There's a trillion dollars-worth stolen every year.

'*Websites* – More than 30,000 are infected by viruses or malware every day.

'*Businesses* – 90% suffered computer hacks in 2016, costing over a billion dollars, mainly using "ransomware" where they block the systems until a ransom is paid.

'*Identity Theft* – 10 million Americans had their identities stolen last year.

'*Personnel Data Theft* – over 70 million records stolen from US healthcare providers this year.

'*Consumer Fraud* – $16 billion was stolen from 15.4 million US consumers in 2016.

'*Espionage* – At NATO, we neutralise over 2,000 cyber-attacks each year and it costs a fortune of money.

'*Fake News* – This is the latest fashion. Announcing on social media or specialised Internet groups news, events that never happened, or happened in a different way to what's presented. We'll talk about that later.

'*Major Heists* – I'll mention only one. Last year, the Bangladesh central bank's account at the Fed was hit by a series of transfer instructions totalling $951 million. Almost a billion dollars! Talk is, it was Pyongyang trying to accumulate dollars for arms purchases. In the end, $81 million was stolen in that one Internet hacking event. That's almost as much as some of you guys make in a year.'

He paused for the inevitable nervous laughter, then brought up another slide with a chart showing a hockey-stick rise in value. 'Here's my last item:

'*Crypto-currencies* – These crypto-currencies, like Bitcoin, Ethereum and Blackcoin, let you buy anything you want in total anonymity: drugs, weapons, trafficked prostitutes, you name it. Sites like *AlphaBay* and *Hansa*, operating on the Tor network, a filthy corruption of the Internet, turn over millions of dollars a day in their immoral dealings. And over the last year, the Bitcoin has almost tripled in value from $375 to $1,055, so you get a double whammy: anonymous crime with a fictitious currency that looks set to outdo any of the old-fashioned kind. Talk about tulips from Amsterdam,' he added, wondering if anyone present would understand the allusion.

Chillicott looked round at the young executives; women in T-shirts and short skirts, crew-cut men, in short-sleeved shirts and blue jeans. *The Digital Generation*, he thought to himself. *They've never known anything else. How can we expect them to understand?*

He stood tall, commanding their attention. 'That's just a few examples of the millions of Internet crimes occurring just about every day and it brings me to the reason for this conference. In the considered opinion of Dr Middleton and myself, in addition to all this crap we already have to deal with, the world is facing two new threats with grave potential consequences that deserve our immediate attention.'

He tapped the screen. 'Here's the first.' A *Financial Times* headline came up, entitled 'The Internet of Dangerous Things'. The sub-heading was 'Cyber Security Breaches Threaten Global Infrastructures'.

'It's this new phenomenon, IoT, The Internet of Things. Or Connected Living, as some people call it. You all are involved in it and know more about it than I do, but our guest will show you some real scary parts we think are being neglected.' He turned to the second screen, 'OK, Hugh, can you take over for a while?'

Middleton stood up and addressed the camera. 'Good morning, ladies and gentlemen. Our purpose today is not to try to convince anybody that the Internet isn't a valuable and efficient tool for twenty-first-century communications. It's to highlight the existing and potential dangers of this technology, and to create awareness of the need for better and new management, security and control. The truth is that despite its obvious advantages, the Internet is already a minefield of potential disasters, and this new technology will make it more and more dangerous. So, let's get straight to the point.'

He tapped his laptop and a map of the US filled the main screen, showing a single large edifice in the centre with no doors or windows. 'This building looks like an impenetrable fortress, you can get neither in nor out, impossible to find out what's inside. Now I'll put in one IoT application, an automated meter reading system.'

He gave a tap and a green door opened in the front of the building and a green skylight in the roof. Two more buildings appeared on the screen, each with a green door wide open. A dotted red line appeared, connecting the green doors and the skylight together.

'The green doors and window are the vulnerable entry points created when an application is implemented. The red line is the

Internet. It connects the meter reader to the energy company, and the billing system to the customer's bank for the direct debit payments. With that one application, you've just opened up two entry points into the customer's confidential online information, and an entry point into the bank and the energy company.

'Now let's list a cross section of businesses, service providers and government departments that the average person is likely to deal with.'

A number of services appeared across the bottom of the screen, each enclosed in a black box with the lid shut:

Energy   *Tax/Pension Departments*
Banking   *Defence & Military*
Telecommunications   *Air, Rail & Road Transport*
Information & Television   *Hospitals & Health Services.*

'I'm going to put in another application, a credit card or direct debit instruction to a bank to settle the charges for any of these services.'

Immediately he hit the *Enter* key, green doors and windows opened in every box and the screen was filled with buildings, all with multiple green entry points. A spaghetti-like mass of dotted red lines connected them all together and led into each of the open boxes. The US map was almost obliterated by the Internet red line, showing how ultimately any application became interlinked to the customer, the banks and the industries involved.

Middleton paused for a moment, letting his audience take in the implications of his slide. 'And nowadays, more and more data is stored in what we call the *Cloud*, which is a global network of remote physical equipment whose information is stored and managed in a virtual fashion on the Internet. Let's imagine that it actually looks like a cloud sitting over the US.' A silver network appeared, floating over the map.

'Now, let's see those applications being connected to virtual networks in the Cloud.' The screen was now entirely covered by the buildings and boxes with green doors and windows, all linked by red spaghetti lines in each direction and going up and down to the menacing shape of the silver network, hovering above the US map like a spider's web.

'If a hacker breaks into any of the hundreds of green entry points on this map – and frankly, it's not that difficult – he opens up access to the global Internet Banking Network and to most government, industrial and business entities all over the country. And, of course, what applies to the US, applies to the whole world, because the Internet links all global information networks. And the IoT is multiplying these entry points at an exponential speed, every single minute of every day. The truth is that any clever hacker with a malicious intent, or even just looking for a thrill, can penetrate the information system through these entry points. And once inside the system, that person can cause untold damage, and especially damage to our essential services all over the world: power, water, communications, banking, defence, hospitals, food distribution. You name it, it's vulnerable.'

Middleton waited a moment, then said, 'I've just showed you two applications. There are millions more.'

SEVEN

San Diego, California, USA
April 2017

Leo looked around the room. It seemed that everyone started speaking at the same time. *Looks like he got their attention*, he thought to himself.

Chillicott went back to the screen and brought up another headline:

WHAT'S BEHIND THE DARK WEB?

'When we talk about the Dark Web, we're usually referring to the most sickening and terrifying perversions of the Internet: violence, pornography, children and people exploitation and trafficking, aiding and abetting terrorism and other despicable activities that hide in that impenetrable space in the ether. Those areas are already getting attention, because they're real and specific. That forces us to prepare and execute a plan of counter-action in a targeted, focused way. But today, our objective is to get you to think about the non-specific threats and dangers, the vast areas of Internet activity we just take for granted. All the stuff we do every day that we wouldn't be able to do without the Internet. Let's look at a few current statistics.' He brought up another slide and read off the items:

'GLOBAL INTERNET ACTIVITY – 2016

'*Data across Internet (Global IP Traffic)* – 1.2 Zettabytes/Year = 1.2 Trillion Gigabytes

'*Number of Internet Users* – 3.8 Billion – 50% of World Population

'*Number of IP Connected Devices* – 17 Billion – 2.4 x World Population

'*Number of IoT Connected Devices* – 6 Billion. Projected 2025 – 75 Billion.

'*Number of Digital Payments* – 480 Billion. Increase over 2015 – 10%.

'*Value of E-Commerce Sales* – $1.9 Trillion. Increase over 2015 – 20%.

'*Number of Apps Available (Business & Consumer)* – Over 5 Million.

'*Number of Facebook Users, 2017* – 2 Billion – 25% of World Population.

'I guess I don't need to show these statistics, you should know them off by heart. But something that most people never think about is this: whether we like it or not, unless you're in the middle of the Amazonian jungle, everything that you and the businesses and folks around you do, gets done courtesy of the Internet. There's hardly a single activity that doesn't involve transmission of data between two points, and that means via the Internet. So, the corollary is kinda self-evident. If you cut off the Internet, you cut off the world's activities.

'Dr Middleton has just shown you some of the vulnerable points created by a couple of common applications. But you development experts know that the constant increase in Internet users and applications flooding out every year are making it more and more vulnerable and impossible to control. To put it another way: nowadays, we don't govern the Internet, it governs us! And it's way past the danger point.'

He paused and took a sip of water. 'The fact is, the Internet is already out of hand, and you guys have to remember that in your development work. What's more, in our opinion, you have a responsibility to help us take action to create and enforce security controls around this world-changing phenomenon. We're gonna explain why and how you can do that.'

He looked at the TV screen. 'Your turn again, Hugh.'

The slide of the US map covered by the buildings and boxes, all linked by red spaghetti lines in each direction and up and down to the silver network – the Cloud – was now entitled:

INTERNET AND CLOUD. A VICIOUS CYCLE.

Middleton said, 'The threat to our modern world doesn't come from credit card payments or automated meter reading, or any other application, existing or yet to be invented. Nor does it come from illicit activities, radical preaching or horrific violence shown online. It comes from all of them, because they all travel the same path and end up in the same place. Today's threat is the matrix that brings together all of our essential services, every part of modern transactions, especially mobile transactions, and all the perverse corruption and abundance of hate available for the radicalisation of ordinary citizens, into that single place. It is the Internet itself, the greatest threat facing the world today. We can obtain or provide online just about any information we choose, truth or lies, for good or for evil. And behind the Internet is the Dark Web; a corrupt, impenetrable hiding place for sickening perverts and insanely dangerous fanatics hidden beneath shadow sites. But we don't know who uses these sites, nor what they use them for, and there is no way we can find this out.

'The Internet fills the ever-expanding Cloud with data, but again we have no idea how much data or information it contains. Like the Internet, the Cloud is vulnerable, from the users who send and store their data there, and from all of the "accidental" points of entry and hidden portals we talked about earlier. As the number of computer users and applications expand exponentially, we no longer know what is real and what is virtual. But we do know that the amount of data they produce and store is filling up this Cloud with valuable and potentially dangerous information, and that the Internet is the key to the Cloud.'

On the screen the silver network over the Earth broke apart and a large key, labelled 'Internet', appeared in the centre.

'At the institute, we spend all our time worrying about the security of the Internet. It's the one common connecting point into every aspect of our lives and businesses, and it's the entry and communicating point for those who would like to hurt us. And it's going to get worse, because there is nothing we can do about it, since we have no control whatsoever.

'What's more, we know from our experience of hacking attacks that the attackers are much cleverer than the defenders. And in a strange way they are more motivated to succeed. They are often young people who sit in their bedrooms with a PC or laptop, either because they have been left to their own devices, or they prefer remote relationships to real-life contacts. They become insulated from reality, addicted to the technology, and they relate to like-minded youngsters, in a digital way, online, people they have never physically met.

'These young people often start hacking, not because they are criminals or want to do any real damage, but just because they can, just for the thrill of doing it. It's their way of proving something to themselves. Proving that they have worth, that they can beat the system, the system that they often feel has let them down. So they group together and they become a clever, multi-functional group of, for want of a better term, 'Cyber Terrorists'. Then, several years ago the situation worsened, because now they can go around with a mobile device in their hands and no one can check what they are doing. Communication is becoming more and more anonymous, from one handheld device to another over an Internet transmission spectrum and into a global Cloud that we can't control or even see.'

The US map came back up, showing the buildings, the open boxes and the red Internet connections running in and out of the Cloud in every direction. A young girl and boy were communicating with tablets from either side of the screen. Yellow lines snaked out into the nearest boxes, then progressively through the others.

'As I just said, most of these youngsters mean no harm, they're just showing off, opening up boxes to prove how clever they are. However...' He pressed his monitor again.

The image of the girl morphed into that of a bank robber wearing a mask.

Then it morphed again into a robed Jihadist.

'Over the Internet you can insert any image you want in the mind of the other person. Now this robber or terrorist has got a tech-savvy kid to open doors for him. Not for the thrill of it, but for criminal or murderous intent. Or a naïve, vulnerable kid he can convert to some nefarious cause without him even realising who he's communicating with. You don't have to be a technical genius to use the Internet for criminal purposes. You don't even have to employ one. You just have to find one and play the game. Let them do the work then plan the result you want, financial, political, murderous, whatever is your objective. Thousands of these amateur hackers are out there, and it's not difficult to link up with them.'

Two newspaper headlines from the *New York Times* came up on the screen: 'Hackers Could Cripple West, Says US General'; 'Nuclear Sites in 20 Nations Seen Open to Cyber-Attack'.

Dr Middleton removed his spectacles and looked wearily at the camera. 'We believe it's only a matter of time before a coordinated cyber-attack occurs. A massive, multi-pronged attack which could cripple government, defence, financial, energy, communications and who knows what other possible targets. Imagine the chaos which would ensue. The financial and human damage could be greater than a military war. Because that's what we are looking at, a cyberwar, caused either by accident or by design, and if we are to avoid it, we must take urgent and effective action now, while we still have time. Thank you for your attention.' He stepped back from the camera and sat down.

EIGHT

San Diego, California, USA
April 2017

General Chillicott stood at the screen again, looking sternly at his audience. 'It's time for some plain speaking now, and I guess some folk won't be too pleased with what I have to say. We all know the number of cyber-crimes and attacks is growing exponentially; that terrorist entities and perversion thrive on access to the Dark Internet; that the new threats we've outlined will worsen until the situation reaches breaking point.

'Then there's the "elephant in the room" that no one wants to discuss. The hacking and publication of government and public records by traitors like Snowden, Assange and other well-organised groups. And along with the release of hacked genuine information, we've now got all the misinformation that hits the Internet every day, deliberately intended to make people confused and suspicious of respectable organisations and people that are being slandered without cause. This hacking and fake news outbreak is just the tip of the iceberg, it's going to get bigger and bigger.'

He counted on his fingers. 'The White House, the Democratic Party, the Joint Chiefs, the Bundestag, TV5 Monde, UK political parties. They've all been hacked in the last couple of years, and sensitive information published to destabilise governments and undermine public institutions, elections, and so on. And the governments of Ukraine, Estonia, Lithuania and other Eastern European countries have suffered sustained cyber-attacks on their administrative and military network infrastructures. We've just uncovered attacks and misinformation campaigns carried out in France, Germany, Bulgaria and Sweden. The Brexit referendum was surrounded by millions of fake social media posts which probably influenced the outcome of that vote. And during our elections last year, we saw a build-up of hacking of US election targets, both Democrat and Republican, and it seems highly likely that the election campaign and results might have been prejudiced. But I can't comment further on that.' He gave a cynical smile.

'The crazy thing is, we know who's mainly responsible and we're doing nothing about it. You've heard the names of some of these hackers: Guccifer 2.0, Fancy Bear, Cozy Bear. Well, all our leading cybersecurity firms, from ThreatConnect to Fidelis, have traced them all back to the same source, but no one wants to say it out loud. So, I'm going to say it for you. We've got beyond reasonable proof that these attacks were organised by cybercriminals working for GRU, the Russian Federation's military intelligence agency. The objective couldn't be more obvious. It's the destabilisation of the Western Alliance, the breakdown of NATO and ultimately the resurgence of the Soviet Union as the leading world power. And this is happening now, under our noses, and we're allowing it to happen and ignoring the devastating consequences that will ensue if we don't take urgent action right now, today.'

There was a lot of shuffling of feet and rustling of papers, some quiet mouth-to-ear comments in the room, but no one interrupted Chillicott.

'Let me get to the point of this whole roadshow.' A new slide came up, titled:

EXTRACT FROM UNITED NATIONS SECURITY COUNCIL INTERNET GOVERNANCE REPORT.

Underneath this heading the screen was blank, apart from one phrase:

UP UNTIL NOW, NO RESOLUTIONS CONCERNING CYBER SECURITY ISSUES HAVE BEEN ADOPTED BY THE UNSC.

'Despite all the dangers the world's facing because of the Internet, the Cloud and cyber-warfare, I've gotta tell you that up until now the UN Security Council has taken no effective action to avoid or mitigate a potential catastrophe. Over ten years ago, the Secretary General convened an Internet Governance Forum. That was the first time the UN showed any acknowledgement of the potential dangers we've described today. But since then, absolutely no progress has been made. None! What little work has been carried out for monitoring the Internet and the prevention of cyber-attacks has been made by individual entities and member states on their own initiative, like us at Homeland Security and at NATO, not by the UN as a body. And it's no good appealing to the companies that control the Internet: Google, Apple, Facebook, Microsoft, these companies know exactly what's going on, but all they're concerned with is getting more customers and making bigger profits. It's a vicious circle, and somebody's got to break it at the highest level, or it will never change.

'Dr Middleton and me, we've had two sessions just like this one with the UN Security Council in New York, and what's the result? Zilch! Under the UN Charter, member states are obliged to accept and carry out the decisions of the UNSC. That means they can force governments to implement a cyber security plan. Some kind of plan. Any kind of plan. And they can tie a budget to that plan, a budget that has to be met by all concerned. But right now, there's no plan and there's no budget. In the face of all the dangers we've outlined, and the daily evidence that these dangers are not virtual, but are real and deadly, we think it's high time the UNSC took some concrete steps to define a cyber security programme and a budget to get it agreed and implemented by the governments of the world, before it's too late.'

Chillicott looked around the room. It was silent, and every eye was upon him. 'I'm asking you all, here and now, to help us to get something done! The leaflet you'll find on the table as you leave explains our plan for a cyber security programme. We're asking for your support; please read the leaflet and subscribe to our website, in your own names and those of your companies. It's called *cybersecurityawareness.com*. It's part of our public information programme, and we want to use it as a platform to make the UNSC finally get off its ass and do something concrete. Please write, personally or on behalf of your company, to your local senator's office, or directly to the UN or UNCS, anywhere you can, to make a noise and help us to get something done about this imminent threat. We're also looking for people, high-level technical and admin employees to help in defending the US against these attacks, as well as volunteers to spread the message through the website and other measures.

'Thanks for coming here today and listening. Dr Middleton and I will take questions now.' He sat at the desk and poured himself a glass of water, and the silence in the room became a babble of sound as people switched their phones back on and started talking, texting and tweeting. Hugh Middleton's voice came over his earpiece. 'Rather impressive, Billy,' he said. 'Let's see if they got the message.'

When Leo took out his mobile, he saw he'd missed three calls from a number with a 971 country code. There was also a text message, *Please call this number urgently. Thanks.* He had no idea where the calls had come from, but it would have to wait. He wanted to listen to the Q&A session, it promised to be controversial. He put the phone back in his pocket to make the call later.

A hand went up in the audience and Chillicott got up again. 'Hi there. What's your name, position and question please?'

Before the invitee could answer, everyone looked in Leo's direction as his phone rang out loudly. It was same 971 number. He stood up, all six-foot-four of him, trying not to look too concerned. 'I'm sorry, sir. I'd better take this call, it seems to be urgent. Do I have your permission?'

'Go ahead, kid. Good luck.'

'Just a moment please,' he said into the phone and walked quickly towards the door, ignoring the curious glances around him, his heart suddenly in his mouth. *Something must have happened to my mum, she's sick or had an accident.'*

He went into the corridor. 'This is Leo Stewart. What is it?'

Leo was sitting with a Coke in the café/bar when General Chillicott walked in. He ordered a drink then, recognising him, he brought his glass over and sat beside him.

'Leo Stewart. I saw from the attendee list you're a programme development manager with M2M. Pretty damn good at your age. Congratulations.' He toasted him with his glass.

'Thanks, General. And I'm sorry about the interruption. I had to take the call, so I thought it best to leave.'

'Well, I hope it was more important and fruitful than my appeals for help with those idle sons of bitches at the UNSC.' He appraised Leo with a cynical, querulous eye.

'It wasn't life or death, but it was a pretty cool phone call.'

'You want to tell me about it?'

'I'm still a bit in shock, actually. And I don't want to take up your time.'

'After that question and answer session, I need at least two whiskies and then some supper. We've got plenty of time if you'd like to talk.'

'Was it that bad?'

'Let's just say I'd rather listen to your news 'til I calm down.'

'OK. I need to get my head around it, so here goes.' He took a swallow of Coke. 'It was kind of surreal. I answer the phone and a woman puts me through to some guy I don't know, and he starts talking to me like we've been friends forever. I'm like, *who the hell is this?* He's reviewing my school results in the UK, my time at UCLA, my finals, my internship with M2M, some news items about me, very embarrassing actually, and my work with them since I joined. He goes on for about five minutes. Finally, he takes a breath and I say, "Who is this calling?"'

Chillicott laughed uproariously. 'What a start to a conversation. Everything ass-backwards. What did he say?'

'Turned out the woman hadn't told him I didn't know who was calling, and he thought I'd be prepared.'

'Prepared for what?'

'He quizzed me for fifteen minutes then offered me a fucking fantastic job! Sorry, sir, but he'd never even met me before and offered to make me a Senior VP over the phone. I'm still in shock.'

'Now we're going ass-first. Who the hell is this guy, and what's the job?'

Leo stood up. 'I'm going to get a beer. You want another whisky?'

He returned from the bar and the two men toasted each other. Leo was beginning to like the bluff, outspoken army man, and the feeling was mutual. He continued with his narrative. 'The guy is called Tom Connor, and he's CEO of XPlus Circuits in Dubai.'

'That's the subsidiary of the Chinese outfit, isn't it?' Chillicott looked thoughtful.

'Right. Very strong competitor, well established in both conventional assets and IoT. I hear they've got huge funding.'

'And he wants you to be one of his Senior VPs? The whole business?'

'Only the microprocessor development division, there's another SVP running the network and support services, but it's still a massive task and it's what I'm best at. And they've got what could be the most valuable asset in the industry, if they develop it right.'

'The new encryption system?'

'ACRE, that's right. It's unbelievable. It's a goldmine waiting to be dug out, and I could be a part of the mining team. It's an awesome offer and if I told you the salary, you'd shoot me and take the job yourself.'

Chillicott gave another huge roar of laughter. He opened his coat. 'See? I'm not carrying. So, they want you that bad, eh? What happened to the previous guy?'

'Connor told me there was an accident and one of their team leaders died of food poisoning. They have to get a replacement in asap.'

The general sat thinking for a moment. 'Why was it so urgent he had to yank you out of a conference? He could have called back, nothing's that urgent.'

'He told me they've got a September 1st launch date for their new products, and they need someone right away. They've done their homework. He knew my contract with M2M is up for renewal this week, and M2M has already signed it, but I haven't yet.'

'How did he find that out?'

'I have no idea, and that's what's weird. There's a lot of things here that I can't figure. He made me a firm offer, only it's subject to me flying there this weekend to meet him on Monday. Seems like he's trying to rush me into a decision, and I don't like being pushed around. Even for an offer like this.'

'He wants you to drop the M2M contract and ship over to Dubai asap?'

'If the interview is OK, I have to answer next week and be ready to start in two weeks. I'm not so worried about M2M, they've got a lot of smart guys queuing up for my job. But if I let the guy push me around now, it'll only get worse, and no job is worth that kind of hassle.'

Chillicott looked at his watch. 'It's almost seven. If you don't have anything better to do, why don't we go along to the brasserie and have a bite? We can talk about this some more if you'd like.'

Leo was staying at the hotel and knew no one in San Diego. He didn't hesitate. 'Thanks, General, sounds great. I'll give my mother a call first. It's eleven in the morning in the UK, I know she'll be at home, writing.'

They finished their drinks and walked out of the bar, an incongruous pair: a disillusioned sixty-four-year-old, battle-hardened, four-star US Air Force General and a bright, optimistic and ambitious Rwandan man just twenty-three years old.

NINE

Durham, England
April 2017

'That's incredible news. Well done darling. I'm so proud of you.' Emma Stewart hadn't heard from her son for a week, and here he was announcing a fabulous job offer over the phone. Then she added nervously, 'Are you sure you want to move to the Middle East?'

'I haven't really had time to think about it, Mum. It came out of the blue, and they want me to go there this weekend and give them an answer next week so I can start in May.' He explained the reason for the rush and heard her draw a quick breath.

'How sad. Do they know how it happened?'

'Tom Connor told me the verdict was accidental death, so I guess they don't really know. Anyway, I suppose things like that happen, it has nothing to do with the job offer.'

'You don't sound convinced about it. What is it?'

'It's all the urgency around it. The guy calls me out of a conference, offers me a really senior job, and wants me to start in three weeks. It's just not normal.'

'Is it a very big company?'

'The Chinese parent is enormous, but the Dubai business is just at the point where someone could do really well if they get on board now. They're growing fast, and they've got a fabulous product and loads of cash to fund them.'

'You need to sleep on it. Things are always clearer in the morning.'

Leo smiled. He loved it when his mother came out with these old-fashioned sayings, as if he didn't know how a good night's sleep could help. He said, 'You're right, as usual, Mum. I'll sleep on it and call you when I've thought about it properly.'

San Diego, California, USA

General Chillicott was sitting at a table for six by the window, with another glass of whisky in front of him. The restaurant was almost full, but apparently no one had plucked up the courage to invade his space. Leo sat opposite him so the table would appear more occupied.

'Drink?'

'I'll just have a beer, General. Thanks.'

Chillicott ordered from the waiter, then said, 'If we're going to be talking all night, it'll be easier if you call me Billy. I'm not in the forces now.'

'What was the problem with the questions and answers, Billy?'

'We'll order first, I don't want to ruin my appetite.' He called the waiter back and asked for a burger, well done, with everything and double fries. Leo ordered the same, medium.

He took a sip of whisky. 'It's always the same problem. Same like we've got with those schmucks at the UNSC. Nobody's paying attention. All we're asking for is a sensible and well-funded programme to implement some proper security around the Internet and the Cloud, and it's like we're asking for funding to go on a trip to Saturn. The world's facing the biggest threat we've ever known, and nobody gives a crap. Hugh Middleton and me, we've done everything bar organise a street demonstration, but we can't get the message through.

'And those techies in that conference room. Nothing personal, Leo, but talk about vested interests. They've got their salaries, expense accounts, bonuses, stock options, and they all depend on one thing: making a shitty situation even worse. Because that's exactly what they're doing, and either they're not aware of it or they're just turning a blind eye. The evidence is there, right in front of them, but it's being ignored. You know what one of those "goody two-shoes" leftist pricks said after you'd gone? He stood up and he said, "Snowden and Assange have the same right as anyone to make public any knowledge that they possess, if they feel it's in the public interest." Fucking idiot. We're talking about national security here.'

Leo hid his smile. The general was clearly irritated. 'What did you say?'

Chillicott laughed loudly again. 'I said, suppose I was having an affair with your wife. I'm aware of it, she's aware of it, but no one else is. How would you like it if I told all the folks here then went on national TV and social media to announce it? How does that help anyone, especially you, the injured party?'

This time, Leo joined his uproarious guffaw. 'I hope it's nobody I know. Don't tell me. I might not be able to resist a dig next time I meet him.'

'Seriously, Leo, this is not a laughing matter. Middleton and me, and a few people like us, we're busting our balls to try to get something done by the UNSC, and it's a totally futile exercise. How many government secrets leaked, or banks or gullible people screwed out of their money, or harmless folk blown up, or innocent children trafficked need to happen for them to see what lack of Internet security is doing to the world? They just don't get it.'

He finished his whisky and sat back in the chair as the food arrived. Neither said much while eating. Chillicott was nursing his wounds from the conference, and Leo was sifting through that afternoon's presentation. He knew he was included in the 'techies', but it didn't bother him. Chillicott needed to vent his frustration and he happened to be the one listening. Leo had his own way of analysing, understanding and rationalising complex matters.

His experiences in South Africa years ago had helped him to mature quickly, and later helped him in his studies in foreign countries, competing with other students, often years older than him.

He waited until they'd finished eating, then asked, 'Billy, d'you mind if I say something?'

'Fire away. I've been taking a beating all day. No need to stop now.'

'Sometimes people don't want to notice, they don't want to see what's happening, to be confronted by the truth, however bad it is. Most times they don't react until something really terrible happens, or until it's too late. My mother was an aid worker in Rwanda after the genocide in 1994. She told me that for one hundred days, while a million people were being slaughtered, the whole world – the governments, the UN, everybody – just refused to acknowledge what was going on. They had a few people on the ground witnessing the atrocities, but they couldn't act, wouldn't act. Why? Because no one wanted to use the word "genocide" or the Genocide Convention would kick in, and would involve sending in troops. After the "Black Hawk Down" disaster in Somalia, the US wouldn't risk their soldiers on the ground. Then the UN was too late and too weak and so nothing was done until it was too late.

'Maybe it's like that this time. The Internet is such a powerful innovation for good that they don't want to face up to the bad side of it and create the security measures that you and Dr Middleton are asking for. If you're right, it's going to take something really bad to happen before something gets done. Meanwhile, all you can do is to prepare for it, and I'm sure that's what you're doing. But I wouldn't hold out too much hope of intervention from the UN or other organisations. They've been wrong before, and they'll certainly be wrong again.'

'Nice speech, Leo. Were you personally involved in that Rwandan tragedy?'

'I was just a baby, but my mum has told me a lot about it.'

Chillicott replied, 'Well, unfortunately I agree with you. I've done a lot of arm wrestling in my career, and you can't wrestle committees. They have to learn the hard way and it's usually a very expensive and destructive experience. Let's talk about the XPC offer. Can you do the job?'

'I don't know for sure, but I'm doing a similar job at M2M without the title, so I guess if I was able to do this job a year ago, I can do that one now.'

'But you're reticent. Why?'

'I guess a few things worry me. It's a fairly new company and it's owned by the Chinese. I don't know how dedicated they are to the business; they can afford to make it really successful, or they can retreat to Shanghai if it doesn't fly. Then, it's in a place I know nothing about, the Middle East. I've heard Dubai is a great place to vacation, but I don't know what it's like to live and work there. And then there's all the hurry-up because of the poisoning accident. This guy Connor comes out of nowhere and I'm supposed to run after him to solve his problems. What about me? I've got my own agenda, and he wants me to change it.'

'What do you think you'd do in his position? He's lost a key man, he's got a problem to solve with a tight deadline, he thinks you're the solution and he wants to meet you to be sure. It's a natural reaction from him and a terrific compliment to you.'

'So you think I should go to meet him on Monday?'

'That's the only way you'll find out what it's all about.'

'OK, you're right. I've got more to gain by going than by refusing, it's only a flight and they're paying the ticket. Thanks for the good advice, Billy, it's been a pleasure and a privilege to spend the evening with you.'

'Promise me one thing, Leo. If you take the job, keep in touch with me and Hugh Middleton. OK?'

Leo laughed. 'You trying to enlist me to the CIA now?'

'Just offering a lifeline if you need it. Here's to a good decision and a great future.'

'And here's to you somehow winning your arm wrestling contest.'

TEN

Malaga, Spain
May 2017

'There he is! Hi, Leo!' Emma Stewart called out and waved at the young man exiting the door of the arrivals hall at Malaga airport. At six foot four, he was easy to spot amongst the holidaymakers arriving for a shot of Spanish sunshine. Leo waved back, struggling to push his overloaded trolley through the crowded hall towards them.

'Hello Mum, Aunt Jenny, you both look great. You've got suntans already.' He embraced the two women and shook hands with Juan, Jenny's gardener-cum-chauffeur-cum-handyman. He mumbled a reply, then took the trolley and pushed it away towards the car park.

'It's been beautiful every day here since I came down,' said Emma. 'Nothing to do but sit and chat with my sister and sunbathe.'

'Get me warmed up for Dubai,' he laughed. 'How are you, Jenny?'

'All the better for seeing you back in Spain. How long can you stay?'

'I've got to be there for Saturday, to start at XPC on Sunday. Seems weird, their Sunday's our Monday.'

'Well, you're here for three days which is marvellous. In fact, the whole Stewart-Bishop family is together again for the first time in quite a while. We'll make the most of it.'

'How's the old man?' Leo asked with a cheeky grin.

'Alan's fine, thank you. And if he's an old man, that's not saying much for me.' Emma looked put out.

'Sorry. Just joking, Mum, is he down here?'

'He's in Edinburgh, busy signing up a new author. Jenny and I are having a sisters reunion week and you'd better not spoil it.' Two years ago, when it was clear that Leo would be settling in the US, Emma had married her publisher and long-term on-off boyfriend, Alan Bridges. They bought a house in Durham on the riverside, near the cathedral, and she gave up the cherished flat in Newcastle where Leo had been brought up. She knew that he had never warmed to Alan, so the 12,000-kilometre transatlantic separation helped to avoid any family disruptions.

'Great. I'm happy if you're happy. You know I never liked you living alone.' As soon as the words came out, he cringed inwardly. *That's going to upset Aunt Jenny.*

Jenny didn't seem to notice the remark and a few minutes later they were sitting in her Bentley, cruising smoothly along the A7 towards Marbella. The car had belonged to Charlie Bishop and was ten years old now, but thanks to Juan's devoted care and attention, still like brand new.

Juan stored Leo's three suitcases in the garage while he took his wheelie bag upstairs to a room overlooking the golf course and the Mediterranean. Encarni, Leticia's mother and Jenny's housekeeper, was nursing a cold at home, and knowing Leo would be hungry as always, Jenny and Emma went to prepare something to eat in the kitchen.

Emma took her sister's hand. 'Leo didn't mean what he said about being alone. It was just a thoughtless way of saying he was happy I married Alan.'

'Don't worry, Emma, it didn't upset me at all. I'm not exactly pining away from lack of attention. You know how busy I am with the private equity business. I travel a lot and mix with some interesting people, including eligible bachelors – well, divorcees more often – so I haven't given up hope.'

'Is it my imagination or did I hear a *sous-entendre* in that reply?'

Jenny laughed. 'Let's just say that I've had a few dates which might develop into something more.'

'Well don't leave me hanging out like the washing. Who is it?'

'Here. Bring the tray out and I'll tell you, but promise you won't say a word to anyone.'

Emma poured the tea. 'Right. I'm all ears.'

'You remember the bankers I work with in London, Fletcher, Rice? Well, one of the partners, Bill Redman, has a house on the beach at Los Monteros. It's just a few kilometres from here, along the A7 towards the airport. He's in the middle of a divorce and comes and goes from London by himself, the same as I do. We've seen each other there and here in Marbella. He's a lovely guy, clever and very funny.'

'And here I am, writing blogs for *TWM* and seeing you every month and you haven't breathed a word about him.'

'There's not a lot to say, except that,' she paused dramatically, 'last month I slept with him, for the first time in about a hundred years, and we've managed to get together a few times since then. Apart from that, nothing's happened. He hasn't gone down on one knee or anything like that, but I really do like him.'

'Wow, wow, wow. My sister's having sex again!' She grabbed Jenny in a tight embrace. 'What's it like?'

'It's marvellous, actually. But I don't want to make you jealous. And I don't want you to say a word to anyone. Promise?'

'Not a word, guide's honour. I hope you're on the pill? You don't want any accidents.'

Jenny frowned, 'I thought you knew. After Ron and I lost our baby, the doctors told me I wouldn't be able to have another. That's why we were thinking of adoption.'

Emma felt like biting her tongue off. 'I'm sorry, Jenny, how stupid, I wasn't thinking. Of course I remember.' She tried to hide her embarrassment. 'Does Bill have any children?'

'Two, a boy and girl. They live with their mother, although they've been down here and we had lunch together at the beach. They're nice, normal kids. I think it's a very civilised divorce from what I can tell, but it's taking a long time to get sorted.'

'Do you know what brought it about?'

'He hasn't said much about it and I don't pry, but from what little I know it sounds like she met someone else. He was travelling a lot until a couple of years ago and I think she just got lonely. It happens.'

'Well, I want regular reports in London when we have our publication meetings. If I have to buy a new wedding outfit, I'll need plenty of warning.'

'Don't rush out and spend your money yet. Never forget I've been married before, and I know it's not all milk and honey. Men are just overgrown little boys and they take a lot of looking after. At the moment, I've got the perks without the problems, so we'll just wait and see what happens.'

After a quick shower, Leo pulled on a T-shirt and shorts and went down to the terrace. It was now four in the afternoon and the sun cast a warm, friendly sheen across the sea.

'Back to paradise,' he said, sitting on a rattan chair beside the women. He took a sandwich from a plate on the glass-topped table, biting hungrily into it. 'I haven't had anything to eat since this morning. Slept all the way to London and again on the Malaga flight.'

'Right,' Emma said, 'if you're not too exhausted, let's have an update on why, when and how you decided to take the job.'

'Hmm. Good tea, Jenny, you still can't get a decent cup over in the States. Do I really have to undergo a cross-examination so soon after arriving?'

'We've heard nothing since your email about coming here, so we're bound to be inquisitive. Anyway, it's to show we care about you. We're waiting.'

'OK, Mum. Where to start? You remember I hadn't decided to go down for the interview when I called you right after speaking to Tom Connor in San Diego. Well, I had dinner that night with a retired US Air Force General, called Billy Chillicott. He's a big wheel at the Homeland Security Agency and he's sure lack of Internet security will bring the end of the world. I was actually in San Diego attending a lecture given by him and an English guy called Dr Hugh Middleton when Tom called. Billy talked me into going down for the interview, and I'm glad he did. The XPC people are working on some really cool stuff and I want to be a part of it.'

'Is it the same work you explained to me? Building billions of microprocessors to manage machines all over the world?'

Emma looked querulously at her sister. 'You'll have to explain it to me when you have time. I haven't a clue what he does.'

'It's similar. Except I'll be responsible for the whole process: development and design.' He gave them a simplified explanation of the job. 'And they've also got a really neat encryption-transmission technology, called ACRE, that could revolutionise the whole Internet industry. Tom wants me to oversee that project as well. He's appointed me as a Senior VP, to give me seniority over the other VP of product development.'

'You mean you'll be helping to make the Internet safer?'

'I'm gonna try my best. Chillicott and Middleton made a very convincing job of putting the frighteners on everyone at the conference. The whole Internet and Cloud computing scenario is an accident waiting to happen, according to them.'

'I'm not surprised,' said Emma. 'We know lots of people who've been defrauded online. It makes you afraid to use a credit card.'

'They're not talking about just credit cards. They think it's a lot more dangerous, that there's a big disaster brewing, ready to explode. The stakes are very high. That's why this job is a really good opportunity to make a difference, to create technology that helps to make things safer.'

His mother went quiet. 'What're you thinking?' Leo asked.

Emma replied, 'Did you hear what happened to the other man, the one who died?' Jenny looked at her in surprise. She hadn't been aware of the death.

'I asked Connor about that. It was just a fluke accident, the guy, Scotty Fitzgerald, got food poisoning from a curry dinner and it was very virulent and killed him.'

Jenny suddenly had a vision of a young man lying on his bed with his mouth open, trying in vain to scream for help. A cold shiver went up her back, but she hid the feeling and asked, 'I suppose there was an inquest?'

'Of course, Aunt Jenny. It's not a tin-pot dictatorship or a Third World country, you know. The verdict was accidental death by poisoning. I heard he'd had a lot to drink and they think that was part of the reason. Anyway, I don't like curry and I hardly drink at all, so I doubt it'll happen to me.'

She tried to lighten the conversation. 'Where will you live when you get there?'

'They've got a really cool apartment for me, I went to see it. Brand new, fully furnished with everything you can imagine, including a great sound system.' Leo was a heavy metal fan, starting with Led Zeppelin and moving on to Metallica, whose gig at San Francisco's AT&T Park he'd attended in May the previous year. Emma, a classical music lover, didn't understand his passion, even when he had played her their 2014 version of 'One' with Lang Lang on piano, but Jenny had fond memories of the music. Ron, her husband, had played guitar quite badly and spent hours practising Jimmy Page's legendary solo on 'Stairway to Heaven'.

'It's right by Jumeirah Beach,' he continued enthusiastically, 'very posh, a concierge and cleaning lady. A bit like Aunt Jenny's lifestyle.' He avoided her attempt to slap his face. 'I'll get a motorbike so I can get through the traffic and to the office easily. There's a great gym with a fight ring, squash, badminton, everything you could want.'

'Have you kept up your training?' Jenny was referring to Leo's Black Belt in Chun Kuk Do, a form of Taekwondo developed and taught by the American actor and martial artist, Chuck Norris.

'Three times a week without fail. Oh, I don't think I told you, I went in for the UFAF world championship tournament in Las Vegas last year.'

'How did you get on?' Now, Emma was intrigued. Leo had taken up self-defence sports after hearing tales from Leticia da Costa about Jenny. Her sister would never talk about it, but Leticia described how she bested a knife-wielding mugger in the park, then later saved all their lives by throwing the Angolan murderer, Ray d'Almeida, down the stairs of the house.

'I got kicked to shit, sorry, in the second round, which was cool, those guys were so much better than me.'

'I hope you won't need to do anything except practise it in Dubai.'

'Some chance. It'll be fine, don't worry. I'll be paid a fortune to enjoy myself. What more could I ask for?'

Relieved to have gotten over that hurdle, Leo decided to change the subject. He picked up the *Daily Telegraph* from the table. 'What about Brexit? It's not going so well, is it? Are you sorry for voting out?'

Both women started speaking at the same time and it was obvious they didn't agree. *Safe and sound*, he said to himself. *They'll have forgotten all about my job by the time they get through their arguments.* After a while he went up to his room to listen to his all-time favourite music, Led Zeppelin's fourth album, with 'Stairway to Heaven'. He put on his Bose earphones and lay on the bed, enjoying the present moment, full of hopeful anticipation for the future. He couldn't wait to get to Dubai.

ELEVEN

**London, England
May 2017**

The brass plaque outside the office entrance read *Institute for Global Internet Security*, and General Billy Chillicott pressed the intercom button and announced his name. The door was opened by an attractive woman of about forty. 'Good morning, General. Welcome back.'

'Hello Ilona. You're looking very beautiful this morning.'

The woman smiled. She was used to Chillicott's unsubtle approach, which she found flattering, but he wasn't her type. 'Thank you, General,' she replied. 'Dr Middleton is waiting in the small conference room.' She led the way through a large open plan office populated by a series of earnest-looking men and women at workstations with multiple computer screens in front of them.

'How's business? Seems like you've hired a few more people.'

'Looking up. The consumer side of the business is growing nicely. We've had a lot of success from our magazine and newspaper articles on bank fraud. And the governmental contracts are growing nicely. We just received a mandate to do a study for the

World Bank in Washington. They're worried about banking security in developing nations.'

He laughed. "'To do a study". So they're still paying lip service. We know what usually happens to the study: it gets published, they have a big meeting to discuss it, it gets filed away, nothing gets done. No change there.'

Chillicott knew that Ilona Tymoshenko was more than just the institute's receptionist-secretary. She was Middleton's minority partner in the business and had been instrumental in obtaining many of their contracts. He wasn't surprised. *She could charm the apples off the trees*, he said to himself. *When she feels like it.*

Hugh Middleton was sitting at the conference table, drinking tea and reading the *Financial Times*. 'Billy, how nice of you to visit.' He jumped up and they shook hands. 'What brings you to London?'

'The short answer is Brexit. It looks to us more and more likely you guys will crash out of the EU without a deal in place. You know what that means in terms of security and defence, NATO, the whole works. And even if you do come to an agreement, when it finally happens it'll still affect just about every defence agreement we have with Europe and the UK, and especially NATO. Jim Mattis is in the middle of a pretty big shake up of the Defence Department and he's got those shitholes, Iraq and Syria, to worry about, so he asked me to pay an informal visit to talk with some of your MoD people. We had a session all day yesterday and I didn't sleep a lot last night. I guess you'll understand I can't say much more than that.'

'Perfectly understandable discretion, which I applaud. If you slept badly I expect you need a gallon of weak American coffee. Ilona dear, can you arrange that?'

She left the room and the two men sat at the table. 'I hear you're going to get some money from the World Bank. You should set up a small country, you'll get even more.'

'Amazingly, we currently have twelve small countries paying us. It's becoming quite a trend.'

'To write reports they light the fire with?' Chillicott smiled cynically.

'Unfortunately, we cannot force them to actually do anything that we recommend. I'm not even convinced that they read what we send them. In any event, I'm quite sure that they request reimbursement of our not-unsubstantial fees from some supra-national organisation which is partly funded by them in the first place. So it's like all circular discretionary government spending, what I refer to as "OPM, Other People's Money". In the end, you and I pay for it with our taxes.'

Ilona heard this last comment as she came back into the room with the coffee. 'My, my, aren't we becoming cynical?' She poured a cup for Chillicott.

'Mm, thanks, hot and sweet. What Hugh means is our constant bitching and moaning is having no effect at all, *nichts, rien, nada,* but they keep paying us to do it. It's insane.'

'As long as we can cover the salaries and costs, I don't mind the insanity. I've got jobs to do, call if you need me.' She left the room.

'By the way, I thought our San Diego presentation went quite well. How many of those hi-tech executives signed up on the website afterwards?'

'Don't even ask. There were about a hundred and thirty attendees, and twelve of them have signed up. That's less than ten per cent, including the kid I met for dinner after the presentation, so maybe we need to do one-on-one sessions in future.'

'You must have forgotten to tell me about that. Is the story worth relating?'

'It was the young guy who had to leave the hall to take a phone call. Just when we were starting that crappy question and answer session.'

'I didn't notice the incident. You're forgetting that I was in London, and although the audience could see me, I couldn't see them.'

'Right, sorry, I guess I'm trying to forget the whole fiasco. It was a young African kid, Leo Stewart. He got a phone call offering him a new job in the middle of our Q&A. At least something good came out of it.'

Middleton gave an imperceptible blink. 'Leo Stewart, you say? That's not a very African name.'

'He was a Rwandan genocide baby, apparently. I didn't go into that. Too personal, bloody dreadful time. He's one hell of a smart kid, he'll do well.'

'What was the job? Did he tell you?'

'He asked my opinion about the offer. XPlus Circuits in Dubai wanted to make him a Senior VP. He's only twenty-three, hardly old enough to vote, for Christ's sake.'

'XPC, that's the subsidiary out of Lee-Win in China? What was the reason for the frantic phone call, it seems a little impetuous?'

Chillicott gave a quick resumé of his conversation with Leo, including the death of the previous VP at XPC and the imminent deadline for the new software launches.

'An unexplained death, you say? How did it happen?'

'It was an accidental death by food poisoning. Why the sudden interest, Hugh?'

'No special reason, Billy, I have a curious mind, that's all. Death in all its various manifestations interests me, especially the accidental variety. Enough of such talk, where was the boy previously?'

'At M2M in San Francisco. He seems to be a bit of a prodigy. I was talking to the president and he told me they tried everything not to lose him. Offered him a promotion and big pay rise, but he left a couple of weeks ago when his contract was up.'

'I see. So XPC needed his encryption expertise for their new software products and he took the job and moved to Dubai, just like that.' Middleton looked thoughtful. 'What advice did you give him?'

'It wasn't much in the way of advice. I told him it was worth going over there to check things out. Seems like he did that and the trip paid off.' He took another swallow of coffee. 'Thing is, Hugh, the kid gave me some very smart advice himself. His mother was in Rwanda after the genocide and she told him a million people were slaughtered while the rest of the world stood by and watched it happen. Nobody was prepared to say that genocide was being committed until it was too late.

'His opinion was that it could be the same thing with the Internet, that people don't want to be confronted by the truth, however bad it is. They concentrate on the good it can do and do jack-shit about the security measures we talk about until it's too late. So we're just spinning our wheels until some global catastrophe occurs to wake them up. Then they'll come crying to us to fix it.'

'It sounds as if that young man is a very intelligent and mature person, and I agree with his analogy. Unfortunately, we are like Aesop's fabled boy who called wolf too often. When finally the wolf comes, no one believes it until the whole flock of sheep is ravaged. I fear that is what may happen, and all of our warnings will have been of no avail.'

'It made me think, if we can't convince anyone by our words, maybe we should organise a catastrophe of our own. That might get the world's attention and finally force governments to take some action.'

Middleton smiled. 'It's fortunate that I know your sense of humour. Such remarks could be interpreted as treason or instigation to commit heinous crimes. Are you still in touch with young Mr Stewart?'

'I gave him both our email and phone details, but I'd be surprised if he ever makes contact. He's got his hands full in a shit-hot job with a fast-growing company, too busy for old farts like us.'

Dr Middleton invited Ilona Tymoshenko to join them, and they talked about global developments; Brexit, the increasing threat of African immigration, growing political instability in Europe and the uncertainty caused by the US election results. International cyber security concerns were discussed at length, Ilona cleverly gleaning from the conversation a number of potential business opportunities for their Internet consulting practice. Finally, they discussed the planning of yet another visit to the UN Security Council's New York headquarters in July. It was becoming difficult to find anything new to say at these events, although, as Chillicott reminded them, 'There's bound to be plenty of new disasters to talk about, but probably none bad enough to get their attention.' As usual, the Englishman apologised that he wasn't able to come over in person, he'd have to participate by teleconferencing again.

Chillicott declined an invitation for lunch at Middleton's club, he'd been before and hated the staid atmosphere and English food; not a hamburger on the menu. Ilona took him to the door and he embraced her, then climbed into the car waiting to take him back to Whitehall.

As she closed the door, Dr Middleton called, 'Ilona, could you come back in here please, I'd like to dictate some notes.' She sat at the table beside him. 'Oh, and I'd like you to find out everything you can about a young man named Leo Stewart and his immediate family. He's with XPlus Circuits in Dubai.' He thought for a moment. 'And do some research on XPC as well as their parent, Lee-Win Micro-Technology in Shanghai, please.'

TWELVE

Dubai, United Arab Emirates
May 2017

'Apart from a few points I want to cover this morning, things seem to be going fine, but I don't have to remind you the timing's really tight. First off, I had to find a new VP to replace Scotty on the Mark VII firmware development, and we've been really lucky with that. His name's Ed Muire, he was a senior programmer with ARM, and he'll be here in ten days. With his experience, I'm betting he'll be up and running in no time.'

Leo Stewart was reviewing his first two weeks as SVP at XPC with his immediate boss, Shen Fu Liáng and their CEO, Tom Connor. At just twenty-three years of age, Leo was responsible for three work-teams, thirty-six people in all, including Sharif, the VP who now reported to him. They were sitting in Tom's office on the fourth floor of the building, looking out onto a terrace area with a small swimming pool and bar. *Reserved for VIP guests,* Leo imagined, feeling quite flattered to have been invited up. The air conditioning was hardly noticeable, since a violent storm had come in the night, bringing the temperature down from thirty-eight Celsius to a more tolerable twenty-five. The African blood in Leo's veins meant that he could withstand the hot weather better than most, but it was a lot hotter than San Francisco and he was still acclimatising to it.

Leo had asked for this meeting for two main reasons. The first was that, probably due to Scotty's disappearance, the reporting structure between Tom, Shen, Sharif and himself wasn't working and needed sorting out. Then there was the planning system, or rather, lack of it. At M2M he'd been used to a well-defined work programme, with constant performance reviewing and measuring, rewarding or correcting where necessary, but planning at XPC was almost non-existent, with no clearly defined separation between the immediate priorities of delivering Mark VII and ACRE. The final specifications and designs had to be in Shanghai by the end of July for the 1 September launch date, just three months away, and they were running late, but Tom and Shen seemed to take the approach that 'it'll be alright on the night'.

This meeting was not going to be easy, but he didn't think he'd been hired to take the easy way out and that wasn't his way of working. It also wasn't his way of viewing life, you either did things properly to the best of your ability, or you didn't do them at all. He plugged the projector into his laptop and addressed the second problem first:

THREE-MONTH WORK PROGRAMME

'Here's the short version,' he said. 'If we want to deliver the full software package to Shanghai by July 31st we need to create, right now, a critical path work plan, as well as a review and correction procedure. It's necessary and urgent, so if there are no comments, I'll just get on with it and sort it out.'

The three men spent the next two hours going through the report and discussing Leo's concerns. He had expected little or no input from Shen, but he was disappointed with Tom Connor, who seemed to be ambivalent about what Leo considered to be a black-and-white choice of alternatives. He kept repeating the same simple message time after time until he got it across, 'Either you plan properly then measure and correct regularly, or you have no idea of how or when you'll be able to deliver your assignment, if you ever do.' He finally got the others to agree to create a planning committee of Shen, Sharif, Ed Muire and himself. Daniel Oberhart would also be involved when necessary. By the end of the week, the committee would issue a plan for the three months up to the launch date.

Relieved, Leo moved onto his most pressing worry:

REPORTING STRUCTURE

Here, he was even more dismayed at the CEO's lack of decisiveness and apparent dithering. It seemed he didn't want to clarify the relationship between the four people principally involved: himself, Leo, Sharif and Shen.

When he saw he was getting nowhere, Leo said, 'Listen guys, this is a very simple problem. I don't want to spend my time running around making sure that Sharif is doing what I tell him to and not what Shen tells him. And Tom, the same thing applies to you and Shen, you have to remember he's my boss, otherwise it will be just one enormous crapshoot. That's not the way to run a corner shop, never mind a hi-tech, multimillion-dollar business. If it doesn't change I won't have time to get close to the development teams to do the job I was hired for, so I should simply get on the next flight back to SF and let you get on with things without me.'

Tom could see that Leo was serious. After the business with Scotty, he couldn't afford another screw-up in the new products division, it would cost him his job. 'What exactly do you want us to do?'

'OK. First, no offence, Tom, but I don't want you to talk to me about operational matters and I don't want to receive any direct instructions from you. Anything you want to say to me you should say it through Shen, or we have a three-way meeting to discuss it.

'Second, Shen, I want you to stay away from Sharif and his team. Please make it clear to them that they report to me and we'll avoid any further confusion. If you have something to suggest or discuss, you do it with Sharif and I together. The same rules will apply to the Mark VII team. Ed Muire will be arriving next week and that'll simplify everybody's life.

'Third, to make sure that you guys are up to speed on everything and can kick my ass when I screw up, I suggest the planning committee meets with Tom every Sunday to catch up on the previous week and plan for the current one. I'll prepare a weekly summary report so everyone's on the same page.'

Tom and Shen finally agreed Leo's proposals, although he could see Shen wasn't happy to cut his ties with Sharif. *He'll get used to it,* he said to himself, *and I can forget all the political crap and get on with some productive work.* 'I'll get Daniel Oberhart on board. I know he feels the same way as I do, it's not what he was used to in Zurich.' Privately, he wasn't enjoying working with the Swiss man. He was uncommunicative and inflexible and could be cold and hostile when he felt his area of responsibility was being infringed, but Leo knew he had to toe the line to make the whole programme work.

Finally, Leo brought up the ACRE upgrade programme. He insisted on being personally tasked with this project, heading the separate four-man team. 'Otherwise it'll just get lost in the rush to get the Mark VII products finished. I think it's by far our prime go-to market asset, and encryption happens to be my strongest suit. We should aim to bring out a new version at least every two years. Each upgrade is an uptick in our monthly revenue and makes our customers feel warm and cosy and looked after by XPC. Once Ed takes over Mark VII, I'll be able to work on nothing else but ACRE. We have to prove we can fulfil our timetable, just like we promised.'

Shen began to argue the matter, but surprisingly, Tom supported his proposal and called the meeting to a close.

'Thanks guys,' Leo said. 'You won't regret this. Now we can get on with our jobs.' Back in his office, he circulated the email he'd already written, with the reporting chart, to everyone concerned, including Tom and Shen. Then he went to see Daniel Oberhart, hoping this organisational change wasn't going to upset their working relationship.

Tom Connor was sitting in his office reading Leo's message when Shen came back in. 'What did you think of all that?'

Tom walked to the window. An Asian man in overalls was pushing a vacuum cleaning hose around the pool. He kept his gaze downwards, didn't look towards the office. Tom always felt sorry for the manual workers in the Emirates. They had no real status, worked at menial jobs, earned a pittance, sent money home to their families and lived in crowded, shitty little apartments in compounds with others like them. *What kind of an existence is that?* he asked himself. *And we westerners are living off the fat of the land. No wonder there's so much trouble in the world.*

He sat back at his desk. 'What do you mean by "all that"?'

'That kid, Leo. Taking over the whole show and you just sat there and let it happen. He's the youngest employee in the division and now he's suddenly telling us all what to do. Why did you let him get away with it?'

Tom had been expecting this reaction and had already considered his response. 'Three reasons, Shen. First of all, he's right. He's right on the reporting, he's right on the planning and he's right on the button in prioritising our work. Secondly, we can't afford to have him walk out and look as if we completely screwed up. It would be a catastrophe for the company and for us personally. And the third reason is, no one else has come forward with a clear plan of action and the balls to present it like he did. You haven't done it, I haven't done it either and frankly, it had to be done.

'Let's face the facts, Shen. We fell into sleepy mode when Scotty was here. Between him and Sharif we didn't have to worry about any of that, they were a great team combination. They made it happen and as long as they delivered we just went along with it. I spent all my time on marketing, operations and finance and I didn't have to worry about development. But since he died we haven't faced up to the situation. Things on the development side are out of hand and we've got to get it sorted. Leo's right, it's not a way to run a business. I don't give a shit how old he is. If he's got the balls to talk to us like that, to see what needs to be done as clear as he does and be ready to take it on, then I'll back him, and I want you to do the same.'

Shen seemed not to notice the CEO's indirect criticism of his stewardship of the development division. 'OK, I'll go along with your decision, but I want it to be noted that I disagree with you. If things go wrong, I want to be on record that I warned you and you ignored my warning. Understood?'

'Understood. I'll dictate a minute of this discussion to Nora to type up and we can both sign it. But what do you mean by "things going wrong". What do you expect to go wrong?'

'Let's just wait and see. That kid is young and arrogant. He's taking on an awful lot and he doesn't have the experience of running multi-project programmes. I hope it works out, but I'm not convinced.'

'I'm fine with that, so long as you don't try to step on my toes. Just sort out the programming side and leave me to worry about my responsibilities.' Daniel Oberhart had listened to Leo's summary of the meeting and delivered his fairly lukewarm opinion of the result.

'I know how to respect boundaries,' he replied. 'I've done a lot of that in my life.'

Oberhart said nothing. He filed away the chart and Tom's memo and looked back at his computer screen, apparently waiting for Leo to leave.

Strange guy, he thought to himself. *He doesn't seem at all interested in anyone. Never asked me a question; where do I come from, what have I done, how did I get the job, nothing at all. Maybe it's my fault, I've been too busy to get to know him. Well, someone has to make an effort.* He said, 'Tom told me you've been with XPC since the start-up in 2014?'

Daniel tore his gaze away from his computer. 'That's right, I was in the set-up team.'

'Came over from MicroCentral in Geneva, right?'

'Zurich. I'm *Suisse Allemand*, not *Romand*, different mindset altogether.'

'Sorry, Daniel. I guess that's like calling a German an Italian.'

He gave a slight smile. 'Something like that.'

It took Leo ten minutes to prise any personal information out of the Swiss man, finally learning MicroCentral had been founded by his father and was now majority owned by a Chinese hedge fund. He'd been with them for ten years before leaving to come to XPC.

'Wow! That must have been one hell of a decision, what made you check out of the family business?'

Oberhart's expression didn't change. 'Money.' He saw Leo's eyes widen with surprise and added, 'Have you ever worked for your father?'

'I didn't even know him. He left my mum when I was a baby.'

'Oh, well, ten years was enough, believe me. When Lee-Win asked me to come over here, it was just a question of what's in it for me? Then, how quickly can I come?'

'Do you see your folks, now that you're out of the stress of working together?'

'My mother died five years ago and no, I haven't seen my father since I came down. Now, I've got to get the night schedule out, so I'll see you later.' He turned back to his keyboard and started typing.

Leo went over to the elevator, *What a character, he's just like a cold fish. To walk away from your father and not even go to see him.* He calculated that Oberhart was in his mid- thirties, that meant his father would be coming up to sixty. *How can you not visit your only remaining parent for almost three years?* He'd lied to Oberhart about his own father leaving his family, it wasn't like that at all. His mind drifted back to his childhood in Newcastle, living in a tiny flat with his mother, wondering who his father had been, where he'd gone, where he was, if he was even still alive and why he was just another one-parent kid at school. It wasn't until after his abduction in 2010 that Emma had decided it was time to tell him about his Rwandan mother, Mutesi, and her rape at the hands of a Hutu genocider. How after her death, Emma had smuggled the newborn baby into England and somehow managed to get him registered as a UK citizen.

Leo had known there was a great mystery around his birth, but for sixteen years Emma had kept her secret, and when finally he learned the whole story, the dreadful truth was almost too much to cope with. But the one thing he had to cling on to, the only thing that mattered, was that his adoptive mother had moved heaven and earth to find him, and with Aunt Jenny's and Marius Coetzee's help had brought him back to safety and a loving, stable home. Leo knew he could never give up his adoptive family for anything, or anybody.

He felt sorry for Daniel Oberhart. *He still has his father, but he's lost that magical family love, and it doesn't sound as if he's very bothered about it.*

That afternoon, Sharif came to see him. 'Shen told me you're taking over the ACRE programme. There's no need, I can do it, I worked with Scotty on the encryption development.'

'I haven't really had time to look at the progress on it, Sharif, so I'm not criticising or even commenting on the status. My thinking is only that you've got a huge job to get the new product out and it's our top priority, even more important than ACRE,' he emphasised, hoping that would defuse Sharif's disappointment. 'Ed Muire's arriving next week. He comes from ARM, so he should be shit-hot. He'll work alongside you and we'll have two really strong teams to deliver Mark VII, and I'll have time to look after ACRE properly.'

Sharif supressed his annoyance at Leo's decision and the two men shook hands on the matter. Leo wasn't very happy about the conversation. *Why would he want to try to manage two massive projects at the same time? He knows he can't do it.* He was having trouble understanding the players in the game; what were their motives, why were they being so counter-productive, what were their real objectives? *Don't we all work for the same company?*

The first meeting of the planning committee was called for the following afternoon. Sharif seemed to have put the previous day's argument behind him. He was positive and keen to take responsibility for his team's input, and Leo was impressed with his contribution to the discussion. Daniel Oberhart was also a useful contributor, with his expertise in network planning and scheduling. Shen, on the other hand, said virtually nothing, and Leo was obliged to run the meeting himself. *I wonder why the guy was sent down from Shanghai? He adds no value at all.*

THIRTEEN

Dubai, United Arab Emirates
June 2017

It was nine at night and Leo Stewart was still working in his office on the second floor of the XPC building. Apart from the night shift customer support staff, he and the man sitting opposite him were the only people in the building. He'd just finished marking up the critical path chart prepared by his planning committee against the status from the week's performance report. After two weeks, they were two days behind schedule. At that rate they'd be a week late by the end of July. Unacceptable, and not what he wanted to tell Tom and Shen at their management meeting on Sunday. He'd have a serious talk the next morning with Sharif and Kurt Reiner, the senior programmer in the firmware team.

He turned his attention to the second report on his desk, from Ed Muire, who'd arrived from the UK that week to take over Mark VII as soon as he was settled in. Leo had given him a test mission to assess the ACRE upgrade status and produce a 'warts and all' report for him. It should tell him a lot about the technology, and probably a lot more about Ed. As far as he could find, this was the first report ever produced by the team, he'd been unable to discover any other.

Once again, he despaired at the lack of organisation and control he'd faced when he arrived, and vowed he'd either lick everyone into shape or leave them to wallow in their own incompetence. He was glad he had only the development division to worry about, *I certainly hope the rest of the business is better organised*, he thought. *Tom can't leave everything to chance as he seems to have done in this area.*

Leo glanced quickly through the update. He wasn't expecting much, but was pleasantly surprised at the sparse but clear summary prepared by the Liverpool man. 'Better than I expected, Ed. How much time did you have to give it the once over?'

Ed chewed on his gum a moment. Leo assumed he must have given up smoking recently, since he seemed to consume a lot of chewing gum. He made no comment, waiting for the new man's answer. 'Not a lot, frankly. By the time I got settled in and did the "Hail fellow, well met" routine, I've had a couple of days to go through the files and run a few basic tests on the new software. I wanted to make sure it's stable, but I haven't worked through the test logs so I can't substantiate any of that. It's a work-in-progress for the minute.'

'What's your gut feeling about the recurring encryption algorithm?'

'The short version? It really rocks. I've never seen anything so cool in my life, it'll totally change the way the Internet works and I bet it'll make Lee-Win and XPC unbeatable in the marketplace.'

'It already has. Scotty Fitzgerald was a genius, a legend. He wasn't very organised, but I would have loved to work with a maverick like him.'

'Yep, tragic accident and a great waste of talent, it's up to us to carry on the good work. Anyway, so far I've got a good idea of the overall envelope and it looks sensible, subject to any surprises when I go through the test logs. My main concern is the remote implementation; it's still in the solution stage and that's not my speciality.'

Leo knew that all Lee-Win processors were built with the same constant foundations, so that any improvements in future models were backwards compatible to upgrade previous versions. They also incorporated a connectivity module that, when activated, would permit all their devices and machines to connect together in a mesh network using any form of local transmission. In the new Mark VII product with ACRE, the connectivity module would be activated before deployment from the Shanghai factory, but Ed was referring to the remote Internet process for the billions of Lee-Win processors already installed all over the world. The upgrade of Mark VII had to activate the connectivity modules and the new version of ACRE would be uploaded at the same time. The combination of the two upgrades would provide customers with a totally encrypted communications network throughout their devices and systems, wherever they were installed.

'OK. I'm starting to see the trees from the forest now and I know a little bit about the remote side of things, that was my main focus at M2M. I'll start looking at the upgrades and that connectivity problem. If you can spend a little more time in the lab this week to finish your tests on *ACRE*, I'll be ready to take it over from Sunday. That'll let you get involved full-time on finishing the rest of the Mark VII development with your new team. It's the fastest way to make progress on all fronts. Thanks for writing up this initial assessment for me, it's saved me a lot of time. If I need your help, I'll shout. Deal?"

'Deal.' Ed was pleased to have his situation clarified. He wanted to get on with his principal job: managing the firmware team.

'Cool. What do you say to a beer and a quick bite at the Corner House?'

Ed hadn't yet acquired a vehicle, and a few minutes later he was hanging on to Leo's waist as they roared along the coast road on his Harley to the most popular café on the stretch.

'Fabulous ride,' Ed admired the bike as Leo parked it outside the restaurant. It was black with red trim, old-fashioned styling that reminded him of the English Triumphs and Nortons of the fifties and sixties.

'Thanks, it's a Softail Slim. I got it in SF before I left and had it shipped over. Saved about ten grand.'

'If I'd known you then, you could have brought two.'

It was still too hot to sit outside, and they found a table in the air-conditioned interior from which they could see the action. As usual, the music from the speakers was so loud they had to shout to have a conversation. An English-looking waitress, about twenty, came for their order and they both asked for medium hamburgers and beers.

'What's your name?' Ed asked the girl when she brought the drinks.

'Lynne,' she replied. 'I'm new, haven't even got a name tag yet. I just arrived at the weekend.'

'Hi, Lynne. This is Leo and I'm Ed. You English?'

'From Wrexham, just on the Welsh border. My name is Welsh, but my mam and dad are English. How about you guys?'

'Leo's just come from California and I was almost your next-door neighbour, from Liverpool, but you probably already guessed that.'

Leo was impressed with Ed's introduction routine. *He must have spent a lot of time picking up waitresses*, he figured. The girl left them, and he asked, 'Where did you get the chat-up lines?'

'I'm twenty-six and you learn that in junior school in Liverpool, so I've picked up a few more birds than you. And the US doesn't prepare you for English totty. Totally different ball game.'

'You're right, American girls really are different from Europeans, even I noticed that.' Leo had gone out with only three girls in the US. None of them had been memorable experiences. He'd had sex a few times with Joanna, the last one, but it hadn't been serious enough for him to stay in San Francisco. She'd driven him to the airport and he'd promised to write, but so far he hadn't found the time, or the inclination, if he was honest.

Lynne brought their hamburgers with two more beers, and Leo chatted with Ed over their meal. He was a grammar school boy who'd gone through a three-year apprenticeship with British

Telecom and stayed there until he was twenty-two. He'd then spent four years with ARM, the largest microchip software designer in the world, in their Cambridge headquarters. He was already looking for a new challenge when Leo spotted him on LinkedIn, and after seeing his CV and references he approved Ed's job offer proposed by the HR department without even meeting him. Prior to his showdown with Tom and Shen, he felt under such pressure to deliver Mark VII that he had to cut some corners if he was going to make it happen.

After talking with him for an hour, Leo was convinced he'd taken the right decision. Ed had specialised in the same development areas that Leo was managing and was well qualified for the job. Lynne brought them a couple more beers, and by the time they paid the bill, Ed had fixed up a date with her for the following Sunday, her day off.

FOURTEEN

London, England
June 2017

'I couldn't manage another mouthful, thanks, Emil.' Jenny Bishop took a last sip of Savigny les Beaune and regretfully watched the head waiter wheel away the dessert trolley. She was having dinner with her sister Emma and Jo Greenwell, her partner in *Thinking Woman Magazine*, at the Langham Hotel on Portland Place, where she stayed when Bill Redman wasn't in town. They hadn't yet got to the stage when she gave up her independence and stayed in his flat. The evening was ostensibly to celebrate the latest company numbers, which were starting to go through the roof, but there was another, more personal reason that Jenny and Emma hadn't disclosed to the younger woman.

She opened up the subject. 'Where's Alan, Emma? I thought he was coming this week.'

'He's in Stockholm, signing up the Scandinavian rights for one of his up-and-coming writers. Too busy as usual, but otherwise fine. We're coming down together next week and we've got a couple of shows booked. The summer exhibition's on at the RA, so there's plenty to do. London in July, paradise. Then it's back to Durham to finish the latest tome by August. How about you and Bill?'

'I was with him last night and he surprised the life out of me. He's booked us on a cruise in September, from Venice to Istanbul. Three days in Venice in a six-star hotel that I can't remember the name of, then ten days in a grand suite on the *Silver Dream*, floating down the Dalmatian coast, through the Greek Islands to Istanbul.'

'Wow! Seems like he means business.' Jo grabbed Jenny's hand. 'Well done you, about time.'

'Speaking of which,' Emma came, not too subtly, to the point of their pantomime, 'what news from you, Mademoiselle Greenwell?'

'You mean, in the romance department? No news is good news for the moment. I've got too much to do, and you both know that as well as I do. I can't afford to lose my focus now the magazine is really starting to take off, or we'll be back to where we were last year at this time. If the business continues to grow like this, Jenny and I have agreed to take on another editorial assistant in September to free me up a bit. So you can ask me the question again in October.'

'I'm only concerned that you work too hard and play too little. You're a young, beautiful woman and you shouldn't be stuck in an office all day and night. You've got to get out and have some fun, meeting people of your own age. A healthy balance is what we all need.'

'You sound just like my mother,' Jo laughed, a little uncomfortably. 'Would you two get off my case? I'll decide when I've got the time to go man-hunting, and I promise you'll be the first to know when I find myself one. Now, Emma, I want to know all about your new book.'

London, England

Hugh Middleton was studying the dossier on Leo Stewart and XPC given to him by Ilona. It was extremely complete and confirmed what he already knew. It was too much of a coincidence to imagine that there was another Leo Stewart with a mother who had been in Rwanda.

His mind went back to the aborted abduction in July 2010. It had ended in complete catastrophe, and the young boy had somehow managed to escape when he should have been safely transported and held in Zimbabwe. Middleton, or as he was known at the time, Lord Arthur Dudley, was fortunate there was no definite proof linking him directly with the kidnapping or the associated murders, nor with a drug smuggling plot in France which he had deliberately sabotaged, but an unlucky coincidence had led the UK police to his door. After a long and complicated investigation, and a very distasteful public trial, he had finally been convicted of money laundering. Since there was no proof that the funds in his Lugano bank account came from any criminal activity, and the recipients of his transfer of $25,000 to a Panamanian account could not be identified, the judge's decision was fairly lenient. But Dudley suffered the shame and embarrassment of being convicted and imprisoned. After serving six of his twelve-month sentence in Ford Open Prison in West Sussex, he emerged in June 2011, a changed character in many important ways.

His conversion was partly due to one man, the Rev. David Morpeth, the prison chaplain, who befriended Dudley and took it upon himself to convince him to use his considerable intellect in the service of good, rather than evil. Morpeth, a petty criminal, had undergone a similar change when he'd been jailed for manslaughter for killing a young woman while driving away from a robbery. Both men were proof that prison doesn't always change villains for the worse. But in Lord Arthur Dudley's case, the motivation to go straight was a primitive emotion: pride. He was an exceptionally intelligent man and his long, successful criminal career had given him a feeling of superiority and invulnerability. Outwitting the inferior intellect of international police forces had become a game to him; until he was caught. Being incarcerated was, for Dudley, a sign that the game was up; he had no doubt that he was still superior, but he knew he was no longer invulnerable. He couldn't face the prospect of a return to prison, and determined to find a way of using his particular skills to make an honest and profitable living.

Before acquiring a taste for criminality, Dudley had held the post of Professor of Connected Machines Eco System Studies at Cambridge College of Digital Computing, and he was an extremely competent and innovative head of department. The college achieved a number of outstanding academic firsts and business start-up successes in Machine-to-Machine Communications, and the board of governors were greatly saddened when they were forced to ask for his resignation after complaints from a number of students, both male and female.

The world of M2M had evolved enormously since then, and Dudley spent the last three months of his 'holiday' in the open prison swatting up on what had become IoT, the Internet of Things. Dudley's conviction, due to an online transfer of funds from an account he wasn't supposed to have, had marked him. Now, every day he saw newspaper and TV stories exposing the lack of Internet security that was causing loss and damage all over the world. An idea formed in his mind and gradually became a concrete project for his next vocation. He would re-enter the world of IoT, this time not in the academic arena, where his reputation might create unsurmountable barriers, but in a commercial environment where he could help to protect the world from the inherent dangers of the Internet.

For the next six months, Dudley continued his IoT studies and transferred his offshore cash to the UK to fund the new business. He realised he needed a competent and experienced partner to 'front' the company, and in this he was rewarded by a fortunate coincidence. Ilona Tymoshenko was an information security official at the Ukraine Security Service, whose investigatory work had led to the arrest of five Ukrainian hacker kingpins in 2010. The hackers had used *Conficker*, a fast-spreading worm, to steal over $70 million from US bank accounts, and faced up to six years in prison. Within a year, all five were released, the official explanation given as: 'A lack of modern legislation covering cybercrime.' Distraught at this result, Ilona left the world's Cyber Crime Centre and moved to London. Dudley struck gold when she saw his job offer on an online employment site. As well as her native language, she spoke Russian, English and French, and had more experience of the real dangers of the Internet than anyone he'd ever met.

In January 2012, Lord Arthur Dudley, now reincarnated as Dr Hugh Middleton, opened his consulting practice, the Institute for Global Internet Security, in Bolsover Street, London WI. The first contract signed by Ilona Tymoshenko was with the Security Service of Ukraine.

Ilona's report on the Stewart family was ten pages long, starting with Leo's school, college and employment history. It was an impressive account, and Middleton read it with increasing admiration for Leo Stewart. *Thank God he didn't end up in Zimbabwe, I almost deprived the world of a very clever young man who might make a real contribution.* General Chillicott had a high opinion of him, and he could see why. *Someone to watch closely,* he told himself.

He was amused to read that Emma's writing career had taken off after the publication of *My Son the Hostage.* The book had come out while he was in prison and he'd been unaware of it. He had no doubt he'd recognise the storyline and decided to acquire a copy. There was no information in the report about Leo's birth or his father, and he wondered once again what the real truth was. It had caused a number of deaths. *Admittedly, all bad people who deserved their fate,* he rationalised. (Dudley's conversion didn't include the past, only the future.) *Although,* he remembered, *there was one exception.* An exception that he regretted and, strangely, was what had put him in prison. The fatal transfer of $25,000, his last act before the police had arrived, was from Lugano to his contact in Harare, to buy a contract on the life of Marius Coetzee, the South African security man who had derailed Leo's abduction. He learned subsequently that Coetzee had been executed by two Zimbabwe agents at his farm in Delmas. *A foolish thing to do,* he chastised himself, *for many reasons.*

Jenny Bishop's story brought him few surprises. He'd known from the beginning that she might prove to be the fly in the ointment. Now she'd become a successful entrepreneur, investing in private equity opportunities. He knew she had inherited a substantial fortune and a thought flashed through his mind: *She might be interested in investing in my business.* Middleton laughed out loud at the idea. *Ships that pass in the night.* He suddenly saw an image of Esther Rousseau, the only woman he had ever loved and who had caused him to lose his usual *sang froid*, with far-reaching and life-transforming consequences.

He took the second document from the dossier, the report on Lee-Win Micro-Technology and XPlus Circuits. It comprised only two pages and revealed very little that he couldn't have found online. Although Dubai corporate law required a fifty-one per cent majority ownership by UAE nationals, this was circumvented by a pledge of forty-seven percent of the stock to Lee-Win against a billion-dollar loan, required to build the new facility. In reality, Lee-Win was clearly the beneficial owner of ninety-six per cent of XPC, the remaining fraction being owned by a Dubai lawyer, who presumably also held these shares for their account. However, it was quite impossible for him to ascertain who owned Lee-Win.

Middleton was a complex character, full of contradictory motivations. Having unsuccessfully attempted to abduct Leo Stewart and ship him off to a fairly certain death in Zimbabwe, he now felt a kind of responsibility of care towards him. Chillicott's story about the poisoning of Leo's predecessor at their Dubai facility was still fresh in his mind. As he had previously informed the general, death intrigued him, and he was not a great believer in accidental death by poisoning. He would find out what he could about Leo's new employers and try to ensure that the young man didn't risk suffering the same fate.

He called Ilona back into his office. 'Thank you for the Stewart report, it is most exhaustive and informative. However, I see that the ownership of Lee-Win is shrouded in mystery. Were you unable to discover more?'

'About the company history, yes, but virtually nothing about the ownership. It looks as if it changed hands about five years ago, and behind the entities listed on my report, there is a complex web of companies, all over the world, which own various other companies and so on, until it's impossible to know who the ultimate owners are. I don't know why you asked me to do this research,' she paused, waiting in vain for a response, 'but I think you've stumbled on an interesting situation. You know I'm usually quite good at digging into puzzles and finding what I'm looking for, but this one seems unsolvable, if there is such a word.'

'Insoluble is an alternative word, if you wish,' from habit, Middleton corrected her and she nodded appreciatively. 'I vaguely remember a story about the Lee-Win family, is that what you refer to?'

'Possibly. It's a fascinating but peculiar story. Over several generations, the Lee-Win family built a number of manufacturing plants in China. White goods, car components, industrial equipment, all kinds of machines. They started the microprocessor business in the mid-seventies, and in the eighties Chongkun Lee-Win, the great-grandson of the founder, took over the dynasty. He was quite a visionary and he made an amazing prophesy which was the key to their success. He forecast that the growth and diversity of applications requiring solutions would quickly exceed the memory and speed capabilities of Central Processing Units. Machines would become like businesses, with a CPU as general manager and several microprocessors as specialised members of the management team, like a corporate structure. More and more secondary processors with specific software would be needed to perform these tasks alongside the CPU. This would have two effects: it would reduce the need for CPUs to double or triple in speed or memory every year, and create a whole new industry to build processors to manage solutions for specific applications.'

'And he was absolutely right. In fact, the CPU has mostly been replaced by one extremely complex microprocessor, or several of them. So, he started designing and building them for specific industries?'

'Exactly. He concentrated on machines used by the biggest businesses in the world, multinational manufacturing and banking institutions and, of course, government departments, infrastructure and essential service providers. That's why Lee-Win now has such a huge international client base and a great reputation in those vital areas.'

'A brilliant pioneer. I was aware of the company's virtual monopoly in such hallowed circles, but I didn't know it was down to one man's foresight all those years ago. However, what I was trying to recall had somehow to do with his death.'

'That's what's peculiar about the history. In 2012, when the company was achieving great success, he was killed in a car accident. He was only sixty, such a tragic waste of a brilliant man. What you probably remember is that his widow claimed he was murdered, but nothing was ever proved. A short while later, she left Shanghai with her two sons and moved to Macau, and they're now involved in the gambling and casino business. It seems certain that the ownership changed hands after Chongkun's death, but I can't get the details of what happened; if the family did sell the business, who bought it and why she left Shanghai.'

'Very well, we'll spread our net a little wider. Can you call your friend, Billy Chillicott, and ask him to assist in our research? He does still owe us a debt of gratitude, if not more.'

For several years, Washington had been aware of Russian intentions toward Ukraine. Until 2012, they were limited to cyber espionage attacks, using a 'Trojan Horse' named *BlackEnergy*, which opened up a back door to hack into Ukraine industry and government computer control systems. In 2013, increased protests against the pro-Russian President Viktor Yanukovych and calls for his resignation resulted in mass demonstrations, with the death and injury of thousands of protestors. Yanukovych's ousting in February 2014 caused Vladimir Putin to immediately execute the annexation of Crimea and Sevastopol by the Russian Federation, on 18 March 2014. The pro-European candidate, Petro Poroshenko, was inaugurated as Ukranian President in June 2014 and Ukraine and Crimea entered into hostilities. Russian cyber-attacks on Ukraine began in earnest and Soviet–US relations hit an all-time low. That was when General Billy Chillicott contacted Ilona Tymoshenko.

The US and Ukraine had been less than friendly since the early 2000s, when the Americans were suspected of accidently 'losing' the plans of a Ukrainian defence system which had somehow fallen into the hands of Saddam Hussein, ruler of Iraq. With Ilona's help, Chillicott gained access to the head of the Ukrainian Security Service, Bohdan Kolisnyk, and information began to be exchanged. Relations between the two nations improved and the Ukraine's long and painful experience of Russia's cyber-warfare was of great value to the US in creating defence mechanisms against such attacks. At the same time, Dr Hugh Middleton's Institute for Global Internet Security became a valued partner of the US Homeland Security Department and GGE Cyber Security. Shortly afterwards, Dr Middleton was invited to join General Chillicott to make their first joint presentation of their concerns about cyber security to the UN Security Council, albeit to no avail.

Chillicott's friendship had been of great value to their business. His network of contacts was impressive, and Ilona was expert at wheedling out of him bits of information which often generated new business, especially at governmental level – the most profitable level of all.

Now, she replied, 'I'll drop him a note about the August meeting with the UNSC and tag the request on the end. And if it's that important, I'll contact an old friend at the Ukrainian SS to take a look. They're very good at looking into complicated structures. With the Russians up their noses, they have to be.' She waited for Middleton's response to 'if it's that important', wondering why he was so interested in Leo Stewart and his employer.

'Thank you, Ilona. That will be very helpful,' was his only reply.

Disappointed, she left him and went to compose a message to Chillicott. *There's more to this than just simple interest,* she thought. Nothing in the Stewart family file seemed of the slightest importance, certainly not enough to justify asking a US general to look into Leo's employer, *but for some reason it is to Hugh. I'd better go through it again and try to find what I'm missing. No secrets between partners,* she said to herself.

FIFTEEN

London, England
June 2017

'What about proxy shareholder names? Any that you recognise?'
Ilona Tymoshenko was speaking with Ilya Pavlychko, one of her
ex-colleagues and a former lover at the Ukrainian SS. He had been
doing some digging around the ownership of Lee-Win and had
so far drawn a blank.

'None. All the proxies I've found are offshore companies
or trusts and, before you ask, the shareholders or trustees of
those entities are also companies or trusts. Lee-Win has thirty
shareholders, of whom fifty-one per cent are domiciled in China,
according to company law. But that means nothing, the Chinese
shareholders are also companies and behind them are other proxies,
so we don't know who controls them. The forty-nine per cent is
owned by six offshore companies and it's the same there, multiple
proxies behind each one. Lee-Win was definitely sold, but on the
face of it, there's not one beneficial owner who is a human being.'

'And the board of directors?'

'There are ten of them. The two top guys are the chairman,
Bohai Cheong, a sixty-five-year-old businessman who was appointed

after the apparent change of ownership, and the managing director, Han Wang Tāng. He and two other technical directors were part of the previous board, but the others are all new. Shen Fu Liáng is in Dubai managing XPC, and the other five are Chinese lawyers. Probably all straw men controlled by the same interests as the ownership. It tells us nothing about who really owns or runs the company.'

'OK. It's pretty well what I found myself. For some reason the real owners are desperate not to be identified. That makes me even more inquisitive. Can you put what you've found into my Dropbox and let me think about it some more? Thanks Ilya, talk soon.'

Hugh Middleton was on the telephone with General Chillicott, and gestured to her to sit down. The speaker was on and they were discussing their upcoming meeting with the UN Security Council. 'Ilona just came in, Billy. I suggest you send your draft topics and text to her, and she can arrange for one of our people to mock up a presentation package that we can play around with to perfect. We have enough time and might as well take advantage of it. The meeting may not produce any results, but at least we'll present a convincing argument.'

'Hello General, Ilona here,' she said into the speaker. 'Just send me what you've got and I'll add the recent items that we've unearthed on our end. The problem with these reports is not finding enough material to add, it's looking through the dross to find the gold. There have been over 100 million stolen records offered on the dark web in the last few months.'

'What kind of stuff are you seeing?'

'You mean apart from the "WannaCry" ransomware attack?' She was referring to the global cyber-attack the previous month, where an estimated 230,000 computers in 150 countries were blocked until ransoms were paid.

'Don't remind me, Ilona. That was the scariest attack we've seen. It cost world businesses, including your own NHS, billions in costs and ransoms. We're pretty sure it was organised by the "Lazarus Group", that Russian outfit, working on behalf of North Korea, raising more dollars for arms purchases.'

'Indeed,' interjected Middleton, 'and since they have very few Internet connections in their own country, the west can't even make a "tit for tat" response, most regrettable. What else have you uncovered, my dear?'

'Take your pick: WikiLeaks published 9,000 documents stolen from the CIA, 77 million accounts exposed on the Edmodo Education platform, more than 250,000 at Wonga, the payday loans company, and 14 million at Verizon Telecoms, £2.5 million stolen from 9,000 online customers of Tesco Bank, and about $150 million has been stolen from 30,000 investors into ICOs, Initial Coin Offerings, using the Ethereum crypto-currency. The latest industry projections are for global cybercrime damage to hit $6 billion by 2012, even though they expect cybersecurity spending to exceed a trillion dollars over the next five years. Is that bad enough?'

'Well, we're starting to get some traction with the SEC. They're publicly agreeing with us that the biggest risk faced by the financial system is cybersecurity. And, just like we've been doing, they're calling for more stringent management and controls. Our people are also uncovering a lot of very interesting social media activity around our elections. Everyone knows there was a whole lot of crap went on that seriously disrupted the process and could come back to bite you-know-who. Maybe that kid, Leo Stewart, was right. It's going to take a massive catastrophe to get people's attention and that's certainly where we're headed. Anyway, thanks for your help, Ilona. I'll get Lloyd to send our draft over to you today.'

'Speaking of Leo Stewart, General, I dropped you a note about the Lee-Win ownership. Did you make any progress on it? We've made none at all.'

Chillicott's tone changed. 'I was coming to that, Ilona. I've got somebody on it and the whole ownership issue looks like a can of worms. You mind telling me what this is all about?'

Middleton interrupted, 'Just commercial information, Billy. In view of the lack of support from the lower echelons who attended the conference in San Diego, I'm considering contacting the companies directly at a much higher level, to try to bring them onto our side in keeping up the pressure on the UNSC.'

Ilona raised her eyebrows, but said nothing as Chillicott replied, 'So this is nothing to do with Leo Stewart and XPC?'

'Billy, since I had never heard of Leo Stewart until you mentioned him to me the other day, I don't know why you'd make such an assumption. However, if there is anything untoward about that company, I think it's in the interests of everyone concerned to be aware of it.'

Ilona Tymoshenko left the room with a frown on her face. *I don't believe that's Hugh's motive. He's looking for something specifically about Leo Stewart and XPC that has nothing to do with our programme.* She was even more determined to find out what it was.

Dubai, United Arab Emirates

'How are you getting on with Ed? He's quite a guy, isn't he?' Leo Stewart had called in to the Corner House for breakfast on his way to the office and Lynne, the Welsh waitress, was on duty.

'He's a typical Scouser,' she laughed. 'All those Liverpool guys are the same, it's like they think they're the Beatles reincarnated. But he's intelligent and really funny. I like his company, reminds me of home.'

'I'm glad to hear it. He's doing a great job for us, so I don't want him to get homesick and leave me in the lurch.'

'Oh. I didn't realise you're his boss. He just said you work together at XPC.'

Leo could have bitten his tongue off. Ed would be bound to brag about his job, it was in his nature, especially when there was a girl involved. He didn't want to dispel anything he might have told her. 'I'm not exactly his boss,' he answered a bit too quickly. 'Just different responsibilities and I have to check some work he does for the team, so I kind of think of him as working for me.'

It didn't sound very convincing to him and it obviously didn't fool her. She flashed him a smile, 'I'd better be extra nice to you then, it might do Ed a favour. Want another coffee?'

I'd better get out of here before I screw Ed's chances, he thought. 'No thanks, got to run for a meeting.' He put some change on the plate. 'Thanks, Lynne. See you next time. Ciao.'

Leo raced back to his office on the Harley, cursing under his breath. He hated making mistakes, and had possibly hurt a new-found friend in the process. Professionally speaking, he also couldn't afford to upset Ed. With everything that was happening at XPC, he needed every asset he could muster if he was going to get the job done. *No point in trying to fix it,* he decided, *it'll only make things worse. Just let it go and hope for the best.*

London, England

'You seem very preoccupied, anything you want to share with me?'

Jenny Bishop was having lunch with Bill Redman, her boyfriend, in Mario's Trattoria, a popular Italian restaurant in the city. They had spent the morning looking over the results from her growing collection of shareholdings in BPE and she was in a mood to celebrate, but Bill seemed ill at ease, constantly checking his mobile and chewing the ends of his glasses.

'Just something at the bank. Nothing to worry about.'

'You're a terrible liar, Bill. Come on, a problem shared is a problem halved, or something like that. You know I don't talk, I just listen.'

He looked around. The restaurant was full, which meant that no one could hear anything over the decibel level of the crowd. 'We've taken a big hit,' he said with a frown. 'Both Fletcher Rice and the BIP.'

'Oh dear, I'm so sorry. Was it a fine?'

'No, not that, we've never been involved in anything we could be penalised for, thank God. It was an Internet fraud, altogether it cost almost 200 million.'

'My God, not another? Seems like there's one every day now.' Jenny could sympathise with him. Her mind went back to 2008, when $12 million was stolen by an Internet transfer from one of her accounts in Geneva. It was a miracle she and Leticia hadn't also been murdered by the culprit, Ray d'Almeida, the Angolan killer. Then she'd had to manage another near-miracle to recover the funds from the bank, after baring her teeth in a fraught battle with lawyers and bankers alike.

'It's the first we've ever had and it's entirely the fault of those bloody fools at the BIP in Paris. Bunch of incompetent idiots.'

'Would I understand how it was done?'

'It was as simple as child's play. They launched a marketing campaign with some holiday vouchers as prizes. You know the kind of thing, "*Tell us why BIP is your favourite bank in less than twenty words. Send to email address, etc.*" All the European subsidiaries were involved, including us. The customers had to have at least 2,500 Euros or equivalent in their account to qualify, so the BIP hoped there'd be an influx of funds from people topping up their accounts to qualify. Then some half-witted IT twit linked the email address to the client account database, so they could compare them as they came in and disqualify any accountholders with an insufficient balance.'

'And someone got through to the clients' accounts and emptied them?'

'You see, Jenny. You're not a computer expert but even you can spot the stupidity of the link. The forensic people said there was a virus in his system. He must have been looking at porn websites or the like and he'd been hacked without knowing it. When he checked the customer account list to verify the details, the virus sent the list to the hacker and *Hey Presto*, he had access to the accounts and there was at least two and a half grand available to be stolen from every one. I've never been so bloody annoyed in my life. That money has to be repaid from reserves, it's not insured of course, and part of it'll come straight out of our bonuses. And I bet whichever genius was responsible has been promoted or paid off with a golden parachute. Bugger!'

'That works out at about 80,000 accounts, right?'

'And counting. But I don't want to talk about it any more, sorry if I got a bit rattled. Let's have another glass of wine.' He called the waiter over.

Jenny remembered her conversation with Leo in Marbella. 'It's a mystery to me how the Internet is one of the most valuable tools of my business and millions of other businesses, and yet it seems to create almost as many problems as it solves.'

'T'was ever thus. Man is capable of corrupting the purest of thoughts or intentions. Anyway, you were right about one thing. I feel a lot better having told you about it. Thanks for listening to my woes, darling.'

Zurich, Switzerland

'Good morning, Daniel, how's everything going?' The caller was speaking in Swiss German.

'It's getting back to normal, thank God. Since Leo Stewart put his foot down and got some organisation into the development division we're starting to see measureable results.'

'So you think we'll make the deadline?'

'He's hired another English guy, Ed Muire from ARM. That's just the background we need for the Mark VII firmware. If Stewart can get ACRE sorted out, we should be OK. It'll be tight, but I think we can make it.'

'Does anyone suspect what's going on?'

'Not a chance. I gave Leo the cold shoulder the other day and we hardly ever speak. The only guy I'm friendly with is Sharif, and he's not very intuitive.'

'Was there any further noise about Scotty's food poisoning?'

'Nothing I've heard. Tom and Shen never mention it. It's strange, as if it never happened.'

'I've got to take another call. I'll ring you next week unless I hear from you. Good luck, Daniel, keep it up.'

SIXTEEN

London, England
Friday, 2 July 2017

'Hugh's not here right now, he's in Cambridge for a weekend conference and won't be in the office until Monday morning. If you email him I'm sure he'll see it sometime over the weekend.' Ilona Tymoshenko was on the phone with General Chillicott. He was calling about Lee-Win and XPC, and she was more interested than she sounded.

'It's not a great idea to put this in writing. That's why I'm calling on the encrypted line, it's very sensitive information.'

Now she was really intrigued. 'I'll record the call and play it for him on Monday.'

There was a pause, as though Chillicott was weighing up her answer. 'This is ultra- confidential, Ilona, it stays with you and Hugh. Anything you write gets shredded and you erase this message as soon as he hears it, understood?'

'I understand, no records of any kind. This call never happened.'

'Agreed, so here goes. You were right about the secrecy around the ownership of Lee-Win Micro-Technology. The short version is that after Chongkun Lee-Win died in 2012, or more likely was assassinated from what I can tell, a short while later his widow sold the business. The family kept the other manufacturing companies, but not the microprocessor unit.'

'I knew it, that's when she moved to Macau. How did you confirm that?'

'I had to call in some really serious favours to find a back door into the shareholders behind the offshore holding companies. There's dozens of proxy companies spread around just about every crappy little offshore jurisdiction in the world. Seemed like looking for a needle in a haystack for a while. Then we found four of the sub-proxies located at a registered agent's office in Delaware. I know, don't say it. We're not supposed to harbour those kinds of shady outfits, but Delaware still has the most business-friendly legal system in the US, especially for offshore companies. They can't operate in the States, but they don't want to anyway, it would defeat the object. These companies still don't give us the identity of the ultimate beneficiaries, but it might get us one step closer.'

'It does sound promising.'

'We've had stuff on one of the directors of that outfit for a couple of years, nasty stuff he won't survive if it gets out. I won't give you the agent's name, 'cos I'm not finished with them and I don't want them to get cold feet, OK?'

'Understood.'

'Well, this week I had a friendly pow-wow with him and he gave me just one name, nothing more. I know I had the guy frightened for his life, but he was even more scared to give me anything more than that. It's the name of the person who instructed them five years ago to set up the proxy companies as shareholders in the next level of ownership of Lee-Win. He told me he's set up dozens of companies for that same person over the last six years. He's never met them, and the only thing he knows about those companies is that person was the common denominator.

'It didn't take me long to find a connection on our side. Several of our departments have got files on the name, big files, with nothing in them we can prove. For five years it's been cropping up in investigations of drug-running, people trafficking, money laundering, cyber-fraud; you name it, the dirtiest businesses you can imagine, and all linked to offshore companies and the same name behind the scenes. We know so little about this person I can't even tell you if it's a man or a woman; we just don't know. But there is one fact we've found out and we're sure of it. There has been a direct connection between this anonymous person and GRU since 2011, still continuing as we speak.'

Ilona's mind was racing as she analysed Chillicott's revelations. 'You're saying there's some kind of link between XPC and the Russian foreign military intelligence agency?'

'That's not what I said, Ilona. You might jump to that conclusion, but I'm not in a position to agree or disagree with you. We have a brittle level of entente with our Russian friends and I can't be seen to be sabotaging it. Not unless I have some specific knowledge in my possession, but I have no such knowledge.' He spoke quietly and carefully, weighing every word, emphasising his enforced neutrality on the subject, but leaving her to draw her own conclusions.

'I understand, General. I understand your predicament, it was foolish of me to make such a suggestion.'

'Good. All I can do is to give you the name I was given by the guy in Delaware.'

Ilona waited, hardly breathing in her anticipation.

'The name is Tsunami. Did you get that?'

'I got it, Tsunami.' She stopped the recording. 'Thank you, General, thank you very much. Is there anything else you need to say to Dr Middleton?'

'One last thing, Ilona. I want to know from Hugh the truth behind his interest in Lee-Win, XPC and Leo Stewart. I don't buy this "commercial information" crap. There's something he knows and if I'm going to be useful in this business, I need to know it too.'

Exactly my feelings, Ilona thought. *Hugh won't be too happy with that. Fortunately, it's not on the tape.* 'I understand, General,' she answered. 'I'll give him your message word for word.'

'Good. That's all for now. By the way, thanks for your clean-up of the presentation, it looks great.'

'I'll have the June data ready before your meeting, so we can include that and bombard them with current warnings they can't ignore. Goodbye General, and thanks for your help.'

Ilona sat back and reviewed the unexpected news. *2011, that's just after General Piotr Gavrikov took over as head of the Russian Main Intelligence Directorate: GRU. The following year, Lee-Win was sold into unknown hands and the Delaware proxies were created. Chillicott said it's still continuing, that must mean Gavrikov has maintained the relationship with Tsunami. He said he needs specific knowledge before he can take any action. He's asking me to help him to find something he can act on. He helped me, now he wants my help to get Tsunami. And somehow, Lee-Win and therefore XPC are involved in the jigsaw puzzle.*

She sent the call to Hugh Middleton's laptop and to her personal tablet, then erased it from the main phone system. *That's what I promised,* she rationalised. *I've erased it and I didn't write it down.*

Dubai, United Arab Emirates

'Right, Ed. You've had enough time this week to discover the origin of the universe. What do you think?'

The two men were in Leo's office, looking at the logs and results of the tests run by Ed with the ACRE upgrade group over the last couple of days. He had now officially taken over the firmware team, and this was his last look at the encryption software before Leo took it over completely.

'Frankly, apart from a couple of specific areas that need attention, it's looking very good. Sharif made some good progress over the last few months before you arrived, well done him.'

Leo made a mental note to compliment the Pakistani, he still seemed a little unhappy with all the changes that were going on around him. 'What's worrying you in particular?'

'I think the algorithms still need tweaking, I have a feeling there's a bug in there somewhere. But it's mainly what I mentioned about the connectivity module and the remote implementation. If we want to upgrade all the previous models out there, we need a totally ubiquitous set of instructions, and we don't have that. There's so many moving parts involved, we need to have a catch-all solution to get through to all the Lee-Win pieces in the networks. Like I told you last time, that's not really my area, I haven't had a lot to do with the IoT.'

They talked over Ed's concerns, and Leo prepared a list of ideas and tests he would carry out himself the following week. 'Right, you can forget about ACRE and get on with the last upgrades for the final Mark VII firmware. Leave the connectivity module to me as well, I've got it under control from now on.' He looked at his watch, it was almost ten p.m. 'What about a quick beer at the Corner House and then an early night? You must be shattered.'

Ed walked to the door, 'Sorry, no can do, I'm going straight over to pick Lynne up. Big night out. We're going to Club 27.'

Leo had heard a lot about the club, on the beach near the Burj-al-Arab hotel. The venue was renowned for its visits by celebrity DJs, and the star of that week's *Dubai Summer BeachFest* was the latest club-busting record spinner from London, Deejai D.

'You'd better get moving. Have a great night and say hi to Lynne for me.'

'Why don't you come with us? It's a fabulous gig and you've been working hard enough to earn a good night out.'

'You know that's not my kind of music. I'm a classics man. Metal or nothing.'

'Leo, you're never going to get a metal concert in Dubai, it just won't happen. So does that mean you can never go out and party? You've been here for five weeks and you haven't seen anything except the office, the gym and a couple of restaurants. Forget what kind of music it is, just come and see people and enjoy yourself. You never know, if we get a request in, he might play a Robert Plant track for you.'

'OK, if you really want a hanger-on I'll join you, but don't expect me to strip off and dance to some puerile crap with no lyrics or recognisable tune.'

'Cool. We'll take the rental and pick Lynne up at home. She'll be chuffed, she thinks you've been avoiding her.'

'Bullshit. I don't have time to avoid anyone, I'm too busy.'

Leo was impressed with Club 27, more impressed than he'd like to admit to Ed. The scene wasn't as wild as some of the parties he'd been to in San Francisco, where some kids ended up half naked and out of their minds on drugs. Here, they were loud and flashy, obviously a crowd of wealthy young people, but much more respectful and well behaved. Although there was alcohol available, and he thought he could detect the effect of drugs on some people, there was no roudiness or brawling. *Being in a police state has its advantages*, he realised. He also liked DeeJai D, a London-based musician turned party host who had a very esoteric taste in music. He proved to have a talent for picking out great individual tracks from otherwise unmemorable albums and produced a constant sequence of musical vignettes, each one leading into the other, even when they were totally disparate music types.

Leo nursed a beer, enjoying the show and glad he'd let Ed twist his arm into coming. During a quieter moment, he went up to the podium and managed to have a few words with the host. To his surprise, he detected a Geordie accent.

'Newcastle, Jesmond actually,' DeeJai answered to his question.

'I thought so, I lived there 'til I was seventeen,' he told him.

'So how come the west coast accent?'

They chatted for a few moments and Leo asked if he was a Led Zeppelin fan. 'Don't tell me,' he said. 'You want "Stairway to Heaven".' Leo just smiled and he went on, 'It'll have to be my interpretation, I'm the only guy who can play that song the way it should be heard. Trust me, OK?'

The resulting production blew Leo's mind. DeeJai D had created a multi-tracked, multi-rhythmed and multi-danceable version of the song that twisted and turned through its full ten minutes, two minutes longer than the original. Midway through the number, a young, coffee-skinned woman came up to Leo, who was standing near the podium, lapping up the ever-changing variety of sound and rhythm.

'Hi,' she said. 'I saw you ask for this, it's cool isn't it?'

'Sure is, I love Led Zeppelin. Are you a fan?'

'My father was, so I was brought up with it. I'm Angela.'

He noticed an accent, *Sounds Spanish or Portuguese*, he thought. 'I'm Leo, Leo Stewart, nice to meet you.'

'Do you dance?'

'Only when I'm asked.'

'Come on then, I'm asking.' He let her pull him onto the crowded floor and they gyrated for a while. They made a good-looking but incongruous pair; at five-eight she was shorter than him by eight inches, but she didn't seem to notice. Leo wasn't a bad dancer but he felt a little subdued, he'd never been comfortable with pushy women, although it wasn't unusual for him to be targetted in clubs. He managed to find out that she was from Sao Paulo and had been in Dubai for six months, before DeeJai's gradual increase in volume prevented any further conversation. Angela was like a contortionist, seemingly moving in every direction at the same time, and after a while he began to mimic her moves. She was wearing a close-fitting dress with shoulder straps and a short skirt which showed off her beautifully lithe, dark-skinned limbs. He realised it was the first time he'd let himself free his mind up and forget his work since he'd arrived at XPC, and he gave himself up to the enjoyment of the moment. Now DeeJai was piling on the sound and the mood, with a reverberating effect on Jimmy Page's final guitar solo, building up the pace until the whole room was a mass of cavorting bodies.

As the last chord faded away, Angela collapsed into his arms. '*Deos*, that was awesome, thanks Leo.' She brushed his cheek with her lips then walked away. He watched her sway across the floor. *She's beautiful*, he decided.

'Who was that?' Ed and Lynne had come over to him.

'That was Angela, and that's all I know about her, she just picked me up.'

'You looked great together, she loved every minute,' Lynne said. 'Everybody was watching you, what a mover. Who would have known?'

'It's my African blood,' Leo laughed. 'Come on, I need a beer.'

Leo looked around the club for the rest of the evening, trying to spot the woman again, but she seemed to have disappeared. Disappointed, he left with the others at two in the morning, wondering who she was, what she did, where she lived, and why she'd walked away like that.

SEVENTEEN

**Ipswich, England
Sunday, 4 July 2017**

Jenny Bishop was on a ship at sea, not far from the shore. She could see sand dunes and a huge expanse of desert leading off to mountains in the distance. Leo and Emma and an attractive coffee-skinned, brown-haired woman she didn't know were sitting at a table with her. There was a white cloth and cutlery on the table and she realised it was a restaurant ship sailing off the North African coast. Leo and the woman were holding hands and murmuring to each other in a romantic way. In the centre of the table was a laptop, the screen showing an old-fashioned water boiler with a pressure gauge on the front like an antique clock, with two hands and pressure measurements in Roman numerals around the face. The heading at the top of the screen was 'INTERNET PRESSURE POINTS' and she knew it was Leo's computer. The hour hand was moving to twelve and the other was at quarter past, showing 250lbs of pressure. At 600lbs, two-thirds of the way around the face, was a red line, with the word 'DANGER' written in large red capitals.

Jenny looked around her and saw there was only one other table, occupied by a couple on the other side of the deck, although every table had a 'Reserved' sign on it. They had their backs to her, but Jenny thought there was something familiar about the woman. A large golden cage stood in the middle of the deck with a green and red monkey in it. An old Arab man in a turban was turning the handle of a music box and she recognised the tune, it sounded like the first part of 'Stairway to Heaven', with the acoustic guitar and recorders. The monkey was dancing around inside the cage, juggling plates in the air.

The woman with Leo took her hand away from his, snapped her fingers, and a waiter rushed over, dressed in jodhpurs, an old-fashioned pleated linen jacket and a riding helmet. She barked out an order and he ran off to the kitchen. Taking the mouthpiece of a hookah standing by the table, she sucked in a deep breath, blowing some of the smoke into Leo's face. Jenny recognised the waft that blew past her: it was cannabis, something she hadn't smelled since her days teaching difficult students at Sunderland Secondary School. She looked disapprovingly at the woman, who drew another deep swallow and blew it out across the table at her. Before she could say anything, the waiter came back, carrying a polo stick and pushing a trolley loaded with dishes of curried meat and vegetables, which he placed on the table. The woman put aside the hookah and served the food onto their plates, while the waiter poured red wine from a decanter into large crystal glasses for each of them. Jenny looked at the pressure gauge on the computer screen, the minute hand had moved further round the face and was sitting over the red 'DANGER' line.

'Bon appétit,' said Leo, raising his glass. As the others responded, a tall man walked across the deck to the table. Incongruously, he looked Chinese, but was dressed as an Arab sheikh, in a long flowing cape and robes. The woman stood up and he kissed her passionately.

'Do you have the money?' she asked him.

'Here it is.' He took his hand out from the robes and showed her a wad of $100 bills.

'Good,' she said. 'Let's go, I've had enough of these stupid people.' He picked up the wine decanter and they walked towards the entrance. At the same moment, the old man stopped playing the music box. The monkey dropped the plates, which shattered all over the deck. Jenny glanced across at the table on the other side of the deck. The couple had disappeared. She looked back at the laptop just in time to see the minute hand reach twelve and the water boiler explode into smithereens.

Jenny awoke with a start, trembling and sweating. This was the first dream of this kind she'd had for several years, since the time of Leo's abduction. She had inherited a sixth sense from her mother and come to dread the moments when strange and disturbing images came to her in the night, heralding some unknown event, future, past or present. On several occasions, the gift had helped to discover hidden secrets or provided clues in the problems she had been faced with, but the experience wasn't a pleasant one and it always left her feeling worried and vulnerable.

Jenny had spent Friday night with Bill in London, and after dinner in Covent Garden they went back to his flat. He was still furious about the bank Internet fraud and the evening wasn't a huge success, he was obviously having difficulty in putting the matter behind him and making the most of their time together. On Saturday, she took the train back to her house in Ipswich, had a quiet day and evening on her own, then watched some TV and went to bed at eleven. Bill's story was still on her mind and it had taken her a while to fall asleep, only to be woken by the dream. She knew this particular dream was a warning, a warning about the Internet and about Leo. Something had happened or was going to happen to him, but as always, she didn't know what it was, and Jenny didn't like not knowing things. She got up, drew the curtains back and shivered. It was a grey, miserable rainy day. Going into the kitchen to make her morning cup of tea, she checked the clock. It was six-thirty, ten-thirty in Dubai. She put the kettle on, then picked up her phone.

Dubai, United Arab Emirates

'Hi, Aunt Jenny. It's great to hear from you. I was just thinking of calling you, great minds, you know. How are things? Where are you right now?'

'Hello Leo. I'm at home in Ipswich and it's raining and cold, so please don't tell me how lovely it is there or in Marbella.'

'I'm sure you'll be going down there soon. You lead a charmed life between the UK and Spain, lucky lady.'

They talked for a while about his job, Emma and Jenny's business interests until she asked, innocently, 'So, how's your love life down there? I hope it's not all work and no play.'

Leo was immediately suspicious. 'Is that you or Mum speaking?'

'I haven't talked to your mother for over a week. Can't I take an interest in my favourite nephew without being accused of conspiring with her?'

'OK, sorry Jenny. It's getting frenetic here. We've got an impossible deadline to meet and we're already a week late, so I guess I'm a bit on edge. Anyway, I haven't had time to check out the local talent yet, so no news is bad news on that subject. Give me time and I'll be scoring like my new guy, Ed.'

'Ed? Who's he?'

Leo brought her up-to-date on Ed's talent for picking up girls. 'He's a Scouser, so I guess he was born with the gift of the gab.'

'Well, watch out he doesn't talk his way into trouble and take you with him.'

'OK. What exactly does that mean?' Leo knew his aunt's reputation for thinking outside the box, but she had never tried to influence anything he did, or if so, he'd never been aware of it.

'Just that Dubai isn't Newcastle, or even California. There's an awful lot of get-rich-quick scam artists and dubious characters, and they're not trustworthy. I've met a few in my investment business and I haven't yet known one I would trust with my money, never mind my nephew.'

'Got it, message received and understood. Leo is not to speak to or accept sweets from strangers without consulting Aunt Jenny. That right?'

Jenny laughed. 'Let's just say your mother and I worry for you. You happen to be our entire next generation and you're in a new, foreign country surrounded by all kinds of risks and strangers, so I'm just saying please be careful. Promise me?'

'Fair enough, Jenny. I know you and Mum are concerned about me, and I'm a very lucky guy. But believe me, I'm fine, and I'll make sure I stay fine. Is that OK?'

They said goodbye and Leo put away his phone, wondering, *Now what the hell was all that about?*

Ipswich, England

Jenny sat thinking for a few minutes, then she went through her old handwritten phone book, looking for the name of someone she hadn't called in a long while. The number was still valid, and after exchanging some catch-up small talk, she said, 'I can't explain why, but I have a feeling we may be needing some help in the not too distant future. Can I count on your assistance if it turns out that way?'

'No need to ask, Jenny. Just call when you need me, tell me where I should go and I'll be on the next plane.'

Jenny saved the number in her Contacts list. She knew she would need it before too long.

Dubai, United Arab Emirates

It was eleven on Sunday evening and Leo was back at Club 27. He'd left Ed in the lab, still wrestling with the Mark VII testing, but after a fourteen-hour day he needed a break. He had two other motives, the first being DeeJai D. It was the disc jockey's last performance and Leo yearned for another dose of his Led Zeppelin mix; it was unique, genius and mind-blowing, and he might never again have the chance to enjoy it. Then, of course, there was Angela. He was intrigued by the woman and definitely attracted to her. A potentially dangerous combination, he knew, but it beat reading, checking and rewriting code until his eyes were crossed. Ed had come in the afternoon, so his punishment was to take over for the night shift. Time was getting short and there was a seemingly inexhaustible list of things to get done.

The club was much quieter than it had been on Friday, and he got himself a beer then hung around DeeJai's stand until the Englishman recognised him. 'Hey, Leo. How you doing? Where's your girlfriend? I guess you want another dose of Jimmy Page?'

'Cool, if you can get round to it. Last session before you go home?'

'Not yet, not for a while. Got a few gigs in Asia en route for Oz and New Zealand. No time to rest.'

Leo laughed. 'Sounds really tough, how'd you like to swap jobs? I hope you have a great trip. It's great to see yet another Geordie making good music. I'll sit it out until you press the button.'

'Let me get them in the mood, it won't take too long.'

'Thanks, DeeJai.' Leo went and sat at the bar. He was lost in thought, thinking about Angela, wondering if she would come in tonight, when he heard a voice.

'Hi, Leo. I didn't know you hung out here.'

He looked up to see his boss, Shen Fu Liáng, standing there alongside Daniel Oberhart and a young woman. 'Shen, what a surprise. Nice to see you out of the office. Hi Daniel,' he said, as pleasantly as he could.

The Chinaman turned to the woman. 'Elodie Delacroix, meet Leo Stewart, he's my new resident prodigy at XPC.'

Leo noted the 'my' ownership claim, but just smiled at Elodie and shook hands. She was a very attractive woman, dark hair, thirtyish, with a voluptuous figure clad in a red and gold silk shirt hanging over black stretch trousers, and a diamond bracelet on her wrist that looked to Leo to be worth a million dollars.

'Nice to meet you, Leo. I hope you don't mind me saying you don't look or sound very Scottish. Where do you come from?'

The comment didn't bother Leo. He was used to this reaction when he met people for the first time. 'I was born in Rwanda, but I've lived in the UK and US all my life, so that may explain my appearance.'

'Rwanda, eh? How exotic.' She gave him a seductive smile and toasted him with her glass. He had an uncomfortable feeling she was toying with him.

Shen insisted on buying drinks and he accepted a glass of champagne. Daniel had a beer in his hand and refused a top-up. Leo thought he seemed annoyed at having his one-on-one time with his boss interrupted by the company newcomer.

'Cheers, Elodie,' he toasted her. 'Have you been in Dubai long?'

'I came with Shen when XPC opened up. It seems like just yesterday. I really like it here. And you?' She had a soft, throaty voice with a hint of a French accent.

Leo was surprised that Shen hadn't told her of his arrival to replace Scotty. *She must know what happened*, he reasoned, *it's the kind of thing you'd tell your partner. New SVP from California working for me and all that.* 'Just five weeks,' he replied, 'and it seems like five years.' He laughed, in case she didn't understand his English sense of humour.

'Is working for Shen that bad?' she riposted.

'Not really, but we're real busy, so it's good to take a night off.'

'You chose the right place to cool out.'

'Which part of France are you from?' he asked.

Shen intervened, 'Close, Leo. Elodie's Belgian actually, from Brussels.'

He avoided making an obvious Brexit joke, and instead asked, 'Is French one of your languages, Shen?'

'*Un petit peu,*' the Chinaman answered with a self-deprecating smile.

Leo chatted with Elodie and asked her about her life and travels. She was an interesting woman with a great sense of humour, and he almost missed the intro to his song. He was about to excuse himself to go over to DeeJai's podium when she looked over his shoulder and said excitedly, 'Angela, *chérie*, you decided to come after all.'

Leo couldn't believe it. His mystery woman was standing right next to him, hugging both Elodie and Shen and shaking hands with Daniel, obviously a good friend of them all. 'Hello Angela,' he said, before they could introduce him, 'it's good to see you again.'

She kissed his cheek, 'Hi Leo. It's time for our dance.'

This time, after another exhausting exhibition of frantic gyrations, Angela agreed to have a drink with them. Leo was impressed to see that Elodie was also a good dancer, affecting a jive style with Shen which he found cool to watch. *He's not bad either,* he noticed. *Strange combination of contradictions, that guy.* His boss ordered a bottle of Laurent Perrier and they sat in the bar. It was quite empty since everyone was on the dance floor; DeeJai had upped the volume, so they ended up shouting at each other across the table. After a few minutes of this, Angela stood up and announced she was tired.

'Me too,' he said. 'Can I take you anywhere?' She was wearing a shirt and shorts over leggings and it was a very warm night. He figured she was dressed appropriately for the bike.

'You have your car here?'

'My Harley. But the back seat's really comfortable. And I've got Led Zeppelin on the music system.'

'We'll take you in the car, it's more relaxing,' Elodie interjected, while Shen went over to the bar to pay the bill.

She thought for a moment, 'No thanks. It'll be my first time on a Harley.' She winked at Leo.

Angela rented an apartment in the Dubai Marina, between the club and Jumeirah Beach, where Leo lived. The sensation of her face pressing against his back, and her arms around his waist, made him wish the five-minute ride was much longer. It was twelve-thirty when they rode up to the building and he reluctantly helped her off the machine.

He walked her to the entrance and she kissed his cheek. 'Thanks, Leo. That's a really cool ride. Will you be going to the club again, now that DeeJai's leaving? No more "Stairway to Heaven".'

'That depends,' he replied enigmatically.

'On what?'

'Whether you'll be there.'

'You don't know anything about me,' she said. 'Do you want to come up and find out all my dark secrets?'

He hesitated. He did want to get to know her better, she was an intriguing and captivating woman, but Ed was expecting him at six in the morning and he had to read the evening's test results before the meeting. 'I've got an early start,' he replied reluctantly. 'Can I take a rain check and call you later in the week?'

'Sure. Don't wait too long.'

She gave him her number and he put it in his phone. 'You want to tell me your full name?'

'Angela da Sousa, that's it.' She gave him a chaste kiss on the cheek. 'Drive carefully. Goodnight, Leo.'

London, England

Emma said, 'I haven't spoken to Leo for a while. Too busy trying to finish my bloody book, I haven't got a minute to spare. How is he? He'd have called me if there was anything special.' She and Jenny were in Jo Greenwell's office for their regular Monday editorial meeting of *Thinking Woman Magazine*, and her sister had mentioned her call with Leo.

'He seemed fine, no problems. But he sounded very busy, he's just hired a new man from the UK, a Liverpudlian called Ed Muire. He likes him.'

'I'm pleased to hear it, I know he's up against a tough deadline and he'll need help to deliver on time. I've got the same problem, mother and son, both in the same boat.'

'Except you can't hire someone to help you write your book. How's it going?'

'I'm about fifty pages away from "The End". It doesn't sound a lot, but I'm finding it harder and harder to get the words on paper. I think I'm running out of ideas.'

'Nonsense. Your last one was the best so far, the sales proved that. Biggest success since the one about Leo. Oops, sorry, shouldn't have said that.' She looked around, but no one was paying attention.

'Don't worry, that's past history now, Leo's twenty-three and there's no more possibility of him or me having a problem. And no one's interested in what happened in South Africa seven years ago. By the way, what did you call him about?'

'Oh, I don't really know, no special reason. Just making sure my nephew's happy down there in the desert.'

'Thanks, sis.' Emma squeezed her sister's hand and they went back to their meeting with Jo, Jenny hoping this time her dream was just a dream.

Washington DC, USA

'I believe I owe you an apology, Billy,' Hugh Middleton said. It was Monday afternoon and he'd called the general as promised.

'Oh, Ilona told you what I said about the XPC enquiry?'

'Exactly. Apparently you suspect me of some infamous, ulterior motive in my research into the company and in connection with young Master Stewart.'

'Either that, or you should have been a clairvoyant. There's more suspicious circumstances surrounding that outfit than a bunch of hyenas around a wounded antelope.'

'Quite remarkable, I agree, but I assure you, purely coincidental. It's simply a consequence of our conversation about Leo last month. When you told me that he was urgently summoned from California to Dubai to replace a predecessor who died of poisoning, my protective instincts were aroused. I am a great believer in cause and effect and in my humble opinion, a suspicious death followed by an unusual event deserves investigation.'

'Well, looks like your instincts might be right on the button, this time. This Tsunami character is closely linked to the Soviets, and I'd like to know what the involvment is with Lee-Win and XPC. Are you doing any more investigating on your end?'

'I have asked Ilona to look into the XPC senior management. If we can't find anything at the top, we may succeed further down the pyramid. I promise to reveal whatever we discover, if and when we do so. Are you content with that?'

Chillicott seemed mollified by the apology and they ended the call in agreement. Middleton put down his phone. *I hope this matter doesn't end badly for Leo Stewart,* he reflected. *Or for me.*

NINETEEN

London, England
Tuesday, 6 July 2017

'I think we've had a stroke of luck with XPC.' It was ten o'clock on Tuesday morning when Ilona Tymoshenko went into Dr Middleton's office with a printout in her hand.

'From your ex-colleague in Kiev?'

'Ilya Pavlychko, yes. He's a bloodhound once he gets on the trail of someone or something. He hasn't found any trace of General Chillicott's Tsunami character, but he's got a lot on XPC.'

'And what has Pan Pavlychko sniffed out that may interest us?'

'He was following up your suggestion actually, so well done your lateral thinking. We already know that Lee-Win is the beneficial owner of XPC. In terms of local management, there are six registered officers in Dubai. I'll discount their lawyer, the CFO and COO and one SVP, none of whom are involved with Leo Stewart or his area of work. That leaves: Tom Connor, the CEO who hired him, he's an American from Boston; Shen Fu Liáng, the Executive VP who Leo reports to, he's a Chinese national from Shanghai; and Daniel Oberhart, a Swiss SVP from Zurich who was with MicroCentral.'

'An American, a Chinaman, a Swiss German and an Englishman! It sounds like the beginning of a typically English joke. I hope it has an amusing ending.'

Yesterday he was in his erudite mood, today it's slapstick. What's going on in Hugh's mind, Ilona wondered. She ignored the interruption and went on, 'Oberhart was one of the rising stars with MicroCentral, his father was founder of the business and he'd been there for ten years since he left university. I understand Lee-Win had to give him a substantial golden handshake to get him to Dubai.'

'Does his family still retain a large stake in the Zurich company?'

'They were bought out by Hai-Sat, a Chinese hedge fund, four years ago with a $3 billion valuation, but I understand they kept a minority shareholding. His father is still chairman.'

'Hmm, interesting. The son of the chairman and a substantial shareholder of a large competitor owned by Chinese investors came to XPC, itself owned by the Chinese, when they were developing a revolutionary new encryption technology. Then, just when they are preparing to launch the product on the market, the senior programmer dies of poisoning. Most intriguing, don't you find?'

'Perhaps, but I think the man who interests us most is Shen Fu Liáng, and I'll explain why.' She read from the printout. 'According to Ukrainian intelligence, Shen was the second of two brothers born to a family in Chengdu in 1978 and 1980. Unfortunately, he was born after the one child per family rule was introduced by Song Jian in 1979. His father, Qiang, was Chinese and his mother, Olga, was from Minsk in Belarus, as you know at that time part of the Soviet Republic and still today a close partner of Russia. Quiang was governor of Sichuan Province, an important and presumably corrupt and wealthy government official. Because of his lofty status, he could have kept both sons, but he decided to show an example by giving up one of them. He chose Shen, and shortly after his birth he was taken to be adopted by Olga's family in Minsk. His adopted name was Grigori Vedeneyev.

'The family stayed in Minsk, where the adoptive father, Akmal, was vice president of the Ministry of Energy, until the break-up of the USSR in 1992. They then moved to Moscow and he retired there, because of ill health. His widow and daughter are still in Moscow but Akmal died in 2000.'

'Do you know the cause of death?'

'There's a newspaper cutting stating that he had been suffering from lung cancer. They all smoke like chimneys there.'

'And what happened to Liáng after Akmal's death?'

'He was twenty then and went back to live with his parents and brother in Chengdu, and attended college there for three years. By now he had a Russian passport in his Belarus name, Grigori Vedeneyev, but while in Chengdu, he obtained a Chinese passport in his original name of Shen Fu Liáng. I've got copies of all of these documents.'

'But he didn't remain there either, I suppose?'

'Correct. In 2003, he went back to his second mother and sister in Moscow until 2008, and I can even tell you what he did there.' She paused, but this time Middleton didn't intervene. 'He was employed, as Grigori Vedeneyev, by SITRA, the State International Trade Research Agency.'

His eyes gleamed behind his spectacles. 'Which we know is part of GRU, the Russian foreign military intelligence agency.'

'Exactly, he was with GRU in Moscow for five years then he was sent to Washington DC as head of the Russian Trade Delegation, also part of the secret service. He was there for four years, and then in November 2012 he went back to China and joined Lee-Win in Shanghai, as Shen Fu Liáng, of course.'

'Which is when Tsunami was creating proxy companies, presumably for GRU, and shortly after the Delaware people set up the proxies for the acquisition of Lee-Win. A most provocative coincidence, one might think.' Middleton was silent for a moment. 'Did he come down to Dubai when XPC was set up?'

'Yes. He was sent by Lee-Win from Shanghai as their board representative in 2014.'

Middleton looked at her in astonishment. 'He's the only person in touch with the Shanghai board?'

'I don't know. As CEO, Tom Connor should be the official contact with Shanghai, but he's not on the Lee-Win board. Shen Fu Liáng is the only person in Dubai who is a board member.'

'So, despite his title of CEO, Connor actually reports to Liáng?'

'I don't know how it works in practice, but it's certainly an unusual arrangement.'

'And is he married, children, anyone else in his life?'

'He's unmarried, but I don't know about any other relationship.'

'Do you know if his Chinese parents and brother in Chengdu are still alive?'

'I'll have to check on that, it's not mentioned here.'

'And his adoptive father, Akmal. Was he a wealthy man?'

'I can enquire, but as vice president of a Communist state organisation, I'd be astonished if he wasn't extremely wealthy. If not, he must have been completely stupid.'

'Quite, well reasoned. That means both his first and second fathers were probably wealthy and influential men. Please continue, Ilona, this is fascinating.'

'There's one more peculiar thing Ilya hasn't yet found out.'

'And that is?'

'Between leaving Washington in May 2012 and joining Lee-Win in the following November, Shen Fu Liáng vanished off the face of the earth. For six months Ilya could find no information about him, no trace at all. He flew from Dulles International Airport to Paris Charles de Gaulle on 12 May then disappeared, turning up again at London Heathrow on 15 November to fly to Shanghai. In the interval, no one seems to know where he was.'

Dubai, United Arab Emirates

'Nailed it!' Leo Stewart had just finished the last in a series of tests of his rewritten versions of the upgrade and Internet upload programme suites for ACRE and Mark VII, and they worked. The instruction to switch on the connectivity module was also now incorporated. Finally, he'd investigated Ed's concerns about the encryption algorithms and had found and rectified a rare error of logic in the basic formulae. He didn't know if it came from Scotty's original work, or had been caused by Sharif's subsequent intervention, but it didn't matter. He'd found it and fixed it and that was all that counted.

He was in one of the basement labs at XPC, where he'd linked up several pieces of equipment containing Lee-Win processors from all versions prior to Mark VII, some with the previous version of ACRE, all with the connectivity module, but some without the encryption software at all. A wireless router was connected to create a mini mesh network. He had also included devices without Lee-Win processors, so he could observe how they reacted to the new software. He labelled the network, *Leo 1*.

Next to this arrangement were two more networks, *Leo 2* and *3*, comprising different pieces of equipment linked by other types of router. He had uploaded the new versions of the software from his laptop to a wireless hub similar to the main XPS hub, as it would be done on a general deployment. The hub was instructed to pass the uploads to the three routers, which downloaded them to each mini-network. He then tested the networks with messages in many different forms: alphabetic, numeric, formulae, coded, etc.

Leo spent the day mixing and replacing the routers and equipment with other devices, right up to network *Leo 10*, almost two hundred variations, always with a mix of Lee-Win supported devices and others. He ran hundreds of tests and messages, each time examining the data running through all these primitive mini mesh networks. Every Lee-Win managed device on the network was now running Mark VII and the updated ACRE encryption and transmission management, which tested perfectly on every type of message. When activated by the connectivity module, ACRE caused the data to pass from one piece of equipment to the next and so on, of its own volition, a perfect data stream, perfectly encrypted.

He sat back, considering what this meant; that he, Leo Stewart, had just created the first truly secure encrypted mesh data network in the history of the Internet. ACRE was no longer a live test innovation. After being deployed around the world by the Lee-Win hubs, it would become the future of encrypted data transmission.

Leo texted his colleagues with an invitation to attend a demonstration of his rudimentary 'Heath Robinson' mini-networks test environment at five o'clock. He knew that Tom and Shen were leaving for New York the next day, and he wanted their buy-in before they left so the production and marketing teams could get moving.

'Brilliant!' 'Incredible!' 'Well done, Leo!' The accolades from Tom, Sharif, Shen and Ed were embarrassingly loud and enthusiastic. Even Daniel looked a little less unhappy than usual and patted him on the back. The demonstration had gone just as well as the tests, and there was a palpable sense of excitement and relief in the lab.

'Guys, I've just arrived here. Scotty started this development and you've been working on it for two years, I just walked in and dotted the I's and crossed the T's. And I was lucky that the last links in the chain were the connectivity module and the upload software, 'cos that's all I really know how to do.'

Tom Connor shook his head. 'You may be right, Leo, but someone had to get it sorted and you've certainly lived up to your reputation. This means we've got almost a month to tweak and test the whole end-to-end process before sending Shanghai the final design and spec. Can we make it, Ed, Sharif?'

'We're bound to now. Leo's got nothing more to do on this end, so he can help us sort out the rest of our problems.'

'No rest for the wicked. OK, I'm at your disposal every afternoon after I've looked at your test results. And guys, I want you both to test and tweak my code to death tomorrow, before we put it into the remote upgrade envelope. I'll prepare complete files with everything you need this evening, so you can start first thing.'

Tom was beaming with delight, 'How about we celebrate with a drink up on my terrace? There's champagne in the fridge.'

Leo nursed a glass of champagne, and at eight o'clock he came back down to the lab. He printed out three sets of his test logs, so that Ed and Sharif could run their own tests with the copies the next day, make sure he hadn't screwed up somewhere. He took all the documents up to his office then went home to get changed. He had a date with Angela, and he had something to celebrate.

Zurich, Switzerland

'That's great news. So we picked the right man for the job?'

'It looks like it, thanks to your contacts.' Daniel Oberhart was speaking to his father, Max, chairman of MicroCentral, one of Lee-Win's largest competitors. 'It didn't take him long to pick up Scotty's theories and convert them into practical solutions. It's an impressive set of software. Our customers are going to be delighted.'

'Not to mention the effect it will have on the company's reputation, and value.'

'Right. The demo I saw today still needs some cleaning up, but Leo told me we'll deliver the final package on time.'

'And he still doesn't suspect anything?'

'Nothing. I'm still unfriendly with him and he doesn't like it much. It's a shame actually, he's a likeable guy, but I guess it's necessary.'

'Once the deployment is done successfully, you'll be able to drop the act.'

'The sooner the better, I need to come home. I've had enough of Dubai.'

TWENTY

London, England
Wednesday, 7 July 2017

'Your lateral thinking seems to be working overtime.'

'Thank you, Ilona. To which particular example are you referring?' Middleton was impervious to the faintly sarcastic tone of Ilona's compliments.

'I've got some interesting news about Shen Fu Liáng's Chinese father and brother.'

'I see, as I was expecting. May I be permitted to disclose to you my presentiment before you reveal all?'

'I suppose I can't prevent it. What were you expecting?'

'Simply that they both died between 2008 and 2012, most likely 2012.'

She was silent for a moment. 'I must admit, that was quite impressive, Hugh. How did you guess, or did you know?'

'I'm afraid it was nothing more than a logical conclusion, sadly based on my very cynical view of the world in its present iteration. Please continue with the inevitably gory details.'

Ilona looked at her notes. 'Liáng's father, Qiang, owned a summer palace on the Tuojiang River, near Zigong, about 200 kilometres south-east of Chengdu. He kept a light aircraft, a Beachcraft four-seater, which he enjoyed piloting himself.' She put down her notepad and looked at the ceiling. 'I was surprised at this when I remembered that he was sixty-five at the time, it seems quite old to be still flying a plane. I'd love to learn to fly, myself.'

She was silent for a moment until Middleton's harrumph, then continued, 'In September 2012, Qiang was flying to Zigong for the Mid-Autumn Festival, with his wife and son, a servant and bodyguard. The plane came down on a mountainside near the river and burst into flames. Everyone was lost, Shen's father, mother and brother were killed along with the two retainers.'

'September 2012, yes, that fits with my theory. That was during the mysterious six-month gap between Shen leaving the Russian Trade Delegation in Washington in May and starting at Lee-Win in Shanghai in the following November, if memory serves.'

No longer surprised, she nodded in agreement, and he asked, 'The verdict was accidental death by misadventure, I imagine?'

'Which you don't agree with? How did you work all this out?'

'It was not as clever as you would like to imagine, Ilona. Let me ask you a question. Were you a happy child in a happy family?'

She thought for a moment. 'On the whole, I'd have to answer yes. We didn't have much money, but we were a very close and loving group. In Ukraine, the family usually includes grandparents, lots of uncles, aunts, cousins and almost anyone who lives nearby. I have three brothers and we got on really well, even after they married. They're still there, all with decent jobs and kids. My dad died two years ago, but my mum lives with her sister, who's also a widow, and we're always in touch and they're planning to come to London to see me next summer. So, yes, I was and still am a member of a happy family. Why did you ask?'

'Because that's the reason that you were unable to see the emotional scars that must have festered for years in the mind of our Chinese friend, Shen Fu Liáng. Can you imagine the pain and mortification of being separated from your natural family shortly after birth and growing up in a different country with another family, not even of the same nationality, speaking a different language? Being unable to see your mother or your brother, just two years older than yourself? Learning, when you are old enough to understand, that your parents had the choice of keeping you with them and your brother, or sending you away, just to ingratiate themselves with the fashionable political insanity of the day, and they chose the latter?'

'I hadn't thought of that. You're right, he must have ended up hating his parents.' A thought flitted across her mind, *I wonder if Hugh is relating to his own childhood experience?* She asked him, 'And you think he eventually got his revenge?'

'I'm beginning to think that was only the first of a sequence of revenges.'

'And XPC is the next?'

'I'm not yet sure. As you know, I find accidental death by poisoning to be something of an oxymoron, it happens seldom except in novels with badly constructed plots. But apparently we have a case in hand at XPC, and that concerns me. If it was not an accident, on the face of it there may be two persons on whom suspicion could fall.'

'Shen Fu Liáng and Daniel Oberhart, I suppose?'

'Exactly. One can easily imagine that Oberhart's family and their hedge fund investors are worried about the launch of this ACRE encryption software. They have a lot to lose if XPC increases its share of the very substantial processor market at their expense. And don't forget there's a Chinese connection there. Perhaps that is the reason that the son came to work with XPC, to keep his eye on, and possibly try to prevent, the development programme.'

'You mean by getting rid of their top encryption expert?'

'That was not what I expressed, but you must agree it's a possibility? However, the death, again by accident, of Shen's natural father during the period in which he was missing is highly pertinent. It may well have resulted in him inheriting a second fortune, assuming his adoptive father was also as rich as Croesus. I don't imagine we can discover any details, these wealthy people have many ways in which to obfuscate their true situation, trusts and similar arrangements, but I think it's highly likely and may be of significant importance to our enquiries.'

Middleton added, 'I think we should keep this information to ourselves, for the moment at least. If I'm right, we don't want to alarm anyone into an impetuous burst of action which could have unfortunate consequences. Thank you for your excellent research, Ilona. I may occasionally conceive a few interesting theories, but theories are only as good as the research work which proves or disproves them and that is your great skill.'

Dubai, United Arab Emirates

Leo had spent the morning looking at the results of their Mark VII testing while Ed and Sharif were in the downstairs lab, trying vainly to knock out his primitive wireless networks. For the first time since he'd arrived at XPC, everything was working as it should. They met in the canteen at lunchtime to review their progress. Tom and Shen had flown off to New York that morning, safe in the knowledge that their teams were delivering the project.

'You know what, guys?' Leo took a swig of his Coke.

'Tell us, oh Lord and Master.' The Liverpudlian unwrapped another pack of chewing gum and popped a piece in his mouth.

'Well, thanks to your terrific efforts, I think we're going to make the launch date. We've got three weeks to tweak and refine and get the final package to Shanghai.' He held out his bottle to clink with the others.

'I think we'll beat it by at least a week. Ed and I have prepared final testing on the end-to-end process for the teams tomorrow, and if it goes well, I'll have the design and mask ready to print what should be the definitive card next week. After that, from where we're at, a few days' testing is more than enough.' Sharif clinked his bottle with a beaming smile. He was enjoying his moment in the limelight. 'But I've got a favour to ask.'

'Ask away, you've earned a lot of favours.'

'My brother's flying in from Lahore this afternoon and I'd like to go and pick him up. But that's not the favour. He's only staying for three days and he's never been before, so I want to show him around tomorrow and Friday, if that's OK. I've already got the tests ready to give to my guys, and they don't need me to look over their shoulder. I can come in to check everything on Saturday after he leaves.' He looked at Leo hopefully.

'What do you think, Ed. Can we cope without this genius?'

'We'll try our best.'

'Go see your brother, Sharif. Then no more rest until we sign off the beta testing and get Shanghai started on Mark VII production.'

London, England

Ilona Tymoshenko was reading through her notes from the various meetings she'd been in that day. She had an excellent memory, but always wrote them immediately afterwards, while the events were still fresh in her mind. Before leaving the office in the evening, she would go back over them to look for any points she might have missed, or to add thoughts which had occurred to her later. The notes were well hidden in the private, encrypted personal files in her tablet, which was not connected to the general office system. Ilona was an expert in concealment, it was part and parcel of her upbringing and training in Ukraine, under the shadow of their Russian neighbours.

The last item was her discussion with Hugh Middleton about Daniel Oberhart's involvement with XPC, and his theory around the consequences of Shen Fu Liáng's birth and the death of his parents. *Hugh seems to have spent a lot of time thinking about this*, she reflected. *It's not at all related to our business and yet he's becoming obsessed by it.* She remembered his phrase, 'an impetuous burst of action which could have unfortunate consequences'. *He must have meant Leo Stewart. There's some connection there that he doesn't want to reveal. But what?*

Ilona wrote, '*Previous relationship/connection with Leo Stewart? Rwanda, mother — author, aunt Jenny Bishop — private equity*'. She decided to do further research on the subject when she had time. Once again, she suspected there was something that her partner was concealing from her, and she didn't like it.

TWENTY-ONE

Dubai, United Arab Emirates
Wednesday, 7 July 2017

Leo finished the paperwork that had accumulated in his inbox over the last few days and went along to put the file on Nora's desk. He had refused the offer of an assistant, since he didn't feel the small amount of admin work he had to cope with at XPC justified the cost. Tom's PA had the time available and was more than happy to help him out. He had no further plans for that evening, so he could catch up on the less stimulating side of his job.

He'd taken Angela out for dinner to the Crystal Lagoon the previous night and it hadn't been an unbridled success. She was a complicated woman, with very changeable mood swings. Halfway through the meal she told him she had a headache, was bored and wanted to go home. Spurning a ride on the Harley, she called a cab, gave him a perfunctory peck on the cheek and disappeared into the night. Leo hadn't had the chance to share the good news about his successful day at XPC; she wasn't in a talkative frame of mind, she was rude and disinterested and then she was gone. He rode home wondering what he'd done to deserve such a miserable end to a great day, and went to bed in an unhappy state of mind. He still found her mysterious and beautiful and was sexually attracted to her, but he couldn't cope with what he decided was simply a selfish and spoiled attitude to others. He would leave her alone until she called and apologised, if she ever did.

It was not yet nine o'clock and he decided to re-run Ed and Sharif's latest Mark VII upgrade tests on his *Leo 1, 2 & 3* networks, which were still in place. This might save time the next day when the teams ran the suite of test programmes that Sharif had left for them. He would use the printed logs of the morning's work from their files. This was another innovation he'd introduced since his arrival. Previously, test logs were often not printed and cross-checking was almost unheard of. He wanted fresh eyes to check every test, both the written code and the physical results.

Down in the lab, Leo ensured that the networks were running correctly, then he recreated their morning's upgrade test codes in his laptop from the file logs. He ran the upgrades together with his upload programme on *Leo 1*. The result was the same, Sharif was right, they would beat their deadline by several weeks. He felt justly proud, not only for his own work, but for the great performance of the teams under his two new friends.

Leo pressed *Print* to get his test log and results, and have them checked over by Ed and Sharif. The printer didn't respond, and he saw it was out of paper. It took him a moment to renew the supply and it immediately spewed out six pages of results. He checked the sheets and saw there were two pages numbered five. The additional log sheet carried Sharif's ID code and yesterday's date with an eleven-thirty p.m. timeline. The machine had obviously run out of paper after printing page four of his tests and he hadn't noticed. *He must have been working after I left to see Angela,* Leo realised. *That's dedication.* He put it to one side while he put the printouts of his own work into his master file then took everything back up to his office.

Replacing Ed and Sharif's morning's test logs into their files, Leo had a momentary doubt. *I don't remember seeing a log of Sharif's testing last night.* He checked the file again; there was no log for testing at eleven-thirty the previous night. He pulled out the Pakistani's morning log again and compared it with page five from the printer. The two logs seemed to be identical, showing that Sharif had run the same tests last night as he had this morning. *That's odd, why would he do the same tests last night and again this morning, with exactly the same results?* He continued comparing the sheets down to the last instruction, then stopped with a shock. There were three extra lines of code on last night's sheet, three lines that were not on this morning's log. *Why? What was in those lines that Sharif didn't want me, or presumably anyone else, to see?*

It was now after eleven, and Leo's head was aching after the long day and the concentration needed to recreate the coding and multiple testing he'd just executed. He decided to call it a night and leave that problem for tomorrow. *There must be a good explanation for it*, he told himself. He rode home on the Harley, went straight to bed, and was instantly asleep.

Dubai, United Arab Emirates

Club 27 was quiet for a Wednesday night. Since DeeJai's final show the previous Sunday, there had been a noticeable drop in customers. The club director was already talking to his management company about getting him back as soon as he'd finished his stint in New Zealand, he was the most successful act they'd ever had, and takings and profits had reflected that.

Ed Muire and Lynne had got there at ten and had the place almost to themselves. They knew the regular DJ and sometimes dropped in for a drink and dance, when Lynne wasn't working the evening shift at the Corner House. The disc spinner was less creative than DeeJai but he played a lot of eighties music that they both loved. Right now, they were dancing to a slightly upbeat version of Bonnie Tyler's 'Total Eclipse of the Heart', with Ed's added lyrics in her ear. Ed was a genuinely funny man who fancied himself as another Jimmy Tarbuck, and what he lacked in talent he made up for in spontaneity. She liked his light-hearted approach to life and they got on well together, making life in the Emirates an enjoyable experience for them both.

The DJ moved to a more romantic mood and they went over to sit in one of the alcoves at the back of the bar. They ordered drinks and talked for a while, Ed keeping an eye on the action in the club from his vantage point facing the dance floor. After a while, an attractive woman came in and sat in one of the side alcoves. Ed recognised her.

'Don't look now, but Angela just came into the bar, alone.'

Lynne managed to refrain from turning to look. 'Something happened with Leo?'

'I don't know. He said they had a date last night, but he didn't want to talk about it today. I guess it wasn't what he was hoping for.'

She laughed and punched him on the arm. 'You mean he's just like you. What do you think he was hoping for?'

'Wait, someone else has joined her, another woman. I don't believe it.' Angela stood up and embraced the woman fondly, kissing her on the lips. They sat down side-by-side at the back of the dim alcove, close together, holding hands and talking quietly.

'Ed, if you don't stop being so mysterious, I'll turn around to see what's going on. Who came in?'

'It's Shen's partner, the Belgian woman. Looks like they were expecting to meet up.'

'What's so strange about that?'

'I just didn't know they were such good friends. Shen's away in New York, so I suppose it's only normal to have a girls' night out, but...'

'You know I haven't got eyes in the back of my head. I'm going to the ladies. I can't stand being told about something I can't see. Get me another glass of wine please, I won't be long.'

Lynne walked on the other side of the room to the toilets, looking surreptitiously across at the two women. They were sitting right at the back of the alcove, invisible to most of the room, heads close together as they talked, still holding hands, looking into each other's eyes. *While the cat's away,* she said to herself. *Almost as if they're an item. Well, well, who'd have guessed?*

* * *

Ed whispered, 'Look, she's stroking Angela's thigh under the table.'

'You mean like this?' Lynne stroked her hand along the inside of his thigh. She was now sitting next to Ed on the other side of the alcove, from where she could partially see the two women.

'I think it was bit higher,' he said hopefully.

She smiled coyly, 'That's turning you on isn't it? Two women we know, being friendly in a bar. It might mean nothing. Not everyone is as unromantic as a Scouser.'

Fascinated, they sat watching Angela and Elodie for another half hour, saying hardly a word. They were still sitting in the same pose, holding hands and looking lovingly at each other. There was a lot of kissing and stroking going on and they moved apart only when the waiter fetched their drinks, martinis for each of them, two lots. By now, Ed was convinced they were lovers.

'Definitely a very involved item,' he said to Lynne as they watched the two women walk out of the club at midnight.

'Where do you think that leaves Leo?' she asked.

'Between a rock and a hard place, I'd say. It's his boss's partner, and it would be very nasty for him if he really falls for her and then finds out she prefers women, especially Elodie. In any case, we'd better not say a word about this to Leo, it's not our business and he's likely to get upset when he finds out.'

'I don't understand. Shen must know about this. I mean, if we've just seen them in the club together, we can't be the only people who know.'

'It depends on what his feelings really are for her. Maybe he doesn't care, or she could be just arm candy. Shen's a very peculiar character, cold and aloof, doesn't show his emotions at all. You know, yesterday Leo managed to find a solution to deliver the upgrades that Sharif and I just couldn't work out. It was the first time he'd really looked at the problem and he solved it in a few hours, just like that.' He snapped his fingers.

'Well done him. What's that got to do with Shen?'

Ed thought he picked up a slightly caustic tone in her remark, but went on, 'He said absolutely nothing to Leo. No congratulations, no smile on his face, nothing. We were all like, wow! Cheering and thanking him, but Shen, nothing. Kind of like he's jealous, or just doesn't appreciate what other people do.'

'So, you think he might know about Angela and Elodie and it doesn't bother him?'

'I think the real problem is he's Chinese and they're trained to hide their emotions. She's a great looking woman and when we met her, she seemed smart and likeable, but to him, she might just be someone to show off with.'

'Well, I think you're smart and good to show off with. Take me home and you might find out how much you're appreciated.'

TWENTY-TWO

Dubai, United Arab Emirates
Thursday, 8 July 2017

Leo went down to the lab at ten a.m. After a good night's sleep and breakfast at the Corner House, he had examined page five of Sharif's test log again. The last three lines of code sent a single instruction thousands of times within the space of a few seconds to cell S470C887,999: Sector 470, Cell number 887,999. A single cell among almost a billion components on the circuit card, all measuring less than a thousandth of the width of a human hair, impossible to identify without a complete diagram of the circuits and cells. Only Sharif, who managed the design of the physical unit, could explain why it was there and what its function was.

I need to know what that instruction actually does, if anything. It could be just some kind of additional testing procedure that Sharif has designed and hasn't mentioned to me.

He tagged the last three lines of Sharif's code onto the test programme he'd run the previous evening on the *Leo 1* network in his laptop and sent it to his mini-hub. A sense of relief flooded over him when he saw the network was running just as before. *Maybe it's some kind of redundancy test he was running, to ensure the network wouldn't break down under a barrage of commands to the same cell,* he reasoned. He was about to close the test environment when he sat back in shock.

Within a minute, every device incorporating a Lee-Win processor, eighty per cent of the network, had shut down. Not simultaneously and not in sequence, but sporadically here and there until nothing in the network was functioning, since those few pieces of non-Lee-Win equipment which were still running had no data to send because the transmission had been blocked further up the line.

His heart started racing, and he realised he was sweating and breathing deeply. *Hang on,* he told himself. *I must have screwed up somewhere. Let's have another go.* He changed the configuration to set up *Leo 2,* the second set of equipment, then sent the modified instruction to the hub again. He watched in horror as exactly the same thing occurred. All the Lee-Win supported devices closed down and the others were sending no data at all. He followed the flow of data in his mind. *I must have messed up the hub somehow. There's no data coming from it, so it's not acting on the instructions from my laptop.*

Leo went to get himself a coffee in the canteen. He sat for a while, sipping the hot sweet liquid, thinking and rethinking the situation, going over every connection, every link in his network, trying to find the flaw, but he couldn't. The network had worked perfectly until he'd introduced Sharif's additional codes. *But why?*

'Hi, Leo. How are things going with the final testing?' Daniel Oberhart brought his coffee over and sat at his table.

Leo was astonished. It was the first time the operations director had ever approached him in a friendly manner. 'Morning, Daniel. I'm still working through the last clean-ups from Sharif and Ed. Still a few bugs to sort out.'

'Anything I can do? I've helped manage a shitload of projects through the final stages, I know how tricky it can get.'

Leo thought for a moment, *Why not? He might know something about Sharif's test routines that I don't, he's worked with him longer than me.* 'Do you know anything about a special redundancy test that Sharif uses to test a programme's resilience? He's off on a few days' holiday with his brother and I'd rather not disturb him.'

'You'd have to tell me exactly what you're referring to, he uses a lot of techniques to test resilience.'

'Something to do with a specific cell instruction?'

'Do you know the cell he's testing?' The Swiss man took a pen and a paper napkin.

'It's in sector 470, cell number 887,999. Ring a bell?'

Oberhart looked thoughtfully at the scribbled number and said nothing for a moment. 'It means nothing to me, but I can look up his recent tests on the network if you like. That might tell us something.'

'Don't bother, Daniel, it'll be easier if I just call him and sort it out. Thanks.'

Oberhart left him and Leo went back down to the lab, racking his brains to work out how to find the reason for the extra code. Finally, he decided to recreate the tests he'd carried out successfully the previous night on *Leo 1*, with his original code. *That'll tell me if the hub is down or it's due to these changes.*

He loaded his own instructions again, sent them to his hub and crossed his fingers. He hardly dared look, but once again, as if by a miracle, the *Leo 1* network was up and working perfectly. A cold shiver ran up his spine. *It's not the hub and it's not an error on my part. It can only be Sharif's instructions to cell S470C887,999. What the hell is going on? Why did he change the test codes and run them at night without informing me?*

Leo was trying to push aside a word that kept entering his mind. *Sabotage. Is it possible that Sharif is trying to sabotage the project? We're two months away from launching the new products and he's testing some kind of Doomsday function behind my back.* Then another chilling thought came to him, even more far-fetched and sinister than the first. *Is that what happened to Scotty? Did he discover too much?* His experiences in South Africa six years ago had taught him there were many evil people in the world, especially where large sums of money were involved. Had he somehow become embroiled again in some kind of illegal activity?

He forced himself to think calmly. *All I know right now is that Sharif was testing something that knocked out the Lee-Win supported equipment. It could have simply been a resilience test.* Then another thought occurred to him. *Or it could be something that Shen asked him to do. Some new idea they might have come up with in Shanghai.* He knew that despite the new reporting structure, the two men often talked over a coffee or had lunch together in the canteen. He sympathised with Sharif's predicament; if Shen had asked him to do something, he couldn't refuse, so he might have worked on it at night to avoid creating a difficult situation between them. *I have to have a session with them to find out what's going on. If there's another item on the agenda, we can all work together to achieve it.*

Whatever the truth of the matter, he needed to get to the bottom of it immediately. Tom and Shen were coming back from New York that night and he had to bring them up to speed on the status tomorrow morning. If there was a problem, he had to get it resolved before meeting them. To do so, he had to get Sharif into the office and ask him some difficult questions face-to-face, see the Pakistani's reaction when he realised his subterfuge had been discovered. It would either be an innocent reaction or a guilty one. He hoped and prayed it would be the former, and there was some rational and convincing reason for the coded instructions that knocked over a wireless network in less than a minute.

Leo went to his office and pressed Sharif's number on his contact list. A woman's voice told him the phone couldn't be reached for the moment. He kept trying.

In the network centre, Daniel Oberhart was searching for Sharif's tests from Tuesday night, but he could find them nowhere. It looked as if the Pakistani had erased the files after running his programmes. He ran a trace through the Pakistani's previous test procedures, then through the whole network database, and failed to find any record of cell S470C887,999 in the XPC system at all. The test codes would be in Leo's mini-network, but the lab was locked and he didn't want to ask him any further questions.

It wasn't his area of responsibility and might only serve to arouse his suspicions.

Why would Sharif be testing a cell that Leo doesn't know about and then erase the files? How come there's no record of that cell anywhere in the system? If there's something going on here, I need to know about it, and fast.

He called a Zurich number. 'Hi Dad, how's things?' He listened for a while, then said, 'Great, I love those numbers. If you can keep it up for another few months, this deal's a no-brainer. But listen, I think there might be something weird going on here.' He related his conversation with Leo and his search for the apparently non-existent cell. 'Leo's smart and he's worried about Sharif's testing. If the guy's hiding that cell, it has to be for a reason. We can't afford the risk that there's something funny going on that could screw up three years of planning. I didn't agree to come to live in this dump for the fun of it. What do you think I should do?'

Oberhart listened again for several minutes. 'OK, I guess you're right. I'll play it cool and get closer to Sharif, he might let something drop. And I'm going to try to find his log sheets, either in his office or on his laptop.'

He rang off and went up to the Pakistani's office. It was locked, and he knew he couldn't get a key card without it looking suspicious. Back in the network centre he forced himself to concentrate on the week's scheduling. Sharif would be back in a couple of days, it would just have to wait.

London, England

'I think we're going to have to come in over the weekend, otherwise we'll never catch up on things,' Ilona Tymoshenko said to Dr Hugh Middleton. She was looking at her list of outstanding tasks. Business at the Institute for Global Internet Security was growing faster than they'd anticipated, and there never seemed to be time to plan ahead for staff and accommodation requirements. 'If we're not careful, we'll bite off more than we can chew,' she added worriedly.

'I have time on Saturday afternoon. Will that suffice?'

'Well, it's a start. We'll see what we can get through and if necessary, arrange another session. We can't afford to fall behind.'

'Very well, just as you say, Ilona.' Middleton was happy to let her manage his time for him, she was better at it than he. 'Meanwhile,' he added, 'I think it may be time to communicate our suspicions about Lee-Win to General Chillicott.'

Ilona looked at him sceptically. 'Yesterday, you said we should keep them to ourselves, and now you want to share our findings with Homeland Security. Any particular reason for your change of mind?'

'I still believe that we should refrain from mentioning the deaths of Shen Fu Liáng's family in the plane crash, and the possible financial consequences. However, the other facts about him and Oberhart are highly relevant to his investigation into the mysterious person, Tsunami, and to the ownership of Lee-Win and possible nefarious activities which he should be aware of. Between you and I, Ilona, of the two alternative theories I feel more inclined to favour the Chinese version.'

'Alright, let's talk to him. He'll be in his office in a couple of hours, I'll get hold of him then.'

Dubai, United Arab Emirates

Sharif called back after a half hour, to say he was in Sharjah for the day with his brother and was about to get on a boat to go out to look for dolphins. The rest of their day was similarly booked up. 'Is it something I can sort on the phone? I've still got a few minutes before we set off.'

'No, I was doing some more testing and I had a question about your last logs, but it'll keep 'til tomorrow. Enjoy Sharjah.'

Leo was about to put the phone away when it rang in his hand. 'Hi, Leo, it's Tom. I'm just about to leave for JFK. How's everything going over there? Still on target?'

Leo thought for a moment before replying. He now had a dilemma on his hands. His boss was asking how things were;

he couldn't pretend everything was hunky-dory after what he'd discovered that morning, he had to say something, but carefully.

'Everything's going well on the testing of the upgrades. I've had one hundred per cent results on all my test networks, so unless something unexpected happens we'll probably beat the deadline for the Shanghai delivery.'

'Terrific, that's great news.' Tom was a shrewd man and sensed some reserve in Leo's voice. 'Is there anything unexpected that could happen, anything you can think of?'

Leo hesitated, then decided to phrase his concerns in the form of a question. 'Do you by any chance know what the function of cell S470C887,999 is?'

'You're asking me if I know the function of one of the billion cells on the card? I haven't got a clue. Why do you want to know? What's special about that cell?'

'It's probably nothing, but that component seems to be giving me some problems. I just thought it might have some special significance that you'd know about.'

'I'll note it down and ask Shen when I meet him at the airport. He's bound to know, if anyone does. What was the ID again?'

Leo repeated the number slowly. 'How did things go in the Big Apple?'

'Some great business coming along. They're excited about Mark VII and ACRE. We'll brief you tomorrow. Gotta run now. Cheers.'

'Cheers Tom. Travel safely.' Leo closed the phone and sat back in his chair. He felt better, he'd told Tom, so now it was his problem. Both teams were running the tests prepared for them by Sharif and Ed the previous day, and there was not a lot he could do before the Pakistani returned. He walked along to Ed's office to invite him for lunch at the Corner House. He said nothing about the strange cell. It was sunny and hot, and sunbathers were lounging on the beach, soaking up the rays without a care in the world. They ordered a couple of beers and chilled out for a while.

London, England

'Sounds like you've worked out a theory around this. Want to tell me what it is?' Hugh Middleton and Ilona Tymoshenko were on the encrypted line with General Chillicott.

'Ilona will explain. She's done all the research, a quite remarkable exhibition of lateral thinking.'

The woman looked at him in amazement. *He never pays compliments. What's going on?* She rallied her thoughts. 'We have two possible theories, involving either Daniel Oberhart or Shen Fu Liáng, both senior officers of XPC.'

First, she outlined the connection between Oberhart's family, MicroCentral, Hai-Sat the Chinese hedge fund and the possibility of sabotage to prevent the launch of XPC's new encryption technology.

Chillicott's response was succinct. 'I don't buy it. The sabotage motive for the murder of a genius programmer could hold water if they're desperate to avoid the new product launch, but the rest doesn't hang together. You really think a Swiss company owned by a Chinese hedge fund could be involved with a Russian agent, offshore company subterfuge and ownership of a Chinese microprocessor company in Dubai? It just one of those peculiar coincidences that happen. It doesn't connect with what we've discovered to date.'

'Our opinion is that you're probably correct, Billy, but we're attempting to evaluate all possibilities with all the evidence available. Please continue with our theory about Liáng, Ilona.'

'Very well. First of all, General, it's the timing. From your side we've learned that Tsunami became active five years ago, including setting up well-hidden companies for the acquisition of Lee-Win for reasons which aren't clear. And from our side, we know that Shen Fu Liáng left his job with GRU and started with Lee-Win, also five years ago. Then there's an empty six-month time slot in Liáng's history just before that which we can't explain. The Dubai facility took eighteen months to build and was opened two and a half years ago. The decision making, planning and approvals must have taken at least a year, which means it was probably conceived at about the same time, five years ago.'

Following Middleton's instructions, Ilona omitted to mention the suspicious deaths of Liáng's Chinese family in September 2012, and the probability that he had inherited a substantial fortune.

She went on, 'Then there are the unusual facts around ownership and management. XPC is owned by Lee-Win Micro-Technology in China, but after the death of Chongkun, his family sold the business in 2012. The current ownership of that company is a mystery and Tsunami is somehow involved with that. And Liáng was sent down from Shanghai to be their man on the ground in their new microprocessor design business in Dubai, even though he's not a computer technician. He was with Lee-Win for only two years before going down to Dubai, but for eight years before that, he was trained with the GRU in Moscow and Washington as what you would call a "spook". So why was he appointed as an Executive VP in XPC?'

Ilona looked at Middleton, who nodded his head. She took a deep breath and said, 'Our theory is that there may be a connection between Tsunami and Liáng, and they are involved in some kind of conspiracy in XPC through Lee-Win. Maybe the two of them were introduced or met in some way during that "lost" six-month period, and they've been working together for the last five years since then.'

'Doing what?' Chillicott's reaction was that this was a wild goose chase. There was no proof that Tsunami and Liáng had ever met, never mind worked together.

Middleton intervened. 'We think there may be a potential source of information to provide the answer to that question, Billy.'

Chillicott suddenly understood the reason for the call. 'Leo Stewart?' he said.

TWENTY-THREE

Dubai, United Arab Emirates
Thursday, 8 July 2017

Leo decided to take the rest of the day off. Sharif wasn't there, the teams were doing their testing, he'd advised Tom of his concern and he'd worked almost every single day since he got to Dubai. He was due a break.

'What about chilling out on Palm Jumeirah?' he asked Ed. 'We should see it once at least.'

An hour later, they were riding along the 'trunk' of the artificial island, shaped like a seventeen-fronded palm tree, which had taken ten years to create. The broad avenue was lined with luxury hotels, restaurants and shopping malls, many of them still under construction, not a patch of sand in sight.

Leo was looking around and up, mainly up. 'Have you ever seen so many half-built skyscrapers in your entire life? We're on an artificial island in the Persian Gulf and it's like being in Manhattan or Vegas. What a downer.'

'I've never been to Vegas, but it's not exactly Crosby Beach in Merseyside,' laughed the Liverpudlian. 'Probably can't get decent fish and chips.'

The leaflet they'd been given about the island gave some impressive numbers: 3 billion cubic feet of sand dredged from the sea floor, 7 million tons of mountain rock to form the seven-mile crescent-shaped breakwater, a six-lane undersea tunnel connecting the island to the beaches on the crescent, and the Middle East's first monorail running the length of the island. Less impressive was the estimate of a square mile of coral killed in the Persian Gulf, although the developers had apparently dropped two American fighter jets on the sea floor to create new reefs. The second and third islands were still on the drawing board and no one was sure whether the project would ever be completed.

They rode the Harley to one of the beach hotels and spent a lazy afternoon admiring the bikini-clad girls posing around them. Leo was chilling out and feeling more relaxed than he had for a while. He realised that meeting the July 31st deadline had become an all-consuming passion with him, and now he knew they could make it, it was like a massive weight lifted from his shoulders. Ed was good company and they swapped stories and made the most of their day off.

It was seven in the evening by the time he dropped Ed off at his apartment and continued to the XPC building on his bike. He worked up a sweat in the gym with an hour of kicking and punching to keep his hands and feet hard, then went home to prepare for tomorrow's meeting and do the things he'd been neglecting lately, like sending emails to his family and listening to his favourite music.

His mobile rang as he let himself into the apartment. 'Hi Leo, it's Angela.'

'Oh. Hi there.'

After their last encounter he wasn't sure what to expect, and was surprised when she went on, 'Listen, I'm really sorry about the other night. I'd had some bad news from home and I wasn't fit company for anyone, especially not you. Can you please forgive me and let's try again?'

At the sound of her contrite tone he felt himself relenting. *Maybe I was too hard on her, everyone has a bad day from time to time.* 'What did you have in mind?' he asked.

'How about calling in at 27 for a drink? We can chat a while, then see what we feel like?'

'Sounds cool. See you there at ten?'

'Great, can't wait to see you again.'

Leo prepared an agenda for the next morning's meeting and sent it from his mobile to Tom and the others. When he got to the club, Angela was waiting at the bar, and she jumped up to kiss him when he came over. She was wearing a white cotton shift with a black and gold thread running through it that almost reached her knees. Her coffee-coloured skin shone under the dim club lights. She looked stunning and he felt great.

At eleven-thirty, Angela said, 'I've had enough of this for tonight. Let's go back to my place.'

She clung to him on the bike, arms around his chest, her hands grasping his shirt. After a moment, she undid the buttons and held his bare chest, her fingernails digging deep into his skin. Again, the ride didn't take long enough for his liking.

Her third-floor flat in Dubai Marina was miniscule compared to his, but furnished in a comfortable way with giant cushions and colourful wraps on the floor and a couch in the living room. A big table lamp of painted porcelain threw a soft light over the room. She went to the kitchenette to get him a beer and he spotted a Jenson record player on the dresser. Adele's *25* was on the turntable and he switched it on again.

'Feeling romantic, are you?' She clinked her glass against his. 'Here's to us.'

'You made me feel romantic the first time I saw you.'

She put their glasses aside and pulled him to her, kissing his face and lips. He responded, their tongues intertwining in a passionate kiss.

'Wait,' she pushed him away. 'I've got something for you, to show how sorry I am about Tuesday.' She took off the Adele disc and put on 'Stairway to Heaven', then switched the lamp off and went into her bedroom. After a moment, she emerged again, her body silhouetted by the light behind her. 'Here's your stairway to heaven,' she said. Angela pushed aside the straps of the cotton shift and it fell to the floor, exposing her small, high breasts, the nipples aroused, and her shaved pubes. Leo felt the blood rush to his penis. She came over to him and pulled him to his feet. 'Come here,' leading him into the bedroom.

Angela's lovemaking was like her personality, a strange combination of tenderness and malice. She kissed and stroked his body until he was mad with desire, then slapped his face. 'I like rough sex,' she said. 'Hit me.'

Apart from a tragic accident in South Africa, Leo had never hit anyone outside of the fight ring, and he wasn't about to start. Instead, with one hand he pinned her down by her wrists, and with the other he opened her legs and thrust his penis inside her. She screamed and pulled his face to hers, biting his lip until it bled, then pushing her tongue into his mouth again. He plunged himself into her again and again until their bodies were joined like one, then with a massive final thrust they climaxed together and she cried out and clasped him to her, her nails clawing into his back.

'Oh, *Dios mio*, oh my God!' she gasped as he fell by her side. 'That was *maravilhoso*.'

Jimmy Paige's last chord faded away behind Robert Plant's final wail, and he kissed her lips gently. 'If that's Portuguese for awesome, I agree.'

After their second session of frantic sex, Leo called time. 'I've gotta get home. It's almost three o'clock and I've got a meeting with my boss this morning. I'm sorry, but I have to go.'

'Are you really sure? Can't I tempt you one more time?'

'You could tempt me, but you'd be very disappointed.' He went to pick up his clothes from the living room floor. 'I couldn't take any more of that rough sex. I'm hurting everywhere.'

At the door, he said, 'How about I pick you up tonight to go to 27?'

'If you can make it, that'll be cool. Goodbye, Leo.' She pecked his cheek.

'See you tonight, Angela.'

Leo's mind was racing as he rode home, reliving the night's surreal events. *What an incredible woman. Whatever's happening between us, it feels great.* He dumped his clothes on a chair, fell on his bed and was asleep a minute later.

TWENTY-FOUR

Dubai, United Arab Emirates
Friday, 9 July 2017

Leo was riding a dolphin across the calm, azure Mediterranean.
Angela was clinging on behind him, her nails digging into his chest.
A guitarist was riding another dolphin alongside him, playing
the solo from 'Stairway to Heaven'. His dream was shattered by a
violent banging sound, and he realised it was someone knocking on
the door. He struggled to clear his head then looked at his watch
and went over, still in his boxer shorts, and called, 'It's six in the
morning, who is it? What the hell do you want?'

'It's the police. Open the fucking door,' a voice shouted back.

He fumbled with the lock and pulled the door ajar with the
safety chain still attached. 'What's going on?'

Two men stood outside; they wore olive green shirts and berets
and had guns holstered at their hips. One of them had a baton in
his hand that he'd been using to bang on the door. 'Are you Leo
Stewart?' he shouted.

'Yes. What is it?'

'*Aftah, aftah.* Open the door up, nigger. You're under arrest.'

Leo's mind couldn't function for a moment. 'What do you mean?'

He banged the baton against the door. 'Open this fucking door now or we'll blow it open.' His hand went to his pistol.

'OK, OK.' Leo unfastened the safety chain and he pushed the door wide and strode in, followed by the other man, who had now drawn his gun.

The policeman shoved the baton into his chest, pushing him towards the open bedroom door. 'Get your clothes on nigger, you're coming to the station.'

'What are you arresting me for?'

'For raping a woman.' He smashed the stick across Leo's back. '*Taharruk!* Get dressed and bring some clothes, *khinzir qadhar,* filthy black rapist.'

Leo staggered and almost fell. 'What the fuck are you talking about? When am I supposed to have raped a woman?'

'You know when, last night. I can see the marks on your face and body. Your cock must still be burning. *Akhris!* No more talking, get ready.' He hit him again with the baton.

Leo's mind suddenly cleared, and the answer dawned on him. He felt sick at the realisation. *It's a honey trap. Angela's cried rape against me. Rape is a death sentence. What the fuck's going on?*

His shirt and trousers were on the chair where he'd dropped them and he picked them up, thinking furiously, forcing himself to stay calm, remembering the events in South Africa when he had turned the tables on his captors. *I need a minute, that's all I need.*

He went towards the bathroom, and the policeman hit him again and screamed, 'Get dressed here, stay where you are.'

Leo's muscular fighter's frame easily withstood the blows, and he mentally calculated the height of the two men at five ten or eleven. Both of them could be disabled with two swift Taekwondo kicks, but he knew it would only worsen the situation. He needed to avoid a fight, to think clever.

'I have to use the toilet. Unless you want me to shit in your car.' He had to get a message to someone before they took him to the prison. He'd heard enough stories to know that once in their custody, it would be too late.

The man hesitated, '*Hasanana.* Be quick, filthy pig. I'm standing here. Leave the door open and don't try to be clever.'

Leo went into the bathroom and half closed the door. He sat on the toilet seat, took his mobile from his trouser pocket and found Ed's number, typed *prison Hatim help*, pressed *Send* then switched it off and shoved it back into his pocket.

Standing up, he caught sight of himself in the cabinet mirror. There was a purple welt across his cheek where she'd slapped him, and his lip was cut and bruised. *Crafty bitch*, he thought. *She's set me up for a fall.* He flushed the toilet and the policeman pushed the door open. The room stunk of their sweat.

'Get ready and bring your stuff, or I'll cut your balls off,' he shouted. 'Where's your mobile?'

Leo handed it over and the man shoved it in his shirt pocket. He grabbed some toilet things and another shirt and shorts and was pushed out of the flat, the baton smashing into his back as he walked to the elevator.

Dubai, United Arab Emirates

Ed Muire's flat was in a nearby building in the park. He checked his phone when he got up at six-thirty and saw the text. There was no reply when he called Leo's mobile. Panicked, he rang Tom Connor's number. The American had arrived late the night before and was still in bed. He rubbed the sleep from his eyes as Ed read the message to him.

'Wait a minute, Ed. I can't understand anything you're saying. Tell me again.'

'It's a text from Leo, he sent it at six-fourteen. It just says "prison Hatim help", nothing else, and he's not answering his mobile. I didn't know what to do, so I called you.'

Tom's brain woke up with a start. 'He'd only ask for Hatim's help if he was in trouble. Why is he talking about prison? I'll get Hatim on the case to find out what's going on. Meet me at the office in half an hour, and we'll take it from there. And Ed, call

Sharif and get him back in here. This sounds like we need all hands on deck.'

At eight-thirty, Tom received a call from Hatim. Ed, Shen and Daniel were in the office with him and Sharif arrived during the call. He didn't speak for several minutes, making notes, his face becoming paler as he listened to the lawyer.

Finally, he asked, 'Is there any proof, or is this just a money-making stunt?' He listened again, then put the phone down, a worried look on his face.

'What's going on?' Ed asked.

'Leo's in jail for rape.'

'What? That's bullshit. He wouldn't rape a girl if she asked him to, it's total rubbish.'

Shen sat silently, his face as inscrutable as always.

'OK, here's the situation.' Tom assembled his thoughts. 'This morning at three-thirty, a woman called the police to say she'd been raped by Leo. They'd been for a drink to Club 27 and came back to her flat and he raped her there. The police came to her apartment and she was distressed and hysterical, so they took her to a police doctor who confirmed she'd recently had sexual relations. Her wrists and legs were bruised as if she'd been held down, and she had a black eye she said he'd given her when she wouldn't do what he wanted. She named the man as Leo Stewart and gave them his address. They went round to arrest him and saw he was bruised on the face and had fingernail scratches on his arms, back and shoulders. He was taken to the Bur Dubai police station and checked by a doctor, who confirmed the marks on his body were consistent with a woman defending herself against him.'

'Where is he now?' Shen spoke for the first time.

'He's in a holding cell at Bur Dubai until they take him to the magistrate later today.'

'Is he OK?' asked Ed. 'I mean, all this is a heap of crap, but I've heard the stories about police brutality here. And if he could only text me three words and then couldn't answer the phone, he must be in bad shape.'

'Hatim said it's a miracle he was informed immediately. He told them Leo is an executive at XPC which is a billion-dollar Chinese investment and they'd better not treat him badly, or Shanghai is going to be very pissed off, so they let him see him. He's been beaten up a bit by the police, but he's OK. He admits he was with the woman last night in her flat. But he says it was at her invitation, and they listened to music and they had sex twice before he left her with a goodnight kiss and went back to his place.'

Daniel Oberhart asked, 'Did he tell you who the woman is?' Ed was sure he knew the answer, but he waited for the CEO's confirmation.

Tom consulted his notes. 'Angela da Sousa. She's a Brazilian woman who Leo met a few nights ago, and they fixed a date last night.'

Oberhart said nothing, but he gave Shen a querulous look.

Shen managed to show some emotion. 'Angela? She's a very good friend of my partner and me. Daniel knows her as well. There's no way she'd lie about a thing like that, she's a fabulous person. I knew there was something about that kid. Pushy, arrogant fucking know-all. I told you so, remember? And now he's raped a beautiful woman who trusted him enough to invite him home. I'll kick the shit out of him if I see him again.'

Ed had been observing Liáng for a while in his own quiet way. His opinion of the Chinaman was that he was irrelevant and divisive, continually undervaluing Leo's contribution while praising Sharif to the skies. He knew there was history between them, and it showed. This was the longest – in fact, the only – speech he'd ever heard him make, and he wasn't going to let him get away with it.

'What in Christ's name are you talking about, you ungrateful tosser? He's just saved your whole fucking Chinese business by sorting a problem that no bugger else could fix, especially you. You were in deep shit before he came, and you know it. He's worth more to this company than you'll ever be. And don't go accusing him of raping that woman, because she was just as keen on him as he was on her.' Ed stopped, thinking about Angela, Elodie,

Shen, whatever their relationship was. 'Unless she's into women and not men, that is.'

Shen gave him a vicious look, but reverted to saying nothing.

Tom held up his hands. 'Guys, no one here knows what happened, so let's stop being judge and jury about it and work out what we can do to help.'

Sharif spoke for the first time. 'I agree with Ed. There's no way Leo would have raped a woman, he's a respectful kind of guy. And we'd still be stuck with the remote upgrades if he hadn't come up with the solution.' He looked at Shen. 'I got a call in Sharjah yesterday from him about some extra tests he was doing. He's smarter than any of us, and we need him to be involved in the final testing and design to be sure we can deliver the job on time.'

'He told me the same thing yesterday morning, but I couldn't help him,' Daniel said. 'He was going to call you right away.' The Swiss man was nervous, there was definitely something not right about this situation. Yesterday Leo had asked him about a cell that he couldn't find in the network, and now they were discussing his arrest on a rape charge. *What the hell's going on?* He looked again at Shen, who was wearing his most inscrutable expression.

Tom snapped his fingers, 'That's right. He asked me about a cell function as well. Did you check it out, Shen?'

The Chinaman looked uncomfortable and shot a glance back at Sharif, who made no comment. 'I haven't had time yet, I just got in. I'm going to look at it with Sharif later on. But you're right, I'm sorry, we have to try to get Leo out of there as soon as possible.'

Ed looked at him in astonishment, but just said to Tom, 'What happens next? Did Hatim tell you?'

'He said the appearance in front of the magistrate is a formality. They've agreed for him to represent Leo, which is a blessing, because none of us understands a word of Arabic. He'll plead not guilty and make a statement, then they'll hold him to await trial.'

'Which prison?' Ed knew there were two options, Port Rashid and Dubai Central Prison. He'd heard very bad stories about the former, but he knew whichever it was it would be a life-changing experience for his friend.

'Hatim thinks he can wangle things to keep him in Bur Dubai until the trial, but that's not the problem.'

'Can we visit him? I can drive down there now. There must be stuff he needs, I can get it and take it in for him.'

'Apparently nobody except his lawyer will be permitted to visit him until after the trial. He's virtually incommunicado.' He looked at his notes again. 'Hatim says the case will go very quickly, and unless Leo can provide some kind of proof, or this woman Angela withdraws her accusation, there's no chance of him avoiding a guilty verdict.'

'Which means?'

'The official penalty for rape is death by firing squad, but that would only be in an aggravated case, something involving torture or murder for example. It's usually commuted to life imprisonment or less, and sometimes it can be settled by a financial arrangement. If it's not, he'd be sent to Port Rashid or Dubai Central. That's all I know, everything Hatim told me.'

Ed shuddered. 'Do you have any idea of what would happen to him if he went to one of those hellholes on a rape conviction? He'd be sodomised by every bugger in the prison and dead from AIDS in a year. Fucking hell! This is an insane situation.'

'One thing is sure. I have to call his mother and give her the bad news, before they get it from the press or the embassy. It'll probably be all over the papers tomorrow, "*Englishman arrested on rape charge in Dubai*", that kind of thing.'

'Hang on, Tom. Can't we keep a lid on this?' Oberhart asked. 'I mean, this is a pretty serious charge, and Leo's a Senior VP of an important foreign-owned business in Dubai. This could become a big issue and do a lot of damage to XPC. Neither the company nor any of us will benefit from that.'

'Shit, I wasn't even thinking about that aspect. You're right, we've got to do everything we can to keep this quiet until we know exactly what happened, the likely outcome and what the collateral damage looks like. Nothing gets out of this room unless and until I say so. I'll tell Hatim and Ms Stewart the same thing, nobody talks about this to anyone.'

Ed couldn't believe that everyone seemed to be putting the company's interests ahead of Leo and his family. 'Hang on a minute, Tom. We need to get Hatim over to get a clearer idea of what's likely to go on before you speak to his mother. We can't just call and say, "Hi there. Leo's in jail for rape and we don't know what's going to happen to him, sorry." There must be something we can do to help.'

'OK, you're right, Ed. This is a new situation for all of us, I'll get Hatim to come over now.' Connor looked at his watch. 'I can't call anyway for a few hours, it's only five-thirty a.m. over there.' He looked worriedly from Sharif to Ed. 'The next question is, though, if we can't get Leo back quickly, can you two guys get the final testing and design ready for Shanghai by the end of the month? That's in just three weeks' time.'

Ed answered first, typically giving his friend the kudos for their present status. 'Leo ran a successful, fully redundant end-to-end solution, so if I take his final logs, I can write the definitive code. I'll test it to death myself to be doubly sure, but if everything runs as it did for him on Tuesday and there are no bad surprises, the firmware should be OK. You, Sharif?'

'Same here. The design is finished except to incorporate Leo's remote upgrade requirements, but I don't see any problems with that. If Shen clears up the question about that cell he asked about, I can deliver without Leo. I don't want to, but I can if I have to.'

'No problems on the network side,' Oberhart added. 'I've cleared the decks for the next few days, so get testing.' He tried to sound relaxed and bullish, but he was a very worried man.

'OK, guys. I feel a lot better hearing that. I'll let you know what Hatim has to say.' Tom breathed a sigh of relief. He was going to have to write a report for Shanghai, and every positive response made the task a little easier.

TWENTY-FIVE

Bur Dubai Police Station, United Arab Emirates
Friday, 9 July 2017

Leo was pushed into a cell with four other men and two double bunks. No washbasin or toilet, but the cell still smelled like a cesspit and it took him a long time to ignore it. There was no place to sit other than on the bunks, and since he was the last occupant, he had no bunk. Behind him the guard locked the barred door and walked away along the corridor. Leo had just undergone a humiliating medical examination by what he suspected was a gay doctor, and had blood and urine samples taken to check for drug use. He now had a lot more bruises on his body from the beatings the police had given him on the way to the station and while moving him around inside. They were incapable of letting him walk without smashing a baton into his back or kidneys.

Hatim Ackerman had arrived as the doctor was finishing the examination, and he'd been allowed five minutes with him to give his account of the night's events.

Leo's first question was, 'Have you spoken to Angela?'

'We're not allowed to speak to her until the hearing, and I doubt she'll be there. They'll have a signed statement from her and the doctor will say she's too distraught to appear. Meanwhile, we just have to wait.'

'You know this is a stitch-up don't you? She invited me to her place and we had sex twice, and she enjoyed it as much as I did. She even played my favourite Led Zeppelin number for me while we made out. If anybody got raped last night, it wasn't her, it was me. You've got to find out why she's done it and get her to withdraw the charge. It's probably to blackmail money out of me and I can raise some through my family, but you need to see her as quickly as you can. I've got responsibilities at XPC and I can't afford to spend any more time in this shithole of a prison.'

'I'll try to contact her, but I don't think she'll agree to see me, especially if it's a false accusation.'

'Then you've got to get Tom or someone from the office to see her. There must be a way to convince her to see reason.'

The lawyer agreed to this, then said, 'I have a strategy to maybe get you released as quickly as possible. You'll appear in front of the public prosecutor this afternoon to make your not guilty plea and sign a written statement. It's in Arabic, but I'll make sure it's correct. I'm going to ask for bail but it'll be refused, so I'll propose house arrest with a corporate assurance until the trial. They're very wary of upsetting foreign investors, especially Russia and China, so I think they might consider it.'

'What does that mean?'

'They'll either agree to house arrest, or more likely keep you in Bur Dubai Station instead of moving you to one of the other prisons. If they send you there, you'll be forgotten for a very long time, so I'm trying my best to keep you here where we can keep tabs on you until the trial.'

'How long will that take?'

'It's impossible to say, but with some pressure from XPC it might be within a month.'

Leo was incredulous. 'You mean, even in the best of circumstances I might be stuck in this stinking dung heap for a month?'

'I'll do my best, but things here aren't like the UK or the US, and we just have to work with the system as best we can.' Hatim went on to explain the house rules to Leo, the only ones he registered being: 'Stay up here on the ground level and don't go down to the basement area, that's where the druggies and serious criminals are housed. Assert your authority quickly but don't get into fights, it doesn't matter how tough you are, they can be fatal. They've got some very nasty ways of hurting you, like gang rapes and with HIV-infected blood.'

The guard came to take him to the cells, and Leo asked, 'Has anyone called my mother? They won't let me use the phone. Can you make sure someone calls her?' The lawyer assured him that Tom Connor would call Emma that afternoon. 'Please ask him to be gentle with her, she'll be horrified to hear I'm in jail. It'll be the worst thing she's ever heard.'

Ackerman left, promising to keep the CEO informed of everything and to be back for the hearing in the afternoon.

Leo pushed the few items he'd brought under one of the bunks and sat on the end of a bed near the door, sizing up the situation, working out how he could assert his authority. The first problem was that he was the only African, which he knew probably spelled trouble. There were two Asian men and two who looked like Europeans, so he addressed them all.

'Hi, I'm Leo. What're your names?'

A blond guy in a vest with spectacles, an earring and tattoos covering his arms and neck said, 'Phil. You got any cigarettes?' He was sitting on an upper bunk and spoke with an American accent. A bloody gash ran across his forehead as if he'd been hit hard with a sharp instrument.

'Sorry, don't smoke. You guys?'

One of the Asians answered, 'He's Tony, and I'm Rafa. We're from Karachi. What's it to you, anyway?'

'Just getting to know my neighbours. How come you're in here?'

'We just got here this morning to look for work. Fucking cops put drugs in our bags at the customs and arrested us. They beat the shit out of us and now they want $200 to let us out, and we don't have it. You?'

Leo wasn't convinced the drugs had been planted, but he replied, 'I was in a street fight, somebody got hurt so they blamed me. I've got to go up for trial, maybe then I can pay a fine and get out.'

The fourth man stood up, looked European, about five-ten with a ragged scar running around his throat. 'Who the fuck do you think you are, quizzing everybody like you own the place?'

'Who's asking?' Leo asked, standing up to his full height of six-four.

The man stood his ground, looking up at Leo. 'Fighter, eh? Marquis of Queensbury rules? You'll need to be careful here, there's some real vicious brawlers around.' He spoke excellent English with an Eastern European accent.

'*Du bist Deutsch, oder?* You're German, right?' Leo dredged up a few words from his college language studies.

'Good try. Polish, Gdańsk. Oskar Novak.' He leaned over and shook hands. 'Good to meet someone with an education in this shitty country.'

Dubai, United Arab Emirates

'You don't know Leo very well, do you?' Ed Muire was speaking to Daniel Oberhart.

The Swiss man was immediately on the defensive. 'I'm not sure what you mean. I hardly know him at all, why?'

'Is that why your first reaction was to worry about the reputation of the company, and not about his shitty situation?'

Oberhart was quiet for a moment, thinking about his role in Leo's appointment. 'You're right, Ed and I'm sorry, I got my priorities completely wrong. I apologise, and I hope you won't mention it to Leo, it was just thoughtlessness.'

'OK, no harm done. I suppose you don't know about his family life, not that there's much to know, but he hasn't had it easy.'

'I was talking with him the other day. He told me he'd never known his father, but that's all he said.'

'As far as I know, Leo's family is his mother and her sister, his aunt Jenny. They're the only relatives I've heard him mention. He's never had a father, so his mum's going to be blown away when Tom calls her. And there's nothing she or his aunt can do, they'll be completely whacked by this fake accusation. So, forget about the company's reputation, and let's try to help get Leo back from that shithole prison and finish the job he's been doing really well.'

'I don't think there's much I can do, but if there is, just ask and I'll be happy to help.' The two men shook hands, and Ed went out. Oberhart took out his mobile and called the Zurich number. His father answered, and he said, 'We've got another problem.'

TWENTY-SIX

Dubai, United Arab Emirates
Friday, 9 July 2017

Hatim Ackerman arrived at one o'clock and was shown up to Tom's office. Shen and Ed Muire were already there. Tom hadn't invited Daniel or Sharif, but he felt that Ed should attend since he'd been the first to be contacted by Leo.

'Before we go any further, Hatim, this whole business must be kept completely under wraps. We can't afford anything to get into the public domain and cause a scandal for XPC or Lee-Win. Can that be managed?'

'Actually, Tom, nobody's really interested in a case like this, they're pretty common. We're not talking about a murder here. I'm sure the woman doesn't want any publicity either, it would only weaken her position, make her vulnerable. If you can keep it quiet on your side, there's no reason why it should be known outside of the people in this room.'

'Great, thanks Hatim, that's quite a relief. Now, what's the latest situation with Leo?'

The lawyer repeated everything he'd explained on the phone, adding, 'Leo seemed in pretty good form, despite the circumstances.

I gave him a few tips on surviving Bur Dubai, but that place is an accident waiting to happen. If he steps out of line, he'll pay for it, and possibly with his life.'

Ed was struggling to contain himself. 'I hope you agree that this is all bullshit, that there's no way he could have raped that woman?'

'Unfortunately, what I think is of no importance whatsoever. My job is to try to get Leo out of jail and back into XPC, that's what I'm paid for. As a matter of fact, I don't think it's likely that he actually raped Angela, he seemed too calm and collected about it, like remembering she put on his favourite album before they had sex. She's having a complete medical examination right now, which might shed more light on what happened, but I wouldn't count on it. If she's smart, she'll know how to fake the evidence and we can't argue.'

'So, this afternoon Leo pleads not guilty, and if she doesn't change her story, he stays in jail until whenever the trial is held, then he's found guilty and shipped off to die in some godforsaken pigsty of a prison.'

'It's not exactly like that. There's a chance he'll be bailed with house arrest under a corporate assurance. But that would still probably take a week.'

'And in the meantime, he might get gang-raped or beaten to a pulp or even killed. I don't fucking believe this country.'

'OK, Ed, we know you and Leo are good friends, but you're not helping right now.' Tom tried to assert some authority. 'Hatim, when and how can we get in touch with Angela to talk turkey? There must be a number, an amount that will compensate her for whatever reason she had to put Leo in jail.'

'She won't want to talk to me, since I'm representing him and XPC, so it'll have to be a friend or acquaintance, someone she knows and maybe trusts. A contact could be made tonight or tomorrow, there's no law against that.'

'Right. Shen, you said she's a good friend. Go see her and find out what it would take for her to withdraw her accusation and drop the whole business. I'll get approval for the payment, if it's not too outrageous. It seems like it's the only way we'll get Leo out of there, for his own safety, and back in here to tie things up before we run out of time.'

The Chinaman didn't seem too keen on the proposal, but he agreed to try to meet Angela and do what he could. Ed wasn't convinced that he'd succeed, or even try. He started thinking about what he might be able to do, if anything.

Bur Dubai Police Station

'What happened to you?' Leo was getting to know Oskar Novak. The Pole had an interesting educational background, having graduated from Gdańsk University of Technology then obtained a Masters in Finance at the London School of Economics, before working at Rolls Royce for ten years. He had been in the cell for a week and was awaiting sentencing for forgery. A small matter of a cheque for $10,000 made payable to himself, which of course was merely a misunderstanding with the account holder. It seemed the LSE's motto, 'to Know the Causes of Things', hadn't quite been understood by Oskar.

'You mean this?' He indicated the scar around his neck. 'I slept with a guy's wife and he slit my throat. Didn't do a very good job, missed the carotid and just left me with an interesting scar. The thing is, I did him a favour. His wife was actually screwing a friend of mine, and I kind of slipped in one night and got caught. But then he hired a private dick to watch her and found out she was doing him wrong, so he saved a fortune on the divorce. And before you ask, I didn't get a commission.'

Leo laughed. Oskar was a villain, no doubt, but he was a likeable villain. 'You know,' he said. 'I've got a great theory about how sex is responsible for everything that's wrong in the world.'

'OK, let's hear Leo's theory of sex.'

'Simple. It's because it's enjoyable. If it wasn't, there'd be fewer people having sex, because they didn't like it. They'd only have sex when they wanted a child, so they'd have fewer children and the world population would be manageable, there'd be no sex crimes, no two-timing, no pornography and so on.'

'And there'd be no fun.'

'Yep. There's a defect in every theory, and that's it.'

Dubai, United Arab Emirates

Sharif was talking to Shen Fu Liáng in his office. 'It's a strange coincidence, Leo being arrested.' The Pakistani sounded worried.

'How do you mean, a coincidence?'

'I think he found out about the redundancy test on cell S470C887,999 that was commissioned by Shanghai. I'd been testing it the previous night, and he must have noticed it on my log. That's what he said when he called me in Sharjah. I don't think he ran a test, or he'd have said so, but he wanted to know what it was.'

'I guessed as much, he called Tom about it, but I wanted to explain it to you anyway.'

'Shen, you asked me not to tell Leo about those tests, and you've never told me why. That's the coincidence, because you asked me not to tell Scotty when you gave me the codes on the flash drive. I told you Scotty saw it and asked me what it was. Then the next thing is, he dies of poisoning, and now Leo's in jail. I'm really wondering what's going on around here.'

Shen went and closed the door. 'Well, the first thing that's not going on is anybody poisoning Scotty or getting Leo arrested. That's so far-fetched it's too ludicrous to even consider. There's absolutely no connection between that cell and those unfortunate events.'

Sharif looked dubious. 'The cell's not on my design spec. It's something they've added in the manufacturing process in Shanghai, and I've got no idea what it's for. And all the redundancy test seems to do is to temporarily close down the network. I don't see the point. I mean, what exactly is that test for?'

'It's not exactly what it says on the box, but it has nothing to do with anything in current production. It's for a highly confidential development I'm not supposed to talk to anyone about, and I wouldn't tell Tom, or Leo, because I don't know them, and in my book you don't trust people you don't know. You and I have worked together for five years and I trust you, but you've got to promise me it won't go any further.'

'You know I never talk about things. That's one of the reasons you hired me.'

'OK, here's the heads-up, and it stays with you. Over the last three years, Shanghai has been developing another innovation to introduce after ACRE, something just as world-shattering. That cell was added only to test the concept, and the codes I gave you are for that and nothing else. It's simply to ensure that we can put the system on hold for a moment when we're ready to launch the next development. Don't worry, it won't be included in the package you send to Shanghai, it's only for your testing here.

'I'm not permitted to tell you exactly what it is, but right after the upcoming launch, we'll receive the specs from Shanghai to write the new firmware and build the next design. And you'll be leading one of the teams that brought Mark VII, ACRE and this new technology to the world. That's why I came down to Dubai and why I chose you and your team, to give you a chance to make history with us.'

Shen was watching Sharif's reaction to his speech. He saw the Pakistani's eyes shine and his chest swell at the thought of achieving greatness. He went on, to try to seal the deal. 'Tell me something, quite honestly. Could you, without Leo and with or without Ed, bring the project to a successful completion by the end of the month? Naturally, the increased responsibility would come with extra remuneration, I'd make sure that you're very well rewarded, you know you can count on me.'

Sharif took his time to answer. He still resented the way Leo had been brought in above him. Instead of getting the top job as he wanted, he'd been demoted. Now Shen was offering him that chance. He knew that if Leo didn't return, Ed might jump the boat, and he'd be the only man with the experience and knowledge to take over. The last tests he'd run showed that all the new software was working perfectly. As he'd just confirmed to Tom Connor, his design work was almost finished, and that was something he was uniquely capable of executing.

'Honestly, Shen, I could do it. I'd prefer to do it together with the others, but if I have to, I can do it alone and it will be before the end of the month, I can promise you that.'

'That's great, Sharif, I was sure of it. I'm going to try my best to get Leo back, but I doubt it'll work. I think he's going to be stuck at least until the trial, and we have no idea how long that will be. Now I know we can manage without him, I feel confident we can fulfil our obligations to Shanghai. At the end of the day, that's what really matters. And just as important, you're going to get the credit you deserve for the great job you've done.'

Sharif left the office walking on air. He was going to be the leader of the team which built the two most innovative and valuable Internet developments of the decade. His family would be proud of him, and so would everyone who knew him.

Public Prosecution Office, Dubai

'Not guilty, sir.'

The Public Prosecutor rattled off something in Arabic, and Hatim translated for Leo, 'State your version of what happened last night concerning the woman, Angela da Souza.'

Leo summarised the events of the evening as succinctly as possible, while a male secretary typed up his statement in Arabic. Hatim read it over and nodded for him to sign it. He asked for bail, which as expected was refused, then he proposed house arrest with the corporate assurance of XPC; a billion-dollar Dubai company, subsidiary of a multibillion Chinese enterprise, where Leo was a highly valued executive.

The prosecutor called over another official and they talked for a few minutes, then he answered Hatim. He relayed their answer to Leo. 'Remanded in custody in Bur Dubai until trial. Date to be set in due course.'

Back at the station, they walked to the cell block. The lawyer saw the disappointment on Leo's face. 'We didn't get house arrest, but there's no mention of the other prisons, so you'll stay here until the trial's called and I'm sure it won't be long. The discussion with the other official was about the damage XPC could do with media reports in China. They don't want to cause an incident, and I think that will weigh in our favour to some extent.'

Before they left for the hearing, Leo had asked him for his mobile, so he could call Emma, but Hatim didn't have it. 'I had to leave it at the entrance,' he'd explained. 'Everyone does, they're not allowed in here.'

Now he said, 'Is anyone allowed to visit me now?'

'Not until after the trial. I'm the only person allowed to communicate with you.'

'What about my mother? Has anyone called her?'

'I'm going to get hold of Tom now, to tell him what transpired here, and he'll call her straight away. He wanted to wait until the hearing to tell her everything he could, it's still only midday in the UK. It's good news, so I hope your mother won't be too worried.'

Leo was astounded at the lawyer's lack of understanding of a mother-son relationship. He couldn't bear to think how Emma would react when she heard the news. He said, 'You must get a phone to me, so I can speak to her myself. You'll have to smuggle one in. Bring one tomorrow and shove it in your shoe or your underpants or something. Just get me a phone so I can call her. She'll be going crazy not hearing from me.'

'I'll do what I can, but I can't promise. They're not as stupid as they seem here, they're used to all kinds of tricks.'

As they re-entered the cell block, a huge black man in handcuffs being escorted by two officers came towards them in the corridor. He was struggling with them, and didn't seem to even notice that they were both beating him mercilessly. His eyes focused on Leo, and he shouted out, 'Hey bitch. You like to fuck? Come and get some here.' They came closer and he tried to grab Leo, licking his tongue around his lips. The guards smashed their clubs into him and yanked him away, almost tearing the skin off his hands with the manacles.

'I'm busy right now with these fucking Arabs. See ya' tomorrow, bitch. Don't fuck around with nobody else. Just you save ya' ass fa' Razza.'

The guards pulled him past them along the corridor, and Hatim said, 'That's the kind of fight you don't want to get into. Stay away from crazy prisoners like that, they really do rape people, anyone they can.'

'I'll be fine.' Leo tried to sound relaxed, but he was counting the number of bad options that surrounded him. He knew he'd be lucky to get out without having to protect himself from someone like that guy, and that might cause more harm than good.

Dubai, United Arab Emirates

Tom Connor ended his call with Hatim. He was relieved to hear that Leo would be held in Bur Dubai, but it wasn't going to make his call to Ms Stewart much easier. He thought back to the Fitzgeralds, Scotty's parents, who had come to collect their son's body. It seemed like it was only yesterday. He was trying to make sense of the situation, wondering why this was happening to him. From what he knew of Leo, his work ethic, his sense of respect, responsibility and dedication, he couldn't believe the man was capable of such a foul crime. *But if he wasn't, why has Angela da Sousa accused him? What motivation could she have to put a man's life in danger if it isn't true? It can only be jealousy, revenge or blackmail.*

Ed had described Leo and Angela's first meeting, and he doubted there could be any element of revenge or jealousy from a Brazilian woman he'd just met in a place he'd never been before. It didn't make any sense. *That leaves blackmail. She must know he's an important executive with XPC, she may even know the new products launch depends very much on him. Is this a stratagem to get money out of us to withdraw her accusation, just a honey-money trap?*

Clearly, nothing could be achieved via the legal process in Bur Dubai. The only possible way to a solution was through the woman.

Shen has to find out if that's what's going on and work out a financial solution with her, before it's too late.

Tom was making notes as he worked through his thought processes. He went back over them, adding further ideas and 'To Do' items. Tomorrow he was going to have to tell Shanghai that they might not meet the deadline, and he had to make an announcement to the staff. There were already rumours circulating around the building again, just as they had in Scotty's case, and he didn't know how he was going to explain another inexplicable catastrophe. *If Shen manages to sort something out with the woman, maybe I'll know more by tomorrow.*

He sat back in his chair and pushed the problem away, to think constructively about the September 1st upgrades launch. From what Sharif and Ed had told him, he wasn't sure they were out of the woods with the remote activation of the connectivity module. And Leo had asked him and Sharif about this single cell, S470C887,999, he still had the scribbled number, and he'd said it was a source of concern. At this late stage of the project, with just three weeks to deliver the final prototype so Shanghai could meet the launch date, they couldn't afford to have any concerns. Everything had to be one hundred and fifty per cent right.

Strange, Tom thought. *Both these men, Scotty and Leo, were inextricably linked to the new product's launch, and both very difficult to replace. It's a miracle I got to persuade Leo to come in at short notice and was lucky enough to pick the right guy for the job. And now I've lost him too. It's as if they were targeted, as if someone didn't want the product to be developed.* Unknowingly, the same word came into his mind as had come to Leo the day before. *Sabotage.* He could think of a dozen competitors who would probably kill to destroy or acquire the Mark VII technology with ACRE. *Is that what's happening?*

He forced himself to put aside this line of thinking, it was self-destructive and would take him nowhere. *I have to call Leo's mother. It's time to give her the dreadful news. At least I can tell her he'll be in Bur Dubai until the trial, that's some small comfort in the whole disastrous business. I just hope she can handle it, because I'm having a hell of a time myself.*

Bur Dubai Police Station

'How did it go?' Oskar Novak made space for Leo to sit on the end of his bunk.

'Pretty much what you told me to expect. Remanded here until the trial.'

'That's better than going to Port Rashid. I hear a lot of people don't come out of there vertical. Plus, you get to keep me company for a while.'

Leo couldn't tell the Pole he had a lawyer who was trying to speed up the process. It didn't fit with his story about being arrested for fighting. He said, 'I guess there are worse ways to spend a few weeks of my life. I can't think of any for the moment, but I'll work on it.'

Novak laughed. 'Not high up on your bucket list, right?'

'Wrong. It's right up there with having all my teeth pulled out.'

'What are you doing here anyway, are you working somewhere in Dubai?'

Leo hesitated, the less he said the better until he knew what would happen next. Oskar seemed like a harmless guy, but it wasn't worth taking the risk. 'I'm travelling on a student discount ticket from London to Mumbai, and I had an option to stop over here. It was free, so I took it. Seemed like a good decision at the time.'

'Student discount ticket? Hmm, bad luck.' Novak didn't sound convinced, but he said nothing further about it. Leo figured he was probably used to being discreet, it came with the territory.

TWENTY-SEVEN

Dubai, United Arab Emirates
Friday, 9 July 2017

Tom Connor's call to Emma Stewart was as bad as he expected, in fact worse. Naturally, she couldn't believe that her son had been accused of such a heinous crime, and it took him a while to convince her it was true. Then she became hysterical at the thought of him being mistreated in a prison, especially in a Middle East country. Bursting into tears, she cried, 'Oh, no. Not again. Dear God, not again.'

His natural reaction was to ask, 'Has he been in jail previously?'

'Of course not,' she replied angrily. 'Don't ask such stupid questions. He's never done anything remotely illegal in his whole life and he's certainly not guilty of attacking anyone, especially a woman. This is a pure fabrication and she should be locked up for perjury instead of him. I'm going to call him now, I have to help him to sort this out, hire a lawyer and get him out of that prison. The whole thing is a monstrous mistake and I'm his mother, I need to speak to him and tell him I'm at his side and taking action.'

'He doesn't have his phone, Ms Stewart. They took it away from him, but he was smart enough to get a message to us immediately.

Our company lawyer has been to see him and he's unhurt and in good spirits. No one believes Leo's guilty of the accusation, but that doesn't change the situation. He knows everything possible is being done to get him freed, and we will, but I'm afraid it won't be a fast process.'

At this, she started weeping again. 'Why not? How long can it take to get this woman to tell the truth? Or to prove she's lying? Leo's stuck in some filthy prison and you're telling me it won't be a fast process. You have to get him out of there, immediately.'

He explained as patiently as he could that unless Angela da Sousa withdrew her accusation, the case would go to trial, and that could take several weeks. 'Leo's immediate boss knows the woman and he's trying to get her to back off. Believe me, we need Leo here at XPC as a matter of urgency. I'm concerned that without him our new product launch could be jeopardised. That's how much it means to us to get Leo back.

'And please don't worry about publicity or damage to Leo's reputation. We're keeping this whole business very quiet, only a few key people know about it and that's the way it will stay. Our lawyer is doing everything possible and he's very optimistic. I can imagine how you must feel about this Ms Stewart, and I feel terribly responsible, but I'm just as helpless as you. As soon as there's any more news I'll call you straight away.'

Finally, Emma seemed to calm down a little, and he ended the call with the usual useless placations, 'Please try not to worry too much. I'm sure we'll get to the bottom of this and I'll keep you informed at all times.' He called Shen in, to urge him to contact Angela da Sousa as soon as possible.

Ipswich, England

It was not yet midday, but already pleasantly hot, and Jenny Bishop was watering her garden before she lost the shade from the trees. She enjoyed looking after the small square of lawn surrounded by flowers and bushes. Hosing down the paths, she almost didn't hear the house phone ring, and quickly turned off the tap to run inside before the answering machine kicked in.

She saw Emma's number come up. 'Hello, darling sister, how are you on this beautiful day?' she joked. Then she listened for a moment and sat down, her face gradually drawing into a concentrated frown.

The memory of her dream flashed through her mind. *It's happened,* she realised. *Now we have to stay calm and fix it.* 'Right, Emma. Please take a deep breath and hang on for a moment so I can get my iPad. I need to take notes, don't go away.' She fetched her tablet. 'I'll put you on speaker, so I can type.' She started noting down points from Emma's tearful and erratic explanation.

Her sister finally drew breath, and she said, 'Right, I understand. In fact, although Leo has obviously been framed in a despicable manner in a dangerous place, it's actually a very simple situation. A woman who had sex with Leo says he raped her and he's been arrested. Nobody believes he's capable of such an act, and I'm certain that's the case. That means the woman is lying for some reason we don't yet know, but the chances of him being acquitted are zero unless she recants. XPC need him back to get their new products launched. Their lawyer has managed to keep him in a jail which is better than the alternatives, but Dubai prisons are violent, and we have to get him out quickly before something happens to him. The legal process is not a viable option, so we have to find a way to make this Angela da Sousa recant quickly, and that's what we'll do.'

She paused, deciding how to tell Emma what she had in mind, what she'd decided after her dream and the reason for the phone call she'd made afterwards.

'Emma, you know how I sometimes get these premonitions, like Mum did? Well, I had one last week about Leo. Somehow, I knew something was going to happen to him, something involving a woman. I had no idea he'd be attacked in such a vile fashion, but I did take action to prepare the ground, to make sure we'd be ready. Please let me take charge of this problem and I'm sure we can get it solved very quickly.'

She heard her sister cry, 'Can you Jenny? Can you do something? I have no idea what to do. I just can't believe it's happened to him again. After his abduction in South Africa I thought nothing could be as bad as that experience, we'd all suffered enough, but I couldn't have imagined this in my wildest dreams. It's just dreadful.'

'Emma, this is nothing like South Africa, nothing at all. Leo's working for a prestigious company which has a local lawyer, we have the resources to take whatever action is necessary and I know just the person to sort this out in double-quick time. Please stop crying and don't worry, it's not going to help. We've been through worse situations than this and we're still here to tell the tale. Take a deep breath and calm down. Leave it to me, and I'll get things moving right away.'

They talked for a few minutes more, Emma thanking her repeatedly. Finally, she reluctantly put the phone down. Now Jenny could concentrate on what she had to do. She found the name in her Contact list and called immediately. When the number answered, she said, 'It's happened. We need your help.'

Dubai, United Arab Emirates

It was eight in the evening, and Tom Connor was ready to call it a day. He switched off the lights and was about to leave when his office line rang. *It might be news about Leo,* he thought, and picked up the phone. 'Tom Connor here.'

The operator said, 'There's a call for you from the US, Mr Connor,' then a man's voice, 'Please hold for General Chillicott.'

Tom had no idea who was calling, and he was exhausted and short-tempered after the day's disasters. He'd hardly had time to say good morning to his family before he'd been called out by ED and all he wanted was to get home, have a whisky and share his problems with his wife.

'Tom Connor?'

'Who is this please? It's late and I was just leaving the office.'

'My name is General William Chillicott. I'm calling from Homeland Security in Washington. I'm sorry to trouble you Tom, but I'd like your assistance.'

Tom Connor almost stood up to attention. He was a proud American and had the utmost respect for members of the armed forces, especially a senior officer. 'I'm at your service, General. What can I do for you?'

'Thanks, I appreciate it. You have a kid called Leo Stewart working for you, right?'

This was almost too much for Tom. Leo Stewart had been arrested for rape this morning and now Homeland Security were calling about him. What the hell was going on? 'That's right, sir. Is there a problem?'

'It's no big deal, Tom. I know Leo, spent an evening with him couple months ago, great kid, smart. You're lucky you talked him into joining you. Anyways, I need to speak to him and he's not answering his mobile, so I figured you'd be able to get me in touch with him.'

Now Tom's brain was spinning. Leo was a friend of this US general, was he the answer to their problem? But Leo's case was still *sub judice* until the trial, how much could he tell the officer? Then another thought occurred to him, *How do I know he's actually a US general?*

'General, the reason you couldn't get hold of Leo is very complicated, and I'm afraid I can't discuss it in a public manner. Since I don't know you, I'd be acting inappropriately to give you any details. Is there a way you could prove to me who you are, because I think you might be of great help in resolving a problem we have down here, if I can speak frankly with you?' He waited anxiously, expecting an earful from the general.

'This sounds plenty bad. You'd better tell me all about it. My PA will send you an email now with proof of what I told you, and a number you can call me back on. It's an encrypted line, so you can spill the beans on what's going on down there. I'll wait for your call. Thanks.'

* * *

Ten minutes later, Tom had related the day's events to Billy Chillicott, ending with his conviction that Leo was innocent of the accusation and that they needed him back to ensure the successful new product launch.

'That's quite a story, especially after what happened to the previous guy, right?'

'You know about that?'

'Listen, Tom. When I met Leo you'd just offered him the job, and he wasn't sure about taking it. We talked and he decided to come down to meet you. Sounds like he was the right guy for the job, but I sure didn't expect it to turn out like this. Makes me feel kinda guilty.'

'So, you think the two events are connected?'

'If they're not, it's one hell of a coincidence. Two guys are doing very confidential, high- security work developing valuable technology, and in three months they both get whacked out of their jobs. One dead, the other in prison. Go figure.'

There was silence at the other end of the line. Chillicott knew he had struck a raw nerve and his antennae were aroused. *There must be something going on at XPC.* Ilona Tymoshenko had dug up the suspicious history of Shen Fu Liáng and here he was, a senior executive at XPC where it seemed probable that two key brains had been savagely supressed. *But why, what the hell are they doing down there?*

'What exactly were they working on, Leo and the other guy?'

Tom recovered his composure. 'It has to do with our new processor model and encryption-transmission system, but I can't disclose more than that. I'm sorry, but it's proprietary development work and we have strict confidentiality rules. All I can say is that we have an upcoming launch date for new products and Leo's contribution has been vital in meeting the deadline. Without him, I'm not sure we can make it.'

Now, Chillicott was quite certain that foul play was involved, and that Shen Fu Liáng was implicated. He looked for another avenue to progress. 'You must be very tied up with handling this mess. Is there anyone else there who was working with Leo and knows about what happened here?'

Tom saw his stratagem. 'He's very friendly with one of his team, Ed Muire, another Englishman. He's one of the few people who know about this, and that's the way we want to keep it. If you can guarantee total discretion, I'll give you his mobile number.'

'Thanks, Tom. It'll go no further than me. Good luck with sorting out your deadline. I'll call back if I find anything worth reporting.'

After he put the phone down, Connor realised he'd revealed quite a lot, but the general had told him nothing. *Why was he trying to get hold of Leo?* He was starting to feel out of his depth.

TWENTY-EIGHT

Delmas, Mpumalanga, South Africa
Friday, 9 July 2017

'I'll need an address. Good, text it to me on this number. Don't worry, I'll sort something out. You're welcome, Jenny, and tell Emma not to worry.'

The man Jenny had called walked back into his office at Advanced Security Systems (Pty) Ltd, housed in a sprawling farmhouse complex about fifty kilometres north-east of central Johannesburg. There were eight people in the two rooms next door, but only one woman in his office. He sat back in his chair, a worried frown on his face.

'Bad news?'

'Certainly unexpected. Very odd business.'

His wife Karen was used to his uncommunicative ways, but she insisted on trying to change him. 'Come on, Marius, stop being mysterious. Who was it?'

'A friend from the past, Jenny Bishop.' Marius Coetzee turned to see the look of surprise on her face. They'd last heard of Jenny five years ago and had never met her face-to-face.

'Well, well,' she murmured. 'To what do we owe the pleasure?'

'Briefly, it seems Leo's in trouble again and she wants me to sort it out.'

'I don't believe it! That boy's really unlucky. What's happened to him this time?'

As Coetzee repeated what Jenny had told him, their adopted African daughter Abby came into the room. 'What's going on?'

He finished his synopsis and Abby gasped with shock. 'Oh my God! That's horrible. Poor Leo, he must be mortified, being in a prison on a disgusting charge like that.'

Her mother added, 'And Emma and Jenny must be frantic with worry.'

'So you don't think he's capable of rape?'

'Absolutely not,' they both answered in one breath.

Abby went on, 'Leo's probably the coolest and dishiest guy I've ever known. Why would he have to rape a girl? This is a stitch-up for sure.'

Coetzee and Karen exchanged glances. 'OK, Abby,' he said, 'thanks for the unbiased sexual assessment, but apparently Leo hardly knows the woman. He met her at a night club last week and now she's accusing him of rape. Why would she do that if it wasn't true? Leo could end up in prison for the rest of his life if she doesn't withdraw it.'

Unknowingly, Karen voiced the same motivations Tom Connor had considered, 'Normally, I'd say jealousy, revenge and/or just money, but here, I think it has to be money.'

Her daughter nodded her head in agreement. 'Someone has let her know his aunt Jenny is loaded and she's indirectly blackmailing her, just like the last time. We can't let this happen to him after everything he's been through. Dad, you have to help him.'

Abby was referring to Leo's abduction in 2010 when, thanks to Coetzee's change of mind and subsequent intervention, his kidnappers failed in their attempt to take him to Zimbabwe and extort a fortune from Jenny. His reward for saving Leo's life was to be shot in an assassination attempt by a Zimbabwe gunman, ordered by an anonymous Englishman known to him only as

'The Voice'. After a month in hospital, Coetzee emerged with just a slight limp to show for the attack, where one of the shots had broken his right hip bone. Of the two remaining bullets in the three-shot, left-to-right pattern, the first smashed his left shoulder and the other was found wedged in the body armour vest he was wearing under his leather jerkin. It was lodged exactly over the position of his heart. After being targeted in two previous visits by the Zimbabwean thugs, Coetzee had decided to take precautions. And he had been right.

A year after those events, Leo had come back for the best holiday of his life, three weeks filled with travel and safari visits, and since then, he and Abby had remained in regular online contact. And although they hadn't heard from Emma or Jenny for a long time, Marius still felt a debt of honour towards them; if it hadn't been for his stupidity, Leo wouldn't have needed to be rescued in the first place.

Coetzee was still in the security business, though he'd been on the verge of bankruptcy at the time of the abduction. While he was recovering from his injuries, his wife managed to sort out his non-existent accounting system and collect enough unpaid bills to keep the company from going under. Six months later, she convinced him to move out of the physical side of the industry and reinvent himself as a computer security specialist.

Karen had been an award-winning journalist before retiring to the countryside, and she was fully aware of the Internet's effect on the way people and businesses communicated and the potential for damage that could result. 'It's the fastest-growing business around today, there's more than two billion machines in the world and because of the Internet, the number's increasing exponentially,' she told him. 'An industry that's growing and changing like that needs specific security systems that keep pace with the changes, and they're in short supply.'

To prove her point, she signed them up with several UK and US companies as SA distributors for pre-packaged security systems, and she was right: it was a great business. This success encouraged them both to enrol for a two-year course at the Joburg Academy of Computer Science and Software Engineering. Six years after taking that decision, they now had a medium-sized, tightly staffed company designing custom-built computer and Internet security systems, which was easily manageable and profitable, and they loved it. Abby had followed in their footsteps, and graduated from the same college earlier in the year with a BSc Hons (IT) degree to become a partner in the flourishing business.

Now, Coetzee said, 'I'm not so sure about the blackmail angle. I know Jenny's got lots of cash, but XPC, the Chinese company he works for, has got an awful lot more. She says Leo's a key player in the launch of some new technology they've invented and XPC might be in trouble if they don't get him back. You're probably talking zillions of dollars in a case like that. If anybody's being blackmailed, it's more likely to be them.'

'So what are you going to do? We can't leave Leo in prison thousands of kilometres away from his family when we know he's innocent. Every day must be sheer hell for him.'

'You'll have to book me a flight to Dubai asap and I'll go talk to the woman, see if I can buy her off. Jenny's prepared to pay what it takes, and I might have to upset her a bit to get her to agree, but...'

'That's what you're best at, Marius. We know.'

Half an hour later, Coetzee was booked on an Emirates flight from Joburg to Dubai, leaving at eight-fifteen the next morning, arriving, with the four-hour difference, at six-twenty in the evening. He immediately texted Jenny with the flight details.

The family talked over supper about the bizarre situation Leo had got himself into, and later, Coetzee received a thank you text from Jenny with Angela da Souza's address. Now he was set to go, secretly looking forward to getting to grips with a real-life problem and not some potential scam over the Internet. Coetzee's reputation had been built on action and reaction. He'd be back where he belonged.

Dubai, United Arab Emirates

'I don't believe it! She was all over him at the club, and now she's claimed he raped her?' It was Lynne's evening off, and she'd prepared a salad for them at Ed's apartment. It had been a scorching day and they were sharing a bottle of chilled rosé on the terrace. After her agreement to tell no one about it, Ed had confided Leo's predicament to her. She remembered Leo's embarrassment at the café when she made a joke about sucking up to him. 'He's definitely not a woman-abuser, he's absolutely not the type. It can't be true, she's been put up to it by someone.'

Ed liked her shrewd Welsh approach, and it was good to know that another woman didn't subscribe to Leo's accusation. 'But why would she do it? She must know he could be locked up 'til hell freezes over on that charge. And she's probably ruined his career with XPC, in fact, his career full stop.'

'We don't know anything about her, Ed. The other night she was schmoozing with the Belgian woman, I don't trust her as far as I could throw her. And she's supposed to be going with that Chinese creep Shen, he's a bad guy if ever I've seen one.'

Ed was trying to come to terms with the situation. 'You don't suppose they could be behind this whole fiasco? But that wouldn't make any sense, it jeopardises the whole XPC launch programme.'

Lynne took a sip of wine. 'Maybe that's the point of the whole thing.'

'You mean someone's trying to sabotage the launch? That's a bit far-fetched, you've been reading too many whodunnits.'

Her remark resonated in his mind all evening, as he worried the problem to death. *There must be something I can do to help Leo, he'd do the same for me.* He decided to circumvent Shen and talk to Tom Connor the next morning.

Bur Dubai Police Station

The prison was quieter than during the day, but it still resonated frequently to screams and shouts from the cells around. A would-be rap artist was practising his vocabulary, ignoring the insults and warnings to keep quiet and let people sleep, or else.

Leo's four cellmates were snoring, and he was sitting on the floor, trying to make sense of the last couple of days. *On Wednesday, I fix the upload problem and see Sharif's test log on the sector 470 cell. Yesterday, I find the network shutdown and call him and Tom. Then, last night Angela phones me, seduces me, accuses me of rape and now I'm in prison. So basically, everything went wrong once everyone knew the system worked and we could meet the launch deadline.* He added the other components. *Angela's a friend of Shen, Daniel and Elodie, whoever she is, I don't know why Sharif was testing that cell with my remote update programme running, and we're three weeks away from the definitive firmware and design spec for Shanghai.*

His mind jumped to the same conclusion as the others had reached – *Sabotage! This has to do with XPC. Angela's just a tool, just a diversion. For some reason I've been shoved out of the way while something happens at XPC that the others won't spot. It must be something to do with that S470 cell. That means Sharif must be involved, because he designed the chip layout. He's connected to Shen and Daniel and they seem to be connected to Angela. I asked Daniel about that cell yesterday morning, and I was stitched up by Angela last night.*

Then Leo remembered that Tom intended to ask Shen about the cell when they got aboard their flight. The realisation hit him like a thunderbolt. *They're all involved; Shen, Daniel and Sharif, that's who's behind the rape charge!*

No point in trying to get Angela to change her mind, she's being bribed by, or working for them and they set up the whole sex scene. Then the next revelation hit him. *That's why Scotty died. He found out something about that cell and they got rid of him. He's dead and they're probably hoping I will be soon.* He wondered momentarily if Tom Connor might be involved, but quickly discounted the idea. *Tom's too decent a guy, an old-fashioned family man, and he's not competent enough to understand that kind of complex technology. Shen must be running the show, maybe he's smarter than I figured. It must be something to do with him and Shanghai.*

Leo folded a blanket on the cell floor and lay down. He'd been offered a share of a bunk by both Phil and Oskar, but he didn't want to start off by accepting favours. He knew he'd probably need one soon and he preferred to keep it in reserve. His mind was spinning like a dervish at the implications of the sinister plot, and he doubted he'd get any sleep. But after last night's exertions and being roused by the police at six, he could have slept on a window ledge. His last thought before unconsciousness was, *This is not about sabotaging the launch, it's about hiding something that will happen when it occurs, something to do with the cell 470 shutdown code. It has to be something big, something so big that two lives don't count in the equation. But I can't go public with it without proving it and I don't trust anyone at XPC except Ed, and if I tell him, he'll be in danger too. I might be the only person who can prevent whatever it is from happening. I have to find a way to get out of Bur Dubai, and fast.*

London, England

At six in the evening, Hugh Middleton's mobile rang. 'Good evening, Billy,' he said. 'I'm just going over your final draft of the UNSC presentation. It's rather good. "Hard-hitting stuff" is how I think you Yanks would describe it. How are things on your side of the Atlantic?'

'Don't want to be rude, Hugh, but I'll cut straight to the chase. You and Ilona were right, there's something shady going on in that Lee-Win/XPC outfit.'

Middleton's ears pricked up. 'I assume that you have managed to learn something from young Leo Stewart.'

'No, I haven't, and that's exactly what I mean by shady.' He quickly recounted his conversation with Tom Connor. 'It sounds like Leo found out something he shouldn't, and he's been framed to get him out of the way.'

The Englishman's startled reaction was, for him, extreme. 'My word! This puts a large question mark over the death of his predecessor. You know how suspicious I am of accidental death, especially by poisoning. Probably my diet of Agatha Christie novels as a boy, but I could be right on this occasion.'

'I'm pretty sure you are, but the question is, what's the motive? Connor wouldn't tell me exactly what they're working on, but

I know from what Leo told me in San Diego that it's a new, all-singing, all-dancing version of ACRE, their data encryption-transmission system. I figure it has to be worth a bundle.'

'And maybe worth killing or false imprisonment to steal, sell or prevent,' Middleton responded.

'I guess so, but I still don't buy that MicroCentral competition theory, there's way too many other flies swarming around this XPC dung heap and it's high time we got to the bottom of it. You've dug up a lot of interesting bones about that Chinese guy, Shen Fu Liáng, and now it looks like there's some fat to put on the skeleton. I want you to send me a copy of the file Ilona put together for you and I'll bring myself up to speed. It's late in Dubai now, but tomorrow I'm going to call Ed Muire, an English guy who works with Leo. He might be able to throw some light on the subject, so if I could have that file tonight, it'll help me sleep. I'll call you back when I get some answers. Thanks, Hugh.'

Middleton put down the phone, a pensive look on his face. He thought about the probability that Shen Fu Liáng had arranged the death of the parents who had rejected him as a baby. Then about Leo's mother, Emma, and the frantic worry she must be going through. *For the second time,* he reflected. *I owe it to her to do whatever I can to help Leo escape from prison and get away from Dubai.* Ilona was still in the office, and he called her in and shared the Chillicott's call with her.

'If you don't mind me saying so, Hugh, you seem very shaken by this news. Is there more about Leo Stewart than you've told me, something I should know?'

He shook his head and asked her to forward a copy of the file to the general. 'Please remove any mention of the deaths of Liáng's family, or potential wealth. I prefer to remain cautious on those fronts.'

Ilona sent Shen's file off to the US Department of Homeland Security, then she re-read her dossier on Leo Stewart, looking for anything she might have missed. She was certain Hugh was hiding something from her.

TWENTY-NINE

Bur Dubai Police Station, United Arab Emirates
Saturday, 10 July 2017

'Showers!' The guard banged his baton against the cell bars. It was six-thirty on Saturday morning, and Leo had managed to get about six hours of sleep on the floor of the cell.

He grabbed a clean T-shirt from his small pile of belongings and stood outside the cell with Oskar. The guard rousted the other three, then followed close behind them with his baton as they walked along to the shower block. Leo stopped and stared, unable to believe his eyes. About fifty men of every colour, in various stages of nudity, were jostling and fighting for a share of the tepid water squirting down from a dozen or so shower heads spotted around a large, tiled square room. Some of the prisoners were still wearing sneakers or sandals, and the water on the basin floor was ankle deep and filthy.

Oskar saw him looking at the scene in amazement. 'Welcome to the Dubai Ritz,' he laughed.

'When in Rome,' Leo replied and stripped off his shirt, keeping on his sneakers and shorts. He figured he'd get them washed at the same time, there was unlikely to be a laundry service.

Stepping into the basin, he elbowed his way to a share of a shower with three other men. He grabbed the soap that was being handed around and was soaping his body when he heard, 'Hey, bitch. I see ya' bitch. Time for my fuck, Razza's comin' over.'

The next moment, a massive arm from behind came around Leo's chest like a vice, a leg pushed forward between his buttocks and a hand grabbed him by the testicles then tried to pull down his shorts. He jabbed his head backwards and stamped down on the foot, and was rewarded by the sound of crunching cartilage. The vice-like lock around him slackened a little and he squirmed out of the man's embrace and turned to face him. Razza was naked, and his huge penis stood out like a third leg.

The crowd around them stepped back to make a circle and started chanting, 'Rape, rape, Razza's gonna rape the bitch.'

Leo measured the man's height as he came forward to grab him again. *Just over six foot, jawline at five two, coming forward slightly crouched. Hit at five exactly.* He took one step back, spun and reverse-kicked him in the jaw with his heel. Razza went down on his back like a felled tree. He sat up groggily, shaking his head from side to side, holding his jaw and looking at Leo through dazed eyes.

He spat out a broken tooth and a mouthful of blood. 'Man. That's some kinda kick ya' got there,' he managed to mumble. 'Guess we won't be fuckin' for a while.'

Leo stood under a shower head and rinsed the soap off his body, and Oskar came to stand beside him in front of the crowd. 'Anyone else want a fuck?' he shouted. They moved away and started chattering amongst themselves, looking back at Leo and the man on the floor.

One of the guards walked over. 'Back to your cells, you two,' he yelled, wielding his baton on their bare backs and shoulders.

Razza climbed slowly to his feet. 'See ya' later, bitch,' he slurred. 'Don't forget, keep that ass for Razza. He's ya' man.'

Oskar handed Leo his shirt and pulled him away 'Great show,' he said, 'but maybe a little provocative?'

'Better than getting screwed by that gorilla.'

Walking back to the cell, Leo remembered Hatim's warning: 'Assert your authority quickly, but don't get into fights.' *I'm going to have to watch my back every minute now*, he realised. *Fastest gun in the West and all that.*

Dubai, United Arab Emirates

Most of the programming staff at XPC were in on Saturday, exhorted by Shen and Tom to ensure they could meet the deadline. Ed Muire was one of them, and right now he was having a coffee alone with his CEO. He'd been pleasantly surprised when Tom had invited him in to discuss the Leo Stewart conundrum. After sleeping on the problem, he found it hard to argue with Lynne's feminine instinct, and he was even more surprised at Tom's opening remark.

'What do you think are the chances of what happened to Scotty and Leo being a coincidence? Both working on vital development work for XPC, and in three months, one's dead, the other's in prison.' Tom repeated virtually word-for-word Billy Chillicott's remark of the previous night.

'If you agree that Angela's story is bullshit, then the only logical conclusion is that they're connected. Someone wanted them out of the equation and that means they want to jeopardise our launch.'

'You think it's sabotage, don't you?'

'I don't know, but if it is, we have to make sure we screw their plan, whoever they are. Let's assume that Leo's stuck in Bur Dubai for a while, poor guy. The last thing he wants to hear is that all the work he did in sorting our problems out was wasted. And we don't want to look as if we can't finish the job without him, because we can. We've got to get the design work and final testing done by the end of the month. Then it's up to Shanghai to get the products launched in time.'

'I was going to warn them yesterday that we may not meet the deadline.' Tom grimaced, 'I can tell you they would not have been happy, not happy at all. But then Shen told me that Sharif's confident he can incorporate Leo's final requirements without any problems. So, all I've said to Shanghai and a few of the senior staff is that Leo's a bit burned out and he's taking a few days off. That's hopefully quelled any dangerous rumours, at least for the moment. I'm praying Shen's right, what do you think?'

'I think he's right, and I'm going to test the shit out of it to make sure the firmware's a thousand per cent. So I think we can do it, but speaking of Shen...' He paused, unsure how to share his concerns with the CEO.

'Go ahead, say what you want. We're in enough trouble as it is, I don't want it to get worse because you felt you couldn't tell me something.'

'Well, I don't want to tell tales or spread rumours, but I think Angela da Sousa and Elodie, Shen's girlfriend, are in a relationship.' Tom looked sceptically at him, and he went on to describe the scene on Wednesday night at Club 27.

'Ed, I've known Shen and Elodie for three years and I've never seen any sign of unusual activities, especially sexual. He seems absolutely devoted to her. But even if there was something, so what? Their private life's got nothing to do with us. I don't even understand why you've brought this up.'

'Don't you think it's a coincidence too many, that Leo got jailed by a good friend of Shen and his partner? I mean, what are the odds? First Scotty, now Leo, and Shen's partner's girlfriend is in the mix. The only common link I can see is Shen.'

'I think you're jumping to conclusions and not being fair to Shen. He doesn't have the most likeable personality, but he's been with XPC since the beginning. He's devoted to it and works a lot harder than you might imagine, looking after a lot of stuff I don't have time for. His marketing network is world-class and he protects us from any static from Shanghai. You might as well accuse Daniel, his family's company is one of our biggest competitors, but that doesn't mean he's come here to harm our business. If someone is trying to sabotage XPC, and we don't have any proof of that, you've picked the wrong guy to accuse. It's partly Shen's baby, he'd never do anything like that.'

Leo hadn't informed Ed about Sharif's testing of the S470 cell and the effect it had, or he would have made a more convincing argument. His theory was all conjecture, and he was too well aware of it. He decided to back off. 'OK, sorry, Tom, maybe I was barking up the wrong tree. I'll drop the subject and hope you're right. Let's concentrate on finishing the job and delivering it on time, then it's out of our hands.'

Connor was relieved to hear this. He couldn't afford to have another upset at this juncture. 'Great, Hatim and I'll concentrate on trying to help Leo. Now, I'm going to confide something to you, and I want you to keep it to yourself and let me know if anything transpires.'

He recounted his conversation with General Chillicott, watching Ed's reaction to see if he showed any knowledge of the relationship. 'Did Leo ever mention his meeting in San Diego, or anything else about this?'

'Nothing. He never said a word. A top brass in Homeland Security wanting to talk to him? Did he say what it was about?'

'He kept his cards close to his chest. I told him about the rape charge, and he also thought it was probably connected to Scotty's death.'

Ed digested this for a moment. *A US general wanted to talk to Leo, and he thinks the two events are connected. What the hell is going on here?* 'So why are you telling me?' he asked, puzzled at the confidential disclosure.

'He's concerned about Leo, said he feels guilty for encouraging him to take the job, so I gave him your number. I figured he might be able to help, but maybe I'm grasping at straws.'

After Ed left his office, the CEO sat for a while, staring out the window at the terrace and pool, thinking of the simple, underpaid Asian cleaner whose only job it was to look after them. Suddenly he was feeling the weight of his responsibilities like a ton on his shoulders. Like an embattled man, he was surrounded by events beyond his control. *Please God, don't let anything else go wrong. Enough is enough.* He pulled himself together and went down to the canteen for a coffee. Tom Connor was wondering if he could cope with the strain of holding things together until July 31st.

O. R. Tambo International Airport, Johannesburg, South Africa

'Listen Marius. If you're right about the reason for this accusation against Leo, it means there are some big interests involved, and that means a lot of money. We both know that lots of money equals lots of danger, right?' Coetzee nodded. 'So, could you just try not to get shot this time? Please come back in one piece, because as unlikely as it might seem, I love you very much and so does Abby.'

Coetzee kissed her fondly. 'Don't worry, I haven't forgotten how to take care of myself, despite you trying to fatten me up and swapping my knife and pistol for a wireless computer mouse.'

Karen watched him carry his overnight bag into the airport, a tear running down her cheek. She still remembered what it felt like to know he was going into a danger zone, but he was a lot older now and she was worried.

Bur Dubai Police Station

'You're not in here for fighting, are you?' Oskar was sitting on one of the bunks with Leo. The other three occupants had been taken away by the guards for some reason.

'What makes you think that?'

'You fight too good, too accurate. You hit that maniac exactly where and how you wanted, a professional job. So, I don't think you got involved in a street fight and hurt somebody by accident.'

'You're right, it wasn't that. But I don't want to talk about it, it's like, a kind of personal thing.'

'No problem, you'll tell me eventually. We all have to get it off our chest in the end.' He lapsed into silence and left Leo to his thoughts.

Hatim had been that morning for a few minutes, but he'd been unable to sneak a phone into the prison. He'd confirmed that Tom had spoken to his mother and assured her that everything possible was being done. He lied and said she'd taken it 'as well as could be expected'.

'Is she coming down? I don't want her to come down and see me here. They probably wouldn't let her in if she did come, so there's no point.' He thought for a moment. 'I want you to ask Ed Muire, he works with me, to call my aunt Jenny, and make sure my mother's OK. Jenny's her sister, so I'm sure she'll know what's happening. She's the most resourceful person I know, and she'll work out something, I'm sure she will. I don't remember her number, but her company's called Bishop Private Equity, it's in London. Will you do that for me?'

'I've met Ed. I'll find Jenny's number and call him as soon as I get my phone back.'

'Oh, and another thing. Tell him to watch out for Shen.'

The lawyer looked startled. 'What's that supposed to mean?'

'Never mind, please just tell him what I said.'

'Alright, I don't understand, but I'll pass on the messages. Meanwhile, remember to stay out of trouble. You're doing fine for the moment.'

'Thanks, Hatim. I'll try.' Leo said nothing about his new 'boyfriend', Razza. It might make the lawyer worry unnecessarily. He'd worry for both of them.

Dubai, United Arab Emirates

'Hi Angela, *chérie*. How are you?' Elodie Delacroix was calling from the apartment she and Shen shared in Jumeirah Beach. It was midday on Saturday, 10 July, two days after the evening of the 'rape'. He was eavesdropping on an extension in the bedroom.

She listened for a moment. 'I can imagine. Especially the medical examination, it must have been awful. But it's over now and everything's going fine, so don't worry. He's in prison and they've refused bail, so there's no way you can get into trouble. You should just relax and take it easy.'

Angela spoke again.

'You poor girl, I didn't know you'd done that. It was a clever idea but it must have hurt like hell. I promise to take the pain away when I see you.'

This time she listened for longer, 'I know, you're quite right. We have to arrange that straight away, so you can see we stick to our promises. Listen darling, the CEO, Tom Connor, has asked Shen to talk to you, so we should do that to keep up appearances and we can make the arrangements at the same time. Why don't you come over this evening, and I'll make us some martinis. We can have a drink, chill out and get things settled, it'll make you feel a lot better. Great, come at eight.'

Shen came back into the living room as she put down the phone. 'She sounds nervous.'

'Don't worry, she'll be fine. $20,000 cures a lot of nerves. As long as she keeps it up until you get the package to Shanghai, we're OK. Afterwards it doesn't matter what happens.' She kissed him. 'Five years' work about to pay off, we should be celebrating, not worrying.'

THIRTY

Dubai, United Arab Emirates
Saturday, 10 July 2017

'Jenny Bishop, I know, that's Leo's aunt Jenny. OK, I've got it.'
Ed Muire looked at his watch. It was four in the afternoon Dubai
time, midday in London. Hatim Ackerman had just related Leo's
request and given him Jenny's number. He listened again. 'Don't
worry, I don't need any warnings, I've been keeping my eye on Shen
for some time. I'll watch out alright, and so should he.'

He rang off then called Jenny's number, and was immediately
put through to her office. A pleasant English voice said, 'Jenny here,
how are you Ed?'

He managed to supress his astonishment that she knew his
name, and answered, 'Not too bad, Jenny, but we're all really shook
up about Leo. I'm so sorry for his mother and you, and the rest
of his family.'

'Actually, we're the only family he's got, so it's up to us to get him
out of that Dubai prison. I'm assuming that's why you're calling?'

'Absolutely. Our lawyer gave me the number with instructions
to call right away. Are you up-to-date on Leo's situation?'

'Unless something has changed since yesterday. Has it?'

Ed liked her direct style. 'I wish, but the answer's no. He's remanded in Bur Dubai awaiting trial, and we don't know when that will be.'

'Right, Ed. I was hoping you'd call me and I'm pleased you did, because I've got a job for you. Are you willing to help me?'

'Ask away. I'm itching to do something useful.'

'This evening, at twenty past six, a man called Marius Coetzee will arrive in Dubai on an Emirates flight from Johannesburg. He's a very trustworthy friend of ours and if anyone can get Leo freed, he can. Please pick him up at the airport and take him wherever he wants to go, and give him any help he needs. At the moment, that's the best possible action you can take to help Leo. Will you do it?'

Ed was noting down the details. 'What's the flight number, and how will I recognise Mr Coetzee?'

Jenny gave him the number, and added, 'Look for a man with a slight limp and built like a brick chimney. That'll be him. Thank you, Ed. It's very reassuring to know Leo has a friend like you down there. Between us and Marius, I'm sure we can get my nephew out of trouble. I'm sorry, but I have to go into a meeting now, so good luck.' She rang off.

Ed looked at his mobile in amazement. 'Bloody hell, what a breath of fresh air!' he said out loud.

London, England

'We'll get the documentation prepared on Monday and courier it over to you for signature. Thank you, Ms Bishop, it's going to be a pleasure to do business with you.' The young couple shook hands with Jenny and Bill Redman, and went to the door. 'And we really appreciate you meeting us on a Saturday, it's most unusual, but very efficient.'

Bill closed the door and turned to her. 'Well done, Jenny. Another feather in your cap. Weekend shopping, you could call it.'

She laughed. 'Any day is a good day to buy into a business like that. With some ruthless cost-cutting and our financial expertise, we should turn it around within six months.'

With Bill's help, Jenny had just agreed to acquire a thirty per cent holding in her seventh business venture, an independent book publisher, based in Cambridge, not far from where she lived. The firm had a solid list of successful authors, but too much money was being spent on promoting lost causes, authors who hadn't and most likely wouldn't make it. Although she'd never said anything to Emma, she'd always been envious of her sister's involvement in the book-writing and publishing world, and now she would have a chance to show what she could do.

Jenny should have been a happy woman, but her mood was overshadowed by worry over the plight of her nephew. 'Can I ask you something, Bill? I need your help,' she said.

'Ask away. As long as it's nothing illegal, I'll do my best.'

'Does BIP have a subsidiary in Dubai?'

'Not a direct Dubai subsidiary, but effectively the same thing, BIP Bank Middle East Ltd. It's a Jersey, Channel Islands subsidiary that was set up years ago, long before my time, and it has offices all over the Middle East. You can't actually own a bank over there, but everybody does the same thing and it works fine. Why do you need one?'

'It's just for a one-off transaction. I need to be able to give someone cash or a negotiable instrument.'

'Sounds mysterious. Do you want to tell me about it?'

'Maybe later. It's a family matter, and the fewer people who know about it the better.' She saw his slightly peeved expression, but didn't expand on her explanation. *Some secrets are better left untold,* she reminded herself, momentarily thinking about the multi-million-dollar cache of diamonds under her control in the vault at Ramseyer, Haldemann's security building in Geneva. *If he knew about that, he'd certainly question the Bishop family's honesty.*

She took his hand. 'Don't worry darling. It's nothing crooked, just a bit sensitive.'

'When do you need this to be done?'

'It came out of the blue, but it could be as early as tomorrow, that's why I'm asking you now.'

'That's a bit short notice. Sunday's a working day there, but they're four hours ahead of us, so I'd have to find a contact today to set it up. We don't need an account or anything like that, just a guarantee of some kind. I'll have to work out a way to authorise the payment from London and take it from your accounts here. Is it a large amount?'

'I doubt it would exceed 50,000. Dollars, that is.'

'I suppose you know the name of the person who'll be collecting the money. Can you tell me that at least?'

'His name is Marius Coetzee, and he's a close friend from Joburg. He'll have his ID credentials with him. He just needs to know where to go and who to ask for.'

Bill noted the details. 'Let me get on the phone and see what I can do. Am I still picking you up for dinner at eight?'

'Of course. Do you think I came to London just to invest in a business? But it'll only be dinner I'm afraid, I've got a few other things on my mind at the minute.'

'I understand. Don't worry, Jenny, I'll try to sort something out before that, and give you a call if I can fix it or if I need any more details. See you later, darling.' He kissed her and left the office.

Bankers have all kinds of uses that I hadn't appreciated, Jenny thought. *I just hope Coetzee needs that money tomorrow and that we can get it there for him.*

She called Emma at home, and gave her an update on Coetzee's trip and her plan to get Leo freed. 'I'm sure we'll have him out of there in a couple of days. You know how efficient Marius is, and how much he loves Leo. Just put your trust in him and it'll all come right.'

In Durham, Emma put the phone down. *Oh God, please let him come to no harm in the meantime.* She steeled herself and finished applying her make-up, taking extra care to try to hide the strained, worried lines that had appeared around her eyes. Waterstones customers expected a bright and witty author at book signings, and she needed to sell books.

Dubai, United Arab Emirates

'I'm seeing Angela with Elodie tonight. We'll try to get to the truth and persuade her to back off from her accusation.' Shen Fu Liáng was in Tom Connor's office, trying to show his concern for Leo's predicament.

The CEO hardly reacted. He looked tired, his face grey and worry lines creasing his forehead. 'That's good, Shen. Do your best, but I don't expect any miracles. We've taken the only decision available, and now we just have to get on with it and finish the job.'

'You look beat, Tom, you've had a lot to deal with. Why don't you take the rest of the day off and go home to your family? There's nothing more you can do today, and I can look after the shop while you have a break.'

Connor demurred for a while, then finally agreed to go home to relax and rest up until the next day. 'Call me if there's any news, or at least any that I might like to hear.'

Fifteen minutes after Tom's departure, Shen was still in his office. He had rifled through the files and papers on the desk, looking for anything of interest. The only item that caught his attention was a Post-it note with the scribbled name, *General William Chillicott*, and a US telephone number. Underneath was written, *Call Ed.*

Shen went down to his own office, unlocked his desk drawer and took out a mobile phone. He called a number and had a fifteen-minute conversation in Russian, then rang Elodie Delacroix. 'Connor's been talking to a US general called Chillicott. I just checked with our people and he's a big wheel in Homeland Security. Seems like he's connected somehow with Ed. Can you ask your contacts to find out what the connection is?'

He listened for a moment. 'I'm not being paranoid, I just want to be on top of the situation, not on the receiving end. I don't think Ed's a problem, but we can't take any chances. Just do as I ask and check him out. I'll see you at home later, before Angela gets there.'

Shen looked at the calendar on his desk. It was Saturday, July 10th, three weeks until they were safe. Twenty-two days to hold things together and get the design and firmware to Shanghai.

Zurich, Switzerland

'I hope you're not calling with more bad news?' Max Oberhart, Daniel's father, said.

He summarised the conversations he'd had over the last couple of days. 'Ed and Sharif are convinced we can make it by the end of the month.'

'That's in three weeks. What's your opinion?'

'The latest tests have been perfect. Leo's last patches fixed everything and Ed is a very competent man. All he has to do is write the the clean code and Sharif can get the design finalised. I think they'll make it.'

'Unless something else goes wrong. That place is like a hospital, casualties all over.'

'Shen's trying to get Leo out of prison, so that would definitely guarantee the job, but we'll see what happens.'

'Keep me informed, Daniel. Especially on any further bad news, we've got a lot riding on this.'

'Including over two years of my life. You don't have to remind me. Bye, Dad.'

THIRTY-ONE

**Dubai International Airport, United Arab Emirates
Saturday, 10 July 2017**

'Mr Coetzee?' Despite Jenny's description, Ed Muire had taken the precaution of scrawling the South African's name on a piece of cardboard and holding it up at the arrivals gate. He needn't have bothered, the man who came over to him fitted the bill perfectly. In Liverpool, he'd have been called a 'hard man'.

'Who organised the reception?' he asked, looking around as if expecting trouble.

'Jenny Bishop. I spoke to her a couple of hours ago. I'm Ed Muire, a friend of Leo's at XPC.'

'I'm surprised she didn't text me?'

He's a suspicious guy, thought Ed. 'She was in a meeting. Probably didn't have the chance.'

'Hmm. So what are you supposed to do?'

'Whatever you tell me to. Jenny said you'll get Leo out, and that's good enough for me.'

'You got a car?'

'A rented Beamer. It's in the parking, five minutes away.'

'OK, let's go.' He pulled the overnight bag behind him and

refused Ed's offer to carry his brown leather holdall.

Coetzee said nothing until they got into the car, then, 'Do you know where Angela lives?'

'I know the urbanisation, but not the exact address.'

'Here it is.' He showed him Jenny's text on his phone. 'How far is it?'

'About thirty minutes' drive.'

Coetzee looked at the time on the phone. 'It's just after seven. OK, we'll go there now and take a look.'

At the apartment building, Coetzee said, 'Park over at the side there, away from the entrance but where we can still see it. Stay in the car, she knows you.' He went to check the postbox names and came back. 'It's on the third floor. No problem.'

Ed was beginning to think he was in a TV cop series. The South African had obviously done this before. *Probably many times,* he thought. 'What happens now?' he asked as Coetzee got back in the car.

'We wait and we observe. Talents that are less and less common in today's fast-track world, but still essential for survival.' For the first time, he smiled, and Ed caught a glimpse of the soft side of this hard man.

They sat in the car for a while, watching the building as one or two people came and went, both observing a civilised silence, until Ed finally cracked. 'How do you know Leo and Jenny Bishop?' he asked, not expecting much of an answer.

'He was kidnapped in SA six years ago, and I was lucky enough to help him get home safe. We've kept in touch. He's a great kid, my wife and daughter know him and they swear on the Bible he would never have done this. It's some kind of blackmail or extortion, and this woman, Angela da Sousa, is probably just a cog in the mechanism. We have to find out why she did it and convince her to undo it. If we succeed, we'll right some wrongs, maybe more than we expect.'

Now, Ed was totally confused. The South African had transformed himself from a monosyllabic Schwarzenegger *Terminator* character into a Gregory Peck *Mockingbird* righter of wrongs. He was about to seek more background when his mobile rang. It was a US number he didn't recognise. He showed the caller number to Coetzee. 'Is it OK to answer?' he asked, not knowing the protocol for waiting and observing.

'Go ahead, it could be relevant.'

'Ed Muire, who's this please?' A moment later, he sat up straight, a look of respect and concentration on his face. 'Yes General, it's an honour to speak to you sir.'

'Hi Ed. I've been trying to get hold of Leo for a day or two, but I hear he's been unavoidably detained and Tom Connor suggested I call you. Is that OK with you?'

'If there's anything I can do or tell you that might help, just fire away.'

'Speaker,' whispered Coetzee. Ed hesitated, then remembering Jenny's instructions, he pressed the speaker button as Chillicott's voice rang out again.

'I'm interested in the Chinese guy, Shen Fu Liáng, who's working with you at XPC. What do you know about him?'

'Virtually nothing, I've only been here for a month. But I don't trust the guy, and I can tell you Leo feels the same.'

'In what way don't you trust him?'

'First off, I think he's a waste of space. He knows virtually nothing about what we're doing, and I don't understand why he's here at all.'

'What exactly are you doing? Can you give me an idiot's thirty-second rundown?'

'Have you heard about ACRE, our new encryption–transmission technology?'

'Leo told me something about it in California. He said it would be a once-in-a-lifetime breakthrough.'

'He wasn't exaggerating, it's incredible. We'll be uploading it with some other new software to the billions of Lee-Win processors around the world.'

Ed quickly described the software upgrade programmes. 'We've got three weeks to get it all finished, and I just hope we can do it without Leo. He's the brains behind the final version of both parts, so if we run into any last-minute problems, we'll be in deep shit, sorry sir.'

'So, Leo being in prison could jeopardise the launch?'

'Maybe not, now. He's already cracked the most difficult pieces. That's what I don't understand. If someone wanted to sabotage the launch, they should have clobbered Leo a week sooner and we'd be in trouble.'

'And you'll be using remote hubs around the world? Still sounds scary to me, but I'm no techy. Good luck with it. Anything else about Liáng?'

Ed described the coincidences surrounding Shen, Elodie and Angela, and was starting on his suspicions of his involvement in his friend's arrest when Chillicott interrupted him.

'Just wait on, Ed. This woman, Elodie, tell me about her.'

'Elodie Delacroix. She's about thirty, Belgian, a real looker. She came here with Shen as his partner when he arrived from Shanghai. But she's a bit too friendly with Angela, if you get my meaning. They act more like an item together than Shen and her. That whole relationship looks dodgy to me.'

Coetzee was listening quietly, storing up the information in his mind. He drew a question mark in the air and mouthed, 'Why Shen?'

Ed caught on. 'What's your interest in Shen, General?' he asked.

'Sorry, Ed, it's a national security issue, no comment. And I think we're through here. You've been a big help and I want to advise you strongly to keep quiet and don't let anyone, especially Liáng, know about this call.'

'Thank you sir, I'll take your advice. He's not going to learn anything from me. Goodbye, General.'

The phone went dead. 'Bloody hell,' he exclaimed. 'I suppose you're used to this kind of cloak and dagger stuff, but I'm not. This sounds like a very big deal, scary stuff.'

'Quiet, Ed. Look, is that Angela?' He indicated a woman emerging from the building.

'That's her. She's got a black eye, sure enough, but I bet it wasn't Leo who did it.' The Brazilian woman waited for a minute until a taxi drove up. She climbed in and the car drove off towards Jumeirah Beach.

'Right. See where she goes and text me.' He shoved a card into his hand. 'Send it to this phone and come back when I ask you. It could be late, but stay up until I call.'

He climbed out of the car with his holdall and walked across to the entrance, as the BMW screeched away to follow the taxi. Ed was quite enjoying this spice-up of his day, he'd have a lot to tell Lynne when he saw her later. *If I see her later*, he realised. *I may be up very late tonight.*

Bur Dubai Police Station, United Arab Emirates

Somehow, Leo had managed to get through the day with no further trouble. They had just eaten the slop that passed for supper and he was chatting with Oskar while doing some muscle stretching against the door of the cell.

'What are you doing in Dubai in the first place? I don't buy that "student travel stop off" bullshit. You must have a reason for being here,' the Pole said.

'I'm with, well, I was with, a microprocessor company.'

'You're a computer scientist?'

'You know something about computers?'

'Not a lot. I know how to fake, or let's say, improve documents. I had a bit of trouble in that department a while ago. It's too much of a temptation, all that photoshopping technology.'

'I've been hearing a lot about that lately, how dangerous our whole computer and Internet business is. I'm starting to believe it.'

'Something go wrong at work?'

'You could say that. It's complicated, but basically I think it's because I discovered something that was about to go wrong.'

'So you got bunged in here to get you out of the way?'

He's quick on the uptake. Leo nodded, 'That's about the size of it.'

'How did they do it? They set you up?'

'I'm pretty sure that's what happened, and it worked. Now I've got no access to the facility and it's only three weeks until it goes bang, whatever it is.'

'You don't actually know what's going to happen?'

'I was close to finding out, but not close enough.'

'Sounds like you were too close. You must have had a big job, how many people?'

'About forty, but only a couple of key guys.'

'They can't all be crooked. Must be someone you could get as your eyes in there.'

The guards called 'Lights out', and they sat on Oskar's bunk in the darkness, Leo thinking of what he'd just said. He concentrated on Sharif's log sheet, seeing it there in front of him, reading the three extra lines of code bombarding cell number S470. He remembered the sector, but he couldn't bring the remaining ID numbers up in the right sequence. And he knew that if his suspicions were right, neither Sharif's log sheets nor his own would be available to anyone now, except maybe Shen.

Wait! he remembered. *I didn't print a log after running my tests because I tried to call Sharif and then forgot to do it. And I don't need a log sheet, the cell number and codes are in my laptop. If Ed can get my computer, it can be retrieved.*

Leo slapped the Polish man on the shoulder. 'Thanks, Oskar. You might have just done something good in your life.'

He laughed. 'There's a first time for everything.'

London, England

'You suspect that Tsunami is this woman in Dubai, Elodie Delacroix?' Hugh Middleton was mildly astonished. He and Ilona Tymoshenko were listening to General Chillicott. It was Saturday afternoon and they had come into the office to try to catch up on outstanding matters, but the general had managed to find them and interrupt their planning session. Judging from his excited tone, it seemed he'd been converted from scepticism of their theory to total conviction after his talk with Ed Muire.

'It sounds too good to be true, but if we're right that Shen Fu Liáng and Tsunami are working together, it makes absolute sense. And it's the only reasonable explanation for what's been going on at XPC.'

'Unfortunately, even if your intuition is correct, it still doesn't help us find out who is behind all these shenanigans. We must ascertain the true ownership of Lee-Win if we're to get anywhere at all. The whole reason for Leo Stewart's imprisonment might become clear and we can take decisive action. But only when we have a clear picture to interpret.'

'I'd bet folding money this new product launch is the key to this business. Ed told me there's millions of companies around the world going to be affected by a remote Internet upgrade that Leo designed.'

Middleton snapped his fingers. 'Just a moment, Billy. Your reference to folding money has reinvigorated this failing brain of mine. We must find out which establishment Madame Lee-Win banks with in Macau or wherever. Remember the old maxim, "Follow the money"? If we discover where it went, it may reveal from whence it came.'

'More lateral thinking, Hugh? Can you get your people to do some research, General?'

'I wish. Even Homeland Security can't investigate people's bank accounts without due cause and a judge's OK. So long as I've got nothing to hang my hat on, I have to sit tight and wait for something to happen.'

'I understand. Then I'll see if I can learn something from my sources.'

'Thanks guys, I gotta go. Let me know as soon as you've got something. I have a feeling we don't have too much time to waste.'

He rang off, and Ilona said, 'You still haven't told him of our suspicions about the deaths of Shen Fu Liáng's family, and that he probably inherited two fortunes.'

'That's exactly why, my dear. For the moment, all we have are suspicions, and Chillicott can't act without definite proof. However, I have a feeling that this treasure chase may throw up more than we expect. I do hope you can find something definitive, I'm becoming quite concerned about the potential collateral damage in this affair.'

Ilona made no comment, but she knew he was talking about Leo Stewart.

THIRTY-TWO

Jumeirah Beach, Dubai
Saturday, 10 July 2017

Angela paid the taxi driver and rang the intercom button in the lobby of Shen's apartment building. A few moments later Elodie opened the door, pulled her inside and embraced her, kissing her lips and face all over. '*Chérie*, look at the state of you. *Mon Dieu*, no wonder they believed your story. I'll put some Arnica on it, come and sit on the couch. Shen, pour a martini for Angela, the poor darling looks like she needs it.'

She went to the bathroom and came back with a jar of cream, smoothed some on. 'Here, this'll clear it up. It looks like you did it with a hammer.' Angela's nose and cheek were red and inflamed and her eye had turned a violent combination of black, violet and yellow.

'I slammed the bathroom door into my face. It was agony, but like you say, it worked.' Shen poured her a martini and she took a swallow. 'Thanks, that's good.'

He said, 'A couple of these will get you back in shape.' Then, without much feeling, added, 'Well done, Angela, you did a great job. Leo's safely away for a while where he can't do any more harm.'

'I was terrified they wouldn't believe my story. You don't know what those policemen are like, they're brutes. Until the doctor confirmed what I said, they treated me like I was guilty and not Leo.' She took another sip, looking concerned. 'But he's not guilty, is he? Are you sure he's going to get out OK? I feel sorry for him, locked away like that.'

Elodie put her arm around Angela's shoulder and kissed her bruised cheek softly. 'Don't worry about him, we'll take care of everything. When Shen's sure the project's finished and ready, we'll get him freed. And by that time you'll be safely back in Sao Paolo. Just relax and everything will be fine.'

'I still don't understand what he did that was so bad, and why you couldn't just fire him or stop him coming into work. It must be awful in that horrible place, he doesn't deserve it.'

'I explained it to you when I came round on Thursday afternoon.' Elodie put on her sincerest voice. 'After Shen found out he was sabotaging the project, he tried to get rid of him, but Leo threatened to go to the press and cause XPC a huge amount of trouble with the other employees and the authorities.'

'That's right.' Shen took over the explanation. 'We're in a vital stage of production; he would have destroyed everything we've worked for and we just couldn't take the risk. This way, he can't damage the business, and when he gets released at the end of the month, it'll be too late for him to do anything.'

'Have another drink, darling.' Elodie filled her glass and clinked her own against it. 'Here's to you getting home to your father. I know it's been difficult for you, but now you can afford to do it in style.'

'Thanks to you and Shen, you've been such good friends.' She took another drink. 'Oh, I forgot to tell you, I've already found someone to take over the flat. They want it right away, so I agreed to move out by the end of this week. I just need to book my ticket and I can leave any time. So I need the money quickly, please. When can I have it?'

Shen looked at Elodie and she took the girl's hand. 'What we suggest, Angela, is that we book your ticket now, for the end of the month, and we give you the cash when you leave. That way, we'll be sure nothing goes wrong with the plan in the next few weeks.'

She put her glass down. 'What are you talking about? No, that's not what you promised. I can get rid of the flat now and leave straight away. My father needs me beside him and he needs the hospital treatment, so I'm not wasting any more time here. And my rent's only paid until the end of the month. If I don't have someone to move in, I'm still liable and I can't afford it. I need the whole 20,000 to look after my dad when I get home.'

Elodie took her hand. 'Alright, *chérie*, don't worry. We'll go to the bank and sort it out tomorrow.'

'You promise? I only agreed to do this because it's my lucky chance to get home, and I have to take it now. And Shen, why did you say Leo might be in prison for a few weeks? You told me it would just be a couple of days, otherwise I'd never have done that to him.'

'It was just a figure of speech. The project is almost completed, we need just a few days more then we can work on getting him released.'

She looked mollified, and Elodie said, 'Let's have a drink to seal the agreement.' Shen filled her glass again and all three clinked glasses. 'Now,' she said, 'just lie back and relax and I'll take away all your pain.'

Angela lay back on the couch and Elodie gently massaged her shoulders and neck, leaning down to kiss her frequently. Soft kisses that became deeper and longer until she gradually pushed her tongue between her lips. Angela responded, opening her mouth and pulling the woman's head to her. Elodie slowly unfastened the buttons on her shirt to reveal her coffee-coloured body, glistening in the lamplight. She lay alongside her, kissing and fondling her breasts.

'*Chérie*, I'll miss you when you go,' she whispered. 'I love your body so much, I wish you could stay longer.' Then feeling the girl stiffen slightly, she said, 'But I understand, you must get home as quickly as possible. So this might be our last moment together.'

When she relaxed again, Elodie took one of her nipples in her mouth, rolling her tongue around it, then the other, in turn. Her hand moved down to the zip of Angela's jeans and slid it open. She pushed her hand inside her panties and explored gently with her fingers. Angela moaned with desire and arched her back as the stroking became more insistent.

'Oh, Elodie, *querido*, I'll miss you as well.' She sat up and pushed the woman down on the soft wool rug, both removing their clothing piece by piece until they were naked.

Shen sat watching in his chair, his martini in his hand. After a while he put down his drink and unzipped his fly. He didn't go to join the two women.

London, England

'Well, that was ridiculously easy.' Ilona Tymoshenko printed off the item from her computer screen and went in to see Dr Middleton. 'The Lee-Win Tower Hotel and Casino has accounts with Macau InterTrade Bank, but the Lee-Win family has a long-standing banking relationship in Hong Kong. Even though Macau's a part of mainland China now, they're hedging their bets by keeping the money outside their main banking system, smart family.'

'Indeed, a wise option. And which establishment is custodian of their wealth?'

'BIP Hong Kong. It's a subsidiary of Banque Internationale de Paris, you must know them, they're all over the world.'

'That was rather quick research, even for you. How did you find it?'

'Actually, I asked one of my ex-boyfriends. He's a prolific gambler from Ukraine and he has accounts with several casinos around the world. It so happens he has one with Lee-Win, and that's where he pays his very substantial gambling debts. The account is in the name of Lee-Win Group Ltd, so I suppose they skim off their profit in Hong Kong before sending what's left to Macau.'

'We're obviously in the wrong business, Ilona dear. Now, how do we find out if that's where the proceeds of sale of the technology business went, and who sent it?'

'I'll get onto that on Monday, Hugh. Now can we please finish our planning discussion? You remember, that's why I sacrificed my Saturday's shopping.'

Jumeirah Beach, Dubai

'Will we see you tomorrow, *chérie*? What about going to Club 27?' It was ten-fifteen and Angela was dressed and ready to leave.

'There's an Emirates flight tomorrow night, so if I get my money early enough I might be able to get a seat.'

Elodie said, a little too quickly, 'I don't think it can be done quite so fast, darling. We'll go tomorrow, as we promised, but we have to make some arrangements to withdraw so much money. It won't be a five-minute transaction.'

A conflicting expression flickered across Angela's face. 'Maybe this whole idea was a mistake. If I go to the police and say I was wrong, it was all a misunderstanding, Leo could be out of prison tomorrow. I could explain to him and everything would be all right between us.'

Shen replied with a malign smile, 'You're right, Angela. Leo could be out of prison, and you'd take his place for making a false accusation and lying to the police doctor. It's your choice.'

Dubai, United Arab Emirates

'She's leaving now. There's a taxi pulling up.' Ed had called Coetzee just after eight, when he saw Angela going into Shen's apartment building. He'd been instructed to stay where he was until she left, then follow her again and report as soon as he knew where she was going. It was now ten-thirty, and he was beginning to understand the 'wait and observe' doctrine. He'd asked the South African where he was and received another monosyllabic answer,

'In the right place.' Since then he'd chewed a half a pack of spearmint gum and struggled to stay awake. Now he was happy to be following her again.

When he was certain of her destination, he called Coetzee. 'She's coming back to her apartment.'

'Wait in the car park for me. I won't be too long. Oh, and could you book me a room somewhere, I forgot to do anything about it.'

'It's a bit late to be looking for a room. I suppose you could sleep on the couch in my flat. Will that do?'

'Sounds perfect. See you in an hour or so.'

THIRTY-THREE

Dubai, United Arab Emirates
Saturday, 10 July 2017

Angela let herself into her apartment. It was almost eleven and she was exhausted, disappointed and frightened. Shen's last remark had stunned her. She vaguely suspected she had been simply a tool in some kind of a plot to trap Leo, but her head was hurting and she couldn't think straight. She went to switch on the table lamp.

'Hello, Angela.'

She screamed at the sound of the voice and spun around to see a man sitting on her couch. He was solid and square and had a suntanned, pockmarked, expressionless face. 'Who are you? What do you want?' She backed away from him to the other side of the room.

'I'm Marius Coetzee. I'm a good friend of Leo's, and I want to ask you a question.'

'How did you get in here? You've got no right. I'll call the police if you don't leave now.'

'It was easy, and I wouldn't if I was you.'

She took her mobile. 'I'm phoning them now unless you go.'

He stood up. 'Fine, go ahead and call. I'll leave as soon as you talk to them. But then they'll come and find all the stuff I've planted around the flat. You know what they're like about abusive substances. I think you'll end up in more trouble than you already are.'

She looked around her in confusion. 'What stuff, what did you hide? Why did you come here to threaten me?'

'OK. Let's start again. I didn't come here to threaten you or hurt you, that's not what I do. I'd like to ask you one question and if I'm wrong, I'll leave. And if I'm right, we can have a talk. Sound reasonable?'

'What do you want to know?'

'How much did they pay you?'

'*O que?* What? I don't know what you're talking about. Who do you mean, paid me? Paid me for what? Nobody paid me anything. *Nada.* That's your answer and you're wrong. Now get out of my flat and leave me alone, you've got no right to be here. I'm tired and I need to sleep, I've got a busy day tomorrow.'

'I suppose you'll be travelling, going back to Brazil, to Sao Paulo?'

At this, she broke into tears and sat on a chair by the door, her head in her hands.

'You're not leaving?'

'That's what I thought. But I can't go, not yet.'

'So they haven't paid you yet. Not even an instalment?'

She stared at him across the room and shouted, '*Nada. Aqueles porcos mentirosos.* Nothing, those lying pigs. They promised me $20,000 and they cheated me. Now I'll be in trouble with the police and with this flat and I can't get back to Brazil. And you're going to hurt me because of Leo. *Mio Dios*, why did I do it?' She burst into tears again.

'I told you, I don't hurt people. I help them, and now I'm helping Leo and it'll probably help you too. Calm down and we can have our talk. Then we'll decide what can be done. OK?'

She looked around the room again. 'Did you really plant drugs in the flat?'

'What do you think?'

'All right, what do you want to know?'

'What did they tell you about Leo?'

'You mean Shen and Elodie? He said Leo was sabotaging a big project at their company and he would cause them a lot of trouble if they tried to fire him. They had to get him out of the way for a few days until they could finish the project.'

Coetzee smiled inwardly at the girl's naivety. 'And who suggested the rape charge?'

She shifted uneasily on the chair. 'It was Elodie. She knew I was mad to sleep with Leo, but I didn't dare. I can't afford to get involved with someone here. My dad's sick in Brazil and I have to get home to look after him and I don't have the money. I've got no job and I'm completely broke.'

'How can you pay for taxi rides if you're broke?'

'Elodie likes spending time with me. At the club, or when Shen's away on business. She gives me some cash sometimes, not a lot, just enough to keep me out of trouble.'

'So, this time she offered you a chunk of money to sleep with Leo, then cry rape and get him out of the way.'

'*Sim*. It was all the money I needed. Enough to pay my ticket and for my dad's hospital treatment. I was stupid and I believed her, and now they keep delaying it and I'm sure they won't pay me and I'll be worse off than before.' She broke down again and Coetzee brought her a glass of water from the kitchen.

'*Obrigada*.' She drank a little and wiped her eyes.

He sat down again. 'They didn't just lie to you about the payment. The whole story about Leo sabotaging the project was a fabrication. I know Leo, he's clever and he's honest, a builder, not a destroyer. The truth is probably the other way round, it looks like it's Shen who's the saboteur and Leo found out too much.'

'What? I don't believe it.' Coetzee just sat looking at her, and she saw the truth in his eyes. 'And they used me to get him out of the way. *Mio Deos*, how could I be so stupid? Now Leo's in that horrible prison and it's all my fault. And there's nothing I can do.

Eu sinto muito, I'm sorry, *Senhor,* I was desperate and I just believed what they said.'

'Why did you say there's nothing you can do?'

'Tonight, they said if I tell the police what really happened I'll go to prison, and I'll never be able to get back to Brazil.'

'They lied to you again. That won't happen if you do it the right way.'

'What do you mean?'

'You do it on this.' Coetzee held up his mobile. 'I video you telling me what happened, and you sign a statement withdrawing your accusation. I show them to the police after you've left for Sao Paulo.'

'I just told you I can't leave. I'm broke.'

'How about we book a flight for you right this minute and I pay you the $20,000 in the morning, and you go home to see your dad tomorrow night?'

'You wouldn't do that after what I did to Leo.'

'If it gets him out of prison, I'll forgive you for what you did. You were stupid and naïve, but you were desperate. Desperate people can do terrible things, I know, been there, done that. So, is it a deal?'

Angela looked at him cautiously. 'I don't believe you, you're trying to trap me into something.'

'That's better, Angela, you're learning. After what happened with those other guys, you need to be sure I keep my word. Call the airline and we'll book that flight right away.'

It was eleven-thirty when Coetzee left her, video and statement accomplished and a flight booked at six-fifteen the next evening with Qatar Airways. Angela was weeping again, but this time tears of joy. She didn't have the courage to kiss him at the door, but took both his hands in hers. 'I didn't know there were people like you in the world any more. Thank you for everything, Sr Coetzee, *obrigada.*'

'I'll pick you up as soon as I know which bank we're going to. It'll probably be late morning or afternoon because of the time difference. Have your bags packed and ready, and don't go out until

I come. Don't go anywhere near those people and if they call, tell them you're sick and you'll see them tomorrow. They'll probably be happy to hear it.'

She nodded gratefully, and he carried his holdall out and went to the elevator. 'Goodnight, Angela. Sleep well.'

Ed was dozing in the car park and they drove to his apartment. He waited as long as he could before asking, 'How did it go?'

'I'll show you when we get to your place. Do you have any whisky?'

'A half bottle of Johnnie Walker.'

'That should get us through.'

Dubai, United Arab Emirates

'That stupid bitch. She's likely to screw up everything if we're not careful.' Shen Fu Liáng poured himself another whisky, his third since Angela had left.

'I think we can keep her under control for a while, but not too long. Certainly not until the end of the month.' Elodie was sipping champagne. She knew she drank too much these days, but it helped her cope with Shen's limitations.

'So what do we do now? We can't remove her, she's too visible, and the body count's getting too high for comfort. You're the brains of the outfit. What do we do?'

She took away his glass. 'That's enough drinking. You'll need your wits about you in the morning. We're going to have to change the game plan.'

'What do you mean? You can't change the plan overnight, it's taken five years to get here, we've got to be patient.'

'We don't have the time to be patient. You told me Leo's programmes are working perfectly, and Sharif is confident he can finish without his or Ed's help.'

'That's what he told me, but I still don't see—'

'Realistically, how long does he need to get the final package ready for Shanghai?'

'He said he could finish well before the deadline, so I'm guessing a week at most.'

'OK, so it's actually a simple situation, and we can manage it if you keep your head and do what I say.' He remained silent and she continued. 'Tomorrow's Sunday. I'll call Angela and arrange to take her to see Louis at the bank the following day. I'll get him to say he can get the funds ready for Wednesday and I'll buy her ticket for Friday. She'll be fine with that, it's what she wants, to get home by the weekend. We keep her busy all week and then she goes.'

'So, it means after Friday we've got a clear run until we finish.'

'No, it doesn't. Just wait. I'll help her to write a letter to the prosecutor, withdrawing her accusation against Leo. That's what she wants to do, and she'll expect it. After getting the ticket and promise of the cash she'll trust me to hold the letter until she's gone. No one will know for a few days that she's gone, let's say until Monday or Tuesday. That means we have about ten days from now to get things finished.'

'How come? Once she's in Sao Paulo she's out of our hair, and we can take all the time we need.'

'Shen, I've been with you for five years and I still fail to understand your total lack of human emotions. Angela likes Leo, a lot. Don't you get it? She wanted him before their night together, and after it she likes him even more. The first thing she's going to do when she gets home is to make sure he's OK. Is he out of prison, how is he, does he still like her? She won't stop until she knows he's out of prison and she can try to forget about what she did.'

'I see what you mean. She'll cause a stink when she finds out he's still locked away.'

'Of course she will. She'll spend the weekend with her family and take her father to the hospital, and on Monday or Tuesday she'll call Leo or me to find out where he is. If she can't speak to him, she'll phone Tom Connor or that lawyer, Ackerman, and the cat will be quickly out of the bag. That means we have ten days maximum.'

He said nothing, and she continued, 'There's another reason we have to move everything forward. This business with Chillicott, the American general, I don't like it. My contacts didn't find any connection between him and Tom Connor or Ed, but there's no smoke without fire, so keep your eye on them and make sure there's nothing there to worry about. But whatever might or might not be going on, it's perfectly clear, we have no choice. We've got to deliver the final package to Shanghai by Tuesday 19th. That's our new drop-dead date. You'll have to speak to Ed and Sharif tomorrow and get their heads straight. Convince them they're ready, and get them to persuade Tom to move the schedule up.'

'What can I tell them that won't sound suspicious?'

She sighed and looked despairingly at him. 'I'll sleep on it and tell you in the morning.'

THIRTY-FOUR

Dubai, United Arab Emirates
Sunday, 11 July 2017

BIP Bank Middle East Ltd. Ask for Manager, Indranil Kapoor. Up to 50k available. The text from Jenny was on Coetzee's phone when he awoke on Ed's couch that morning. She had received the details from Bill Redman in the train taking her home from London, and sent them on to Marius immediately. He texted back, *Only 20k needed. Everything arranged for today. Call you later.* It was still only three a.m. in the UK, but he wanted Jenny to be able to tell her sister as soon as she woke up.

Ed called Hatim Ackerman, the lawyer, to tell him he had important news about Leo. He asked him to come round to his apartment and to contact no one on the way. When Hatim arrived, he introduced him to Coetzee then went off to XPC as normal, with an admonishment from Marius to say nothing to anyone about anything at all. 'Just get on with your testing and keep your mouth shut.'

Hatim watched the video in a daze, then read Angela's letter. 'That's astonishing, Mr Coetzee. I don't know how you did it, but congratulations, this is guaranteed to get Leo released right away, probably today.'

'Thanks, Hatim. First off, call me Marius; second, we don't want Leo released today. Now, please listen carefully.'

The South African gave him detailed instructions of how he wanted events to play out. He didn't mention their suspicions about Shen and Elodie, nor the possible sabotage going on at XPC, but stressed that Hatim should do nothing to compromise Leo or Angela. The lawyer agreed not to inform anyone at the company about the new situation until they were both safely away from danger. Then Coetzee sent him off to the police station to see Leo, Hatim driving off almost in a daze, wondering how anyone could have achieved so much between arriving last night and meeting him this morning.

Bur Dubai Police Station

'I understand Marius Coetzee is a friend of yours?'

'Marius? I haven't seen him for five years or so, but he's a very good friend. How do you know him, what's he done?'

It was ten o'clock on Sunday morning, and Leo was sitting in the prison meeting room with Hatim Ackerman. He'd been brought along by the guard, who for once didn't hit him. He wondered if it might be due to his demonstration of self-defence with Razza in the shower room.

'He's here in Dubai.'

'What? He's here, how come?' Before Hatim could answer, he said, 'I know. Jenny Bishop sent him, right?'

'Your aunt, that's correct. She arranged for him to come last night and he's already performed a miracle.'

'I'm not surprised, they're both miracle-workers. What exactly is it?'

'We have a signed letter and videoed confession from Angela da Sousa that she made a false accusation and she's withdrawing it unconditionally.'

'What? That makes no sense. Why the hell would she do that and then withdraw it?'

'I don't know. She doesn't say why, just withdraws it, but that should be enough to get you released.'

'So you've come to get me out? That's fantastic news. Shit, I wasn't expecting that kind of turn around.'

'Not exactly. For the moment, only you and I and Ed Muire know about this. Angela should be leaving the country tonight and we can't go public with it until she's gone, or she'll be in serious trouble for making a false accusation. We want you to stay in here until tomorrow, then I can present the evidence to the prosecutor and you'll be out within a few hours. I know what she did was wrong and caused you a lot of trouble and pain, but Mr Coetzee said he'll explain it all to you himself tomorrow. Apparently she was desperate and naïve and now she's broken-hearted, but her father's sick and she has to get back to Brazil immediately. Will you do it?'

Leo pondered for a while. Every day he spent in prison was dangerous and reduced the time he had to find out what was going on at XPC and try to prevent it, but he knew he had no choice. *It can only have been about money*, he said to himself. Then to Hatim, 'Can I see the video?'

'Marius has it and won't let anyone have a copy for the time being. He'll give it to me on a flash drive tomorrow morning, to show to the prosecutor. But he showed it to me. It's extremely emotional, very genuine. I think she really likes you. You're lucky, she's a beautiful woman.'

Once again, Leo wondered at the lawyer's lack of understanding. *What's so lucky about this situation?* Aloud, he said, 'What about the letter?'

'I've got a photocopy here.' He took an envelope from his inside pocket. 'Don't let the guards see it.'

A copy of Angela's passport was in the envelope with a single sheet of paper dated the previous day, written in a schoolgirl scrawl with a couple of corrected errors. It was addressed to *The Public Prosecutor, Ryhad Street, Dubai*, and read:

Dear Sir,

On July 9th, I filed an official complaint accusing Leo
Stewart of raping me on the night of July 8th. After reflection, I
realise that this accusation was untrue. I was a willing participant
and the sexual relations were consensual.

I hereby unconditionally withdraw my accusation and wish the
complaint to be annulled with immediate effect. I regret any harm or
injustice that has been done to Leo Stewart as a result of my actions.

Yours faithfully,
Angela da Sousa

Angela's signature reminded him of her. It was extravagant and
feminine, the *A* and *S* in large curling loops around the name. He
thought of her flamboyant dance moves, the sheen of her lithe,
dark-skinned limbs and the feel of her firm, naked, thrusting body
beneath him. *It could have been so good, so bloody good.*

He took his decision and handed it back. 'OK, I can manage
another day of this, so long as you're sure that's all it'll be.'

'I'm positive of that. One more thing. Marius doesn't think it's a
good idea for you to stay in Dubai, and certainly not to go back to
XPC. He didn't explain why, but I assume you know what he meant.'

Leo was astonished at how much Coetzee seemed to have learned
in such a short time. 'I'm pretty sure I do. What does he suggest?'

'He'll also talk about that with you tomorrow. He and I will
come for you when the prosecutor agrees to your release.'

'Do my mother and Jenny know about this?'

'He's going to call them as soon as they're awake.'

'What about Tom Connor? Does he know what's happening?'

'Marius asked me not to disclose any of this to anyone at XPC
until you're safely out of this place. I don't want to do anything to
jeopardise the woman's liberty, nor yours, so I agreed to his conditions.'

'OK. He's usually right. In that case, Hatim, there's an urgent
problem I'm going to be faced with when I get out, and I need to
be prepared. Please tell Ed to do everything he can to delay the

launch until I can speak to him, and ask him to get hold of my laptop. It should still be in my office unless someone's taken it. Tell him to give it to Coetzee so I can get it from him, and tell no one at XPC.' He went to the door, then turned back. 'And ask Marius to tell Angela I understand, and there's no hard feelings.'

Hatim left, and Leo was hustled back to the cell. He wanted to finally confide his story to Oskar and tell him he'd be leaving the next day, but he knew it was better to wait until it was certain. So far there had been too many bad surprises.

Dubai, United Arab Emirates

Coetzee called the bank as soon as it was open and asked for Mr Kapoor, who came on the line immediately and confirmed that he could collect up to $50,000 any time after midday. The South African was impressed, Jenny Bishop obviously had a lot of pull with someone to arrange that in twenty-four hours. 'I'll be there at two-thirty sharp,' he told the banker.

He called Angela. '*Bom dia, Senhorita da Sousa.* How did you sleep?'

'*Muito bem*, Sr Coetzee. I didn't know you speak Portuguese.'

'I was with the military in Angola in 1987, trying to help UNITA, but it didn't work. The war still went on for another fifteen years. All I got out of it was a dozen words of Portuguese and some hand-to-hand fighting experience.'

'That's where my dad got sick in the beginning. He was hurt in the war and came to Brazil in 2002, after Savimbi was killed by the MPLA. You were fighting on the same side as him.'

'We still are. I've got good news. I'll pick you up at two p.m., we're going to the bank.'

'They have the money?'

'They do. Get your bags ready, and I'll take you from there straight to the airport. Once you're there nobody can touch you, you'll be safe.'

'I don't know what to say. *Muito, muito obrigada por todo.* Thank you for everything.' Then, after a moment's silence, 'Have you seen Leo?'

'I'll see him tomorrow when he's released. The lawyer's already seen him and explained everything. He said he understands and there's no hard feelings.'

He heard her take a deep breath, then in a tearful voice, 'Tell him I'll miss him a lot. He's a special guy.'

'I'll see you at two. Don't go out until I ring downstairs.'

Coetzee texted Ed's mobile. *Call me from somewhere safe.*

A few minutes later, his mobile rang. 'Hi Ed, everything under control at XPC? Good. Listen, I need you to pick me up at one-thirty to take Angela to the bank and then to the airport. Can you make it? Great, I'll see you then.'

Dubai, United Arab Emirates

'Sharif, I've been thinking about our talk the other day.' Shen had walked into the Pakistani's office with a couple of coffees, trying his utmost to be likeable.

'Thanks, what's on your mind?'

'Well, I just looked through your log sheets for last night and I see you were testing Ed's final version of Leo's upgrade connectivity solution. How did it go?'

'As perfectly as I could have hoped for. Ed needs to improve one tiny piece of code and we've got it nailed.'

'It sounds like we're about ready to roll everything out to Shanghai, no?'

'If we had to, I'm pretty sure we could, but I always like to use all the time we have available, it's safer.'

'And is the redundancy test still performing?'

'It hasn't changed. We've still got the shutdown when I trigger it and two minutes later the start-up when I stop.'

'That's great. And you've said nothing to anyone about it?'

Sharif looked a little uncomfortable. 'Nothing. But I'm not very happy testing stuff that Ed and Tom don't know about.'

'I take full responsibility for it, I already told you so. It's a really cool concept they're developing, you're all going to love it, trust me.' He finished his coffee and went to the door. 'Oh, I completely forgot. We saw Angela last night and I think we can get her to withdraw her complaint by the weekend. So Leo should be back early next week.'

'That's fantastic.' Sharif shook his hand. 'Well done, Shen, thanks for taking that on, it's great news. It'll be good to have him back for the launch.'

'That's very considerate of you. I'm impressed with your modesty.' Shen watched the Pakistani closely.

'How do you mean?'

'Just that you've worked your ass off for almost three years to bring this project through, but Leo's going to get most of the credit for it when he gets back. I think it's a nice gesture to wait for him, that's all.' He saw the expression in Sharif's eyes and turned to go. 'See you later.'

Sharif sat down at his desk again, conflicting emotions running through his mind. He looked at the calendar on his laptop, *Today's Monday. I'm sure we could get finished by Sunday. That's five full days. I'll have lunch with Ed and see what he thinks.*

Shen went down to the lab, where Ed was running tests. 'How's it going? Sharif told me we're in good shape.'

Ed overcame his surprise; he'd never seen him in the lab except for special occasions, demos, etc. 'It's looking good. I'm cleaning up a couple of things Sharif asked for, but really picky stuff, nothing major. We're basically done with the solutions, it's mostly front end, cosmetic stuff now.'

They talked for a few minutes, then Shen went upstairs to talk to Tom Connor. He was now convinced they could meet Elodie's new timeframe. *I'm sure Sharif's taken the bait. Now let's see how Connor reacts.*

Shortly after Shen left, Ed's mobile rang. It was Hatim. He listened for a moment. 'OK, I'll do what I can, but there's a lot of pressure to get everything wrapped up asap. I'll get the laptop right now.' He made sure that Shen had gone upstairs and walked swiftly across to Leo's office. The computer was still sitting on the desk, and he took it with the connector cable, shoved them into his document case and locked it. He didn't know what was going on, but he was starting to enjoy the cut and thrust of the game.

THIRTY-FIVE

Ipswich, England
Sunday, 11 July 2017

Jenny was up at seven and saw Coetzee's text. She forwarded it straight on to her sister. The house phone rang almost immediately.

'Is it really true? Is Leo being released tomorrow?'

'It looks like it. Coetzee seems to have lived up to his reputation.'

'And you've lived up to yours. Leo and I can't thank you enough, Jenny. I can't believe that's the second time you've saved my son for me. It was a brilliant idea to get Marius to go up there, and how on earth you managed to send that money and have it available for him on a Sunday I don't know. I could never have managed it in a thousand years.'

'All credit to Bill on this occasion. He called in a few favours and it was "Hey presto, money's there".'

'And I owe you another \$20,000. My God, I'm going to have to sell an awful lot more books. What happens next? Is there anything I can do?'

'Marius is calling shortly, and I'm sure he'll give us our marching orders. I'll patch you in when I get the call.'

Dubai, United Arab Emirates

Tom Connor was catching up on paperwork after his half day off when Shen came in to see him. 'Thanks for convincing me to go home yesterday. I crashed out for ten hours. Guess I didn't know how exhausted I was with all this crap happening.'

'Well, you'll feel even better when you hear my news.'

'News about Leo?'

'Yes. Angela came to our apartment last night, and I'm pretty sure we can get her to withdraw her accusation within a few days.'

'That's terrific. How did you do it? Money?'

'If you can authorise a cash payment of $20,000, she'll sign a letter of retraction.'

'I can do that today without any problems. Why wait?'

'She wants to leave on Friday, and knows she'll be in trouble with the police for making a false statement. She'll hand over the letter just before she flies out.'

Tom gave him a worried look. 'That means Leo won't be back until Sunday at the earliest. That's getting a bit too close for comfort.'

'I've talked with both Sharif and Ed about that, and I'm certain we can finish the job even sooner than planned. They've been testing Leo's programmes since yesterday morning and there isn't a problem in sight. Ed is prettying up some of the quick-fit patches that Leo wrote to prove his theories, but that's just cosmetic. Sharif is incorporating them into the final design as we speak. The expectation is we'll be finished by Friday, so my vote is we deliver the goods to Shanghai this week. After the warning you gave them yesterday about Leo being off for a while, they'll be very impressed with our performance. What do you think?'

Tom liked the sound of that. 'If we're ready, then why not deliver? I understand the psychology. Let me think it over, Shen. We'll talk with the guys tomorrow and see where we are. Thanks for the update.'

Dubai, United Arab Emirates

'Hello Angela, *chérie*. How are you feeling?' Elodie Lacroix spoke in her most solicitous tone; she couldn't afford to upset the Brazilian girl, they still needed her for a few more days. 'Oh, my dear, I'm sorry, too many martinis last night? Well, never mind, you can stay home and recuperate. I just spoke to the bank manager, and unfortunately he can't see us today, so I booked an appointment for tomorrow afternoon. Is that alright? Good. I'll call you later to see if you feel like going out this evening. Lie down and rest and you'll feel better. *Au revoir, chérie.*'

Angela put her phone down, relieved she'd got over that hurdle. Elodie hadn't sounded suspicious, but she was terrified of saying the wrong thing now she was so close to getting away. She checked her watch. It was twelve-thirty, another hour before Coetzee would arrive. She sat by the door, her packed bags beside her, nervously checking her watch every few minutes, waiting for the bell to ring. After a while, she decided to turn her phone off. It was safer that way.

Dubai, United Arab Emirates

'How about a sandwich in the canteen, Ed? It's one o'clock and I'm famished.'

The Liverpudlian looked at the time on his screen. 'Sorry, Sharif, no can do. I promised to see Lynne for a quick bite. I'd better be off right now, or I'll be in trouble. See you later.' He grabbed his document case and went out to his car, to drive home to pick up Coetzee.

A few minutes later, Shen came into Sharif's office again. 'I just talked to Tom, he's pretty excited with your progress. He agrees, if we can deliver earlier then we should. How about we go for some lunch with Ed and talk it through?'

'I just asked him, but he's gone off to see Lynne. I'll come with you and we can pin down the last details.' They went down to the canteen together. Sharif could already see his name in lights: *The man who delivered Lee-Win Mark VII and ACRE 2017.*

Ipswich, England

'Hello, Marius. I see you've been busy, well done. Hang on and I'll patch Emma into the call.' It was nine a.m. UK time, and Coetzee had rung to give a progress report.

Emma came on the line. 'Mr Coetzee, I'm overwhelmed. You're another Julius Caesar, "*Veni, vidi, vice*", you certainly came, saw and conquered, in one night no less. You have our heartfelt thanks.'

Knowing that Coetzee didn't like praise, Jenny asked, 'What's the situation now?'

'I'm picking Angela up in a half hour to go to the bank and then straight on to the airport. She has a flight at six-fifteen. I've already got a video confession and a signed withdrawal letter. The lawyer says that'll get Leo out tomorrow morning.' He explained the background to the accusation and the reason for the delay. 'She's a decent girl, just in a desperate situation and she made a bad judgement. I don't recommend putting her in a Dubai prison for making a mistake that she's now remedying. Those XPC people are cunning and vicious, and everything tells me there's something going on there.' He made no mention of the unusual interest shown by the US Homeland Security Department.

'Are you talking about the previous man, Scotty?'

'I think there could be a connection. In my view, Leo shouldn't show his face there again. When he leaves that prison, he should get out of Dubai and find a safe place with people he trusts, on the double.'

Emma said, 'It sounds like you have something in mind, Marius.'

'From what I can work out, Leo was framed because he found something out that he shouldn't. That's his problem, sometimes he's too smart for his own good. Anyway, he'll be bearing a big grudge and try to find out what's really going on. If it's bad, he'll want to prevent it, so he'll need a technical environment to do that.'

'And you just happen to have such an environment?'

'We've got a lot of brainpower and technical gizmos that I don't really understand, but if this turns out to be a serious matter, he'd be safe down there and well-placed to give it his best.'

'What do you think, Emma?'

'Well, as far as Angela goes, I suppose Marius is correct, two wrongs don't make a right. If Leo's prepared to stay there one more day, he should be the judge of that.'

'He already confirmed that, Emma. He forgives her.'

'Of course he does. And as far as taking him down to Delmas, I think once again it's up to him. He'll know what he has to do and where he can best do it. So, as long as you can swear he'll be safe with you, I think we have to agree with his decision. Jenny?'

'He's no longer a boy, and you've always encouraged him to follow his own path. This may turn out to be more difficult than Marius imagines, but I'm sure he'll want to do it.'

'OK, ladies, sounds like we have a decision. I'll collect Leo in the morning and see what he wants to do, no pressure. But just in case, I'll have two tickets to Joburg ready in my pocket.'

Dubai, United Arab Emirates

Shen used his time in the canteen to stoke Sharif's now burning desire to claim the credit for the launch. He left him at one-thirty and went down to see Daniel Oberhart in the network centre. He was in an irritable mood.

'I don't have time to chat, Shen, I'm too busy keeping the network clear for all the continual testing and preparing the customer support team for when we launch the new products. Even if everything goes perfectly, it's going to be hell for a while.'

'Well, I've got great news for you. Sharif and Ed are convinced we'll have a finished package in a couple of days. Tom wants to send it off early, to show Shanghai what we can do, so by the end of the week you should have plenty of time on your hands to worry about customer service.'

Oberhart gave a rare smile. 'I heard you'd been pressing to get it out, prove that Leo wasn't irreplaceable.'

Shen was immune to subtlety. 'Whatever. The main thing is, we've got the job finished ahead of schedule. Get ready for the customer reaction when Shanghai sends it out, it'll be terrific.'

Daniel made a call as soon as he left the room. 'Hi Dad, I finally got some good news. We're back on track.'

Shen went back to Ed's office. It was empty. He couldn't remember the Liverpudlian ever going out for lunch, he usually missed it or grabbed something from the canteen. On a whim, he called the Corner House café and asked for Lynne. After a moment, he heard, 'This is Lynne, who's calling?' He quickly said, 'Sorry, my mistake,' and cut the line.

He called Elodie, 'Have you spoken to Angela?'

'I called her a little while ago, she's not feeling great. Everything's set for tomorrow.'

'So she didn't insist on going to the bank today? Isn't that a little strange?'

'She said tomorrow would be fine. Why the interrogation?'

'It's Ed. He said he was lunching with that waitress, Lynne, but he's not, she's working.'

'Maybe he's sitting with her in the café?'

'OK. I'm a little nervous, I've had a very stressful morning. But I managed to get everyone to agree to send the package to Shanghai this weekend.' He paused, waiting to hear some praise.

Elodie knew him well. 'That's fabulous, darling, well done. So why are you nervous?'

'I don't know. Just a feeling something's wrong. Can you check on Angela again?'

'I'll give her a quick call.' She rang Angela's mobile again. It switched to the message service immediately.

'Merde.' Elodie ran out to the car park and drove to Dubai Marina in record time, vainly calling Angela's number twice more. There was no answer from Angela's intercom, and she had to wait impatiently for ten minutes for someone to exit through the door of the building before she could get inside and go up to the third floor. She rang the doorbell and knocked for a full minutes, but no one answered.

Elodie rang Shen back. 'She's not here. The scheming bitch must be with Ed. But where are they?'

Washington DC, USA

For the sixth week in a row, General William 'Billy' Chillicott was working on a Sunday. He'd woken up to a flurry of FYEO messages from Homeland Security, the US NATO Mission office in Brussels and one of his close friends at the Defence Department. They all said the same thing: satellite surveillance showed massive movements of Russian troops and naval vessels that had started three days ago and were continuing apace. His day off would be consumed by examining and analysing satellite images and related reports from various intelligence services, and participating in the several conference calls he had already been invited to attend.

Since he'd lost his beloved Madelene after a three-year fight against cancer, working weekends was sometimes a welcome option to fill in the time and keep his mind occupied. Teenage sweethearts from high school days, in 2015 they'd just celebrated forty happy and fulfilling years when she finally lost her last battle.

Billy's father had been a military 'lifer' and he had followed in his footsteps, going to the Air Academy High School El Paso, Colorado, where he first met Maddie. He spent four years at the Air Force Academy, the last two involved as a research scholar at the Institute for National Security Studies, his chosen major. They were married shortly after he emerged from the academy as a second lieutenant with a Bachelor of Science degree, and moved immediately to San Antonio, Texas, where he started his career with the 25th Air Force, part of the US Intelligence Community, USIC.

For the next twenty years, as he progressed to ever more senior roles with various parts of the huge USIC machine, eventually becoming one of their key senior representatives at NATO, Maddie was always at his side. They moved all over the US and then around the world, bringing up two sons and a daughter on the journey. Raising small children on the move wasn't easy, but it never fazed Maddie, she loved the life and she loved Billy and she just adapted. He missed her more than he could bear.

General Chillicott's present official title was Special Projects Director for the National Protection and Programs Directorate of the Department of Homeland Security. This custom-made role meant he could do pretty much what he wanted, so long as he was always available to bring his enviable knowledge and experience to bear on whatever new threat presented itself, both inside and outside the borders of the North American continent. What he wanted to do today was watch his grandson's Sunday softball game, but it wasn't going to be possible. When Mother Russia made a move, the world took notice, and usually experts like Billy Chillicott were asked to find out why.

He called his eldest son and made his excuses, then prepared a large pot of coffee. It looked like being a long day.

THIRTY-SIX

Dubai, United Arab Emirates
Sunday, 11 July 2017

Mr Kapoor was a tall, slim, dapper Indian gentleman with a gleaming smile and a firm handshake. He invited Coetzee and Angela into his office, where he had several documents already prepared. His solicitous manner confirmed Jenny Bishop's standing in the bank's clientele and he quickly went through the identity checks, ticking numerous boxes as Marius answered his questions and showed his passport.

'And how much cash do you require, Mr Coetzee? My instructions were to have available up to $50,000.'

'Actually, Angela will be travelling, and cash is too cumbersome and too risky. What we would prefer is a transfer to Banco Santander Brasil. She has the details for her account at the branch in Sao Paulo. Will that be acceptable?'

'Perfectly. It will take a few minutes more, but I agree it is much safer. I'll arrange it right away. For what amount?'

He seemed disappointed when the South African replied, 'Twenty thousand is the agreed amount. Is that right, Angela?'

'*Sim*, Marius. That's exactly the right amount. Please say thank you so much to Mrs Bishop, I will never forget the two of you. And Leo, of course,' she added.

Ed drove around the terminal while Coetzee walked Angela through to the check-in desk. She was crying again. 'I can't believe these last few days. First I do a terrible thing to Leo to get some money, then I find out I've been lied to and I'll be in trouble, and now all my problems are solved. It's like a dream come true.'

'Just make sure it stays that way. I'd be surprised if Shen and his girlfriend don't try to contact you again today. You're still a hot property as far as they're concerned, and they'll want to protect their investment.' He checked his watch. 'It's three-thirty, so you should be through security by four. Your flight's at six-fifteen, so you have about an hour and a half to wait. Have you got any money?'

She nodded, 'A little. Enough for the trip expenses.'

He gave her a fifty-dollar bill. 'I'm taking no chances. When you get through security, go and sit in a busy café near your departure gate and have a coffee or something to eat, and read a book or a magazine. Switch off your mobile. Don't look at anyone, don't talk to anyone, just sit quietly and wait until your flight's called, then go straight to the gate and get on your plane. Understood?'

'*Sim*, I understand. *Obrigada*, Marius. I promise not to get in trouble and spoil everything you've arranged.'

There was a long line at security control, and Coetzee left her there with her carry-on luggage. '*Adeus e boa sorte*, goodbye and good luck, Angela. It's been interesting.'

This time she threw her arms around his neck and kissed him on both cheeks. 'Come and see me in Sao Paulo, Marius.' As he walked away he heard, 'And bring Leo.'

Dubai, United Arab Emirates

It was after four when Ed got back to the office, after dropping Coetzee off at his flat with Leo's laptop. The South African's words were ringing in his ears, 'I don't know what these people are doing, but they're not playing tennis. Watch what you do and say, and stay out of trouble. If there's any sign of problems, call me.'

He went down to the lab and found Sharif running tests. 'How's it going?'

'Same old, same old. Everything seems to be perfect. I like the clean-up you did on Leo's patches, it's made my final design really easy. To tell you the truth, I'm like, just spinning my wheels now, it's as good as it's ever going to be.'

'Cool. We've got plenty of time to spare now.'

'Too much. I was talking to Shen about moving the deadline up. If we don't need the time, let's sign off asap.'

Ed's antennae were alerted. Leo was right. Shen was pushing to release the package early for some reason. 'What did you have in mind?'

'Why not Wednesday? We can run everything by Tom and Shen tomorrow and get their buy-in, then sign off the package.'

'I was thinking of looking for ways to improve efficiency, it's a bloody big bundle. I'm sure we can tighten it and slim it down a little, if we use a week or so of our extra time.'

Sharif looked disappointed. 'I think you should talk to Shen about that, he's pretty keen to wrap it up. Oh, I forgot, he was looking for you at lunchtime.'

'I'll go up and see him now.' Ed went back upstairs, preparing himself for a difficult discussion. Shen's office door was closed, and he knocked and went in. 'Sorry, Sharif said you wanted to see me?'

'Hi, Ed. That's OK. He told me you went to see Lynne, no hassle.'

Ed was immediately suspicious. Shen was never this friendly. 'I forgot she was working today, so I waited around and we had a drink and a chat. I guess I missed the time, sorry.'

'Not a problem, you haven't had much time off and the results are there to see.'

'Thanks. What was it you wanted?'

'Sharif says he's ready to sign off this week. What do you think?'

'He just told me, and personally, I'd like a little more time. The debugging is complete, so we know the package is stable and won't fall over, it's solid. But because we were under the cosh I cut a few corners and it's not as tight and efficient as I'd like. If I have another week or so, I think I can tighten up some areas and slim it down. Daniel says we can test all day and night if we want, so I'd like to take advantage of the time. I'm all in favour of beating the deadline, but I'd like to produce the best possible solution.'

'We seem to have a divergence of opinion. No problem. I'll speak to Tom and we'll get together tomorrow to take a final decision. OK?'

The Liverpudlian left the office, and Shen immediately made a call on his mobile. 'Ed just got back. He says he went to see his girlfriend, but I don't buy it, I'm sure he was with Angela and we don't know where. Now he says he's not keen on releasing the package this week, and that makes me suspicious. There's no reason to delay any longer, it's already wrapped up.'

'OK. Let's think here.' Elodie was tired of Shen's ability to think without any apparent result. 'Angela's not at her apartment and Ed was gone for three hours, right? And you think someone might be influencing him to hold back. There's also this US general in the picture somewhere.' She racked her brain for a moment. 'Has anyone from the office visited Leo in prison?'

'No one. Hatim told us nobody would be allowed to see him until after the trial, and that hasn't even been fixed yet.'

'When did you last hear from him, the lawyer?'

'I've seen him only once, after Leo was arrested, but he called Tom two days ago, on Friday, after the plea hearing.'

'Get him on the phone. Put him on the speaker and keep your mobile on. Ask him if there've been any developments.'

Hatim answered immediately. 'Good afternoon, Shen. What can I do for you?'

'I haven't heard from you in a couple of days, and I wondered if there were any new developments in this crappy business with poor Leo.'

'I intended to call this afternoon. I'll be coming over there tomorrow to give you an update. Could you fix an appointment for me with Tom, at two-thirty?'

'So, there are some developments?'

'Nothing I can discuss today, I'm sorry. I'll be there tomorrow and bring everyone up-to-date. I have to run now, see you then.' Hatim put away his mobile and walked to his car in the prison car park. He had just left a note for Leo, confirming Angela's departure and the appointment he'd made with the prosecutor for eight-thirty the next morning. He was confident Leo would be freed by lunchtime, but he was sticking to his word with Coetzee and saying nothing. Or so he thought.

Elodie had heard the conversation. 'Something's happened. If he's going to update you tomorrow, he knows today. Angela must have recanted and Leo's going to be freed. *Merde.* That little *putain*, she's screwing everything up.'

'But it makes no sense, she knows she'll be in deep shit with the police.'

'Not if she's leaving tonight. That's where Ed's been, he must have bought her a ticket and taken her to the airport, and she's written a retraction to give to Hatim when she's gone.'

'Now it's you who's being paranoid. I don't see how…'

'We've got to find out what's going on. I'm calling the airport, if she's there she'll speak to me. I'll call you back later.'

Ipswich, England

'How did things go with the Dubai bank?'

Jenny Bishop had prepared lunch at home for Bill Redman. He had been visiting his family in Bury St Edmonds and arrived in a taxi. It was pouring with rain, and she'd laid the table in the conservatory at the side of the house, surrounded by her immaculate little garden. They were enjoying a glass of chilled Moët & Chandon.

'Perfectly. Mr Kapoor handed the funds to Marius this morning and everything seems to be sorted out. It only cost 20,000, which is good news. Thanks, Bill, that was really important to me.'

'I'm happy to hear it. So the family problem is resolved?'

'It should be by tomorrow. I might tell you about it afterwards, it's been a bit of a worry, that's why I didn't want to discuss it much. Anyway, thanks again, you really helped me out.'

He let the matter drop, and they spent a pleasant few hours together before he left to take the train to London. Jenny still wasn't ready to share her house with anyone, not yet. She wondered when that might change, if ever.

Dubai International Airport

'Airport central enquiries, this is Mahmud speaking. How can I help you?' The man had a pleasant and considerate tone.

'Good afternoon. This is Doctor Charpentier from the Deira Private Hospital in Sharjah. I'm trying to trace a patient of mine who is travelling to Sao Paulo this afternoon or this evening. It's very urgent.'

'What's the passenger's name and flight number, please?'

Elodie gave Angela's name and said, 'I'm not sure which flight she's on, only that she's travelling today. Can you please look it up?'

'I'm sorry, doctor, I'm not allowed to give any information about a passenger's flight arrangements. You'll understand it's for security reasons.'

'I need to speak to the patient urgently. She needs to take some medicinal treatment before she takes off, or she'll be in danger.'

He was silent for a moment, then, 'May I ask what the problem is?'

'She has a heart condition which is affected by changing air pressure. I just found out she's flying today, and she must take a specific combination of medications I prescribed for her. I'm worried she won't remember to do so and it could be fatal.'

Mahmud's sympathy was immediately aroused, he was on medication himself. 'The problem is, terminals one and three both have flights to Brazil and we don't know which airline she's with.' He decided to bend the rules a little. 'What I can do is make a general public announcement to all terminals that she's wanted on the phone. She may not hear it, but that's all I can suggest. Please hold for a moment.'

*   *   *

Angela was reading a magazine and nursing a second latté in the coffee bar nearest her departure gate in terminal one. It was almost five o'clock, just another half hour before her flight was due to be called. She was shocked when she heard her name called on the public address system, looking around her in the café like a fugitive. The man didn't say who was calling, but she guessed it could only be Coetzee. Apart from Ed, he was the only person who knew where she was, and she didn't think Ed would call. She gathered her hand luggage and walked over to the information desk on the other side of the hall. Both assistants were occupied and she waited at the side, wondering why Coetzee would be calling.

She remembered his last instructions to her. *He said I should sit and wait and do nothing. 'Don't look at anyone, don't talk to anyone,' he told me. Why would he call? He knows my mobile number, he could have texted.* She switched on her mobile and suddenly felt afraid. There were three missed calls from Elodie at around one-forty.

The woman at the desk said, 'Can I help you?'

'No thanks,' she replied. 'I just found what I was looking for.' Angela switched her phone off again and went back to the coffee bar.

Elodie heard Mahmud say, 'I'm sorry, doctor. There's been no response to my announcement. Is there anything else I can do for you?'

'Unfortunately not. Thanks for your assistance.' Elodie closed the call and pressed Shen's number. 'We have to move quickly, the cat's going to be out of the bag very soon.'

THIRTY-SEVEN

Washington DC, USA
Sunday, 11 July 2017

'Can you connect me with General Chillicott? My name is Marius Coetzee.' The South African had obtained Billy's number from Ed. He was hoping to find out more about what was going on at XPC.

'What's your clearance code, please?' The man's voice was polite but brisk.

'I don't have one, but you can tell him it's to do with Leo Stewart and XPC.'

'Sorry, Mr Coetzee, the general isn't here, it's Sunday and I can't call his mobile number unless you have a clearance code.'

'Please tell him I have news about Leo Stewart's release from prison. That's sure to get his attention.'

'OK, I'll try but I don't promise.'

A moment later he heard an irritable voice, obviously used to giving orders. 'General Chillicott here. Who's this? It better be important, it's a Sunday and I'm busier than I've been all week.'

Coetzee introduced himself and apologised for calling on a Sunday. He quickly updated him on what he'd arranged since he'd arrived in Dubai, adding, 'We expect Leo to be freed tomorrow.'

'That's great news, Mr Coetzee. Sounds like you haven't wasted any time since you got down there, congratulations. Sorry I was a little brusque earlier, but there's stuff happening all over right now, and we seem to be running round in circles. I'm relieved to hear Leo's out of that mess, how do you know him?'

'I've known him for seven years and he's been with us in South Africa several times. I love him like my own son, and it looks like he's mixed up in some trouble at XPC. Do you want to tell me about it?'

'It depends on what you want to know.'

'Anything you might know about Shen Fu Liáng and Elodie Delacroix?'

'I'd love to, but protocol gets in the way. All I can say is we're looking into XPC, their owners Lee-Win and some of their people as part of a national security investigation. I guess you know what that means.'

'I'd like to help, and I think I can. How can we resolve the protocol problem?'

'I see you know your way around, Mr Coetzee. OK. Call Dr Hugh Middleton on this number.' He repeated it slowly. 'He runs an Internet security business in London. He knows pretty much what I know, and he's less, let's say, restricted from talking to you.'

Coetzee wrote the number down. 'Thanks, General. I'll keep you informed if anything transpires. I'm sure we'll be speaking again. Enjoy the rest of your Sunday.'

Bur Dubai Police Station, United Arab Emirates

Leo unfolded the note he'd just been given by the guard. It was from Hatim. He'd received confirmation from Marius that Angela had the money and was at the airport.

He read the short message with conflicting emotions. He would be free tomorrow, but Angela was gone, without the chance to talk to her, to understand why she'd acted so cruelly and what she really felt about him. He folded the paper and slipped it into his pocket with a sigh.

'Bad news?' Oskar was watching him from his bunk. The two Pakistanis had shipped out, where and why they didn't know, but Phil was dozing on his upper bunk and Leo now had a bed to himself, though it seemed he'd need it for only one night if everything went according to plan.

'Mixed. Seems like you'll be losing me tomorrow, sorry about that.'

'Oh, I see. As you say, mixed. I'm happy you're getting out, but I'm gonna miss you and your kickboxing. You're entertaining company. How come they're letting you go?'

Leo gave him an expurgated version of the episode with Angela. 'She retracted the accusation today, so I should be free as a bird tomorrow.'

'Wow! Interesting story. And that explains two things. Why you've got this negative attitude to sex; and second, you're right, there's definitely something bad going on at your company.'

'Looks like it. Now all I have to do is find what it is, and work out how to prevent it.'

'Don't worry, you'll manage it fine.'

'What about you?' Leo had gotten to like Oskar, and now he'd walk free but the Pole would still be incarcerated.

'Same thing, mixed. The guy says he'll leave me alone for a grand. That's a ninety per cent discount.'

'Cool. Have you sealed the deal?'

'That's the "mixed" bit. I don't have $1,000, so I guess I'll just have to wait for a bigger discount.'

'You'll work it out.'

'You want me to break the news to Razza for you?'

Leo laughed, but made a mental note to somehow get $1,000 to Oskar. If anyone deserved to get out of that hellhole, he did.

Dubai, United Arab Emirates

Shen and Elodie were at Club 27. After failing to find or speak to Angela, they were now convinced that Ed had somehow arranged for her to leave the country. That meant she had left a letter with him to absolve Leo; he wouldn't have done it otherwise. Ed had left the office at seven as usual, and they were hoping he might come into the club with Lynne to celebrate and relax, and they could find out what was going on. Shen had never contacted him at home and to call his mobile in the evening would arouse his suspicions.

He had also fixed a meeting with Tom Connor the next morning, for all of them to agree on a date to release the Shanghai package. Elodie was now adamant that it had to be delivered within two days. If Leo was free, he would most likely contact Tom Connor immediately, to try to hold things up until he could find out the purpose of cell S470C887,999. She was terrified their five years of planning, work and investment – and most of all, her reward – would be jeopardised. Shen might be able to keep Tom and Leo out of touch, or talk Tom around for a day or two, but after that it would quickly get out of hand. Their heads would be on the block and there would be no place to hide.

By eleven-thirty, Ed and Lynne hadn't showed and they drove back to the apartment. Elodie's last words to Shen that night were, 'Wednesday's the new deadline. You've got to convince them tomorrow.'

Coetzee finished off the Johnnie Walker with Ed in his apartment. He was happy with their day's work. His last words before hitting the sofa were, 'Tomorrow, you have to buy us some time.'

THIRTY-EIGHT

Public Prosecution Office, Dubai
Monday, 12 July 2017

'Where is this woman now?' The public prosecutor had just read Angela's letter and watched her video confession on Hatim's tablet.

As agreed, Hatim fielded the question. 'We understand Angela da Souza is no longer in the country. Apparently, she left for Brazil last night. The letter, passport copy and memory stick were delivered to my office this morning.'

He said to Leo, 'Do you agree with her description of what happened?'

'It's exactly what happened, sir.'

'Do you intend to take any action in respect of her untrue accusation?'

'No sir. She made a mistake and now she's rectified it, I want nothing more.'

The prosecutor called over the same official as he had previously, and they talked for a few minutes, then nodded in agreement. He turned. 'You are to be taken back to Bur Dubai to collect your belongings and sign a statement of release, and you will be freed. That's all.'

At ten a.m., Leo walked out of the police station into Coetzee's vice-like embrace. 'Hi, Leo. I thought I told you to stay out of trouble?'

'Seems like it comes looking for me. Thanks, Marius, I don't know how you did it, but thanks. I owe you. You too Hatim, thanks for everything.'

'Let's get a coffee, we need to talk. Listen, Hatim, it's best if you don't join us. The less you know, the safer you'll be.'

'I don't understand. Why should I not be safe? It's ridiculous.'

'Let's just say that there's more to Leo being stuck in prison than meets the eye. You have to report back to XPC and I want you to be able to tell them as little as possible. Angela signed a retraction and left the country, Leo's been released and he's not coming back to work, right Leo?' Leo shrugged, and he went on, 'You don't know what he's going to do or where he's going to go. You don't have to say anything about me. I'm just a family friend who gave you the letter and video. Can you do that?'

'Of course. If you tell me nothing about yourself then there's nothing I can say.'

'Right, Hatim, that's exactly right.'

'Very well, I'll get back to my office. Good luck, Leo, I hope everything works out well for you. Goodbye, Marius, it's been... educational.' He went off to find his car, and the others walked along the street to a café near the Al Jafiliya metro station.

'Lend me your phone, Marius. I have to call my mum, she'll be so relieved.'

'She knows you're getting out today, both her and Jenny. Hang on for a minute until you hear what I've got to say, OK?'

They sat outside the café and ordered coffees. Leo's first question was, 'How did you manage it?'

'I really was just the messenger. It was Jenny who figured she could be bought off, and she sent the money in twenty-four hours, $20,000.'

'She's amazing, but it seems like I'm costing her money all the time. What was it all about?'

'Angela was desperate to get to Sao Paulo, and sold her soul to two devils called Shen Fu Liáng and Elodie Delacroix.'

'So Elodie's involved in whatever's going on?'

'Dead right. Sounds to me like it was her idea. They spun Angela a yarn about you sabotaging the project, and promised her money to get you out of the way. What did you find out that scared them?'

'I don't know yet. There's some strange code linked to a cell in the processors, and I think it may be a worm they're planning to load into the Mark VII ACRE upload. I'm worried that Daniel Oberhart and Sharif could be involved.'

'When did you make the discovery?'

'Tuesday night. I tested it on Wednesday morning, but I couldn't work out what it was doing.'

'Then I doubt they're involved. Angela said Elodie came to see her on Wednesday, before she called you. Looks like the plan was made off-the-cuff, as soon as you got suspicious.'

'You're probably right. Tom must have asked Shen about that cell, and he got Elodie to talk to Angela straight away. We'd already finalised the software, so I was dispensable.'

'The other pointer is that US Homeland Security's investigating Lee-Win and everyone involved with them, especially Shen and Elodie.'

'Homeland Security? You mean, Billy Chillicott?'

Coetzee briefed him on Chillicott's call to Ed and his conversation with the general. 'There's definitely something very big going on for a senior US security officer to be looking into a Chinese processor company.'

'Shit! I had no idea it was anything like this! I wrote some software, and now it looks like they might be planning a cyber-attack.'

'Ed told me you'd cracked some problems to get it finished.'

'I wish I hadn't. There's billions of Lee-Win processors out there that will be accessed by the upload. It could cause mayhem.'

'Sounds like we've got a problem. I've got your laptop at Ed's place. Can you do anything with what you've got in there?'

'It's possible. I've got the whole package and the last test runs, and that weird code and cell number. I have to try. I mean, I helped them to get this launch airborne, I can't let it cause some kind of world crisis.'

'In that case, Leo, you need a safe place to work in, and it isn't XPC. I talked to Emma and Jenny and suggested you come down to Delmas with me for a while. We've built a pretty good set-up there since you were last down. Small lab, lots of equipment I can't operate, half a dozen clever programmers, plus my brilliant daughter. She and Karen would be delighted, of course, but that's irrelevant. What do you think?'

'What did Mum and Aunt Jenny say?'

'They said you should decide and they'd agree with your decision.'

Leo thought through the alternatives, and they weren't great. In fact, he couldn't think of any at all. 'You don't mind?'

'I've got the tickets here. We leave at six tonight via Doha, and get to Joburg at ten tomorrow morning. Business class, OK with you?'

'OK, let's do it. Thanks, Marius. I've got time to call my mum and pack a few things. And take a shower, I must stink after festering in that pigsty. I'll have to ask Ed to look after some stuff for me,' he grimaced, 'that includes my bike, I suppose.'

'Right. Let's find us a taxi to go get your things and move over to Ed's. It's safer than staying in your place. He can meet us there and take us to the airport.'

Dubai, United Arab Emirates

Sharif and Ed were with Shen and Daniel Oberhart in Tom Connor's office. The Chinaman was playing his cards cleverly. He asked for a status report, and the Pakistani was happy to toe the line. In his opinion, there was no reason for any further delay. They had a fully debugged, tested and operating package ready for delivery to Shanghai whenever it was required, tomorrow if necessary.

Shen was fulsome in his praise, emphasising that 'Leo's unfortunate absence hasn't held us back. Well done, Sharif. Ed, you seemed a little cautious yesterday.'

Daniel stayed out of the discussion, he was relieved they were back on track with the upload, though he wondered what Shen's agenda might be and whether Sharif was somehow tied up with him.

Once again, Ed was more circumspect, asking for some time to clean up his work. 'I don't want them to think we've done a shabby job, just because Leo's not here.' He made no mention of his friend's release, though he'd had a call from Marius to say they'd wait for him later at his flat. He wanted to see what Shen would say on the subject, but he said nothing.

It was Tom who announced that Hatim Ackerman was arriving later. 'He must have some news, or he wouldn't bother coming. But I doubt it's anything immediate, or he would have told Shen when he called. I think we have to assume Leo won't be back for a while and make our decision accordingly.'

Both Shen and Sharif were nodding in agreement; it was clear what the decision would be. Ed made one last attempt to stall things. 'Why don't we compromise on the end of the week? That'll give me four days to spit and polish everything to impress our Chinese masters.'

Tom Connor weighed in with authority. 'Here's what we do. Unless Hatim has some unexpected news which moves the goalposts, we deliver the package on Wednesday.'

Daniel Oberhart went to make a call to his father in Zurich. He knew he'd be very happy to get the news.

Dubai, United Arab Emirates

'Let me see the video please, Marius.' Leo had showered and shaved and was feeling almost human again.

Coetzee found it on his phone, pressed play and Angela's face appeared. It was a short clip, but Leo treasured every second of it. She didn't mention the conspiracy, only that she'd made a mistake and wanted to rectify it without any further damage to Leo or his reputation.

'She looks really awful. How did she get the black eye? I didn't do that.'

'She did it herself, to make sure the police would believe her.'

'I don't believe it! Like you say, "desperate people do desperate things". Poor kid, she must have been terrified when they took her to the prosecutor's office. But how come she doesn't talk about XPC and the frame-up?'

'She does, it's on another clip. No one else has seen it, and I want to keep it that way for the minute. I didn't want to confuse the issues, the objective was to get you released, we can go after the culprits later.'

Leo watched the extra piece, in which Angela told the truth about the reason for her accusation. Tears came to his eyes when she ended, 'Leo's a good person and I'm sorry if I've hurt him. He doesn't deserve that.'

'Send me a copy, Marius. I want to keep it, for old time's sake.'

Coetzee said, 'Seems like you keep getting hurt by people who love you. OK, time to pack your stuff and whatever you need to take to Ed's. We don't have all that long.'

'First, I have to call my mum. It's seven-thirty there now, she'll be up. Can I borrow your phone?' The chief prison guard had restored his phone to him on his release, much to his surprise, but the battery was flat and he hadn't yet charged it up.

He called Emma, trying to get a word in edgeways for a few minutes as she alternated between laughter, tears and annoyance at his stupidity in getting himself 'arrested like that'. Finally, he managed to squeeze in, 'I'm with Marius and I'm fine. We're going down to his place this evening, if that's OK with you?'

After a few more minutes, he said, 'I promise, and I'll call you again as soon as we get to Delmas. Lots of love, and please give Aunt Jenny a kiss and a big thank you for me when you get into London.' He rang off, looking sheepishly at Coetzee. 'She's a bit wound up, thinks I was fairly stupid.'

He shrugged. 'She's your mother, it's only normal. I need to make a couple calls now, so get packing.'

Leo pulled two suitcases from under his bed and started throwing things in, while Coetzee made his calls.

'Marius, where are you? How's everything going?' Karen sounded relieved. She'd received only a text from him since he left, just four words: *everything ok love you xx*.

'I'm fine, and Leo's here with me. He was released this morning. And before you ask, you and Abby were right, as usual. The rape allegation was all about money, but there's more behind it than that and we've got some work to do with him to sort it out. You'll be happy to hear we're coming back down together tonight.'

He gave his wife the flight details, then rang off and called Jenny Bishop. Her number didn't answer, and he left a message. A half hour later, Coetzee was in a cab with the luggage and Leo was enjoying his last ride to Ed's flat on the Harley. He was going to miss the bike and he was going to miss Angela.

Dubai, United Arab Emirates

'Leo was released from Bur Dubai this morning.' Hatim dropped the bombshell without any preamble, then glanced around at the group assembled in the CEO's office. Tom and Sharif looked astonished and delighted, even Daniel Oberhart switched a smile on, whilst Shen seemed to be having difficulty in maintaining his inscrutability. Ed was watching the Chinaman's expression, trying to figure out what was going on in his mind.

Tom was the first to speak. 'That's terrific news. How did you manage it?'

'I did nothing special. Yesterday morning I received a video and a letter from Angela da Sousa, retracting her accusation. This morning I presented them to the prosecutor and he released Leo. It was that simple.'

Tom said, 'Wait up a minute. Angela gave you them just like that? She didn't ask for anything?' Shen had lost his inscrutability, and was looking at Ed venomously.

'I didn't receive them from her. I haven't seen her.'

'So who gave them to you?'

'Someone I've never seen before. I know nothing about him except he's a friend of Leo's family, and he said he was merely a messenger boy.'

'This whole thing is becoming ridiculous.' Connor banged his fist on the table. 'Where's the woman now? First she files a complaint, then retracts it a few days later. She should pay for the trouble she's caused to Leo, and to us.'

'It's certainly a very complicated matter, which I'm having trouble understanding.' Hatim looked at Shen, who had now fixed his gaze on the ceiling. 'As far as the woman's concerned, I understand she left the country last night. That's why I was instructed to wait twenty-four hours before going public.'

'What? I don't believe it. And where's Leo? Why isn't he with you?'

The lawyer looked uncomfortable. 'I have to inform you he's not coming back to XPC.'

'What are you talking about, he's not coming back?' Tom was on his feet now, shaking his head in bewilderment.

'That's what he told me.'

Shen had been waiting for this, and before anyone else could respond, he said angrily, 'What? Never? What in hell is that supposed to mean? He's got a job to finish, an urgent job. He can't just walk away and leave us in the lurch.' For once, the Chinaman was thinking on his feet. He had to discredit Leo with Tom and Sharif.

The lawyer weighed his words carefully, 'I think we have to respect his decision. You didn't see how he was treated in that prison. After what happened to him, it's not surprising he wants to get away. In any event, he is definitely not coming back here.'

Daniel Oberhart was watching the Chinaman's reaction with increasing suspicion. He said calmly, 'I can understand his point of view, Shen. I'm pretty sure I'd want to get out of this country if it had happened to me. And from what I've seen and heard, he finished his job with flying colours before he was imprisoned, otherwise you wouldn't be planning to send the package to Shanghai on Wednesday. I see nothing reprehensible about him leaving.'

Ed gave him a grateful glance. 'Right on, Danny. It's not our place to question Leo's decision. He's just got out of that shithole, for Christ's sake. And he's done here. If he wants to go home, it's entirely up to him.'

Tom couldn't agree. His Senior VP had quit, and he didn't like it. 'We're not responsible for him going to prison, Ed. That had nothing to do with XPC. Shen's right, I'm disappointed with Leo's behaviour. Where is he now, Hatim?'

'I don't know. I left him outside Bur Dubai this morning and I have no idea where he was going.'

Sharif started to speak, but Tom interrupted. 'All right, I think that wraps it up. Thanks for your report. I'm not very pleased with the situation, but we'll manage without Leo Stewart. We'll manage just fine.'

'That's what I was about to say, Tom. We can manage without Leo. Wednesday's delivery day, no more discussions.' Sharif looked across at Shen. He was about to become famous, and the sooner the better as far as he was concerned.

Ed watched the lawyer leave, feeling a grudging admiration for Shen's pantomime. *It's going to be impossible to delay things now,* he realised. *I'd better let Leo know asap.*

THIRTY-NINE

Dubai, United Arab Emirates
Monday, 12 July 2017

'Leo Stewart was released this morning.'

'Really? And Angela?'

'She's gone. Left the country last night.'

Elodie gave a cynical laugh. 'I knew it. I told you so. It must have been Ed who convinced her and bought her a ticket. *Merde*, if only I'd been able to find her at the airport, I'm sure I could have changed her mind.'

'I'm not so sure. The lawyer told us he'd been given a video and letter by someone he'd never met. A stranger, friend of Leo's family.'

'Hmm. He's probably lying to protect Ed, I don't trust lawyers. Where's Leo Stewart?'

'I don't know. Ackerman said he's not coming back to XPC, but that's all. You're probably right, he's obviously been told to say nothing more.'

'You mean Leo's gone as well? Where?'

'I have no idea, but it doesn't matter any more.'

'What do you mean by that?'

'We're sending the package on Wednesday.'

'*C'est vrai*, it's true? *Chéri*, you talked them into it? Well done, darling, I knew you could do it.' She was becoming tired of feeding Shen's ego, but she didn't have much choice. 'Have you told Shanghai?'

'I called them straight away. They said they can move the schedule forward on their side, just a few days testing, that's all. They're very happy with us.'

'Did you have much of a fight?'

'That little prick Ed Muire tried to win more time. But Tom and Sharif supported me, we've got the deadline you wanted.'

'I assume he'll be staying at XPC. Can he cause us any trouble?'

'No. Leo must have told him to try to slow things down, but he's not smart enough to understand why. Even Sharif doesn't know what's going on. Anyway, it's too late for that now. Everyone's red hot to get the project finished, so he'll just have to toe the line if he wants to keep his job. He likes it here and he's got a girl, he won't make trouble.'

'And by the time Leo and Angela get to wherever they're headed, it'll be too late for them to cause us problems.' Elodie was breathing a sigh of relief. It had been a close-run thing getting Angela to take Leo Stewart out of the way. *If he'd been left to poke his nose into things for just one more day, it would have been curtains for the whole operation*, she realised. 'We know she's gone home, but where do you think he's gone?'

'He won't stay here, unless he's looking for more trouble. And I doubt he's gone with her after what she did. I expect he'll go back to the US or the UK, probably already run home to his mother, arrogant, cowardly little African shit.'

Her voice dropped to a whisper. 'Come home early tonight and we'll open a bottle of champagne. I'll have something unusual waiting for you.'

He felt a movement in his loins. 'I'll be there at seven. Put on your special outfit.'

London, England

Ilona Tymoshenko called through to Dr Middleton's office. 'There's a Mr Marius Coetzee on line one. He wants to speak to you about Leo Stewart. He got our number from General Chillicott.'

Middleton almost fainted with shock. *Marius Coetzee? He's still alive? It's not possible. How did he find me? What does he want?* He panicked, thinking, *I can't speak to him, he'll recognise my voice.* Although he had used acoustic software to disguise his speech whenever he had called the man, he knew his vocabulary would give him away, no one spoke the way he did any more. 'What name did you say?'

'Marius Coetzee, I got him to spell it out. He has a South African accent. Do you know him?'

'Not that I recollect. If it has to do with Leo and XPC, then you are equally informed on those subjects. I'm afraid I'm in the middle of researching something rather complex. Do you mind speaking to him to see if you can be of assistance? Please omit our suspicions about Tsunami and Liáng's family and fortune.'

She was immediately suspicious. *Everything to do with Leo Stewart is shrouded in mystery. What's Hugh playing at?*

'What about the possible Russian connection?' she asked.

'You could vaguely allude to it, if it crops up in the conversation.'

'Very well, I'll talk to him.' She took the line back. 'Dr Middleton's busy right now, I'm his partner, Ilona Tymoshenko. Can I assist you?'

'I hope so. I spoke to General Chillicott yesterday, and he said you'd be able to give me the heads-up on Shen Fu Liáng at XPC and his girlfriend, Elodie Delacroix.'

'Can I ask you what your interest is, Mr Coetzee?'

Coetzee explained only that he was a friend of the Stewart family, he'd been asked to come to Dubai to help, and he'd been able to arrange Leo's release from prison. 'It looks like something bad's going down at XPC, and I'd like to help to sort it out.'

'Congratulations on arranging the release, Dr Middleton will be delighted. He's very interested in Leo's well-being, although I don't know how he knows him.'

Coetzee didn't understand this remark, so he ignored it. 'I haven't discussed the XPC business with Leo yet, and I don't know the background. All I know is he was locked up to keep him out of the way for some reason, and we need to find out why. We're going down to Joburg together to try to work on some technical stuff, but I'm sure we can be more useful and effective if you can share what information you have with me. Do you want to help me, or am I wasting my time?'

Ilona hesitated. If this man had somehow managed to get Leo released in twenty-four hours, he must be a close friend, and highly efficient. And if he already knew something was happening at XPC, what was the risk of confiding in him? General Chillicott had put him in touch with them for that reason. She took her decision. 'Very well, Mr Coetzee, I can share some information with you in the strictest confidence.'

Fifteen minutes later, Coetzee knew everything she knew, except for the pieces Middleton had asked her to omit. He was used to looking for the key to a puzzle, but in this case he hadn't spotted it in her explanation.

He asked, 'What single piece of information could be most helpful to you, to find out who's behind whatever's happening?'

'Who provided the funds to buy the technology business from the Lee-Win family.'

'Wait, you said their bank is the BIP, the French bank, right?'

'Yes, we assume the funds were sent there, but we don't know from which bank and who was behind the payment.'

'I think we may be able to help with that. I'll get back to you asap. Thanks for your information and your trust.'

Ilona went into Middleton's office. He had his nose in a highly complex document on a new super-conducting material called Cronimum. Looking up, he said, 'Apologies, Ilona. This is the most fascinating of materials and I was lost in admiration at the almost infinite possibilities it presents. How was your conversation with Mr Marius Coetzee from South Africa?'

'You should have spoken to him yourself, he told me he just got Leo Stewart out of prison.' She waited to see Hugh's reaction.

A beaming smile came to his face. 'Leo Stewart has been released. My word, that is good news. Well done Mr Coetzee.' He paused, looking a little self-conscious. 'What else did you find out from him?'

'I think he's on the level, he's very concerned about helping Leo and finding out what's going on at XPC. I told him everything we know, except for Tsunami and our suspicions around Liáng's parents' deaths. He thinks he can help us track the money.'

'Splendid news. I suggest that since you have obviously developed a positive relationship with Mr Coetzee, you should continue to deal with him. Best not to confuse the issue with too many cooks in the kitchen.'

Ilona went back to her office, still wondering. *What is going on in his head? He never leaves important matters to me, he loves interfering too much. What's this unnatural interest in Leo Stewart?*

Dubai, United Arab Emirates

'I don't believe it, Chillicott and Middleton investigating Shen and Elodie, and possibly Russian connections. This thing's even bigger than I imagined. It explains what happened to me, and probably to Scotty as well.'

Leo was with Coetzee in Ed's flat, and the South African had just recounted his conversation with Ilona Tymoshenko. He had taken very few notes, like everything about him his memory was well-trained and in excellent shape. They discussed the matter for a while, and he said, 'Ilona, she's Middleton's partner in the business, said he was quite concerned about you. Do you know him well?'

'I don't know him at all, never spoken to him. He was on a video link from London at the conference in San Diego where I met General Chillicott, but that's the only time I've seen him. He's an expert on the Internet of Things, machine-to-machine communications. He's like Billy, fanatical about Internet security. They're both convinced the Internet will bring about the apocalypse.'

'If this XPC threat is as bad as you think, they could be right. A virus in the upload could cause a global catastrophe.'

'I've been thinking about that. I told Chillicott that it might take a major event to convince the world to do something about Internet security, but I didn't expect to be a part of that event.'

'If you hadn't spotted that code, we wouldn't be talking about preventing it, it would be happening as we speak.'

'Ed called me. They're delivering the package to Shanghai on Wednesday. They'll want a day or two to run tests, then, bang! What possible reason could anyone have for sabotaging millions of computers? I mean, who would benefit from such a mad global cyber-attack? It makes no sense. Only a maniac would risk the repercussions.'

'According to Ilona, if they can find out who actually owns Lee-Win Micro-Technology, that might show up the motive for what's going on.'

Coetzee's mobile rang before Leo could answer. He looked at the name on the screen. 'Hello, Jenny, how are you?'

London, England

Jenny Bishop was meeting with her sister Emma and Jo Greenwell. It was their *Thinking Woman Magazine* weekly editorial review session, and they were discussing an article on Brexit, being written by Emma for her blog in the July issue. Time was tight, it was due for submission on Monday and Emma was having difficulty getting it right. Although the piece was theoretically a neutral analysis of the current, apparently deadlocked negotiations, the state of play in the office was also stalemate. Jenny and Emma agreed with the referendum result, but for differing reasons. Emma – who, apart from her time in Rwanda, had never lived outside of the UK – was concerned about the lack of border controls and immigration, whilst Jenny was tired of dealing with EU red tape which was impacting all her businesses, slowing down growth and wasting thousands of costly man-hours. Jo, on the other hand, had never known life outside of the EU, and was devastated at the thought of the UK having to cope alone in an unfriendly outside world.

The discussion became a little heated, and Jenny thought it was time to change the subject. 'I have to return a missed call. Try not to get at each other's throats while I'm out.' She stepped into the corridor and called Coetzee back.

'I suppose Emma gave you the good news?'

'We're in London and she told me as soon as she got here. Thanks, Marius, I knew you'd sort it out in no time at all. So it was just a money-grabbing stunt?'

'Not quite, I've found out a lot more since I called. I'll put you on speaker, Leo's with me and he's just heard this latest stuff.'

Leo was suitably apologetic for having fallen prey to the honey trap scenario, and embarrassingly thankful to Jenny for saving him once again. She avoided chastising him about his penchant for getting into trouble, and after they talked for a few minutes, Coetzee said, 'OK, I'd like to give you my assessment of the situation, it's complicated and potentially dangerous.'

Jenny's dream came back to her mind. 'There was a man and another woman behind it, wasn't there? Hold on, I need to grab my notebook and find an empty office. OK, I'm ready, go ahead.'

With interruptions from Leo, Coetzee gave her a detailed account of everything that had transpired in Dubai, including his conversations with Ed, Ilona Tymoshenko and General Chillicott. Jenny finished making her notes, and said, 'So, Homeland Security believes there may be a connection with the Russian Secret Service?'

'That's what it looks like. We just found out about them investigating Shen and Elodie and the Russian angle, so I'm still trying to get my head around that. But there's definitely some kind of conspiracy at XPC. That's why they framed me and maybe got rid of Scotty.'

Jenny had another quick vision of Scotty's last moments, but she said only, 'And you're going down to Joburg to try to stop this attack. Is there any way I can help from here?'

Coetzee took over again. 'Maybe you can, Jenny. Chillicott and Tymoshenko think the key lies in the acquisition of Lee-Win Micro-Technology in 2012. They can't find out who bought the company, and that could reveal who's behind this conspiracy. It set me thinking. That bank I went to yesterday, it's related to your bank, is that right?'

'Yes. It's part of BIP, the International Bank of Paris.'

'That's who Lee-Win's widow banks with in Hong Kong.'

'I see.' Jenny immediately followed his line of thinking. 'You want me to find out who sent the money to her account in 2012.'

'Exactly. It must have been a big number, a few billion dollars at least, and you'd imagine it would show up easily if someone was able to take a look.'

'Let me think about it. I have to go back into a meeting now, but I'll follow it up this afternoon. It's a long shot, but I'll try.'

'Aunt Jenny, according to Ed the software package will be sent to Shanghai in a day or two. We don't have much time.'

'I understand. I'll move as fast as I can, if I can. Meanwhile, Leo, please take care.'

Jenny said goodbye and went back to the meeting room. Emma and Jo had moved on from the Brexit argument and were wrapping up their suggestions for the layout of the August edition of the magazine. Something was nagging at her mind, and she found it hard to concentrate on the conversation. It was something about her dream, Leo and Coetzee's story, some link that she couldn't quite grasp.

After a few more minutes of discussion, they ended the meeting and she and Emma left Jo and went out of the building together. 'Let's go for some lunch, and I'll bring you up-to-date on what's going on with Marius and Leo. There've been some developments.'

Emma grabbed her hand. 'What's wrong? Has something happened to Leo?'

'Of course not. There's nothing to worry about,' Jenny lied. 'Everything's going really well.' *I'll have to get hold of Bill right away*, she told herself. *I hope he's as helpful as the last time.*

FORTY

Dubai, United Arab Emirates
Monday, 12 July 2017

'This is for you, thanks for all your help, to me and Marius. Take care of it.' Leo handed Ed the keys to his Harley Davidson Softail Slim.

'No way. You can't give away motorbikes. I'll keep it safe 'til you come back.'

'I'm never coming back, Ed. I've had my fill of Dubai, XPC and this whole crappy business. I know the reason they got me out of the way.' He related his discovery of the shutdown code and the mysterious cell S470C887,999. 'I was arrested before I could ask Sharif about it, but I mentioned it to Tom and he must have told Shen. We know he and Elodie moved fast to get Angela to do what she did, so he's definitely the spider in the web. What we don't know is what that cell's for, and why he used her to shut me up so quickly.'

'You mean, the way Scotty was shut up?'

'Maybe. Or probably, I don't know. Anyway, if they're sending the package off on Wednesday, I don't think you risk anything. It's too late to stop it now and you should keep helping them to avoid suspicion. You did a great job for XPC and for me, and you should take some credit for it with Tom, I think he's clean. I'm just sorry I got you mixed up in this mess, it's not what you expected.'

'Don't worry, it's been cool, especially the last few days with Marius. So, you don't want me to try to delay it any more? Or maybe I could have a look at that cell?'

'It's too dangerous. From what Marius has told me, Shen and Elodie are playing for big stakes, and anything or anyone that gets in the way is just collateral damage. Let them get on with it. Once it's over, you can decide what you want to do.'

'What are you going to do? Maybe I can still help if I stay. You're not just giving up, I don't buy that.'

'I think we have to play them along until they get the job done in Dubai. Shanghai will take a month to manufacture and send out the first batch of Mark VII processors, but they can deploy the upgrades to the existing kit out there any time they like, so we may have very little time. I'll be in Joburg tomorrow and I can work with Marius's team. I've got everything in my laptop, so we can take a closer look at that cell and try to work out what it does and why. If you're still around, maybe you can help us if we discover what's going down.'

'You're thinking of carrying out a remote attack on Shanghai at the time of the launch?'

'Maybe. I don't know yet. I'll be in touch when I get down there.'

Coetzee checked his watch. 'It's time to move. You want to take us, Ed, or shall we call a cab?'

'I'll put a few more miles on the rental. Come on.'

London, England

'I hope you didn't mind me inviting myself?' Jenny Bishop had found time in her schedule to call in on Bill Redman at Fletcher, Rice.

'That doesn't warrant a response. How is everything with the family?'

'You guessed right. That's what I want to talk to you about, you deserve it after your patience and help.' She explained what had happened to Leo, and about Coetzee's intervention. 'But apparently, that's not the whole story. They called me this morning and they're convinced that behind it there's a conspiracy at XPC.'

'Hmm. How sure are you that your nephew isn't guilty? It's the kind of thing a young man might do when he's a long way from home. A few drinks too many, it happens more than you might think.'

'Of course he's not guilty of this ridiculous charge. You don't know him, or you wouldn't make such a dreadful suggestion.' She tried to supress her annoyance. 'Can I tell you about this conspiracy?'

'The whole thing sounds very unsavoury. I'm not surprised you didn't want me to know about it. But I have half an hour before my next appointment, so go ahead.'

She ignored the sceptical tone of his voice, pulled out her notebook and recounted everything Coetzee had told her. 'It seems the key to the plot is the ownership of Lee-Win Micro-Technology, it's shrouded in mystery. That's where I want to ask your advice.'

'Lee-Win owns XPC, where Leo was working?'

'That much is clear. XPC is definitely owned by Lee-Win in China, and the link man is Shen Fu Liáng, Leo's boss and the only director of the Chinese company in Dubai.'

'And your South African friend, Marius Coetzee, has discovered this conspiracy since he arrived in Dubai two days ago, while he was arranging the release of your nephew from prison for rape?'

'No! I've already told you Leo would never do anything like that. He was imprisoned falsely because he discovered the conspiracy, and now Marius is helping him to try to prevent whatever is being planned.'

'Jenny, in my job I'm used to looking at all the aspects of a problem to get to the truth of the matter. How well do you know this Marius Coetzee? I'm not a great believer in conspiracy theories and it all seems very far-fetched, if you don't mind my saying so.'

She forced herself to answer calmly. 'I can't go into details, but Marius saved Leo's life in 2010. That's how well we know him, and why we trust him absolutely. And look at all the other people investigating this affair, including the US government. It's not something Marius made up, he only became involved because my nephew was arrested and I called him for help.'

He pulled a face. 'I'm sorry, Jenny, but I'm just a boring old banker who deals in provable facts and figures, and this kind of adventure story is beyond my powers of imagination. OK, let's put aside the whole conspiracy thing, and tell me what advice you think I can give.'

Jenny took a deep breath. 'Actually, it's not so much advice, it's more in the way of information.' She explained the banking relationship between Lee-Win's widow and BIP, his parent bank. 'We believe Madame Lee-Win received several billions of dollars from the purchasers in 2012, and it probably went into her account with the BIP in Hong Kong.'

Bill was silent for a long moment. 'You're asking me to disclose confidential information about one of our customers? Apparently a very substantial customer, from what you've said.'

'Yes, I suppose I am. My nephew is convinced he was unknowingly involved in creating what could be an imminent and massive threat to global business and government security. He was wrongly thrown into prison because he found something out, and he believes his predecessor, Scotty Fitzgerald, was killed for the same reason. He must try to prevent it and it's my duty to try to help him. I'm sorry, Bill, but you are the only source of help I can think of.'

His face hardened and his eyes looked bleakly at her. 'I'm sorry too, Jenny. Even if this highly improbable conspiracy theory were to be true, you've asked me to do something which is not only unprofessional in the extreme, it's quite illegal, as you should very well know. If you think I would compromise my integrity for the sake of a personal relationship, no matter how close, I'm afraid you've misjudged me very badly, and it seems I've misjudged you also.'

He stood up and went to the door. 'Fortunately, my office does not have CCTV cameras and there is therefore no record of this conversation. I need to prepare for my next appointment now, so I'll see you out.' Jenny silently followed him to the reception area, her cheeks burning. 'Goodbye, Jenny,' he said, shaking her by the hand. Then he turned and went back along the corridor to his office.

Jenny went out onto the street. The sunshine was bright, and she realised her eyes were watering. She wiped them dry, put on her sunglasses and looked for a taxi.

Dubai International Airport

'OK, guys. This is it. Have a great flight, and text me when you get there and when I can do anything, it's safer than calling.' They shook hands, and Leo and Coetzee walked towards the fast-track security checkpoint.

Ed turned back when Leo called, 'Wait up, I completely forgot.' He counted out ten $100 bills from his wallet. 'Can you give this to Hatim and ask him to find Oskar Novak? He was in my cell. This is his get-out-of-jail money. Tell him it's from Razza's boyfriend.'

Dubai, United Arab Emirates

'Why would Leo just go off like that? After everything we've done for him, he didn't even take the time to say goodbye.'

Shen was in Tom Connor's office, and they were discussing Hatim's visit that afternoon. He said, 'There's only one possible interpretation. He was guilty of the rape and his family paid the woman off. Now he's afraid to show his face and he's slinked off back to the US or the UK. Don't waste any tears on the little bastard, we're better off without him.'

'At least he fixed the problems before he was arrested, otherwise—'

'Otherwise we'd have fixed them ourselves. Don't give him too much credit, Tom. Sharif did ninety-five per cent of the work before he came. We'd have cracked the problems, with or without him, I'm sure of it.'

'Well, it puts paid to the conspiracy theories.'

'What do you mean?'

'Only that after Scotty, it was looking as if someone was trying to sabotage the project. There's been a lot of speculation.' Tom didn't mention the US general's call. He didn't have to: Shen knew about it from the note he'd seen.

'Do you know how ridiculous that sounds, Tom? The project was wrapped up before he was arrested. If it was sabotage, the timing was fairly shitty. We're delivering the goods two weeks before the deadline. Doesn't sound like sabotage to me.'

'Sorry, Shen. I've been so worried about it I couldn't think straight. You're right, we've done the job and we'll get the credit for it. I'll announce the good news to the staff tomorrow. We're delivering Mark VII, the ACRE upgrade and connectivity package on Wednesday.'

'Why not make it even better?'

'How do you mean?'

'Tom, Sharif and Ed are done, finished. The project's wrapped up. They've said so, and we've seen the proof. Leo Stewart's not even in the equation any more. Why don't we send the package to Shanghai tomorrow, and show them what we're capable of?' He watched the conflicting emotions flicker across the CEO's face.

'I guess it wouldn't do us any harm to deliver the package another day ahead of time.'

'On the contrary, it would be a massive statement of confidence in XPC. One they can't ignore. We don't need so-called geniuses like Leo Stewart to fulfil our commitments.'

Tom Connor took a decision. 'You're right, Shen. Let's show them what we can achieve in Dubai. Show them how much they need their XPC subsidiary.'

'And we'll forget about Leo Stewart, he's history.'

'Right. Leo's been a big disappointment. Strange business, but it's all in the past now.'

Shen left the CEO, his usually inscrutable face creased in a broad smile. Everything was back on track, time to go home for one of Elodie's special evenings. He'd buy some flowers on the way, that always started things off well.

London, England

Jenny was in her office, looking at flights online. She had a lot of experience in finding good prices, but on this occasion it was the availability she was interested in. After her rebuff by Bill Redman she had cried for a while, then her steely character kicked in and she thought again about what Leo and Coetzee had told her. As usual, her thinking had brought her another idea. She booked an economy seat on a British Airways flight leaving Gatwick at nine-thirty the next morning and sent an email to Encarni to advise her, and ask Juan to pick her up at Malaga airport. Then she sent another to confirm the appointment she'd just made by telephone with Patrice de Moncrieff, Leticia's husband and the manager of BIP's Spanish subsidiary.

Jenny cancelled all her appointments for the week, and took a cab along to the Langham Hotel. They could always find a room for her. *Good job I didn't move into Bill's flat,* she thought. *That would have been a bit complicated. And I suppose they'll be appointing a new business manager for me at the bank.* She busied herself with her address book and tried to forget her consistently bad experiences with bankers.

Over Saudi Arabia, en route to Johannesburg

'Cheers, Marius, and thanks again.' Leo settled back in his business-class window seat and sipped the glass of champagne Coetzee had requested from the cabin attendant. He had flown in business class a number of times over the last few years, usually when his employer was paying for the ticket – true to his Scottish upbringing, he didn't like to waste money – but the experience was still novel enough that he enjoyed being spoiled for a while. 'A bit of a contrast to Bur Dubai,' he said jokingly.

'Better make the most of it. We've got serious work to do in Delmas. I just hope Jenny manages to find something out about Lee-Win, we need a break, something to get our teeth into.' Coetzee lapsed into silence, thinking, *Why is Dr Hugh Middleton so concerned about Leo? They've never even met before. Wheels within wheels.*

Dubai, United Arab Emirates

'I'm going to miss Leo. It won't be the same without him.' Ed and Lynne were at Club 27. It was a quiet night and they were chatting in the bar.

'Do you know where he is?'

Ed hadn't yet shared the full story with Lynne. If she knew the real reasons behind Leo's imprisonment and his suspicions over Scotty's death, she'd be worried out of her mind. He replied, 'He's gone down to stay with some friends in Johannesburg, lucky guy. That's all I know.'

'And he's definitely not coming back?' He shook his head, and she said, 'I don't blame him after what happened. Are you going to stay at XPC?'

'I'll see how things pan out. Now that Shen's got his way, the work on Mark VII and ACRE is over, so it depends on whether they've got any new projects scheduled for Sharif and me.'

'But you don't trust Shen anyway. After what happened to Leo, why take chances?'

'Once everything gets sent to Shanghai on Wednesday, I don't think there's any risks down here. I told Leo I'd hang around for a while, in case he needs me to look at anything for him, so I'll give it a few weeks to see what happens. The pay's good and I'm not that keen to look for another job again so soon.'

'So I'm not part of the equation?' She gave him a mock vicious look.

'Oops! I kind of took that for granted, sorry. You know I'd be less keen to stay if you weren't here. C'mon, let's have a dance, then I'll take you home on Leo's Harley.'

FORTY-ONE

Dubai, United Arab Emirates
Tuesday, 13 July 2017

'So, what's the new timetable?' Elodie and Shen were having a lazy breakfast. After two bottles of champagne and an exhausting session of rough sex the previous night, they'd slept late.

Shen wasn't in a hurry, everything was under control at XPC, the crisis had passed and he'd talked Tom Connor into sending the package off tonight. Elodie had praised him to the skies when he'd bragged of that latest triumph. If nothing else, it had ensured a passionate reaction from her. He'd go in later to make sure Sharif and Ed had finalised everything, and Tom would talk to the staff that afternoon. Everyone was a hero except Leo Stewart. It couldn't have turned out better if he'd planned it that way.

'No change. For Mark VII, there'll be copies of all the final test runs made by our people, so the Chinese programmers can run the firmware on Sharif's design until they're happy there's no problems. They'll pass the design to the production people, so they can start producing the new module.'

'But that's not our concern?'

'Right, we don't care if it's ever produced and distributed. We're interested in the upgrades to be deployed universally through our wireless hubs to the billions of processors out there already. They'll deliver Mark VII software, running on ACRE encrypted transmission, to all those processors that have a connectivity module. He'll never know it, but Leo Stewart designed the perfect system override delivery method.'

'And when that software is downloaded the customers will be happy?'

'They'll be delighted. It can be sent out as soon as Shanghai's finished testing, I'd say a week at most. Then a couple of days later, our underground guy will send out a minor correction, citing a small debug issue.'

'And that wakes up our cell?'

'Right. The cell that brings us our return for five years of work.'

'I like it.'

Delmas, Mpumalanga, South Africa

'Leo, it's great to see you again.' Karen ran across the driveway and threw her arms around him as he got out of the taxi.

'It's great to be here. Unexpected, but really great.'

'I can imagine,' she said. They carried the bags to the door as Coetzee paid the driver. 'What a time you've been through. Was it really awful?'

'Educational, I'd say. But the kind of education that's best in very small doses. Anyway, thanks to Marius, I'm here in one piece.'

'I know, he's sickeningly efficient, but I love him anyway.'

'Hello Leo, glad you're safe. Nice of you to visit.' A tall, slender African girl walked towards him.

'Abby, it's good to be back.' He kissed her on both cheeks. 'You get more beautiful every time I see you.'

'And you seem to get taller,' she said, looking a little self-conscious. She turned away from him, 'Hi Dad. Another successful safari, well done.'

'Not yet, the real work is just about to start. That's why Leo came down with me.'

She hid her disappointment. 'I made some coffee, come and tell us all about it. It sounds intriguing.'

It took half an hour to bring Karen and Abby up to speed. They were both amazed and appalled at the story. Abby said, 'Do you really think we can do anything from here? If they're sending the package off tomorrow, it seems unlikely.'

'I don't know, but we have to try. We've probably still got a couple of days to work out exactly what's going on.'

'I'll take you up to your room to clean up, then you can show us how all this fits together.'

'OK, thanks. Meanwhile, can you find out how many pieces of kit here have got Lee-Win processors?'

Dubai, United Arab Emirates

Elodie Delacroix took a mobile from a handbag in her wardrobe, and pressed a WhatsApp number. 'Hello darling, latest update. Shen convinced everyone at XPC that the Leo Stewart thing was a red herring and the heat's off.' She laughed. 'I know, even Shen gets it right once in a while. Anyway, they're sending the package today and expect Shanghai to turn it around within a week.'

She listened again. 'OK, I'll try to get it speeded up. Maybe I can get him to go up there and move things along at Lee-Win. I'll keep you up-to-date. I can't wait to be in your arms again, not long now. *Au revoir mon amour.*'

Malaga, Spain

'*Hola, buenos dias*, Juan.' Jenny shook hands with her gardener-chauffeur, and he mumbled a gruff '*Buenos dias*, Jenny'. Due to the hour time difference, it was now one-fifteen and the sun was beating down mercilessly as they walked to the car park. The drive took forty minutes, and she was in time for her meeting with Patrice at the Banco de Iberia. The bank closed at two o'clock and he'd arranged to go for lunch at Da Bruno Sul Mare, near the beach. Jenny was starving, having had nothing since her early morning tea and biscuit.

Patrice was waiting for her in the banking hall and they walked along the busy streets to the restaurant. Her previously difficult relationship with him had improved since she'd set up Bishop Private Equity, and he had steered several opportunities in her direction. He was very enthusiastic in his praise for her business intuition.

'The deal you did with Lady Knick Knack was incredibly daring. I would never have been able to negotiate that, nor to sell it to the bank.' He spoke perfect English with an attractive French accent, which Jenny always assumed he put on to impress.

'One of the best, as it turned out. You can't fight people's inner desires, so you might as well cater to them. Especially if you can make money while you're at it.' She didn't reveal that his wife, Leticia, was one of their most regular customers.

At the restaurant, the banker ordered two glasses of chilled Rueda, from the north of Spain. '*Salud.*' They savoured the hint of apple and lemon flavours on their palettes and he said, 'I know you don't like wasting time on social visits, Jenny, so to what do I owe the honour?'

'Thanks, Patrice. I'm sure you're incredibly busy, but this is an urgent matter which came up just a few days ago and I think you might be able to help me.'

He nodded for her to continue, and she launched into the story of Leo and the XPC conspiracy. He was very quick on the uptake and asked a lot more questions than Bill had done, seeming more and more impressed by her obvious conviction and the detailed background to the events she described.

They had finished their first course when she finally stopped talking. '*Mon Dieu!*' he exclaimed. 'That's quite a story. You and Emma must have been out of your minds with worry when he was arrested.'

Patrice was unaware of Leo's abduction in 2010, and she replied, 'Fortunately, Marius Coetzee is a close friend and a very resourceful man, and we never had any doubt he'd get Leo out. After he talked to Angela, the pieces of the jigsaw suddenly came together, and the picture is pretty frightening.'

Unknowingly, he echoed Karen Coetzee's question. 'Do you really think Leo and Coetzee can do anything from Johannesburg? It seems to me that once the software package arrives in Shanghai, it's too late to stop whatever it is they're going to do. I mean, if Homeland Security can't do anything, what chance do they have?'

'Quite honestly, I have no idea, but General Chillicott and the people in London think the ownership of Lee-Win Micro-Technology might be the key to putting a spanner in the works. Without that, they say they can't take any action until it might be too late.'

'And Lee-Win's in Shanghai? I don't have any contacts there, Jenny. If that's what you were hoping, I'm afraid I can't be of any help.'

'What about Hong Kong? I remember you told me you went there to set up their private equity operations.'

'That's a different matter entirely, I go there two or three times a year to discuss cross-marketing and partnership deals with them. But I don't see how it helps you.'

Jenny explained what they were looking for, praying that he wouldn't react in the same way as Bill Redman.

Patrice laughed, 'Why don't you ask me to burgle the bank while I'm busy.'

'To quote General Chillicott, Homeland Security is conducting a "national security investigation" into Lee-Win and XPC. Surely that gives you the authority to make a simple enquiry?'

'I can't ask them to send me information of that kind, it creates a paper trail and will cause a scandal with the compliance people. Let me think for a moment.'

They continued with their meal, chatting about family and friends, then when their coffee arrived, he said, 'I got an email a week ago from Ho Au Yeung, the PE MD in Hong Kong. He wants me to go over sometime, to talk about one of our European clients expanding in the Far East. How soon do you need this information?'

'Leo told me the new software will be sent to Lee-Win in Shanghai tomorrow, and it could be distributed within a few days.'

'The deadline is this weekend? That's a bit tight. Even if I leave tomorrow, with the time difference, the earliest I can find anything out will be Thursday. What do you think?'

'You'll do it for me?' Jenny almost shouted with relief.

To her surprise, he took her hand in his. 'Jenny, I know we haven't always hit it off, but I have a very long memory. If it wasn't for your bravery and refusal to admit defeat, I wouldn't have Leticia and Emilio today, so I owe you much more than a quick trip to Hong Kong. Right, I'd better get back and sort out my schedule. I'll call you as soon as I've made all the arrangements.'

FORTY-TWO

London, England
Tuesday, 13 July 2017

'Back again so soon, General?'

'I wish I wasn't, Ilona.'

'You look tired.'

'I'm a bit beat up, you're right.' Chillicott dumped himself in a chair and she went to fetch him some coffee.

Middleton came into the hall. 'Welcome back, Billy. Official business again?'

'Unfortunately, Hugh. I wish it was a social visit, but I'm with the MoD guys this afternoon.'

They went into Middleton's office. 'Brexit seems to be infecting everyone with a case of mass hysteria. Is that what is causing even more concern, or is it your new president's apparent schizophrenia?'

'Neither, this time. It's NATO business, problems with our Russkie friends.'

'What has Comrade Vladimir been up to this time? Or is it ultra-confidential?'

'It's going to be common knowledge when the media spies get hold of it, so I don't think I'd be talking out of turn.'

'Is it my country again?' Ilona put a mug of coffee and a tumbler of whisky in front of him. Since the Russian invasion of Ukraine and the annexation of Crimea in 2014, car bombings and assassinations had become almost commonplace, and she lived in dread that the Russians would extend their occupation and effectively take over the country.

'Thanks, you read my mind.' He poured the whisky into the mug and took a swig. 'It's been going on for over a week now in just about every neighbouring country. Large troop movements carrying out "exercises", or "war games", like they always say. They're amassing more troops in Crimea, probably to move against Ukraine again, or as a launching point into the Balkans, so I guess you're right to be worried. And Russian troops are carrying out manoeuvres in the north on the borders of Finland, Estonia, Latvia, Belarus, down around Georgia and Azerbaijan in the south and Kazakhstan in the east.'

'Any estimate of numbers?'

'The analysts say over half a million troops on the move.'

'That sounds quite ominous.'

'It gets worse, there's fleet movements off the coast as well. The *Admiral Grigorovich* is leading a group of six warships sailing down the North Sea off the Norwegian coast. Those ships carry Kalibr cruise missiles. Looks like they could be headed for the Baltic, so they'd have some of those countries in a pincer, back and front. Even Poland and Sweden would be vulnerable.'

'Aircraft carriers, submarines?'

'The *Kuznetsov* and *Gorshkov* are on manoeuvres in the north Atlantic. We've had an unconfirmed report of a nuclear sub leaving Murmansk. And there's two destroyers set off from Crimea across the Black Sea, towards the Balkans; maybe Romania and Bulgaria. The whole shebang. It looks like a blatant attempt to reassemble the USSR, maybe even more.'

Ilona frowned. 'I haven't seen or heard anything about this.'

'It'll be front page news tomorrow. You know how fast bad news travels.'

'Hmm. With the lack of stability and confidence in a constantly changing US government, and the EU-Brexit row just starting to heat up, the timing couldn't be worse — or better, depending on your point of view.'

'You bet. The US is almost in a state of suspended animation, wondering what Trump's gonna say or do next. While he's tweeting and spouting warnings about annihilating Iran and North Korea, the Russians will run rings around him until there's nothing left to tweet about. They know NATO is under threat, since he says it's obsolete, but nobody knows what he'll do about it. While everyone is posturing and parleying, they could grab back their old territories, just like they've always wanted.'

He took another swallow of coffee. 'I was invited to a meeting of the Joint Chiefs of Staff yesterday. The Defence Secretary was there, that's how serious we're taking it.'

'And?'

'Well, between us guys, we're sending in 20,000 troops to beef up NATO forces in Poland, Bulgaria and Turkey. Air force overflights of the vulnerable borders and a few battleships in the North Sea and Baltic. It's nothing but a token response, but it's all DefSec's authorised to do. I think I've persuaded him to convene a meeting of the UN Security Council, but with the Russian veto power it's a total waste of time.'

'I'm surprised I've heard nothing from my friends in Kiev. They're usually the first to spot anything going on.' Ilona looked perplexed. 'It can't be on the airwaves or they'd be rebroadcasting it all over. This must come from very high up, to have been kept under wraps until now.' She went to the door. 'I'll call Ilya now, see what he knows.'

'What are you talking to the MoD about?' Middleton asked.

'It's more of a courtesy call than anything else. The truth is, you Brits have no teeth left in your bite. The military budget has been decimated over the last few years until you need four signatures to buy a paper clip. If all these Soviet movements are serious, we're in deep shit. You might muster a battalion or two to give a show of solidarity with the northern NATO countries, but it wouldn't be a meaningful show of force. The fact is, apart from us, nobody can show any credible reaction at all.'

'I'm unfortunately obliged to agree with you, although your president might not be inclined to react as we might hope. And, of course, Russia's attempts to dissuade their Baltic and Balkan neighbours to enter into the NATO alliance is not improving the situation.'

'It sure doesn't look like a coincidence. We've got proof positive the Russians were trying to manipulate the elections in Montenegro, they were doing everything possible to stop them joining NATO.'

Middleton gave a cynical smile. 'I'm afraid that Montenegro isn't the only election where we should be concerned about Soviet interference. Your people could start by looking closer to home.'

Chillicott took another swig. 'I know, Hugh, but I'm not allowed to interfere in that. I'm just a soldier, not a politician or a special investigator. Anyway, the other reason I called in is to ask if you found out anything further about Lee-Win?'

'So far, nothing, I'm afraid. However, Ilona's new South African gentleman friend, Marius Coetzee, is confident he can uncover something about the transaction.' Middleton paused. He found it strange to be talking in the present tense about a man he'd been convinced had been assassinated seven years previously. He took a sip of coffee. 'As you know, he managed to arrange Leo Stewart's release, so he's obviously a very resourceful man. But we've heard nothing from him yet except a message saying the software package will be sent to Shanghai, probably tomorrow.'

'The global upload is going ahead?'

'So it seems. Apparently, Leo perfected the software before he was imprisoned. That probably means they'll add the virus when they send it out from Shanghai, which will be very soon, I don't imagine they'll delay too long. Coetzee has taken Leo down to Johannesburg to try to work out what they can do to mitigate whatever's going to happen, but unfortunately they don't yet know what that is. It seems to be one of those annoying cases of the cart and the horse.'

Ilona came back into the room. 'They started to see the movements last weekend, without any previous warning. He's worried, this definitely comes from a very high level, they were taken completely off guard.'

'I just had a random thought. May I throw out a speculative suggestion?' When no one answered, Middleton said, 'I don't suppose these events could be more than just coincidental?'

'You mean the cyber-attack, if that's what it is, and the troop movements?' Ilona looked dubious.

'What I'm talking about is what could be described as "the perfect storm". In Europe, we are involved in what will inevitably become a bitter and protracted Brexit argument between the UK, the buffoons in Brussels and twenty-seven countries. This is in addition to recent and upcoming elections in France, Germany, Austria, Holland and Italy, which could destabilise the EU even further. On your side of the pond, Billy, you have uncertainty and paralysis caused by dissension at the very highest level of government, which as we know, may involve NATO. In the Middle East we have several pots of boiling oil which can spill over in any direction, inciting intervention from East and West, and in Asia we have a young, narcissistic, ambitious and ruthless ruler who is determined to show off his explosive toys to the world at any cost.'

'And you throw the Internet into the mix with a cyber-attack that brings down government and business infrastructure, so there's a temporary void in communications. Bingo, World War III!' Chillicott banged his fist on the table.

'Do you recollect what young Leo Stewart told you in San Diego?'

'You mean about crying wolf? I sure do. He said it would need a really devastating event before anyone took notice of our preaching for more control and security of the Internet. Maybe that's what we're looking at here. What's worse is that it seems like the cyber-attack will come from China, and the military threat is from Russia. Very strange bedfellows.'

'Quite, Billy. Very strange.'

FORTY-THREE

Delmas, Mpumalanga, South Africa
Tuesday, 13 July 2017

'Right, I'm ready to go.' Leo had showered and changed and was feeling wide awake. Abby had introduced him to their team of programmers and specialists, and they were now sitting with Rod and Julia, two ex-hackers, in an office repurposed as a lab. 'Did you find some Lee-Win kit to create a mini mesh network?'

'It's actually amazing how many of our machines have got them. We've brought six of them in here. What do you want us to do?'

Leo opened his laptop. 'I've got the software upload here that's going to be deployed from Lee-Win in Shanghai to their billions of microprocessors. We're going to do a test run on this equipment via a wireless hub.'

'How do you know all the processors have got connectivity modules?' Rod, a short, red-haired reformed hacker from Cape Town, looked sceptical. Leo noticed he chewed his nails a lot, his finger ends were red and looked sore.

'OK. You're right. Only the Mark IV to VI models have got those modules built in, they started to incorporate them four years ago. But you only need to have one in any machine for the upload to permeate through a whole mesh network. And don't forget there's also millions of processors in IoT equipment that's already sitting on mobile networks.'

'Wow, that must be hundreds of millions of machines out there that could be infected.' Now Rod looked impressed.

'What's in the upload?' Abby cut to the chase.

'Upgrades to Mark VII firmware and the new version of ACRE encryption-transmission.' Leo explained the background to the upgrades that had been perfected. 'After downloading, the whole network will switch automatically to the new transmission system.'

'And there's a worm, or something you don't like, in the firmware or ACRE?'

'No, I don't think so.' Over the last few days, Leo had had time to think deeply about the tests he'd run in the XPC lab. He explained to the team what had happened, the additional code addressed to the cell he'd discovered. 'It closed down the system, but it started up again afterwards with the clean coding.'

Abby said, 'It sounds to me like the worm is already in the processors. What that instruction is doing is waking it up.'

'That's what I'm thinking. I'll show you the test I did in Dubai. Let's get the network built.'

An hour later, they had created a mini mesh network, linked together and to a wireless router, exactly as he'd built at XPC. Leo's laptop display was projected onto a large screen to let everyone see what he was doing.

'OK, I'm going to upload the clean version of the upgrades via the router. Watch this.'

The screen showed a flurry of commands and a moment later, all the equipment was running with ACRE encrypted transmission. Leo ran some data through the network and showed how the old key-based algorithms and Mark VI encryption version had been replaced.

'Wow, that's really cool.' Rod was biting his nails and examining the ACRE algorithms on an analytics programme. 'It just keeps calculating and recalculating the encryption parameters so fast you can never catch a status for long enough to hack in. Impressive.'

'It was developed at XPC by Scotty Fitzgerald, a real encryption wizard. But last week I accidently found a different version of the upload package. It's identical, apart from three extra lines of code attached on the end. Look.' He showed Sharif's test code on the screen.

'It's just sending the same message over and over again to that cell, S470C887,999,' Abby said. 'I think it must be a sleeping cell that's already in the processors, and it's telling it to wake up so it can do something, but I don't know what. Where did it come from?'

'Sharif, the design guy was testing it, but I'm sure he was doing it for his boss, Shen.'

'You think he was duped as well?'

'Probably. He's not the type to plan anything like this, not enough imagination and too honest. Shen put me in prison, so that cell must come from him somehow. Here, I'll run it and show you what happens.'

Leo ran Sharif's revised test. They could see the flash of the repeat instructions being passed thousands of times per second. In less than a minute, the mini-network shut down.

'That's impressive, but weird.' Abby frowned. 'It must wake that cell up and there's some kind of handover that shuts down the network. If it's to introduce a virus or something, I don't see the point. When the network's down, it can't be instructed to do anything.'

'Maybe that's all it does, shut the system down.'

'You guys are right. That cell's asleep somewhere on the Lee-Win processors.' Julia, a pretty, statuesque Swazi woman with an abundance of frizzy curls, intervened. 'I read about something like this a while ago. See if I can find it.' She started interrogating her laptop.

Abby asked, 'When is this upload supposed to happen?'

'The plan was to launch Mark VII at the same time they deploy the uploads, to get maximum bang from the buck. That would be in a month or so, depending on production.'

'Are the uploads interconnected or independent from the new modules?'

'They're in the same package, but they're not interconnected. All the software will be deployed together to the existing pool of processors, but the Mark VII modules can only be distributed after they build them.'

'So, if the plan is to do something when they send the upgrades, it could be right after they finish testing in Shanghai. Before they even manufacture the new modules.'

'That's what worries me. If they're going to attack the existing pool of machines they can do it as soon as they get the upgrades. They could deploy the modified code this week.'

'It would really cut down our timescale for doing anything. We need to look at that shutdown function right away.'

'I know, but I don't understand how the shutdown happens. That cell is just like any other cell, it can't suddenly take over the management of the whole microprocessor.'

'That's not what it does, Leo.' Julia looked up from her screen. 'I found that item I remembered. It's called an "Analog Back Door Attack", code name "A2". I'll distribute it.' She forwarded an article published by the University of Michigan.

'A2? I've never heard of it. How does it work?'

'It's a physical change to the processor, they add a malicious cell in the manufacture process. It's a capacitator cell that accumulates an electric charge when they trigger it with those multiple commands, then it hands over control to a logical function that's already programmed in the processor. In this case, it just shuts down the system.'

'Shit. All the processors in the devices we've got here shut down, so they've been tampered with. That means someone discovered this A2 backdoor cell idea some years ago. It must be Shanghai that's behind it, and they've been preparing an attack all this time.'

Julia was still reading. 'Hang on, Leo. Stop sending that code and see what happens.'

He terminated the programme on his laptop and they all waited in silence. After a minute or so, the network came back to life. Leo shook his head. 'Now I'm totally confused.'

'That's what's supposed to happen,' Julia said. 'When you stop sending those trigger instructions, the cell loses its electricity and the network reverts to its normal state. Check that it's still running ACRE, Rod.'

'Yep. It's back to where it was before, with the upgrades working.'

As they were reading and discussing the report, Coetzee walked into the room with Karen. 'Hi guys, how's it going?'

'We think we've got it, Dad. Julia, you explain.'

She summarised what they'd found, finishing with, 'We haven't looked at the cell yet, so this is all theoretical.'

'OK, guys. We need to do some strategic thinking.' Coetzee decided it was time to restrict the flow of information. 'We'll break for lunch. See you later.'

In his office, Coetzee said, 'All the equipment in that network is less than five years old. Didn't you tell me they'd been incorporating the connectivity module for the last four years?'

Leo nodded. 'I was thinking the same, the timing of the changes is linked. They started planting that cell at the same time as providing the connectivity capability to contact it later.'

'I suppose you know Lee-Win changed hands five years ago. This plan must have been hatched soon after that.'

'That figures, if they're targeting all the processors built in the last four years.'

'What happened when you stopped sending the trigger commands?' Coetzee asked.

'The network came back to life in a minute or two.'

'So, the command has to be sent continuously to maintain the network shutdown?'

'Exactly. But if it's downloaded by millions of users, their systems will stay shut down until a new command is sent to stop triggering the cell.'

'Is there any way of finding that command and overriding it to make it harmless?'

'We haven't got that far yet, but that's what we need to get the team focused on now.'

'I wonder how they'll do this.' Abby was going through the plan in her mind. 'Will the package they send from Dubai contain the extra code, or will they add it in Shanghai?'

'I'll ask Ed. The final package must be ready now if they're sending it tomorrow, and he knows about that cell instruction. It would make sense for Shanghai to send out the clean version first, get it accepted, then follow it up with the A2 code afterwards.'

'You're right. Once the customers are happy with the upgrades, they'll accept a minor correction without question, then the world shuts down.' She frowned. 'The other thing I can't understand is why they set up the XPC facility in Dubai in the first place? Wouldn't it have been simpler to do everything from China?'

'No idea, but they must have had a reason. It might have been to attract first-rate people who don't want to go to Shanghai, like Scotty. I think the key to this is ACRE. They doubled their sales last year because of it, so the number of networks it gives them access to is huge.'

Coetzee said, 'I think there's another reason. Whoever's behind Lee-Win and this potential attack, they're hiding their identity from the world. They have to remain anonymous because the processors are in top level organisations, hospitals, government departments and the like. It could literally bring everything to a standstill, cause a worldwide panic.'

'While they do what, Marius? Why would the Chinese or anyone else deploy something so devastating, knowing it could start a new war? We'll have to give the bad news to General Chillicott. He knows there's going to be an upload, but he doesn't know what might be in it.'

'And there's this possible link to Russia. Ask Ed for a status report, then we'll call Homeland Security. I don't know what good it'll do, but they need to know what's going on.'

Leo texted Ed, asking him to call when he found a quiet corner. His mind was racing, desperately trying to work out if they could do something, anything, in time to prevent whatever was planned, before it was too late.

FORTY-FOUR

Dubai, United Arab Emirates
Tuesday, 13 July 2017

'The package is assembled. Shen's sending it tonight. He talked Tom into proving to the Lee-Win people how well we can manage without you and moved it forward another day.'

Ed was in the XPC car park, speaking to Leo. He'd finished his last clean-up of the software and signed it off to Shen. Sharif's design template for Mark VII was also delivered. Now it was out of their hands.

'You're not delivering it to Shanghai yourselves?'

'Tom decided that there should be only one person in contact with them, for security purposes. Shen's the direct link, so he's sending it. It's not rocket science, even he can manage to do it right.'

'So, after Shanghai retests everything, they could put the upgrades out without waiting for the Mark VII launch?'

'I suppose so. No one's actually given us a date for the release, but you're probably right, it'll be a fast turnaround. There's nothing to be debugged and we don't expect any glitches. It works fine, thanks to you.'

Leo explained what they'd discovered about the rogue cell. 'We don't know if the upgrades will trigger it, or if they'll do it in two stages. Any thoughts?'

'Fucking hell! That's what Shen's been plotting? That devious, arrogant Chinese arsehole.' Ed sounded apoplectic. He popped a piece of gum into his mouth and chewed aggressively. 'Let's think about the deployment. The package has got our original software, so it would make more sense for them to send that clean version out to test the process. When they know it's been successfully downloaded by the networks out there, they follow it up with the trigger. Sound logical?'

'That's one of the theories we've come to down here, but it's a hell of a risk to take.'

'Well, there's no way I can find out now it's in Shen's hands. We just have to make that assumption.'

Leo thought for a moment, cursing the fact that he'd never been in direct contact with Lee-Win in Shanghai. 'Any chance of getting the address and handshake that Shen's sending to? Maybe the hub network coordinates?'

'I get it, try to get in the back door and take a look. I've never had any contact with them, so the only way would be through Sharif, if he's sent stuff before. He's gone for the night, I'll see what I can find out tomorrow. I'll check with Daniel as well, but Shen probably used his laptop, so there'll be nothing in the main network.'

Washington DC, USA

'Leo, how's it going? It's great to hear your voice. That must have been a hell of an experience.'

'Educational, I keep telling people. Billy, I'm calling you about the Lee-Win upload that's scheduled. I think you know Marius Coetzee, I'm on the speaker with him here in Joburg. We've been running tests on the corrupted version of the software.'

'That figures. Hugh Middleton and I were talking about it in London yesterday. Hello again Mr Coetzee, glad you're looking after Leo down there. This whole thing sounds like it could be that

imminent catastrophe you were warning me about in San Diego, Leo.'
Chillicott said nothing about the Russian troop and naval movements.
No need to complicate things in their minds, he thought. *One thing at a time.*

Leo quickly brought him up-to-date on their tests. 'The package
will be in Shanghai tonight,' he finished, 'and I don't know how to
prevent it from being deployed.'

'That's a new one on me. A physical cell added to a processor.
How do they do that without it being noticed?'

'Maybe you've never seen one of these silicone chips, Billy.
They've got a billion components on a fingernail. Impossible to see
what's there or not. But that cell is definitely there and it's not on the
XPC design, so it must have been added at Lee-Win in Shanghai.'

'You know, guys, the more we find out about that Chinese outfit,
the more it looks like a barrel of worms. The problem is, we don't
have one single solid fact. We don't know who owns it, what's really
going to happen on this upload, and we don't know why.' He asked
the same question as Coetzee had. 'What does it do?'

'They send a trigger command to the cell and something in
the processor switches it off. The whole network goes down, as
simple as that. You'll have billions of devices all over the world
that stop working.'

'Jesus Christ! Lee-Win's main market is government departments,
industrials, banking and essential service industries, correct?'

'Right, the infrastructure of the world's business.'

Leo's words seem to hang in the air as Chillicott was silent for
a moment. 'But if they deploy your original upgrades without that
additional code you found, the new software works fine?'

'Perfectly. We think that's what they'll do, then they'll follow
up the clean version with that code as a minor update and "wham
bang thank you mam"! I've got Ed trying to find out what's going
on up there, but we've heard nothing yet.'

'Is there any way you can find out how to access the hub network
they'll use for the deployment?'

'Ed's on that as well. And we've got a team of people here
in Joburg trying to identify the exact command that does the

shutdown. Then we could try to hack into the hub to override it, or maybe your Homeland people could, you've got a lot more resources in that area than we have.'

'I didn't hear you say that, but it sounds like a plan. See if Ed can get us some kind of link. And while you're at it, ask him if he can manage to get a photo of that woman, Elodie. We know all about Shen Fu Liáng, but nothing about her. If she's on any kind of file, we might have some luck with our image matching kit. And Leo, tell him to be real careful. Those people don't play by the rules, as you know better than me.'

Delmas, Mpumalanga, South Africa

'Hello Jenny, how's everything with you?' Coetzee had gotten to enjoy speaking to Jenny Bishop. She seemed to be like him, didn't waste time talking about things, just got on with it. He regretted what had happened in 2010, but it didn't appear to have left any lasting scars, apart from his.

'I just wanted to keep you informed. One of my family, Patrice de Moncrieff, is a director of BIP in Spain, and he works closely with their Hong Kong subsidiary. He's gone there on our behalf to try to get details of the payments made to Mme Lee-Win.'

'That's great news, Jenny. What are his chances?'

'Honestly, I don't know, but he knows what we need and he's a clever man. He wouldn't have gone if he didn't think he could do it. I'll know in a day or two if he can find out what we want. Is there any progress on the technical side?'

'I'll get Leo to give you an update. He was just explaining it to General Chillicott, so you're in exalted company.'

Leo explained what the team had discovered about cell S470C887,999. 'We just don't know what they're going to do with it, or when they'll do it,' he finished lamely.

'Remember what I told you about those billions of anonymous processors all over the world? "The most terrifying thing I've heard in my life", I said. And I was right.'

Dubai, United Arab Emirates

'I'm ready to send the package off. Anything special you want me to say in the message?'

Shen had just come up to Tom Connor's office, where the CEO was finishing his report to the Lee-Win board.

'I'll email this report shortly, so you don't need to add anything. This is a great result, Shen, and I'm giving you all the credit, you and Sharif. It could easily have gone wrong when Leo went AWOL, but you guys managed to save the day. Thanks for being a trusted partner and getting it done within the timeframe, I won't forget it.'

Shen smiled modestly. 'You're welcome Tom, we owed it to you. After what happened to poor Scotty, and then this episode with Leo Stewart, we just had to deliver to prove the value of XPC. I'll get it off now with the appropriate signature protocols. See you later.'

He went down to the lab with his laptop, and collated the bundle of firmware and connectivity programmes and the ACRE upgrade into a machine-readable executable file with the agreed Lee-Win handshake signature. After further testing in Shanghai, the upgrades would be distributed with that same trusted signature; the customer devices would open them and override their firmware with the new versions. The design spec and mask was a CAD document that could be read by Lee-Wins CAM machinery to manufacture the Mark VII processors, although that wasn't one of his priorities. If everything went according to plan, it might never even be produced.

He called Elodie. 'Everything's finished and ready to go. I'm pressing *Send* now.'

'Well done, darling, it's finally over. When are we leaving? I'm sick and tired of this place, and the people. Can I start booking flights and hotels?'

'We'll wait until the uploads are deployed, then we'll make our move. We don't want to be here when the trigger upload goes out, it's likely to get a little nasty.'

'So, a few more days? Are we going back to Ireland as you promised? It's months since I was there, and you know how much

I love it. And it'll be a long way from the problem areas. We'll wait it out until everything's settled down, then the world's our oyster. I can't wait.'

'Just a few more days, then Dublin. I promise.'

Shen rang off, then called a number on his encrypted phone. 'I've just sent off the package,' he said in Russian. 'Yes, it should be just a few days, not more. I'll keep you informed.'

Dubai, United Arab Emirates

'Hello, darling. The software package was sent off to Shanghai a few minutes ago.' Elodie Delacroix was on her other mobile phone again.

She listened for a moment. 'Yes, Shen sent it. He says it will go out in a couple of days. I know, not long now. I'll keep you informed as soon as I hear anything more. Take care, I'm missing you.'

FORTY-FIVE

Dubai, United Arab Emirates
Wednesday, 14 July 2017

'I hear Shen sent everything off last night? Pressure's off for a while.'
Ed took a swig of coffee. He'd just come from Hatim's office, where
the lawyer had promised to visit Oskar Novak in prison to hand
over the $1,000 'get out of jail' money from Leo.

Sharif nodded his head. 'Just housekeeping until we get the
next project from Shanghai. But it might be sooner than we think.'

The remark made Ed's ears prick up. 'Sounds like you're
expecting something specific. Anything I should know?'

The Pakistani looked away. 'Just something Shen mentioned.'

Ed tried to sound nonchalant. 'To do with that cell,
S470C887,999?'

'How do you know about that?'

'I don't. Only that Leo was trying to work out what it's for.'

'It's something Shanghai's working on, I don't know the details.
Shen thinks we'll get a chance to build something even better than
ACRE.'

'That would be difficult.' Now Ed was sure Sharif had been
hoodwinked by his boss. 'Isn't that one of your cells?'

'Morning, guys.' Shen came into the office. 'What's new?'

Sharif shifted on his seat. 'We were just wondering when we might get the new project from Shanghai.'

'I'm going up there as soon as they send out the upgrades. It's top of my list of priorities, I don't want you guys sitting around with nothing to do.' He gave a mirthless laugh, avoiding looking at them.

In for a penny, in for a pound, Ed thought. 'Is it as exciting as Sharif said? Bigger than ACRE?'

'I'm not allowed to discuss it, but it's quite earth-shattering, I promise you.'

'Strange Tom hasn't said anything about it.'

'You know he's not in touch a lot with head office, he leaves all that to me. Now, I've got a few things to do, so I'll catch you later.' He walked out, leaving the two men looking at each other.

Ed tried to provoke a reaction from Sharif. 'What the hell's going on? He's working with Shanghai on something the CEO doesn't know about?'

'I don't know. I try not to get involved in office politics, it's not my business.'

Shen went straight to his office and called Elodie. 'Ed's poking his nose into things.' He explained what had transpired. 'What do we do? Take him out of the picture?'

She forced herself to be patient. 'That's not a great idea, we don't want another incident, especially right now. Don't forget there's some connection with that general at Homeland Security. We can't afford to arouse his suspicions.'

'So what do you want me to do?'

'Can you get Shanghai to speed up the test procedure and move the deployment date forward?'

'I can try, but it's the regular Lee-Win systems people handling the upload, our guy will only step in after it's gone out. I can't pressure them too much or they'll think there's something wrong. I'll call them and see what the timetable is.'

'Maybe you should go up there and get them moving?'

'I don't know. Let me see what's happening and I'll decide. I'll call you later.'

Elodie put the phone down in exasperation. She couldn't wait until she no longer needed this idiot. Once she got to Dublin with her reward for five years of putting up with him, she wouldn't hang around. A quick change of identity, an airline ticket and she'd be leaving on a jet plane, John Denver style.

Marbella, Spain

Jenny's mobile rang at seven-thirty. It was a clear, sunny morning and she'd already enjoyed a refreshing ten-minute swim in the pool. Encarni and Juan didn't arrive until eight, and she'd thrown aside her inhibitions and swum in the nude. She'd woken up feeling a little bleary and the cold water had helped to clear her head. The coffee machine was spewing out her morning dose of caffeine when she saw it was Patrice's number calling.

'*Hola*, Patrice. *Que tal?*'

'Hi, Jenny, your Spanish is improving, keep it up. I just want to give you a quick update, is this a good time?'

'Fire away, I'm taking my coffee out to the terrace.'

'It turns out that Mme Lee-Win lives in Hong Kong now and she's one of our PE clients, has been for a couple of years. Ho Au Yeung has a good relationship with her. The sad part of the story is that she's ill. She has an untreatable condition, prognosis only a few years to live. That's why she's moved here from Macau.'

'My God, how awful. How old is she?'

'Sixty-two, much too young, but there's apparently no hope. Her sons are taking over the casino business and they've sold off the manufacturing plants the family had in China.'

'She's been sorting out her affairs.'

'Exactly. I spoke to her this morning and she's invited me over to her house tomorrow. I explained what we're looking for and she said she'd try to help. Seems like she wants to talk about what happened, her husband's death and her decision to sell the microprocessor business and move to Macau.'

'Like a last catharsis to cleanse herself of those bad things?'

'I suppose so. I'll try to get as much information as I can, documents, whatever she has that might help us. I'll call you again tomorrow when I know what's available.'

Jenny thought for a moment. 'I don't think you should tell her about the cyber-attack, Patrice. It won't help, and the shock might endanger her health. We don't want her blaming herself because her company is being used for such an awful purpose. Just stick to the ownership angle, I'm sure it will be sufficient.'

They said goodbye and she checked the time. It was just coming up to eight, and she heard Encarni's cheerful '*Buenos dias*, Jenny.' She called Coetzee, it was the same time in Joburg and he would be waiting for her news.

Zurich, Switzerland

'*Sehr gut. Das sind gute Neuigkeiten.* That's good news. When will Shanghai send it out? A few days, excellent.' Max Oberhart was listening to his son's latest report from Dubai. 'I'll pass the message on to Julius at Hai-Sat. He's getting impatient.'

He listened for a moment. 'Just sit tight and let's see how the launch goes. It's too early to make a move yet. We've waited a couple of years, a few days more won't make a difference now that we're so close. If it goes well, I'll set up a board meeting to agree on our strategy.'

Delmas, Mpumalanga, South Africa

'I'll only be here for a few days. Whatever they're going to do, they won't wait long. I'll call as soon as I know my plans.'

Leo was walking in the courtyard behind the farm in Delmas, trying to calm his mother down on the phone. Since Emma had learned the reason for his arrest, she'd worried constantly that something else would happen to him, remembering the story of his predecessor, Scotty. And she still remembered the trauma of the 2010 events in South Africa.

Coetzee came over to him. 'Ed's on the phone, you'd better listen.'

'I have to go, love you Mum.' He switched off and listened to the other call.

Ed was saying, 'First, they sent off the package last night with our original clean coding, so it looks like a two-stage process, and that gives us more time. Second, Sharif let something slip. You were right, he didn't put that cell in, it was done in Shanghai. Shen spun him some crap about being prepared for the next big breakthrough, bigger than ACRE, and Sharif believed him. And he got that A2 code from Shen. Problem is, he came in and heard us talking and knows I'm up to speed, so I'm not sure what to do next.'

'Did you ask Sharif about the hub network coordinates?'

'I didn't get the chance, but I'm pretty sure he won't know. Shen's the only person to have direct contact with Shanghai, he's their board guy and even Tom Connor gives him a free rein. Tom knows nothing about that cell, and neither does Daniel, they mentioned it the other day, but no one seems to know anything about it. That Chinese prick runs the show.'

'Ed, this is a really big deal, we're pretty sure that cell's in all the Lee-Win processors built over the last four years. So it's hundreds of millions of machines.'

'Shit, I don't fucking believe it; these bastards are planning a worldwide cyber-attack? What can I do to help? There must be something.'

'I spoke to Chillicott yesterday, and if we can identify the hub network access he'd have a go at hacking into it before the upload takes place. What do you think?'

'Maybe Sharif knows something. I'll try again to worm it out of him. I would check with Daniel as well, but he'd start to wonder what the hell's going on.'

'I'm sending you a copy of the cell S470 code, so you can run it on my network downstairs and see what happens. The processors stop working and the whole system shuts down after thirty seconds.'

'I'll take a look at it in the lab.' Ed stopped, an idea forming in his mind. 'Sharif must have received that code from Shen in some kind of digital form. Maybe there's some ID on the file, something that might lead us to the hub network. I'll see if I can get him to show it to me. What else?'

'Chillicott asked if you could get a photo of Elodie. They'd try to match it with their database. See if she's known.'

Ed's tone changed. 'OK, Lynne, I'll see if I can find some and we're on for nine tonight, right? Cool. Ciao, baby.' The phone went dead.

'Quick thinking. Shen probably came into the room.' Coetzee laughed, 'I like Ed. He's a complicated mix of back street cunning and naïve high-mindedness.'

'I just hope we're not getting him involved in something he can't handle. I don't want anything to happen to him or Lynne.'

'Abby's got an idea. Let's go back inside and hear what she has to say.'

They went into Coetzee's office, where his daughter was writing on the blackboard. Rod and Julia were there with Karen.

Abby said to the two employees, 'Listen up, guys. Dad wants us all to swear we'll keep this information amongst ourselves. It's a potentially devastating way of hacking into a system, and the fewer people who know about it the better. When we get through this, we all have to wipe everything from our systems, so nobody can try it again in the future. Agreed?'

They nodded in agreement and she pointed at the flow chart she'd drawn. 'What's going to happen here is that, first of all, they'll upload the upgraded firmware and the new ACRE to all the Lee-Win customers out there. When the users download the package, it will activate the connectivity modules and ACRE will take over the transmission management, and interconnect all their equipment in a mesh environment with the new firmware and encryption.'

'I wish I'd had you on my team at XPC, Abby,' Leo said. 'You've described the process just as it will happen, clear and concise.'

She blushed. 'I've had more time to think quietly about it while you've been rushing around. Anyway, I'm sure they'll want to know everything's functioning correctly before they send the A2 trigger.'

'Ed thinks the same, and I guess it's the only logical conclusion. It should give us a few days' extra time.'

'Then you think they'll send the trigger to override ACRE to decrypt all those networks?'

'I don't think that's the plan, Julia. ACRE's not just an encryption algorithm, it also creates a single line of communication from Lee-Win to every device that has their processors. It has to, to maintain encryption in the data flow across all the pieces of equipment.'

She showed the flow of communication on her diagram. 'What Leo designed here is brilliant, it's a totally ubiquitous way to remotely reach all kinds of systems and turn them into mesh networks, intercommunicating with ACRE via their connectivity modules.'

'You can replace "brilliant" with "terrifying". I've designed the most dangerous Internet threat in the world, now we've got to un-design it.'

Abby showed the continuation of the path. 'I'm sure they'll use ACRE to reach the cell we've been looking at and trigger it. But they're not going to override the encryption, that would be self-defeating, it would destroy their line of communication.'

Coetzee looked admiringly at his daughter. 'What do you think they'll do?'

'Just what we did. Close the network down, and keep it closed down with the constant trigger commands.'

'I don't follow.' Rod looked perplexed. 'What would be the point of that?'

'Because, the only purpose of hacking at this level, which is probably on the greatest scale we've ever witnessed, must be to use it for blackmail.'

'You mean, "Pay and we switch off the trigger, don't pay and we leave it on". Simple, but effective.'

'Maybe it's not paying, Rod. With those stakes, it could be political, or some kind of power grab, who knows.'

Coetzee said, 'I assume there's nothing we can do to change that cell? To somehow prevent it from receiving those instructions?'

'It's a physical cell, Dad. It acts the way it was built to act. Unless you can actually remove it from the card, it will always do what it's doing.'

Leo nodded his agreement. 'Our only chance is to work out how to override that command it triggers.'

Abby said, 'Rod, if we run it again and again for you, can you find where that shutdown function is? Where the handover from the cell goes to?'

'I can sure try, but I don't know how long it'll take. If Julia can give me a hand, we'll need to get back in the lab and set things up. Let's go, Jules.'

FORTY-SIX

Dubai, United Arab Emirates
Wednesday, 14 July 2017

Shen Fu Liáng was in his locked office, speaking in Russian on his encrypted mobile. 'If I get the upgrades deployed by Friday, how long do you need to upload the trigger?'

He listened for a moment. 'Sunday, that's his decision? OK, I'll be there on Friday evening. I'll text the flight details once I book the ticket. Send my driver to pick me up, I'll be shot, two long flights.'

He finished the call and pressed Elodie's number. 'I've spoken to Shanghai, but they don't seem to be in a hurry. I'm going to fly up there to kick their asses, I'm sure I can get them to launch by Friday. I'll tell Tom I have a Lee-Win board meeting and I can follow up on the deployment of the upgrades while I'm there. He'll be fine with it.'

She supressed an 'I told you so' remark. 'That's a marvellous idea. When will you go?'

'There's a flight at two-fifty tomorrow morning. It's a nine-hour flight, so I'll go first class and get some sleep. With the time difference, I'll be there by the afternoon to get things moving. I should be back in a couple of days, then we're off to Dublin. OK with you?'

'I'll miss you, that's all,' she lied. A couple of days without him would feel like a break from prison. The thought reminded her of Leo Stewart, and she wondered what had happened to him, where he was.

'I'll be home about seven. See you then.'

Shen went up to Tom's office and explained his plan. The CEO was all in favour of the trip, 'Good idea, remind them who's responsible for the on-time delivery. Nora can make your reservation, give you time to sort things out. I've got a few papers you can take up with you, save me the trouble of scanning them.'

After giving Nora instructions for the Emirates flight to Shanghai, Shen returned to his office and closed the door. He wrote a two-line message, encrypted it and sent it to an email address in China. Then he went online and booked first class on a China East flight from Shanghai to Moscow, leaving on Friday at one p.m., paying from his personal account. It was a ten-hour flight; with the time difference, he would be there by early evening. He texted the details in Russian to the number he'd called earlier.

Shen checked his watch. It was five-thirty. He went along to chat with Sharif before leaving, just to make sure he could still be relied on.

London, England

'Well, Ilona my dear, the whole world now knows that the mighty Russian Federation is rattling its sabres. Our leaders are becoming quite concerned at the president's intentions. Of course, that doesn't mean they'll actually do anything about it.' Dr Hugh Middleton was reading the *Daily Telegraph* reports of Russian troop and naval movements in Eastern Europe.

'You mean until it's too late, just like in my country.'

'Precisely. America is carrying out what they always refer to as "military exercises" in several NATO countries, but we are aware of their president's ambivalent attitude to that organisation, largely funded, as he points out, by the US. He may send out inflammatory tweets and make threatening speeches, but it remains to be seen what action he would actually take, or, more pertinently, be allowed to take. They've also announced a meeting of NATO members in Brussels this weekend, but I anticipate an abundance of rhetoric and an absence of decisions.'

'With twenty-eight member states, all with their own vested interests, it's not surprising. They're usually too late, too selfish or too disinterested to take a stand on any matter which might cause dissent.'

'Indeed. And even though Billy's suggestion of convening the UNSC seems to be gaining traction, I'm afraid indecision and vacillation have become the order of the day when faced with resolution and boldness. It has been ever thus since Reagan and Thatcher were no longer the leaders of our western world, alas.'

'And the Lee-Win global deployment is imminent. Do you really think there could be a connection between them?'

'I'm inclined to believe so, except for one peculiar fact. Lee-Win is a Chinese company, and this military threat is a typically Russian strategy. The 2011 Sino-Russian trade agreements were trumpeted as being the start of a long-lasting love story, but it's a very one-sided affair and I find it difficult to imagine our Chinese friends sticking out their necks to support Moscow in such a potentially damaging scenario. I don't suppose you've received any clarification of the ownership from your South African friend?'

'If you mean Marius Coetzee, he told me he expected news by tomorrow. Do you think that's the key?'

'Based on my interpretation of Mr Shen Fu Liáng's actions over the last several years, I'm quite certain the explanation lies in that single fact. I hope Mr Coetzee's expectations are fulfilled, or we may be facing a rather nasty global crisis which none of us will enjoy.

'By the way,' he went on, 'in that same vein, there's an interesting piece in the business news about cyber-warfare. Apparently, Lloyds of London, the insurance group, has calculated that a global cyber-attack, like the Lee-Win event we are anticipating, would cost the world governments over £50 billion. I'm not sure on what data they can possibly base such a calculation, but it will certainly be a world-shattering event if it is not nipped in the bud.'

'And that's just the financial cost, apart from the political and human disasters that would ensue.'

'Quite right, my dear. It also happens to be approximately the amount that our UK government threatens to spend to leave our European partners in first-class comfort.' He snorted in anger and turned the page of the newspaper, 'And I'm sure you're aware that two Republican Congressmen, Brad Sherman and Al Green (they sound like two jazz musicians), are trying to impeach President Trump for obstructing the investigation into Russian interference in the presidential election. The Democrats want to begin the hearings immediately, but the Republicans favour investigations into Hillary Clinton's emails. Billy Chillicott must be thrilled by these diversions. As the Chinese say, "May you live in interesting times".'

Ilona shook her head as she walked out of his office. *Sometimes I wonder what goes on in that mind of his.*

Dubai, United Arab Emirates

'He's going to Shanghai tonight to kick them up the backsides and get the upload deployed asap.' Elodie Delacroix was speaking on her second mobile phone.

She listened to the other person. 'Maybe tomorrow, definitely by Friday. I'll call you as soon as I get confirmation. Take care, talk soon.'

Delmas, Mpumalanga, South Africa

'Sharif just told me Shen's going to Shanghai tonight to follow up the deployment. He wants it done tomorrow.'

'Crap! Time's starting to get tight.' It was seven in the evening in Dubai, five in Delmas, and Leo and Coetzee were on the phone with Ed Muir.

'Did you test the network in the lab with that code I sent you?'

'Too bloody right. I've never seen anything like it. It would knock over every installation with Lee-Win kit inside. Cause bloody worldwide havoc. Have you made any progress on finding the default command?'

'A couple of the team are setting up a diagnostic programme to find it, but no luck so far. Abby thinks you're probably right, they'll send out the trigger after the clean uploads, so we might have more time than we thought. Did you get anything out of Sharif on the hub ID?'

'He's not very talkative. Shen must have promised him money and glory and he's fallen for it. He won't listen when I tell him why you were kicked into touch, says he lost confidence in you when you didn't come back to XPC. I asked him about the code, where he got it from, but he clammed up. I'll try again in the morning, but it's a long shot unless I can find a way to convince him of what's really going on. I'm still not sure about Daniel, he's a complicated guy to read. I'll get to him after Shen's gone, just to be sure.'

Coetzee interrupted the conversation. 'Ed, I've got the video of Angela confessing the full story about Shen and Elodie. The long one I showed you that night. If Shen's gone, you can show it to Tom Connor and Sharif tomorrow. That'll put the cat amongst the pigeons.'

'OK, great. But you're sure I should talk to Tom as well?'

'Certain. I didn't suggest it earlier because no one would have believed it, Shen had everyone under his thumb. Now he's gone, we can tell them both the truth. Don't forget, Tom knows you've been contacted by Chillicott, he must have suspected something but he didn't want to admit there's anything wrong. When he finds out his company's involved in a major global threat, he'll be shitting bullets, so will Sharif. If either of them knows the hub address they're bound to help us.'

'OK. Send the video to my personal email account. I'll tackle them with it first thing in the morning. See what we can get out of them. And I won't involve Daniel until we can work out whose side he's on, OK? Good luck with the diagnostics.'

Marbella, Spain

The temperature was now unbearably hot, and Jenny didn't feel up to going anywhere, or even leaving the cool, air-conditioned house to sit outside. Encarni had gone for the day and though she didn't have much of an appetite, she prepared a salad then sat in the kitchen to watch the two o'clock news on SKY.

The theme music came on with the headline, 'NATO Convenes Over Russian Troop and Fleet Movements'.

The reporter announced that an emergency meeting of NATO members had been convened for Saturday and Sunday in Brussels to discuss unusually high military activity around the Soviet borders. Live footage was shown of soldiers, ships and aircraft on the move, then a map with animated images showed how Russia's Eastern European neighbours were being surrounded by the relocated military presence.

A new headline came up, 'US Puts on a Show of Strength'.

Similar footage appeared of US aircraft, battleships and troops carrying out exercises in several NATO countries, the North Atlantic and North Sea. A photograph came up of Donald Trump with Andrzej Duda, the Polish president, taken during his visit to that country earlier in the month, followed by a clip of a Polish military parade with tanks, missiles and soldiers marching in front of a US general. The voiceover announced, 'SKY News has received unconfirmed reports that up to 50,000 troops, equipment, aircraft and other military support are on their way from the US to NATO countries with vulnerable borders adjacent to Russia.'

The camera panned back to the reporter, who said, 'After previous forays into Chechnya, Georgia and Ukraine, is Russia revealing new territorial ambitions? Or is this just the president flexing his muscles to remind us of his power. Can the US rely on its NATO partners to stand up against any further incursions into their regions? Whatever the reasons for Russia's power display, it's an impressive demonstration, and a terrifying one,' he finished dramatically.

Jenny poured herself a glass of water, remembering what Leo and Coetzee had told her about a possible XPC connection with

GRU. Thank God Patrice is in Hong Kong and Leo's in Joburg. They're both a long way from Russia, she reassured herself.

Delmas, Mpumalanga, South Africa

'It's impossible to see at the level of a single cell, so we've set up a test to measure the electric charge that's storing up in the processor when the cell gets hit by the trigger code. At a certain level it will trip the command to change the status. When that happens, I'll try to see what address that command is at. That's the hard part, it moves so fast I don't know if I can catch it before it closes down.' They were all back in the lab, where Rod and Julia had been working on various alternative methods to try to identify the shutdown command.

'Right, I'll send Sharif's instructions again. Here goes.' Leo hit *Enter.*

'OK, I can see the charge accumulating. Got it, the processor just moved into a different mode.' The network closed down again. 'Boy, that was really awesome, sabotage in action, real-time.' Rod chewed his finger nails nervously.

'Did you find it, the shutdown function?'

'No chance. I got the exact level of the accumulated charge at the change of mode, but I couldn't follow the path to the command. I'm never going to find it at that speed.'

'Leo, it doesn't say it has to be continuous, it could be sporadic. Every message creates a tiny charge and it accumulates over time.' Julia was rereading the UOM article on A2.

'OK, let's build it up gradually, slow the accumulation down. I'll send smaller bursts continuously.' Leo stopped sending the code and changed it to partially trigger the cell every few seconds. He hit *Enter* again.

'That's better, the charge is accumulating more slowly. It's almost there, coming, coming...' Rod stared intently at his monitor.

'Trigger! Where the hell did it go?' The system crashed again, and he turned away from his equipment. 'Sorry guys, I can't get a handle on it. Even though the charge is coming slower, when it hits the critical level it changes mode so fast I can't see where the command is sitting.'

'Let's give it another try,' Abby said. 'We have to find a way to prevent this attack. Lives might depend on us finding a way. Come on guys, keep trying.'

It was eleven that night when Coetzee's team finally admitted defeat and Leo broke up the session. 'That's enough for tonight. Maybe tomorrow will bring a breakthrough. We really need to find that son-of-a-bitch command.'

Dubai, United Arab Emirates

'Goodbye, darling, have a safe trip and hurry back. I'll miss you.' Elodie Delacroix kissed Shen and waved as the taxi drove away. It was midnight and cold outside. With a shiver, she closed the door, went into the bedroom and took out her mobile from the wardrobe. 'He's just left for Shanghai. Everything's going according to plan. No changes.' She listened for a moment. 'I can't wait. Talk soon, love you too.'

Elodie went into the kitchen. There was a bottle of Laurent Perrier in the fridge. She opened it and poured a glass. Switching on the television, she found *Marseille*, a French political drama series with Gerard Depardieu that she'd recorded from TFI. She put on the first episode and lay back comfortably on the settee. Lifting her drink in a toast, she said to herself, *Thank God for small mercies. Santé.*

FORTY-SEVEN

Dubai, United Arab Emirates
Thursday, 15 July 2017

'Take a look at this, Lynne.' Ed had found Coetzee's video in his Dropbox when he opened his laptop first thing that morning. He'd taken her to the cinema the previous evening and they'd spent the night at his apartment. It was her day off, and since the workload at XPC had suddenly been alleviated, they would have a leisurely breakfast together.

She sat by him on the couch and he started the clip. It was less than a minute long, but she was in tears when it finished. 'My God. I can't believe it. Those bastards blackmailed Angela into putting Leo in jail. What a pair of total shits.' Then, 'Where did you get the video? You must have known about this all along. Why didn't you tell me, don't you trust me?'

'Sure I do, but I didn't want you to worry about me after what happened to Leo and probably Scotty. I talked to Leo last night, and now Shen's gone, we don't think there's any danger.' He told her about Coetzee's visit, the potential cyber-attack and the mysterious call from Homeland Security.

'You mean this whole XPC business is a fake, and they've fooled you into helping to build some kind of secret weapon that the

Chinese are going to use to attack the world's computers? I thought Scousers were smarter than that.'

'That's what I thought, so don't rub it in. I'm still wondering how we all got fooled like this.'

'Who's this other man, Coetzee?'

'He's a close friend of Leo and his family in South Africa. He took the video and arranged Angela's escape to Brazil. He runs a cyber security business in Joburg, and that's where Leo is now.'

'Do you think Tom and Sharif are involved, or maybe that Daniel Oberhart, the Swiss guy? I don't trust that man, he's really weird.'

'We don't think so, but I've got to get them onside, that's why Marius sent me the video. We're hoping Sharif can help us to find a way of stopping whatever it is.'

'Well, I think you've all been pretty stupid to let that Chinese creep run rings around you like that.'

Ed unwrapped a pack of spearmint gum. 'Thanks Lynne, I need all the sympathy I can get.'

Dubai, United Arab Emirates

'She's lying, or there's got to be some mistake. I've known Shen for three years and you've known him just a few weeks. No way would he do anything like that.' Tom Connor had just watched the clip with Sharif and Ed. 'Where did you get that video?'

Ed gave them the same explanation he'd given Lynne earlier, adding, 'It was Shen who put him in prison, and we think he probably killed Scotty as well.'

'What are you talking about? That's a scandalous accusation. Scotty's death was an accident and there's no way Shen has done anything to harm XPC. This isn't the first time you've tried to slander his name, why the hell have you got it in for him?'

'OK, Tom, we'll do it the hard way. Tell him about cell S470C887,999, Sharif.'

The Pakistani squirmed on his seat. 'I don't know anything about it, I already told you that.'

'Wait, that's the cell Leo asked me about, right?'

'That's right, Tom. I want you to come down to the lab and Sharif will show you what happens when that cell is awakened. Then I'll tell you what it is and why it's there. I saw it for the first time yesterday, and it's fucking scary.'

Reluctantly, Tom accompanied him and Sharif down to the basement. Leo's network was still in place and Sharif ran his version of the upload. Thirty seconds later the system crashed.

Connor's face was a study in panic and fear. 'What happened? I thought the upload was one hundred per cent debugged.'

'That's not Leo's upload. It's a different version that contains extra code addressed to that cell, S470. It's a capacitor cell that accumulates electricity, then switches the processor to a different mode and shuts it down.'

'Where did they come from? I mean, the cell and the code?' Bewildered, he looked from one to the other.

Ed said nothing, and Sharif finally blurted out, 'They're both from Shanghai. The cell's not on my design, they add it to the card in China. Shen gave me the code to test it and told me it would be used for another major innovation. He said it would be as big as ACRE.'

'What the fuck? Lee-Win are modifying our processor in Shanghai with a cell that shuts the system down and we don't know why? And you've been testing it and didn't think it was important enough to tell me about it?' He looked at Sharif and raised his fist as if to strike him. Then he looked back at the silent network. 'When did you find this out, Ed?'

'Yesterday, when Leo got out of prison. That's the reason he left, he knew he was in danger here. He went down to Joburg to try to work out what's going on, and now we're all sure it's for a cyber-attack. We knew you wouldn't believe it, so he sent the video to me last night to convince you. He reckons that all the processors built in the last four years have got that cell incorporated.'

Tom's mind suddenly cleared. 'You think they're going to upload this version of the code instead of Leo's? But that means...'

'Armageddon, right. Remember Chillicott, the US general who called you? He's from Homeland Security and they're investigating Shen and his girlfriend, Elodie. This is a major threat Tom, and we're right in the middle of it.'

'Why the hell didn't anyone tell me what was going on? Sharif, I can't believe you've been plotting with Shen to undo everything we've been working for over the last three years.'

Ed grabbed Tom's arm. 'I tried to warn you about Shen last week and you weren't having any of it. I didn't know the full story then, otherwise I'd have made a lot more noise. And as far as Sharif's concerned, he's been duped just like the rest of us. Shen's the villain, not us. Now we have to help Leo and Coetzee sort it out.'

The CEO looked frantically around the room, as if he didn't know where he was. He went to the door. 'No, Ed. I have to call Han Wang Tāng, the MD in Shanghai. Find out what the hell's going on up there. We've got to make sure they don't send out this version of the upload. If anyone can help us to fix it, he can.'

Ed grabbed his arm. 'Whoa. Hang on, Tom. Shen might be with him now, we can't let him know we're onto him. And both the processor card and the code have been changed by Lee-Win, so someone there must have authorised it, and it must come from high up. We reckon they'll send out our clean upload first and we've probably got a few days before the trigger code goes out. If you call Tāng and he's working with Shen, they'll make sure they send it out right away and we're screwed.'

'Jesus Christ! I don't know what the hell to do. Sharif, why in hell were you testing a code from Shen on a cell that you didn't design? It must have been obvious something was going on.' Now Tom was convinced, and he was scared. This threat had been developed on his watch, by his team and under his responsibility.

'Ed's right. I didn't know any of this, I swear. Shen fooled me like he fooled everyone. I'm sorry, I've been an idiot. I just wanted to achieve something for myself. Scotty and Leo were brilliant and I just wanted to get some credit, to show I was as good as them.' Tears came to Sharif's eyes and he turned away.

'Guys, there's no point in going over it again and again, it's all history now. What we've got to do is help Leo to sort it out. Do you know the hub address they'll use for the upload?'

'You mean they can hack into it and change the code?'

'That's the only chance we've got, but it's a long shot.'

'I've never seen any of the coordinates from Shanghai.' The CEO shook his head. 'I was just as stupid, I left all the Lee-Win relations to Shen. He's their board member, it never occurred to me.'

Sharif pulled himself together. 'Me neither. I've never had any contact with them, Shen never allowed it, he did all the communications.'

'How did you get the code from him?'

'On a flash drive. Scotty saw it just before… Shit, that's why he was killed. I told him it was just photos and music, but I know he didn't believe me.'

'Did you tell Shen about it?' Ed could see from the Pakistani's expression that he had.

Tom saw the expression too. 'My God! Shen… You really think that's what happened to Scotty?'

'Probably, Tom. I'm sorry, but there's no way you could have known.'

'That fucking devious, corrupt, murdering Chinese son of a bitch. I'd like to rip his throat out…'

'Join the queue, Tom, but we don't have time to talk about it now. Sharif, where's the stick? Does it have any other data that might help us?'

'Shen gave it back to me after… It's in my desk. Come on.'

Ed refrained from telling him how stupidly naïve he'd been, and they went up to his office. Sharif pushed the memory stick into the USB port of his laptop. 'There are two files on it. This one has the code I added to the upload.' He pointed the cursor at a text file named 'Sharif' and double-clicked to open up a sheet of coded instructions.

Ed explained to the CEO, 'See the last three lines of code? They're sending the same message thousands of times to that cell. That's what sets off the command to close the processor down.'

'And millions of Lee-Win customers around the world will download it, and governments, businesses and whole industries will stop working.' Tom put his face in his hands. 'Oh my God, how could I be so blind.'

'Wait, if they do it in two parts, we might have a chance. What's the other file, Sharif?'

'I don't know, it's an encrypted folder in Chinese and I can't open it. I don't know why it's on the stick.'

'It has to be connected in some way. Let's see.' Ed looked at the screen. The folder name was written in Chinese characters, 金路. 'It can only be for Shen.'

He clicked on it and a new panel came up with a picture of a silver key and more Chinese text, 回车键. A typing box was provided to enter the encryption key, and he knew he couldn't get past it.

'Dead end, at least for me. Encryption's not my thing.'

Tom Connor said, 'Can't you see from those lines of code where the cell is sending that command to?'

'It doesn't work like that. That code just charges the cell then we don't know what happens, it creates a physical switchover in the processor. Let's have a look at that code file again, we might get lucky.' Ed clicked on the file name, then opened up *Properties* on the screen. On the *General* page, the creation date of the file was 26 February 2017.

'That's the month before Shen gave it to me.' Sharif looked as if he wanted to sink through the floor.

Ed brought up the *Details* page. 'Well, well, very careless. Look, the author left his moniker, somebody called Hoi Wei. That definitely sounds Chinese to me.'

He removed the flash drive from the laptop. 'We know who wrote the A2 code and when, but we don't know what's in the other file, 'cos we can't bloody open it.'

'Leo's the king of encryption, Ed.'

'Just what I was thinking, Sharif. Plus, he's got some really switched-on ex-hackers down there. I'll send him the folder right away. See what he can do with it.'

The Pakistani grabbed Ed's shoulder. 'If Scotty died because of this, we have to stop it. I'll work all day and all night to help if I can.'

Delmas, Mpumalanga, South Africa

'Right, guys. We've got some decrypting to do.' Leo had just received the folder from Ed, with a note saying, 'This is from the flash drive Sharif got from Shen. The code was written in Feb 17 by a careless Chinese called Hoi Wei. We can't open the other file. Hope you can.'

He was with Abby and the team in the lab, having failed several more times to catch the elusive A2 command, and now all were resigned to it being impossible. The information from the memory stick might be their only chance of finding a way into Lee-Win's hub network.

'Does anybody here understand Chinese characters?' he asked Abby.

'I don't think so, but you can copy it into an online translation programme. Here, I'll do it.' A moment later, she said, 'OK, the first text means "Golden Path", and the other one just says "Enter Key".'

'Golden Path? So this might be about money after all. And who's this guy, Hoi Wei?'

'Leo, never mind about that, we don't have time. Just send the folder to Rod and Julia and we'll get started.'

Marbella, Spain

The email started, '*Good morning Jenny, greetings from Hong Kong.*' It was midday in Spain and Patrice's message had just arrived. Jenny put on her glasses and read the text.

'*Saw Mme Lee-Win this afternoon. Charming and elegant, you wouldn't know she's ill. Looks fine, but tires quickly. We talked for two hours, mainly about the death of her husband, Chongkun. In 2012 a Chinese man and a French woman came to see them, from a syndicate that wanted to buy the microprocessor business. The business was not for sale, but they returned and phoned several times, making new proposals, until she told them to go away and leave them alone. A few weeks later, Chongkun's car was hit by a lorry and he was crushed to death. The verdict was an accident, but she's sure (me too) that it was murder. The couple came repeatedly, until she was frightened for her sons and finally gave up and sold the business to them. It was handled by her lawyers and she can't remember the details. I'm coming back again tomorrow and one of her sons will be here from Macau, so I'll get the rest of the story and any available documents. Sorry, it's so difficult. Hope this helps. PM.'*

Jenny sent off a thank you note and called Marius Coetzee with the news. Maybe it would start to make sense for him, if not for her. She was still feeling under the weather, and went up to her room for a nap.

FORTY-EIGHT

Shanghai, People's Republic of China
Thursday, 15 July 2017

'We've done all the necessary tests and we're most satisfied with the results. The upload works efficiently, the download procedure is faultless and activates the connectivity module, and the new ACRE and Mark VII versions exceed our expectations. Your Dubai team has done great work, Shen, you must congratulate them for us.' The speaker was Han Wang Tāng, Managing Director and Head of Product Development at Lee-Win Micro-Technology, Shanghai.

'Thank you, Han, I'll do so. As you can now see, our concerns over the departure of Leo Stewart were unfounded. The other members of my group accomplished the work quickly and efficiently, and his absence caused us no disruption.'

The man sitting next to Han, Bohai Cheong, the company chairman, intervened. 'I wasn't aware of that, what exactly happened?'

Tāng responded, 'Tom Connor mentioned this matter to me, but I understood that Leo Stewart had taken just a few days off to rest and was then returning to supervise the final work programme. Was I wrong?'

'Unfortunately, yes. He left XPC last Friday and we don't know where he has gone. But it made no difference, the work was completed under my supervision and we delivered the final package ahead of time. I'm very proud of what we accomplished.'

'And so you should be, Shen. But I'm shocked to hear of the behaviour of that man, Stewart, a most irresponsible attitude. But thanks to you and your other colleagues, the project has been executed to perfection.'

Shen smiled modestly. 'I assume you'll be deploying the upload immediately?'

Mr Cheong said gravely, 'Tomorrow, July 16th, is the anniversary of the birth of our illustrious founder, Chongkun Lee-Win. He would have been sixty-five years of age, if his life had not been cruelly ended in the motor car accident five years ago. We will send out the upload tomorrow morning at eleven o'clock to honour him in the most appropriate manner we can. He was a great visionary, and we would not have the successful business and reputation we enjoy had it not been so. I am only sorry that he cannot be here to celebrate this great event with us. Our directors and staff will mark the occasion with two minutes of silence all together in the main hall.'

Shen listened to this eulogy, a solemn and respectful expression on his face. *At last,* he thought, *it's going out tomorrow morning. I fly to Moscow at one o'clock. Perfect timing.* Aloud he said, 'I am indeed fortunate to be able to join your memorial ceremony tomorrow morning, before I leave. Sadly, the great man is no longer here, but I am sure he is at the side of Buddha, looking down on us as he achieves nirvana.'

Cheong patted him on the shoulder. 'Thank you for those words, Shen. Sadly, you did not know Chongkun. He was a most extraordinary visionary and would have been proud of the way we have continued his great work. When the world sees what we have achieved, it will stop for a moment and marvel.'

It will most definitely stop, and perhaps for more than just a moment, he said to himself. *Let's hope it has the desired effect.* 'I'll call my office now and share this news with them and pass on your congratulations. I'm sure they'll respect that same two-minute silence in Dubai at the appropriate hour.'

He left the room and called Elodie. 'It's going out tomorrow at eleven o'clock, that's seven in the morning for you. I'll text you when it's done and we start receiving reports. I'm missing you, darling. Goodnight and dream sweet dreams, and you should wake up one step away from nirvana, as they say here.'

Next, he called the Moscow number. 'It's confirmed for tomorrow morning. I'll be there in the evening as arranged. Get everything ready for Sunday, we're on the final stretch.'

Shen went along to the canteen, where a group of techies were drinking sodas and talking. He was carrying his computer bag. He glanced over at one of them, a smartly dressed, tall, dark-skinned Chinese with a hair lip, then went to the elevator and pressed the button for the garage level. A few minutes later, the tall man came into the garage and got into a green Toyota. Shen waited a moment then got in the passenger seat. He took an envelope from his bag and handed it to him.

'Here you are, Hoi, the second instalment of your money. Five hundred notes of 200 Euros - 100,000 Euros. That's 150,000 altogether. You want to count them?'

The man shook his head. 'It's OK. If you want me to finish the job, it better be right. How will I collect the rest?'

'Don't worry, we're not dishonest people. I'll find you and you'll get the last hundred.'

He shrugged. 'I'll be around. What's the timetable?'

'You know it's eleven tomorrow morning for the Lee-Win upload. Yours is on Sunday, I'll be in Moscow and I'll text you. It'll be around midnight Moscow time. About five in the morning here, with the time difference. OK?'

'I'll be here before midnight just to be sure.'

As he moved to turn away, Shen grabbed his head and stared into his eyes. 'By the way, Hoi. I've never mentioned this before, but now is a good time. If you fulfil your duty, you'll be paid in full, as I've promised. But if for any reason the deployment fails, for any reason at all, your life and your family's lives will not be worth a single yen. The men behind this attack are the richest, most powerful, corrupt and ruthless in existence and they will find you wherever you try to hide. If anything goes wrong, that 150,000 Euros will buy you nothing but pain, misery and death. Understood?'

His face blanched and he pushed Shen away. 'Nothing will go wrong. I'll make quite sure of it.'

'Good. It's been a pleasure.' He climbed out of the car and went back into the elevator. This time he went straight up to the executive floor. Han Wang Tāng was still sitting with the chairman, and Shen said, 'I've just talked to Tom Connor in Dubai. He asked me to tell you they will be honoured to mark the deployment with two minutes silence tomorrow. It will be seven in the morning local time and everyone will be there to show their respects.'

'Thank you, Shen Fu Liáng. You are a truly devoted colleague,' Han replied, shaking him by the hand.

Dubai, United Arab Emirates

'Shen just confirmed the upload's scheduled for eleven o'clock tomorrow, Shanghai time. Is that what you were told?' Elodie Delacroix was talking on WhatsApp on her other phone.

She listened for a moment. 'Good, then we know it's definite. When will you deploy the trigger? Sunday, as we thought? I'd better get moving then, I don't want to be stuck here by myself when the chaos starts. They'll catch on pretty soon what's happening at XPC, and they'll be looking for scapegoats. I'll book a flight for tomorrow and text you the details. You'll come to meet me at the airport, right? *Fantastique*, I can't wait to see you, it's been too long. I'll dream about you tonight *chéri*, see you tomorrow.'

Elodie booked herself a first-class seat on a two o'clock Emirates flight, arriving in Moscow at six-thirty in the evening. She texted the flight number then went to run a bath. She poured in a double amount of her most expensive bath lotion and lay back, a glass of champagne in her hand, celebrating her masterful handling of the situation. By the time she was dressed and ready to go out, the bottle was empty.

Delmas, Mpumalanga, South Africa

Rod's finger ends were bitten to the quick. He looked at the others in despair. 'OK, I've tried all the tricks I know to break in and every connected word I can think of as a key: Lee-Win, XPC, Shen, Elodie, Sharif, ACRE, Trigger, Mark VII and dozens more. I even tried the cell number, and nothing works. I'm going to have to try to use brute force.'

'That could take forever, and the chance of cracking it is hundreds of millions to one. Has no one got a better idea?' Abby was feeling the pressure. Leo had come down looking for solutions, and so far they were having no success.

'How long will it take to set up?' Leo had never attempted a decryption by bombardment before.

'Maybe an hour to write the parameters. You can help me with them, suggest related fields and logical connections, that kind of thing. It opens up millions of potential keywords. Then my programme just starts sending them to the key field until it takes a liking to one and "Hey presto, open sesame".'

Coetzee said, 'OK, get started. Leo and I need to call General Chillicott to update him and see if he's got any news from his side.'

They left Rod and Julia and went into Coetzee's office. He asked, 'Have you seen the papers this morning?'

'Haven't had time. What's the latest bad news?'

He pointed at a front-page article from the previous day's *London Times*: 'NATO meeting convened as Russian military movements subject of concern at EU Conference'.

'Troops and ships moving into strategic places around Eastern Europe,' he commented. 'Could be Vladimir just flexing his muscles, or maybe something more serious.'

'Dad, we've got enough on our plate without worrying about Soviet plans to take over the world.'

Coetzee shrugged and looked at Leo, making as if to slap himself on the cheek. 'Sorry, Abby. We'll call Chillicott and hear what he has to say.'

After going through the security call-back process, the general's voice boomed out of the speakerphone. 'Gentlemen, got any good news for me? I sure could use some.'

Leo explained about the folder they'd received from Ed. 'It's encrypted in Chinese and we're trying to hack into it.'

'Everything falls into place,' Chillicott said. 'Lee-Win sets up Dubai, they hire Scotty then Leo, and you guys perfect that great encryption system. Shen sends the upload package to Shanghai and we believe they'll deploy a corrupted version in the form of a cyber-attack. And there's nothing we can do about it yet, because the package you sent up there is kosher and we've got no definite proof of anything bad happening at XPC. The whole thing's a perfect set-up. Have you made any progress on the source of funds for the Lee-Win buyout?'

Coetzee explained that a well-placed friend was with Mme Lee-Win in Hong Kong with that objective. 'We're expecting some news by tomorrow.'

'I'm crossing my fingers, guys. Let me know what you find out asap.'

Coetzee said, 'Can I ask a delicate question, General?'

'Fire away, Marius, and call me Billy. If we're gonna save the world, let's at least be on first name terms.'

'Ilona Tymoshenko mentioned something about a possible Moscow connection. Could that explain the military activity around Eastern Europe?'

There was a long silence, then, 'I didn't expect it to be so delicate, Marius. But the short answer is, we hope not.'

Coetzee looked at his daughter's shocked expression. 'Understood, Billy. Now we know what we're up against. Trust us, if there's a way to stop it, we'll find it.'

Dubai, United Arab Emirates

'Don't look now, but Elodie just came in.' It was ten p.m., and Ed and Lynne were in the bar at Club 27. It was starting to liven up on the dance floor, but the bar wasn't yet crowded.

'I see her. She's coming over. Shit, this could be embarrassing.' He stood up. 'Hi Elodie, having a night out on the tiles?'

She laughed loudly. 'When the cat's away, you know what happens. Hi, Lynne, mind if I ask you to keep me company?'

'Sit down, we wouldn't want you pining away for Shen all alone in your apartment. How about a glass of champagne?'

'Actually, I'd kill for a very dry martini.'

Ed went to the bar, and Elodie said, 'You two seem to be getting along very well. How long are you intending to stay in Dubai?'

'I don't really know. I like it here, but it's not a place for a normal life, at least not what I'd call normal.'

'I know what you mean, especially for a liberated woman, very complicated. And Ed? What about him?'

Lynne weighed her words. 'I suppose it depends on whether he continues at XPC or not. After everything that happened with Leo, and now they've finished the upgrade project, I don't know what he's going to do.'

Ed came back to the table. 'What who's going to do? You're talking about me behind my back?'

'Cheers.' They clinked glasses and chatted for a while. Elodie had obviously had a few drinks before arriving and was totally at ease in what should have been an awkward situation.

It's the elephant in the room, Ed thought. *We all know what happened, but no one wants to talk about it, and she doesn't care whether we know or not, because there's nothing we can do.*

He bought another round of drinks and whispered to Lynne, 'Let's find out about her and Shen.'

She said, innocently, 'What about you and Shen? You've been here for over two years, right? It's not exactly Brussels, is it?'

'That's not my favourite town, I don't miss it at all. I've been to lots of countries and cities and there's only one place I miss.'

She sipped her drink and didn't elaborate.

'Where did you guys meet? It's not obvious, a Chinaman and a Belgian lady. It must have been in some exotic location. Hawaii, Los Angeles, London, New York?'

'As a matter of fact, it's not exotic at all. Just my favourite place, the one I miss.'

They waited, but she still didn't disclose the location. Ed changed the subject. 'When's Shen back from Shanghai? I suppose the upload's scheduled pretty soon.'

'They're deploying it tomorrow morning at eleven o'clock. You XPC guys will be famous.' She threw back the rest of her martini. 'We should celebrate that, the champagne's on me.'

The waiter came over with a bottle of Laurent Perrier and poured three glasses. 'Cheers, here's to Scotty, Leo and Ed, a great team.' She emptied her glass and poured herself another.

'You forgot Shen and Sharif.' Lynne sipped her champagne.

'No, I didn't, I ignored them.' She laughed uproariously and downed her drink.

Ed looked at Lynne and shrugged his shoulders. 'She doesn't care,' he mouthed. Leaning over, he filled her glass. 'We should get a photo, to mark the occasion.'

'*Non, non*, I don't want a photo. I hate them.' Elodie tried to stand up and almost fell over.

'Come on, be a sport.' He called the waiter and gave him his mobile, sat between the two women, holding Elodie upright in her seat. 'We can call it "Scouser between Belgian and Welsh Roses". Right, here's to a great team.' They all lifted their glasses.

Ed took his phone and looked at the photos. The waiter had taken five shots and there were two with excellent likenesses of the Belgian woman in full face. 'I'll send them to your mobile now. What's your number?'

It was midnight when they poured Elodie into a cab, then they rode to Ed's flat on the Harley. He texted Leo, Chillicott and Tom Connor, *Upload expected this morning at eleven Shanghai time.* He cropped Elodie's image from one of the photos and enlarged it to give a clear full view of her, then sent it to the general.

Chillicott forwarded it to the UK, to be seen by Hugh Middleton when he arrived at his office in the morning.

Delmas, Mpumalanga, South Africa

Rod's brute force bombardment programme had been running for six hours, with no success. Abby called time, and they left it to hammer away at the key field until they came back to the lab the next morning. It wasn't looking good.

FORTY-NINE

Dubai, United Arab Emirates
Friday, 16 July 2017

Tom Connor hadn't slept at all, and was at XPC at six forty-five,
waiting nervously for Ed. They went down to the lab, and at seven
on the dot a message came up on the main system computer screen:
'New software is available from Lee-Win'. It was accompanied by the
usual certification, description of the upgrades and payment details.

'OK?' Ed looked at Tom and he nodded. The package took
several minutes to download, then he immediately ran Leo's mini-
network to test the ACRE encrypted transmission.

Sharif came into the lab. 'What's happening? Have we got the
new software?' he asked excitedly.

'We have, and it's exactly what we wrote and running flawlessly.
You, Scotty and Leo should be proud, it's beyond fabulous, a
terrific job.'

Sharif looked a little mollified. 'Thanks, and obviously you
were right. They're going to send out the other code later. We've
probably got a couple of days.'

Ed checked the time. 'We'll call Leo later to see if he's
made any progress, it's only five-thirty in the morning there.

I'm going down to talk to Daniel now, see if he can help with the hub problem.'

'Let's hope to God you can find a way in.' Tom went to his office. He felt helpless and stupid, and he didn't want to think about the consequences if they didn't find a way to stop the next upload. *In any case,* he thought, *I'm finished here whatever happens, and maybe XPC is. Better get ready to move on.*

Delmas, Mpumalanga, South Africa

It was six-thirty a.m., two and a half hours after the Shanghai deployment, when Coetzee joined Leo and the others in the lab. Rod's bombardment programme had been throwing millions of keywords at Sharif's folder for fifteen hours and it was still encrypted.

They saw the message from Lee-Win on Leo's laptop screen and downloaded the software. It worked perfectly on the mini-network, as it would in the millions of businesses around the world that received it.

While Abby was examining every detail of the download file, trying to find a way to reverse engineer into the hub, Leo showed Coetzee a two-word text he'd received in the night from Billy Chillicott: *Try Tsunami.* Neither understood the connection, but he said to Rod, 'Switch off your programme. Try putting in *Tsunami.*'

Rod looked sceptical as he typed the word in, then, 'I don't believe it. Where the hell did that come from?' The folder had opened, and inside was a text file with a Russian name: '**Код выключения**'. He clicked on the file and it revealed several lines of computer code written in English.

'It came direct from General Billy Chillicott, at US Homeland Security.' Leo ignored their querulous looks. 'You're the expert on A2, Julia. What do you think?'

'That's it. That's the A2 function. It basically says, "When cell S470C887,999 changes mode, shut down ACRE transmission until mode change."'

Abby looked up from her laptop. 'The translation of that Russian script is *Shutdown Code*.'

'And it does what it says on the box, but where Russia fits in this conundrum is still a mystery to me. OK, all we have to work out now is how to change that instruction and get it deployed to all the existing processors out there via the Lee-Win hub.'

'Sounds easy, Leo, except for two small problems. You can't change the properties of a physical cell, and we still don't know that address.' Abby had given up searching, there was no ID on the Lee-Win download.

'And we've got maybe two days to do it,' said Coetzee.

'We got this far in three days, we just need another break. I'll text Billy that it worked and it's in Russian. It might help him to help us.'

Dubai, United Arab Emirates

'It's every bit as good as we expected, well done Daniel.'

'I didn't have much to do with it. This XPC team did a great job, despite all the challenges they had. I still can't figure out what happened with Scotty and then Leo. A strange coincidence, but it's all worked out in the end. You're all set to go back to Hai-Sat.' Oberhart was speaking to his father Max, in Zurich, when Ed came into his office.

'I'll have to go now, talk to you later.' He put the phone down. 'Hi Ed, how's everything?'

'What do you think of the download?' Ed had come down hoping to find a route to identify the Lee-Win hub address.

'It's fabulous. I've been running it back and forwards, up and down, and it's as solid as a rock. Scotty, Leo and you guys did a marvellous job, well done.'

'Did Shen give you a copy of the package he sent to Shanghai?' Ed asked casually.

'He didn't have to. I've already got everything from the teams. All the testing and the final versions, Shen copied it all onto his laptop to send. And now I've got the downloads, I don't need anything else.'

'So you've got the hub coordinates?'

'No, I've never needed them. Shen handles all the communications with Shanghai. He's their board member, it's his prerogative. What's this about?'

Ed hesitated. He still wasn't sure about Oberhart, and Lynne had a perceptive woman's instincts about people. *But he seems sincere, and he might be the only guy with the answer. What the hell.* He decided to tell him the whole story, and show him the video and the effect of the A2 attack on Leo's network. 'There's something you should know about, Daniel, something to do with Shen,' he said.

Shanghai, People's Republic of China

'Thank you for your visit, Shen, and please remember to thank every member of the Dubai team for their remarkable work. As promised, we will be awarding a special bonus pool to reward them. Our finance director will be in touch with you and Tom Connor to arrange the payments.' Chairman Bohai Cheong and MD Han Wang Tāng bowed then waved as Shen Fu Liáng climbed into the company limousine and was driven off to Pudong International Airport.

The driver dropped him off at Terminal 2 for the Emirates flight back to Dubai. Then Shen took the shuttle bus to Terminal 1 in comfortable time for his one o'clock China Eastern flight to Moscow. A few hours of sleep on the ten-hour journey meant he'd arrive in good shape to finish the last item on his agenda. He accepted a glass of champagne from the cabin attendant, laid back in his seat and closed his eyes. Shen was pleased with his work. It had taken almost five years, but it was almost finished.

London, England

'Good morning, Ilona. How are you this morning?'

'Just fine, thank you, and I've got good news. The new Lee-Win software has been deployed from Shanghai.'

'So they finally managed to send it out, and with what consequences?'

'According to our IT manager, it works absolutely perfectly. No glitches or viruses.'

'So, the diabolical plan, if there is such a plan, must be to send out the virus later.'

'I suppose so. In any event, we don't have time to talk about that now.' She looked at her watch. 'You're a little late, you know you have an appointment at ten-thirty?'

'My taxi was involved in a traffic accident, a minor event, although I found it rather unpleasant.'

'What happened?'

'The driver of the car directly in front of us lost control and veered onto the crowded pavement.'

'How frightening. Was anyone hurt?'

'Fortunately not, but for a moment I imagined I was witnessing a car terrorist attack. There have been so many of them in recent months.'

'You must learn to control your fertile imagination. It's not always productive I'm afraid.'

He sat at the other side of her desk. 'You know I don't drive, don't you?'

She nodded, wondering where he was going with this line of thought.

'There are two reasons for that. The first is simply that I have a fear of travelling, and I can't bear the thought of setting off somewhere with myself in charge of the journey.' He ignored her astonished expression. 'The second is that I've always considered that a motorised vehicle is a lethal weapon, and that anyone in control of one is a potential murderer. I'm mortified that these recent lethal attacks have proved me right, and I fear that it will become the weapon of choice in the hands of these deranged terrorist assassins.'

Ilona thought about his words for a moment. 'For once, Hugh, I don't appreciate your lateral thinking. If everyone who drives a vehicle has the idea of using it as a lethal weapon, the world will be in even worse shape that it presently is.'

'Precisely.' He stood up. 'In any event, I hadn't forgotten my appointment, although I rather wish I had. You know how much I dislike these left-wing journalists and their rose-tinted views of a utopian socialist world.'

'I've sent you a couple of messages that I need an answer to, can you quickly look at them before the poor man arrives?'

Middleton went into his office and opened his laptop. Amongst the several messages, he spotted an email from Billy Chillicott, with the subject 'Elodie' and an attached photo. He double-clicked on the photo, looked at the enlarged likeness of the attractive woman on the screen and froze at his desk.

Dubai, United Arab Emirates

When Ed left him, Daniel Oberhart called his father back to tell him about the probable A2 attack. It was not an enjoyable call.

FIFTY

Dubai, United Arab Emirates
Friday, 16 July 2017

'We haven't been able to find anything on the hub ID. Sharif and I've taken the download data to pieces and there's no clue there. Daniel's here and he's been working with us. I've told him everything and he wants to help us screw Shen and his conspiracy.' Ed was in Tom Connor's office, on the phone with Leo. Sharif and the CEO were listening, as were Abby and Coetzee.

'Hi Daniel, glad to have you on board. I guess you're a bit shaken up by what was going on?'

The Swiss man appeared calm and collected, despite the overwhelming evidence of Shen's duplicity shown to him by Ed, but behind the controlled facade he was seething with rage and shock. He was furious to have been taken for a fool by someone he trusted, and even angrier to find XPC involved in a potentially catastrophic global cyber-attack. He'd already shared the news with his father at MicroCentral, knowing it could ruin their three years of planning and work, but he hid his feelings and said simply, 'You've been through a really crappy time, Leo, so don't shed any tears on my account. What exactly are we trying to do here?'

'We're trying to find an access to the Lee-Win hub, so we can somehow block the trigger download when Shen tries to send it. We've had no joy on that, but thanks to Billy Chillicott we've found the cell instructions.' Leo explained about Tsunami and the contents of the Russian-named file.

'First it's Chinese, now it's Russian? What's Shen got to do with Russia?' Ed was getting lost in the ever-changing events. 'Does it mean anything to you, Tom?'

'I've never heard of any Russian connection. Nothing at all. He was appointed to the Lee-Win board in Shanghai in 2012, after the company changed hands, and then he came down here just before we opened in 2014. That's all I know about him.'

'Chillicott said something about a possible connection with the Russian Secret Service, but I don't think it's a proven theory at the minute.' Leo shook his head in exasperation. 'OK, let's concentrate on the job in hand. Abby's people are working on changing the trigger code. But we need the hub coordinates. Come on, guys, there has to be a way to get them. Any thoughts, Daniel?'

'Shen sent the package from his laptop on Tuesday, with copies to no one, and he's taken it with him.' Daniel was quiet for a moment, then, 'He would have to send it from his XPC address and not his personal account. It's a highly valuable package of confidential software from XPC to its parent, so he'd have to present it correctly, otherwise the Lee-Win people would find it strange. If that's the case, we've got it right here on the company server. Everything he's ever officially sent to Shanghai or received from them. It's all there in the Cloud, the great big filing cabinet in the sky!'

Marbella, Spain

'Patrice, it's good to hear back from you. How is Madame Lee-Win?' Jenny had been dozing on the settee when her mobile rang.

'She's in fine form today, less tired. I think she felt more comfortable with Junjie, her eldest son, being there. He went through her old files and found a copy of the Sale & Purchase Agreement for the business in October 2012, and the bank statement with the payments received by her. It was a huge deal, $2.4 billion, in six payments, although Junjie says his mother reduced the price because she was so concerned about her family's safety. I won't waste your time on the phone, I'll scan extracts with the main items to you right now and you can go through them yourself. You know just as much as I do about such transactions nowadays.'

'Well, certainly not at that level, but the principles are the same. That's great, Patrice, many, many thanks. I'll keep you informed of our progress, assuming we can make any in this complicated business.'

'Is everything OK in Spain, Jenny? You sound a little tired.'

'I'm fine, thanks. Just didn't sleep well and it's unbearably hot here. Don't worry.'

He rang off and Jenny immediately called Leo. 'Patrice has received the documents concerning the Lee-Win sale. I'll forward whatever seems relevant as soon as I get them.'

'Great, tell Patrice I was wrong about him. Things are looking up, Aunt Jenny. We're working on a counter-measure for the next upload aimed at that cell, and they're searching for the Lee-Win hub coordinates on the XPC server. Marius says hI, and thanks.'

Dubai, United Arab Emirates

'There's a call for you on line one, Mr Connor.'

'I'm tied up right now, Nora. Who's calling?'

Ed Muir was with the CEO in his office. They were trying to decipher the conflicting information they'd found on the server concerning Shen Fu Liáng.

'It's Lee-Win, in Shanghai, Mr Han Wang Tāng.'

Connor looked at Ed, his eyes raised. *What next?* 'Put him through, please.'

After exchanging the usual polite Chinese introductions, the Lee-Win MD and Head of Development said, 'Tom Connor,

I am calling you at the request of our chairman, Mr Bohai Cheong, who is listening on the loudspeaker.'

Tom had only met the chairman once, when he'd taken the job, and knew he wasn't comfortable in English. 'It's an honour to have you on this call, Mr Chairman. How can I help you, Han?'

'You have already helped us more than we can acknowledge, Tom. As I said to Shen Fu Liáng this morning, your XPC team in Dubai has done a wonderful job. The new software is now in billions of our processors all over the world and the customer reaction is incredibly positive. Mr Cheong and I are aware that you have experienced several unfortunate events during the last few months, but you have overcome those problems and reinforced our global reputation once again. Thanks to you and your colleagues from everyone here at Lee-Win. Thank you, Tom.'

Connor was trying to find the right words to respond when the Chinaman went on, 'As you know, we sent out the upload at eleven o'clock this morning to respect the sixty-fifth birthday of our sadly deceased founder, Chongkun Lee-Win. Before leaving for his flight, Shen joined us for two minutes of silence at the celebration, and he advised us that your staff did the same thing in Dubai. Mr Cheong and I wish to thank you and your team members personally for your great endeavours, and for the respect and honour you have shown to the great Lee-Win tradition.'

Ed wrote on a sheet of paper, *Shen's gone? Where? Celebration?*

Tom shrugged and said, 'Han, Bohai, on behalf of our great team here at XPC, I thank you. Your call has given me enormous pleasure and I'll be sure to share your remarks with all of them.'

Han continued, 'We want you to share more than just our praise with your team. Next week you will receive a special bonus amount to distribute to everyone according to your own judgement. This is a more tangible way of showing our appreciation and gratitude.'

Ed wrote, *These guys may be clean??*

Tom managed to continue, 'I am so overwhelmed, I cannot find the words to express myself. With your permission, I'll call you back tomorrow when I have had time to appreciate this moment.'

The call ended in mutual thanks and congratulations, and he put the phone down. 'What the hell is going on?'

'You're learning how to be Chinese, that's what's going on. Well done, you gave nothing away. Now we have to work out what it all means. We still don't know who we can trust.'

'Where has Shen gone? I'm sure he's not returning to Dubai, he wouldn't dare.'

'Who was he flying with?'

'Probably Emirates. Company policy, best prices. I'll check with Nora.' Connor called his PA. 'He had an open return with them.'

'Let me take a look on your system.' Ed went online on Tom's laptop. 'If he left shortly after eleven, he would have had a flight in the early afternoon. All the Dubai flights leave in the early morning, that's out.' He kept checking, then looked at Tom. 'There's a flight to Moscow at one o'clock.'

Emirates Airline Terminal 3, Dubai

The Emirates flight attendant showed Elodie Delacroix to suite 1A, in the front of the Airbus A380, and placed her only piece of luggage, her wheelie bag, in the rack above. She'd been advised that morning that the software had been deployed successfully, so her job in the Emirates was over. She hadn't packed anything from the apartment, she wanted to forget Dubai, Shen and the last five years. Elodie was a beautiful, intelligent and experienced thirty-five-year-old woman. *It's time for me to start a brand-new life, without any baggage and with a big bank balance,* she said to herself. She settled down for the six-hour flight to Moscow with a glass of champagne. *Cheers. Here's to a well-earned five-year dividend.*

Dubai, United Arab Emirates

'We could have saved a lot of time if I'd thought of this earlier.' Ed was embarrassed he hadn't remembered that all their email correspondence was stored in the XPC server. Tom and Sharif were listening to the loudspeaker.

'We're rushing about like mad ferrets, so it's nobody's fault. Did you find what we need?'

'There's a whole raft of information on the server. Our upgrades package that Shen sent on Tuesday went to the Shanghai hub and I've got those coordinates, I'm sending them to you right now. Between us and Chillicott, we might be able to find a way in there.'

'That's cool. We'll get working on it right away.'

'Hang on, Leo. There's some weird stuff on there we can't figure out. Tom and Sharif are here with me.'

'We're getting good at doing weird. What is it this time?'

'First, as well as the official stuff Shen was sending to Han Wang Tāng, there were some encrypted messages to another address in China: hoi.wei@sina.com.'

'The guy who we think wrote the A2 code.'

'Exactly. Problem is, we can't see what they're about, the encryption is good, that's maybe why he risked sending from the XPC address.'

Coetzee said, 'Or maybe he just got careless when he thought everything was going so well.'

'Maybe, Marius, he's arrogant and stupid enough. Anyway, we didn't want to send them down to you, you've got enough on your plate.'

'Send them over, and Rod can have a look at them.' Leo added, 'He wrote a bombardment programme the other day, we might get lucky. Anything else?'

'This next piece is really weird. There's a file with a Russian name sent by Shen containing two unencrypted sheets of code. One looks like an early effort, and the other seems to be a corrected version. They're both marked up, not final, which might be why he didn't encrypt them, in case they got corrupted.'

'Did you translate the file name?'

'Sure did. It's called *Hub Manager*, but we haven't had time to try to rewrite the code to see what it does.'

'You think the guy at Lee-Win's been sending code to Shen, and he's been testing and correcting? I didn't think he had the capability.'

'It's not clear who was doing what, but that's not the point. The thing is, he didn't send them to Shanghai.'

'Where did they go to?'

'An address in Russia: patch@rostelcom.ru.'

Coetzee interjected again, 'Another Russian connection, that makes sense. But why would he send messages like this from XPC and not his personal address?'

'Marius, you know better than any of us that everybody makes a mistake some time or another, that's how criminals get caught. Remember?' Leo went on, 'And I guess you're right, Shen never expected anyone to catch on to him until it was too late.'

'Let's get back to the point, guys,' Tom Connor said. 'It looks like there's a definite Russian connection here and I've got some news that might confirm that.' He recounted his conversation with the Lee-Win senior management. 'We've checked the flights and Shen wasn't flying back to Dubai. My PA went around to their apartment and there's nobody there, it looks like Elodie's gone missing as well. Chances are they're meeting up somewhere, and we reckon it might be Moscow.'

Ed added, 'And it sounds like Lee-Win might be in the clear on all this, he was still lying to them today. Maybe they've been kept in the dark just like we have.'

'We're still making too many guesses,' Coetzee said. 'Send us everything you've got and Abby'll get the team working on it, see if we can find out anything more. We'll try to make sense of it, then have another talk.'

Delmas, Mpumalanga, South Africa

'Marius, Jenny just sent me the Lee-Win bank extracts with a note about Patrice's meeting with Mme Lee-Win. What do you want me to do with them?'

'Print them out and we'll have a look at them. And forward everything to General Chillicott, and to Ilona at Dr Middleton's office.'

Leo sent the files on, and while the documents were printing, he said, 'What do think about Shen going AWOL, and this Russian address he was sending stuff to?'

'I don't know, but I'm not surprised. Since we found that file with the Russian name I've been expecting something like this to turn up, Billy was already suspicious. We need to talk to him and Ilona as soon as they've had a chance to look at those documents.'

Abby came over. 'We've been testing our idea for the modified cell instruction, and it works. We can reconfigure it if we can get to it. But...'

'But? It sounds like there's a problem.'

'Not with that, it's something else. Rod's been hammering away at those email files Ed sent over, without much progress, but he's managed to open one file that wasn't properly encrypted. It's a message in Chinese that Shen sent to the hoi.wei address on Wednesday.'

'That's when he left for Shanghai.'

'Right. I think he must have sent it in a hurry. Either that or he thought he'd won and was just getting careless. The translation is, "Expected Sunday, 12 p.m."'

'And your interpretation is?'

'We're wondering if Shen's communications with that Russian *patch* address and this guy Hoi in Shanghai are linked. If Shen's now in Moscow, that *Hub Manager* code might mean the trigger will go out from Russia via Shanghai, on Sunday at midnight.'

'Have you been able to run the code?'

'It's a mess, Leo. We have to reconstitute it to find out what it does, and we haven't had the time yet.'

Coetzee put his arm around her shoulders. 'That's a pretty clever theory, Abby. It fits the facts pretty well. Unfortunately, it's just a theory, and we've no way of validating it without more information.'

'That's the whole problem.' Leo shook his head. 'There's still so many unknowns, and we can't be expected to work it all out without some professional help. I think it's time Homeland Security got involved. We've got to improve our chances of success.'

'Do you want us to try to sort out that code now?'

'You've all been here since dawn, Rod and Julia must be exhausted. If you've finished the work on the cell, send them home. We can start in the morning, fresh and alert.' Coetzee stood up and stretched. 'We'll see what these printouts tell us, then call Billy. It's time he got off the pot. If he can't get the US intelligence machine cranked up over everything we've discovered, then the world's a much less safe place than I'd like. Leo, can you send him an up-to-date summary so he gets up to speed? Then we'll see if he can walk the walk.' He gathered up the documents and went into his office.

'How's it going, Marius?'

'It's going well, Karen, thanks to these brilliant kids. The problem is, I don't know where the hell it's going to end up.'

Marbella, Spain

It was a scorching day and Jenny still wasn't feeling well, which was unusual for her. She had a headache and was feeling tired and listless. The prospect of a cool, shady corner in her little garden in Ipswich beckoned, and she decided to return to England. There was nothing further she could do in Marbella. Patrice had done his bit to help Leo and Coetzee, she just hoped they could use the information to stop whatever it was Shen Fu Liáng was planning. And she decided to have a stern word with her nephew when she got the chance, she didn't like his line of business.

She went online and found a last-minute flight for London the following afternoon. Jenny was looking forward to getting home.

FIFTY-ONE

**London, England
Friday, 16 July 2017**

Ilona Tymoshenko called on the phone. 'It's General Chillicott on the line, with Mr Coetzee and Leo Stewart. Do you want to speak to them, or should I?'

Hugh Middleton had managed to recover from the shock of seeing that face on his computer screen. His interview with the journalist had helped, he'd enjoyed the opportunity to refute the man's basic premise, that the Internet was a government tool introduced by the Conservative Party to create a right-wing fascist dictatorship in the UK.

Since then, he and Ilona had studied the documents sent by Patrice, via Jenny and Coetzee. The sale and purchase agreement told them nothing more than they already knew, the myriad of offshore, onshore and proxy companies behind the acquisition. The bank statements showed the names of six companies, each transferring $400 million on 20 October 2012 to the BIP in Hong Kong for Mme Lee-Win. Middleton remembered Jenny Bishop's comment about the price having been reduced. *They probably forced her to take a bargain offer,* he reflected. The statements gave no details of the names or account numbers of the transferring banks.

'Typical,' Ilona said. 'The less money you've got, the more details you have to provide, even for small bank payments. Obviously, that's not the case if you're a billionaire making huge transfers. Mind you, in 2012 there wasn't so much information provided on bank statements as nowadays.' She immediately sent copies to her friend, Ilya Pavlychko, in Kiev, who promised to pass on any information he could glean from his sources.

Now, Middleton was faced with a new problem: he couldn't let Marius Coetzee hear his voice. He replied, 'Since you have now effectively taken over the investigation, with the assistance of your Ukranian ex-colleague, I think it would be better for you to handle the conversation. I'll listen on the speaker and intervene if necessary.'

She took the call. 'Good afternoon, gentlemen. Dr Middleton is busy, but he's listening in his office.'

'Hi, guys. First off, listen up, Leo. We did a limited download of the Lee-Win ACRE software, and I just got confirmation from our IT folk that it was one hundred per cent OK. You guys at XPC wrote some pretty awesome technology, our people love it.'

'It also confirms our theory about the second upload, Billy.'

'I know. I've had to tell my folks about that, 'cos we've got thousands of machines with those processors, so we'd be a massive target. That's why we downloaded only to non-essential networks until we see what's going to happen. We still have no real proof of anything, but I've got people looking at different scenarios to find a solution.'

'Thanks General, that's good to hear. Between us we've got a lot of smart brains focused on the problem.'

'I just hope they work something out. Anyway, do you have any news for me, Ilona?'

After explaining that Ilya was looking into the bank accounts, she added, 'I suppose you noticed that the six payments came from companies who are not listed anywhere as shareholders or proxies?'

'You bet we noticed. That just might mean we have a better chance of tracking them down if we can find the banks that made the payments. It's easy to set up anonymous hundred-dollar proxy outfits, but hiding huge payments is more difficult.'

'That's why I asked Ilya to look at them. They have a team of forensic banking experts. And all the companies have English names, so he's filtering his search parameters.'

Leo interrupted, 'There's some things you don't know, Ilona.' He brought her up-to-date on the Tsunami file and the hub coordinates found by Ed. 'And there's some emails to a guy called Hoi Wei, in China, mentioning Sunday twelve p.m. We're assuming he's Shen's accomplice in Shanghai. But the text file on the stick is called *Shutdown Code*, in Russian, not Chinese. There's also emails and software coding, called *Hub Manager*, sent to an address in Russia. And it looks like Lee-Win's people are in the clear and Shen may have done a runner to Moscow. There's definitely some kind of Russian link here, but we can't work out what.'

Ilona thought quickly. *That name, 'Tsunami', has cropped up in both Chillicott's and Leo's investigations. There has to be a connection.* Dr Middleton wasn't in the room to countermand her, and for some reason he didn't want to speak to Coetzee or Leo. She decided to tell them everything they suspected about Tsunami, GRU, the death of Shen's Chinese family and him possibly inheriting two fortunes.

There was a long silence on the line, then Coetzee said, 'So, Dr Middleton's theory is that Shen killed his Chinese family to increase his inheritance from his Russian father, then used his fortune to acquire Lee-Win. The purchase was related to GRU, through this Tsunami person, and they're now planning a global cyber-attack. This is linked to the Russian military moves around the Soviet satellite countries, and the beneficiary of this whole complicated conspiracy is going to be Mother Russia, getting her children back?'

'It's starting to make sense, Marius, listen up. We've got Russian connections on all sides of the equation now. Tsunami and Shen arranged Chongkun's death to acquire Lee-Win. He set up XPC as a camouflage in Dubai to develop malicious software, and he's been sending files to Russia to create a cyber-threat via that software. The Lee-Win people have been hoodwinked, just like XPC was.

It looks like the whole Shanghai thing is a red herring to frame China, and the strings are being pulled in Moscow, by some very high-up people.'

'I get the logic, Billy. But why the hell would Shen go to these lengths, investing probably hundreds of millions of dollars into Lee-Win and spending five years of his life preparing a cyber-attack that could start a third world war? If Dr Middleton's right, he's already got more money than he knows what to do with. What's in it for him? Why would he help Russia take back its territories, and set up this whole imbroglio just to frame China for the attack?'

Lord Arthur Dudley, alias Dr Hugh Middleton, could no longer restrain himself. He pressed the speaker button and said, 'Because he was the second son.'

Moscow, Russian Federation

It was seven p.m. local time when the young woman walked out of the arrivals hall at Moscow Domodedovo International Airport. She waved to a man wearing a cashmere overcoat and fedora waiting near the exit door, and he walked across to meet her. 'My darling Tsunami. It's been months since I held you.' He took her in his arms and kissed her passionately.

'Piotr, *mon chéri*. I've missed you so much, I promise I won't leave you again.'

She took his arm and they walked across the hall. 'Is everything in place?'

'Everything is arranged. By Monday, it will all be over.'

'And that idiot Shen doesn't have a clue what's happening. I almost feel sorry for him, he's going to be so disappointed.'

'Don't think about him, think about us. Come, the car is waiting.' General Piotr Gavrikov escorted Elodie Delacroix out of the building to a Mercedes-Benz S 600 bulletproof limousine flying a red, white and blue pennant, the flag of the Russian Federation. He helped her into the spacious interior, and the car pulled away towards the expressway and the city of Moscow.

London, England

'I've received a reply from Ilya Pavlychko. Do you want to see it?' Ilona asked Dr Middleton.

'That was impressively fast.'

'I know, Ilya's people seem to know everything about Russian banks. I suspect they've got a team of informers working in them.'

'You suspect, or you know?' She didn't reply, and he asked, 'Is it conclusive, or does it require what you call my lateral thinking?'

'Here.' She plopped two sheets of A4 paper on his desk.

'Hmm, this is most informative. Behind the companies mentioned on the bank statements are six charitable trusts, based in the Cayman Islands, named "Golden Path", I to VI.'

'That's the name on the folder that Shen gave to Sharif.'

'It had not escaped my notice, my dear. What is fascinating is that each of the six payments to Mme Lee-Win's Hong Kong account transited through the Moscow Trade & Kreditbank. As Ilya points out, that is one of the Kremlin's banks of choice for, let us say, confidential transactions.'

'You mean, government business?'

'Exactly. I'm reliably informed that the oligarchs do a lot of "government business" through MTK. I wonder if that's the link we're looking for?'

'The oligarchs?'

'Time will tell. Have you considered one other aspect of this affair, Ilona?'

'Probably not, I've been too busy. What is it?'

'Simply this. The acquisition of Lee-Win was actually a commercially brilliant strategy, as can be seen by the success of the new software. There is a veritable flood of news items, tweets and messages about it online and in the evening paper. I have no doubt that the value of the company has greatly improved as a result of this development. And you will remember that Mme Lee-Win reduced the sales price due to the threatening circumstances at the time. The purchasers have hedged their bets very well.'

'A good point, but it doesn't help us to uncover their identity.'

'You are, as usual, correct, and I am digressing. Can you forward your note to Billy and get him on the telephone as quickly as possible? And please send a suitable note of gratitude to Pan Ilya, he is a veritable treasure trove of knowledge.'

Marbella, Spain

Jenny went to bed at seven. She'd made a light supper, but had no appetite when she sat down alone at the table. After one glass of Ribuero del Duero, she could hardly keep her eyes open and went upstairs. She tossed and turned for a long while, her mind going back over the recent events; Leo, Emma, Coetzee, the XPC problem and Patrice in Shanghai. When she finally fell asleep, she didn't have one of her strange dreams, but her sleep wasn't as restful as usual.

US Homeland Security Headquarters, Washington DC

'Looks like we're getting somewhere, Hugh. Well done to you guys.'

'Not guilty, Billy. All due to Ilona and her friend Ilya, who discovered the six trusts. They are uncovering the truth layer by layer. It seems there is no limit to Shen Fu Liáng's duplicity.'

'The guy sure turns out to be a bigger can of worms than we expected. This is one of the smartest fit-ups I've ever seen.'

'Nevertheless, our friends in South Africa believe they can thwart the attack with some help from you.'

'I know. Marius Coetzee thinks it might be possible to rejig the trigger code. He suggested that if they can't work out how to hack into the hub, maybe we could talk Lee-Win into letting us access it, but you and I know there's no way I can get that to fly.'

'Diplomatically unlikely, I agree. Meanwhile, the Soviets continue to move their pieces around the chess board with impunity. I'm surprised you're not attending the NATO meeting?'

'Truth is, Hugh, if the shit hits the fan, I'm more useful here in Washington than with those politicians in Brussels. I hate to say it, but NATO is not what it was when I was young and ambitious. I don't expect much from that conference except newspaper headlines.'

'On this point, Ilona and I agree, NATO is in a state of disarray, vulnerable to a strong and decisive move to destabilise its member states. And all of our recent information suggests that the cyber-attack discovered by Leo will come from Russia, who will use it to blackmail their territories back to recreate the USSR. This attack is now a clear and present danger.'

'I think you've hit it on the button. Everything points to a Russian power play that's taken five years to gestate, starting with the takeover of Lee-Win by these six trusts. But we still don't know who owns them.'

'Our belief is that behind them you will find five oligarchs, plus Shen Fu Liáng.'

'I can see why you'd say that, Hugh, if the plan is to grab big chunks of the repossessed territories. But you're still pissing in the dark. Sorry, Ilona.'

'We shall ignore that mental image. In any event, we shall remain so, unless you consider you now have enough proof to look at your files and see who are behind those trusts?'

The American's guffaw roared from the loudspeaker. 'What makes you think we've got stuff in Washington on innocent-looking Cayman Island trusts?'

Ilona and Middleton stayed silent, and Chillicott finally said, 'OK, I think the case is strong enough to take it to the top. I'll get back to you tomorrow. I'm not promising anything, but I'll see what I can find.'

'Thank you, Billy, you're a credit to UK–US collaboration. Long may it continue.'

London, England

At six-thirty p.m., UK time, Ilona Tymoshenko was still in her office, sorting out her emails and thinking about the day's events. She'd called Marius Coetzee and updated him on their conversation with General Chillicott, although she still wasn't confident it would produce anything concrete they could act on. Now, she was reflecting on Hugh Middleton's lack of reaction to one event that morning. As an ex-official at the Security Service of Ukraine, Ilona was suspicious both by nature and formation. She had been copied on Chillicott's email and knew that Hugh had received the photo of Elodie Delacroix, who might possibly be the mystery person, Tsunami, but he hadn't mentioned it. That wasn't normal. Hugh never missed a chance to show off his superior intellect with a sarcastic or witty remark. *Another secret,* she wondered, *possibly connected to Leo Stewart?*

Ilona went to her file of contacts in the western security agencies. If the woman was some kind of Chinese or Russian agent, as they believed, there must be a dossier on her somewhere. *She's supposed to be Belgian,* she remembered, and found the name of Chief Inspector Lucas Meyer, head of the Antwerp SICAD, the Communication and Information Service of the district of Antwerp.

Meyer had been her Belgian contact in 2008, when she had investigated a diamond smuggling operation on behalf of the Security Service of Ukraine. Three high-ranking justice officials had been arrested on corruption charges involving government contracts, and had apparently been paid off with millions of dollars in uncut diamonds. Information from the whistle-blower pointed to Antwerp as the marketplace for the stones. For once, international police coordination had been successful, and the stones were impounded, the officials convicted and everyone involved was congratulated.

CI Meyer didn't answer her call and Ilona left a voice message, hoping he would remember her. Fifteen minutes later, he rang back. He was still in charge of the SICAD and remembered exactly where and when they'd worked together. After exchanging the usual platitudes, she told him a fictitious story about checking out a prospective business partner, and he agreed to put Elodie's photograph through their facial recognition system. If her image was in any European database, they had a good chance of identifying her. She thanked him and sent the photo across, wondering if her action constituted deceitfulness toward her senior partner. Once again she decided, *There's no room for secrets between partners.*

FIFTY-TWO

Delmas, Mpumalanga, South Africa
Saturday, 17 July 2017

'Good morning, Abby. You're up with the larks.'

At six a.m., Leo was trying to fit in an hour's training. It was several days since he'd exercised his body and he was feeling stale and lethargic. He'd fastened an old, hard mattress against a wooden door in the courtyard and was punching and kicking his way to a healthy state of mind.

'You're not the only one who needs a workout. I've been locked indoors for weeks. It might be good for our brains, but not our bodies.' Laying a blanket on the grass, she started stretching, prior to some Pilates exercises and a few minutes of yoga. Abby was wearing shorts and a bikini top, she looked a picture of health, slim and supple, a glowing sheen on her brown skin.

They worked out in silence for fifteen minutes, then Leo threw his soaked cotton T-shirt aside and continued his assault on the mattress.

Abby positioned herself so she could sneak glances at his muscular frame pivoting gracefully back and forwards. 'I didn't know you were an adept. When did you take it up?'

'About five years ago. After I came down here on holiday.'

'Seems like a lifetime ago. Then you went to the States and made your name.'

'Some name. I was lucky enough to be offered a great job. Anyway, how about you? I never thought you'd get involved in IT. Didn't seem like your thing.'

'She did it to help my business and my life, Leo.' Coetzee had come out of the house with a mug of coffee. 'Now, it looks like it's time to help the world. Come on kids, breakfast time, then we've got stuff to do.'

Moscow, Russian Federation

Shen stayed under the shower for five minutes. The water was hot and crystal clear, unlike the sometimes lukewarm, cloudy liquid from the taps in the Emirates apartment. He'd slept like a baby for eight hours and felt on top of the world. There was a pot of breakfast tea in his room when he came out of the bathroom and he poured himself a cup. Looking out the window at the woods surrounding his house in Rublyovka, the most expensive suburb of Moscow, Shen felt as if he'd finally come off a treadmill that he'd been on for the last five years. He felt at one with himself and with the world.

His mother Olga and sister Annika were in the breakfast room when he went down, and they fussed over him as if he was still a teenager. Annika was unmarried, and she and her mother adored their adopted brother and son. They enjoyed a leisurely breakfast filled with stories of government corruption, local scandals and struggling billionaires, then Shen stood up from the table. 'I've got a few things to do. I'll be on the phone in my office and come down later for coffee.'

'Grigori, darling, I thought you'd retired from Lee-Win and come home to run the family businesses?'

'Don't worry, Annika. By Monday, I won't have anything to do. You and mother make a list for me and I promise to get started.'

Moscow, Russian Federation

Elodie's phone woke her at nine a.m. After the most passionate night she'd enjoyed for a long time, she had slept like a baby and felt wonderful.

She heard Shen's voice. 'Good morning, darling, did I wake you?'

Clearing her fogged brain, she said, 'Of course not, it's ten in the morning here. I was just making another cup of coffee, but you're not here to have it with me. I'm missing you.'

'Just a few days and I'll see you. You know the upload was successful?'

'I never doubted it,' she lied. 'You were in charge and it went perfectly. Well done, *mon chéri*. Will the trigger command go out tomorrow?'

'More likely on Sunday, I'm staying in Shanghai to make sure. But it's time for you to get out of Dubai before the shit hits the fan. I can't come back there, and I think you should go straight to Dublin. I'll join you there on Monday.'

Elodie was immediately suspicious. She was supposed to be dumping him, not the other way around. 'Then I won't see you before getting to Ireland?'

'You'll have time to make sure everything is OK at the apartment. Get in more champagne and caviar, fill it with flowers.'

'Well, if you say so. I'll book the flights now and be there when you arrive.' *Some chance*, she said to herself. 'Are you certain we'll be finally through this whole five-year struggle, with our pay-off?'

'Don't worry, by Monday you'll be rich and we'll be as free as two birds.' He liked the metaphor. *Two separate birds*, he thought, *but I'll finally be free of the past.*

Delmas, Mpumalanga, South Africa

'What do you think of Dr Middleton's theory about Shen's second-son complex?' Coetzee was having breakfast with his family and Leo.

'Am I allowed to know what it is?' Karen didn't know what he was talking about.

After he managed to explain it to her over the interruptions from the others, she said, 'I can understand Dr Middleton's point of view. That poor man, Shen, being kicked out of his family and his country like an illegal immigrant. If you had that kind of money, wouldn't you do anything to get your own back? Who's this Dr Middleton, by the way?'

'He and his partner, Ilona, head up a cyber security company in London, very tight with US Homeland Security. It's funny,' Coetzee mused, 'he didn't say much, but I was almost sure I knew him. I seemed to recognise his voice, but I just couldn't place it. Anyway, he seems pretty bright, so if we suppose the theory's right, and that Russian *Hub Manager* code seems to confirm that, it means Shen's going to deploy the trigger from Moscow via Shanghai. How would he do that?'

'If the Lee-Win people are in the clear, he couldn't have set up a transit facility on their hub without their knowledge, so he'll need someone, a physical person, to do it. It has to go out from the Shanghai hub, with their signature, otherwise the download will be refused by the customer networks.' Abby described the problem.

'So, this Hoi Wei that he's been writing to is his accomplice in Shanghai, and he's going to receive the trigger update and send it out from there.'

'Logically, yes. That's why Shen's in Moscow now, if we're right about that. Wei's his mole in Shanghai.'

Leo swore in frustration. 'That means we've been spinning our wheels looking at ways to hack into the Lee-Win hub. If the upload's going to be sent out from Moscow via Shanghai, it will be gone before we could touch it. We would have to actually bring down the hub, knock it over, to prevent the trigger going out.'

'Problem is,' Abby mused out loud, 'how do they keep sending it? If they're in the clear, the people in Shanghai are bound to spot it, and when they do, they can just switch it off. I still don't get how it works.'

'Maybe they're not in the clear after all, but whatever's going on, time's really short. If Shen's in Moscow, it must be ready to send out, so we're probably right about Sunday at midnight.'

'He must be completely mad.' Karen shivered.

'He might be, but he's not acting alone. I'm sure Middleton's right. He thinks it's about money and power, as usual. Chillicott's finally going to look for the owners behind those trusts. Middleton and Ilona are betting they're oligarchs, investing alongside Shen to pick up the pieces when the USSR is reconstituted.'

'That makes sense, there'll be chaos in those countries and that means rich pickings.'

Abby frowned. 'But even if General Chillicott finds the truth, it doesn't help us stop the Moscow-Shanghai deployment.'

'I have a feeling that he's not in a position to act directly. Politically, I mean. He's leaving it to us.'

'In that case, Dad, we've got to get into Shanghai ourselves to derail the upload. But how?'

Abby was quiet while Coetzee and Leo talked the problem over, then she asked, 'What was the name of Jenny's banker who sent the documents from Hong Kong?'

'Patrice de Moncrieff, French guy. He's kind of part of the family in Marbella. I never liked him much, but he's delivered the goods this time.'

'You told me he met with Mme Lee-Win and her son, right?'

'Junjie, yes. Patrice went to her house and met them there.'

'Did he tell them what this is all about? I mean the cyber-attack?'

'No. Jenny specifically told him not to, because she's ill and it wouldn't be fair to upset her. What's your point?'

'Is he still there?'

'You mean Patrice? I don't know. Aunt Jenny probably knows. Why?'

'Wait, last question. How long is the flight time from Hong Kong to Shanghai?'

'I'll check.' He looked it up on his phone. 'It's about two and a half hours. Now, what's the interrogation for?'

'Ed told us the Lee-Win board have huge respect for Chongkun, the founder, they even dedicated the upload to him. If they're not involved in the conspiracy, I'm sure they'd listen to his son and help us find this Hoi Wei, and maybe prevent the trigger upload.'

Coetzee said, 'You mean, Patrice and Junjie should go to Shanghai to talk to the Lee-Win board?'

'That's a great idea, Abby. I'll ask Aunt Jenny to call him, see if he's up for it.'

'Wait on, Leo, not so fast,' she said. 'There are a few problems. Chillicott has produced nothing to confirm a Russian involvement, and Patrice hasn't told Junjie about the cyber-attack. It'll be a huge shock to him and we don't want his mother to know about it. And if the board members really are clean, they'll know nothing about any of this either. It's not the kind of thing you can explain or demonstrate from a distance. They'd need to see Leo's network shutdown to understand the potential catastrophe they'd be involved in.'

'So, we need someone who can explain it and show them what's going to happen?'

'Exactly.'

Everyone looked at Leo.

He said, 'OK, guys, I get it. You're right, as usual. I'll check the flights to Hong Kong. I'd better get moving, time's short.'

Moscow, Russian Federation

'Shen's at his home in Rublyovka, pretending to be in Shanghai, and you're in my apartment in Moscow, pretending to be in Dubai. It's like one of those farces you French people love.' Elodie was on the phone with Piotr Gavrikov at his office in the GRU headquarters.

'I suppose it is, but I have to keep it up until Monday. Why can't you send out the trigger command today, and get it over with?'

'It comes from the very top. Vladimir wants to do it in the middle of the night on a Sunday, while most of the world leaders are asleep or having dinner and can't get hold of their staff. I actually agree with him, it will create more panic when they're woken up to mayhem and start running around like headless chickens.'

'So, it's midnight on Sunday and that's final?'

'You're worrying about your paycheque on Monday, right?'

'Should I be?'

'Have I ever let you down, Tsunami? If the boss and his friends get what they want, we'll all be buying big fancy houses in the sun.'

General Gavrikov called Shen's mobile. 'It's fixed for midnight on Sunday. I'll expect you at eleven. Is your man primed and ready?'

'Midnight, that's what I told him, no problem. I'll confirm it with him again to be sure.'

'OK. One final rehearsal tomorrow afternoon, and it better be perfect. No mistakes, Shen, or we're all history. Understood?'

'Don't worry, Piotr. Monday will be a great day for the New Russian Federation.'

Shen texted Hoi at Lee-Win, *Confirmed midnight Sunday, five a.m. your time.*

FIFTY-THREE

Malaga, Spain
Saturday, 17 July 2017

It was another very hot day, and Juan was driving Jenny to the airport for her two o'clock flight to London. She was still feeling off-colour, suffering from the oppressive heat, looking forward to escaping the Spanish summer temperatures and cooling down at home in Ipswich. Her phone rang as they were leaving the highway. It was Leo. 'Hi, Aunt Jenny, where are you?'

'On my way to the airport to go back to London, it's too hot for me in Marbella. What's new?'

'Is Patrice still in Hong Kong?'

She thought for a moment. 'I would think he'll stay for a few more days, he went on bank business, but with the Lee-Win problem he hasn't had time to do anything. Why?'

Leo explained their theory and Abby's suggestion. 'Do you think he'd go to Shanghai with me, and maybe talk Junjie into coming? I've got a flight to Hong Kong at five-twenty, arriving just after midday tomorrow, local time. It's only two and a half hours from there to Shanghai and there's lots of flights. We think the trigger command will be sent out at midnight tomorrow, so if we get a quick connection we could get there in time to stop this Hoi Wei character and convince Lee-Win to hijack the Moscow update and kill the deployment.'

'I see.' Jenny decided to defer the telling-off she'd been preparing for her nephew. 'OK, I'll call him now and ask him to wait for you and talk to Junjie. If he can go, I'll tell him to book connecting flights for all of you. Text me your flight details and I'll get hold of him before I leave Malaga.'

O. R. Tambo International Airport, Johannesburg, South Africa

Leo went early to the airport and had lunch while waiting for his flight. With all the rush to organise his flights and departure, he hadn't eaten any breakfast. He called his mother to let her know what was happening.

'I'm at the airport on my way to Shanghai,' he answered to her first question, then related the morning's happenings, ticking them off in his mind as he brought her up-to-date.

Jenny had texted that Patrice would meet him at Hong Kong airport when he arrived at midday the next day. He'd booked three seats on a flight to Shanghai at three-twenty, getting in at six-ten. He confirmed that Junjie would join them, which would give them the credibility they needed.

Coetzee had asked Tom Connor to contact Han Wang Tāng to arrange a meeting for them with the Lee-Win board. Tāng had been reluctant when the CEO told him that Leo was coming, and especially when he heard the real reasons for him leaving XPC, but when he knew that Junjie Lee-Win would be with him, he finally agreed to go into the office to receive them at seven o'clock. That gave them just five hours to convince the Chinese of the imminent catastrophe and to access the hub.

Emma listened in silence until he'd finished, then she said, 'Is it dangerous?'

'Maybe if I was going to Moscow, but not Shanghai. They'll be just as keen as us to kill the upload and it's their hub, so I should be able to access it and sort it out before Shen sends his code over. Don't worry, Mum, I'll be with Patrice in China and the bad guys are in Russia.'

He managed to calm Emma's fears and she wished him luck and said goodbye, but Leo wasn't as confident as he had sounded. On the plus side, he had everything he needed in his laptop and carry-on bag to demonstrate the A2 shutdown code, and hopefully convince them to prevent the hub deployment. Middleton's assessment of Shen Fu Liáng's psychological condition, and the documents about his background he'd received and printed out from Ilona, would help him explain the Chinaman's role in the deception. Billy Chillicott's account of the Soviet military strategy meant he could describe exactly what a devastating blow the attack would be to global stability and security. And with Junjie's help, he could probably convince them of the circumstances of their founder's death.

But there were two big negatives. He knew nothing about Shen's accomplice, Hoi Wei, who somehow had to be neutralised. And even though he felt fairly certain the Lee-Win board members were not involved in the conspiracy, if he was wrong he might walk into an ambush. And what he couldn't yet show, the key to the whole conspiracy, were the faces behind the plot. Who had invested almost $2.5 billion to acquire Lee-Win and spent five years in a bid to recreate the USSR and reap even more billions in the process? He couldn't prove who actually owned their company, who the Lee-Win directors were really working for, if they didn't already know. He prayed that Chillicott would turn up some names for them, and fast.

His last call was to Ed Muire, to bring him up-to-date and ask him to share the news with Tom Connor. For once, Ed listened to the plan in silence, then he just said, 'Be careful, Leo.'

Moscow, Russian Federation

General Piotr Gavrikov was in a meeting room in the Kremlin building in Red Square with five other men. Three of them were dressed in smart, expensive suits, one was wearing torn jeans and a sweatshirt, and the fifth looked as if he was still on his yacht, in deck shoes, white trousers and a blue and white striped T-shirt.

He didn't comment on their dress sense. Worth $30 billion between them, they could afford to look the way they wanted. They'd spent the last two hours discussing a list of prime industries, government services and businesses in the countries that interested them. Now they moved on to the execution of their five-year plan.

'It's definitely tomorrow night, you're sure?' the smartly dressed Ukrainian asked.

'At midnight, exactly. Vladimir insisted on that.'

'There's no way it can go wrong? Technically, I mean?'

'We've run it again and again between our own hubs. I'll get one last demonstration tomorrow, but it's a thousand per cent OK. It knocks everything out like getting hit by both Klitschko brothers.'

'And your guys, the military, they're all in place?'

'There's enough ground troops on every border to quell any local resistance. Admiral Bolotnikov says the fleet positioning will be in place to back up the threat, and General Zhigunov will have a dozen squadrons over their airspace immediately after the cyber-attack. NATO will do nothing except call for meetings and it'll be a fait accompli in a couple of days.'

Gavrikov continued, 'I'm having a last session with them tomorrow to ensure they're all one hundred and fifty per cent ready. But in my opinion, it won't be necessary. If our targets want their governments and industries operating again, they'll just have to toe the line. There'll be insurgent resistance for a while, but we're used to dealing with that.

'By the way,' he continued, 'have you seen all the publicity around Lee-Win since the new software was deployed? As well as the primary objective of this operation, it looks like we could make a fortune from the sale of the company. It's being touted as the leading semiconductor business in the world. I was right, it'll be worth billions more than we paid.'

'You mean "more than *we* paid", Piotr. But it's a good point, we have to decide what to do with it when this project is finished. I just hope it's still worth at least what it cost.'

'OK, last item.' The man in jeans from St Petersburg spoke. 'We should talk about the Chinese who thinks he's a Russian.'

'Shen Fu Liáng?' He laughed, 'Or Grigori Vedeneyev, as he likes to be known in Moscow. He'll send the trigger update to his mole at Lee-Win, then he's expendable. All we need to agree on is what happens to him.'

'You mean what does he get for removing the old man from the scene and working for us for five years, while screwing your girlfriend?'

Gavrikov smiled uncomfortably. *Thank God they don't know about Shen's family's 'accident', they'd be really worried about their homicidal partner.* 'When this is done, everyone's expendable, including her. I think the Tsunami programme has run its course. Unless you've got other ideas?'

'We should get rid of them both, they're not part of the club. We've put up a shitload of money and now she'll want a place at the table when the dividend is due, but I'm not feeling generous. As for Liáng,' he laughed and looked around at the others. 'That guy is a gullible idiot. Why would he think that hating the Chinese would make him a Russian? Once a Chinese, always a Chinese, you can't change your skin because you were born in the wrong place at the wrong time. We won't need him, and we won't need Tsunami any more.'

'You're saying it's a one-fifth share for each of us, instead of one-sixth? I'm cool with that. Piotr can earn his commission by removing the both of them.' The Chechnyan in the Giorgio Armani linen outfit put his hand out. 'Agreed?'

'*Soglasovano*, agreed.' The men around the table joined their right hands in a handshake with their left hands on top.

Enviously, Piotr Gavrikov watched them leave. *If this works*, he said to himself, *I won't just be watching them from the outside, I'll be on the inside, mixing with the oligarchs.*

Dubai, United Arab Emirates

Tom Connor said, 'I'm not sure I like the sound of this.'

Sharif and Daniel were in his office, and Ed had explained Leo's plan to them, emphasising that Patrice and Junjie would be with him, trying to make it sound as simple and safe as he could.

'Thing is,' he replied, 'there's nothing we can do about it from here. Leo's right, it has to be sorted in Shanghai, and he's probably the only guy who knows enough to get it done. Plus, he's got the founder's son with him, that should count for a lot.'

'I should talk to Tāng again, explain what we suspect, prepare the ground for him. He and Cheong seemed to be on the up and up when they called, I can't believe they're involved in this business.'

'I'm sorry, Tom, but I don't agree. We still don't know for sure who are the good guys and bad guys up there, and we can't take the risk of harming Leo's chances. Anyway, he's on his way there right now, so my vote is we leave it to him and the others to do their best.'

Daniel spoke up, 'I agree with Ed. We don't have enough information to take any decision here. He'll be the man on the spot and he's smart enough to handle things without our interference. We should let him get on with it.'

Finally, Tom agreed to wait for further news, but he wasn't happy with the situation.

Oberhart went to his office to call his father in Zurich. 'Looks like there might be a chance of avoiding the trigger upload. I'll keep you informed.'

FIFTY-FOUR

Ipswich, England
Saturday, 17 July 2017

It was a warm evening, but compared to Marbella it seemed positively fresh and cool to Jenny. Still feeling tired and a little sickly, she wondered if she'd picked up a bug in Spain and resolved to pay a visit to her doctor in London if she didn't shake it off soon. In the back of her mind, Jenny realised it might simply be a delayed reaction to her break-up with Bill Redman. While in Spain, she'd kept herself too busy to think about her own situation, and she was still trying to do the same. It had been painful, but hopes of a new life with the banker were gradually fading from her mind.

She was sitting in her garden with a sandwich and a cup of tea when her sister called her on FaceTime.

'I hear Patrice worked miracles in Hong Kong.'

'He was brilliant. With hardly any notice he was on a plane, and then found out everything we needed just in time. I was really impressed with his family commitment.'

'It must be nice to have all these international bankers around at your beck and call.'

Jenny laughed and avoided the subject. 'What's the latest news, I've lost touch a bit.'

'I had a chat earlier with Leo. Thanks to your infuriating efficiency, he's on his way to Hong Kong to meet with Patrice and Junjie. They're flying straight to Shanghai to meet the Lee-Win board and try to prevent the download, or upload, or whatever you call it. Apparently the Chinese were duped by Shen like everyone else.'

Jenny was relieved, her arrangements seemed to be working out. 'How much time do they have? Leo said they were under the cosh.'

'They found some kind of message that mentioned midnight tomorrow. He's hoping to get there by seven in the evening, they're seven hours ahead over there.'

'They'll only have five hours? My God, that's much too tight for comfort. I hope they can pull it off. That cyber-attack will cause chaos if it's not stopped. Marius told me the Russians have already got their forces in position to grab back the ex-USSR regions. The western powers won't know what's hit them.'

'They'll think it was a joint attack by China and Russia, a new détente between them to change the balance of power in the world. There'll be a massive retaliation and we'll end up in World War III. It doesn't bear thinking about.'

Jenny put on a confident tone. 'I'm sure Leo will be up to the task and find a way of preventing the attack. If not, don't forget, we're talking about countries a long way away which don't affect us here at all.'

'Well, I suppose there's nothing we can do except "lie back and think of England", as we used to say. Speaking of which, how are things progressing with Bill?'

'Sorry, Emma. There's the house phone ringing. I'll call you back later or tomorrow. Love you, bye.' She put her mobile down and drank a swallow of the now lukewarm tea. *Not a good day to share bad news*, she thought. *It'll keep.*

* * *

Jenny sat thinking about their conversation, and she wasn't happy. She hadn't been entirely honest with her sister, not what she'd said about the international threat and potential consequences, but what she hadn't said: about the risks of Leo's position. He was in China, a far-away, savage country he didn't know, with a company whose director had put him in prison in Dubai, where he would still be festering without the intervention of Marius Coetzee. The man responsible was determined to deploy this devastating cyber-attack and Leo was going to go head-to-head with him to prevent it.

The dream she'd had a week ago came back to her, the woman and the Chinese man dressed as a sheikh. After Leo's incarceration and then release, she'd assumed the couple must be Angela da Sousa and Shen Fu Liáng, but now she wasn't so certain. Worrying thoughts flitted through her mind, shadowy faces she couldn't pin down. She knew there had to be other players in the background. *It's not all as it seems, it can't be, it never is.*

Jenny went online and checked out a number of alternatives, then confirmed the most suitable. She picked up her mobile and made a call.

Delmas, Mpumalanga, South Africa

'How are you, Jenny? I hear you've been busy, and effective, as usual.' Coetzee listened for a while, interspersing her monologue with comments like, 'I see. Maybe. You could be right. You think so? Fair enough.'

After several minutes of this, he said, 'You're right. I should have thought of that. What do you want me to do?'

He listened again and looked at his watch. 'Why am I not surprised? OK, text me the details and I'll get moving. Take care, and I'll get back to you asap. Meanwhile, can you call Dr Middleton's office and update them on Leo's meeting in Shanghai? Thanks.'

Coetzee went into the kitchen to negotiate with Karen. He hated these difficult discussions.

FIFTY-FIVE

**Hong Kong International Airport
Sunday, 18 July 2017**

'Patrice, great to see you again. Thanks for staying on and organising this trip.'

'You're looking well Leo, despite everything. Let me introduce a new friend, Mr Junjie Chongkun Lee-Win. He's agreed to go up to Shanghai with us.'

The Chinese man standing next to him was almost as tall as Leo. He bowed low then shook his hand. 'Leo Stewart, I am happy to meet you, and to help you if I can to save my father's illustrious reputation and our family name.'

'Nǐ hǎo ma? How do you do?' Leo bowed in turn. 'It's an honour to meet you, Junjie, thank you for coming on such short notice.'

'You speak Chinese?'

Leo laughed. 'You just heard my entire vocabulary. I speak three words of several languages, not exactly multi-lingual.'

'Let's get something to eat and you can give us the full story while we wait for our flight.' Patrice led the way to the VIP lounge. It was almost one p.m. local time in Hong Kong and their connection to Shanghai was at three-twenty. They settled down and Leo launched into his narrative, keeping the others' rapt attention for almost an hour.

'So, we're missing one last piece of the puzzle. The names of the people behind this plot, Shen Fu Liáng's partners.'

'The people you think murdered my father and stole our company. It seems my mother was right all along.'

'Probably, Junjie. We think they killed Scotty Fitzgerald as well, the guy who took over the ACRE development. Your father would have admired his work, but he was in the way, like I was. Only I was lucky enough to get out alive.'

'Do you know the Lee-Win board members personally, well enough to convince them of the truth and to take action?' Patrice asked.

'Some of them, but not all,' Junjie reflected. 'There are only five active members, all the others are lawyers. Han Wang Tāng is the managing director, he worked for my father, he's a clever man, helped him to invent the ACRE concept. They were a great team and I know he's still devoted to my family. Bohai Cheong is older, an influential businessman who came in as chairman after the acquisition. He was a close friend of my parents and has an honest reputation, but I don't know him well. Two of the others were also in my father's team and I think they'll listen, but they don't have a lot of influence. Then there's Liáng, who seems to be the mastermind behind this whole plan.'

'If we've guessed right, he won't be there. We know he left Shanghai and didn't go to Dubai, so chances are he's in Moscow.'

'They're calling our flight. We'll see what we find at Lee-Win in a few hours.'

London, England

'I had to call in some serious favours to see these files, Hugh. When I tell you the names, you'll understand why. Like we already figured out, there's dozens of camouflage proxy companies and trusts all over the place, but they made a mistake. Those six charitable trusts are the loophole and I can tell you who are the real money people behind those payments. The guys who really own Lee-Win along with Shen Fu Liáng.'

'It sounds as if our modest predictions have been validated. Please end the unbearable suspense and reveal all.'

Dr Hugh Middleton and Ilona Tymoshenko had come into the office on a Sunday, in the hope that they would get this call from General Chillicott. Besides which, they still hadn't caught up on her list of outstanding matters.

'First off, as usual, you didn't get this information from me. Understood?'

He didn't wait for their agreement, and slowly and distinctly pronounced six names, the last being Shen Fu Liáng.

Ilona was the first to comment. 'It reads like a dinner invitation to the president's five closest friends. I wonder how Shen managed to be the sixth at the table?'

'That still remains to be ascertained, my dear. For the moment, I believe General Chillicott has provided the evidence that young Leo Stewart will require in Shanghai. I haven't yet informed you of this Billy, but Jenny Bishop called Ilona with the news that the Lee-Win board has agreed to receive a contingent of Leo, his banker friend Patrice and Chongkun's son, Junjie, this evening. They're all scheduled to arrive in Shanghai for the meeting in a short while.' Once again, Middleton had difficulty in believing he was on the same side as Jenny Bishop and her nephew.

'That's great news, well done Leo. If the names of these characters don't convince the Chinese to help them, nothing will. I hear their people were worried enough about the Russkies' military intentions to send someone to listen in at the NATO meeting in Brussels last night.'

'Speaking of which, did you have any success in convincing the UNSC to convene to discuss that unusual Russian military activity?'

'I'm still working on it. You know as well as I do how tough it is to get them to do anything except fly around the world making photo-stops in airports.'

Ilona interrupted what she considered to be their idle chat. She wanted to get home and enjoy what was left of her Sunday. 'I'll make a list of these names with photos and a brief description and send them to Leo right away. Thank you, General Chillicott.'

'You guys did more than I did, Ilona, so I guess it's thanks all round. Let me know as soon as there's anything new.'

Dubai, United Arab Emirates

Although he didn't have a lot to do, it was a working day, and Ed Muire was in his office at XPC when he got a call from Abby.

'Hi, Ed, I think I've made a bit of a break-through, how the Russians keep up the triggering without the Lee-Win people seeing it. It's the *Hub Manager* code Shen was exchanging with Moscow. I don't know who wrote it, maybe he was only testing it and it wasn't finished. But I managed to get my head around the changes and produce a final version, and it's pretty neat code. It's a handover of an upload from one hub to another. I tried it out on Leo's network; sent it out from one hub via a second one, and when it was in shutdown mode, I got it to automatically hand the signal back to the first hub to keep sending the trigger signal and maintain the shutdown. Once the code was downloaded, the devices accepted the trigger transmissions from the first hub and the second hub couldn't override it.'

'That's pretty smart, I've never heard of anything like that. Well done you. So, Shen sends the A2 trigger upload from Moscow via the Shanghai hub, and when it's accepted as genuine, that guy Hoi passes the control back to him in Moscow to keep sending it.'

'Not quite. I don't think Hoi actually does anything, because he doesn't have the code, probably to prevent him from trying to blackmail them or something like that. His job is simply to receive the upload and send it out to the regional hubs. Then the control automatically switches back to Moscow and the trigger keeps going out from there until they stop it. Now I understand how they can keep up the threat without Lee-Win seeing it and switching it off.

And why they'd send it from Moscow in the first place. The Lee-Win people must know nothing about this, the automatic handover explains everything.'

'Sounds like you're right on the button. What does your father say about it?'

'He's not here. I was busy reprogramming and he rushed off somewhere without saying goodbye. But I'm pretty sure we know what's going to happen now.'

'Did you find a way to rewrite it, override the trigger function?'

'That was the easy part. We just changed the address from the S470 cell to a different cell and it has no effect on the network at all.'

'Duh!' He laughed. 'Wish I'd been smart enough to think of that. But you can still only do it by accessing the Lee-Win hub?'

'That's right. We still depend on Leo getting into that hub. And there's something else I was wondering. There's five hours' difference between Moscow and Shanghai. That message to Hoi Wei said only Sunday 12 p.m. It didn't specify where.'

'That's five in the morning in Shanghai, a lot more time. He may not have thought of that with all the flying around between time zones. Better drop him a mail, so he's prepared for the two options.'

'Sure. And I'll send him this handover file, so he knows we've confirmed our theory. I'll copy you on it and I'll keep thinking about it. Thanks, Ed.' She was about to ring off, then asked, 'Do you think Leo's in danger over there?'

Ed said nothing for a moment. He was just as worried as Abby. 'It sounded to me as if the Lee-Win people were genuinely in the dark about Shen, so if they can clobber Hoi Wei, the mole, Leo shouldn't be in any real danger. Anyway, I heard about his reaction to danger from a Polish guy called Oskar who was in the prison with him.'

'And?'

'I wouldn't like to meet him on a dark street corner.'

'Really?' Abby tried to imagine what that meant. She rang off, Ed wondering whether he should be worried more about Leo, or Abby.

Shanghai, People's Republic of China

For reasons best known to China Eastern Airways, flight 720 arrived thirty minutes late at Pudong Airport and, thanks to the permanent traffic jam on the S1 into the city, it was seven-thirty in the evening when the three men walked into the Lee-Win building near Century Park in central Shanghai. Although it was a Sunday, the offices were open, employees rushing busily around the enormous entrance and corridors. A security officer took them up to the twentieth floor, where they waited the obligatory fifteen minutes in a luxuriously furnished conference room.

Leo was looking at his phone. He'd received two new messages, from Abby and Ilona. He asked the receptionist for the WiFi password and brought them up on his laptop. Abby had sent him the rewritten *Hub Manager* file with an explanation of the handover process. He read her description of the process then skimmed through the completed code. Shaking his head in admiration, he said out loud, 'Brilliant woman!'

He explained the software to the others. 'I figure that must mean the senior Lee-Win people are not involved,' he told them. 'They won't even know what's going on in their hub, because the control will revert to Moscow to keep the shutdown in place until Shen gets whatever it is he wants.'

'That's good news.' Junjie looked relieved. 'I couldn't believe my father's friends and colleagues would damage his reputation in this way.'

'And it makes our job a lot easier,' Patrice added.

The second message contained Ilona's list with photos of the oligarchs behind the Lee-Win acquisition. The names meant nothing to him, but the others sat back in amazement when he showed them.

'This is being planned from the very top,' the Frenchman said. 'These are five of the wealthiest and most powerful men in Russia, and amongst the president's closest allies. They're playing for very high stakes.'

'So, Dr Middleton was right again. It's all about money and power.'

'And that's why my father was murdered. If he had agreed to sell, he would still be alive today. These men made this plan five years ago and for some reason they needed to start with the purchase of our company, and they killed him to achieve it.'

'I think it was Chungkin's invention of ACRE and the huge number of government and industrial networks with Lee-Win processors that was the attraction,' Leo answered. 'If they introduced the A2 cell into millions of those installations and perfected a downloadable version of ACRE, they'd create a link that could be used to blackmail just about the entire world.'

'And XPC was set up in Dubai to develop and test this cyber-attack capability without it being seen by the Lee-Win people here in Shanghai.' Patrice shook his head. 'What a terrifying and ambitious long-term plan. Billions of dollars and five years to get to this point.'

'I was fooled into helping them. ACRE is now running on millions of networks all over the world, so their plan is ninety per cent done. We've got to stop them from finishing it. It's up to us now, guys, there's no one else who can stop this happening.'

Patrice put out his hand, 'I'm in. Whatever it takes, let's get it done.'

'Me too. I want nothing more than to avenge my father's death.' Junjie reached out and they shook hands.

Leo looked at the time. 'Abby's pointed out another thing I didn't think of. We don't know if Shen's sending the upload at midnight local time here or in Moscow. If it's here, we've got only four hours; if it's Moscow, it's nine. But whichever it is, we're running out of time.'

At that moment, four men came into the room. Han Wang Tāng, the MD, introduced himself, Chairman Bohai Cheong, and the two previous colleagues of Chongkun, Junjie's father. They greeted Junjie like long-lost friends, asking after his mother and their families. Patrice, they welcomed respectfully, and with Leo they were barely courteous. 'We have not disturbed the other directors,' Tāng said. 'If this is a technical matter, they would not be helpful.'

They sat on opposite sides of the conference table and Leo weighed up the two senior men. The chairman carried an air of wisdom and gravitas, scrutinising the visitors through thick-lensed spectacles. Tāng appeared to be in his forties, slim and fit-looking with sharp, shrewd eyes. He murmured something to Cheong, who nodded his agreement.

His manner became frigid and his tone severe as he addressed his remarks to Leo. 'What is the purpose of your visit, Mr Stewart? We have agreed to this meeting only as a courtesy to Junjie and to Tom Connor, since we have a great respect for the CEO of our Dubai subsidiary. However, he informed me that you have made allegations against our fellow director, Shen Fu Liáng, whose successful work at XPC created the most innovative software in the history of microprocessing. And this was done despite you, Mr Leo Stewart, leaving the company at the most vulnerable and crucial moment of the development. Before you begin to malign our good friend and colleague, who is not here to defend himself, kindly explain your actions and we will decide whether or not to continue with this discussion.'

Leo saw their chances of getting past this stone wall by lengthy explanations were negligible, and time was short. He decided to take a risk to get their attention quickly. 'I understand your position, Mr Tāng. Like you, we didn't want to believe the truth, because it is frankly unbelievable. I'm going to show you a video which was the evidence that convinced us, and you can judge for yourselves. Tom informed you that I was shoved in prison in Dubai to get me out of the way. Well, that's because I discovered something that pointed to a sabotage attempt at XPC. Or at least, that's what I thought. Let me show you what actually happened.'

The room was silent as Angela's confession played on his laptop. He ran it all the way to the end, including her last message to him. Then he said, 'You're right that Shen was instrumental in delivering the new software, but that was only the first step in his plan. After my arrest, we realised he was planning something else, but we didn't know what it was.'

Bohai Cheong leaned over and whispered something to Tāng, who nodded and said, 'So you expect us to be convinced by the words of a young woman who prostituted herself for money? We Chinese are not so gullible as you may believe, Mr Stewart. If this is all you have to show us, then we can end this conversation immediately.'

He started to rise from his chair, and Junjie said, 'Please wait one moment, Han. What do you know about Shen Fu Liáng?'

He sat down again. 'I'm not sure what you mean. He's the son of Qiang Fu Liáng, who was governor of Sichuan Province, until he was sadly lost in an aeroplane accident with Shen's mother and brother. That was just before he was proposed by the new owners of our company to join us as a board member, and he was immediately involved in creating our successful Dubai subsidiary.'

'Leo, show Mr Tāng the copies of the passports I saw this morning.'

Leo took out the printed copies he'd made from Ilona's attachments, the Chinese document in the name of Shen Fu Liáng and the Russian passport of Grigori Vedeneyev. Tāng's eyes opened wide and he passed the photocopies to his chairman and the other two directors. 'I don't understand. Who is this man Vedeneyev? His picture is the same as Shen's.'

'That's because he's the same man, Mr Tāng.' Leo rapidly described Shen's life history, ending with, 'We believe that's why he's implicating Lee-Win and China in this conspiracy.'

'What conspiracy, Mr Stewart? You haven't yet told us what this is all about, and you've given us no proof that Shen has done anything but enhance our company's global reputation. How do we know this photocopy isn't a fake?'

'OK, you're right. I can demonstrate the proof of the plot if you let me use one of your test networks. It's easier to show it than to explain it.'

Junjie said, 'I would like to see this proof also, Han. I haven't seen it and I think we owe it to my father's memory to find out what this is really about.'

They sat silently as the Chinese began to argue around the table, Junjie and the two ex-colleagues of Chongkun wanting to see the demonstration, with the chairman and MD remaining loyal to Shen. Finally, Tāng said, 'Very well. You have come all this way to show us something and it would be discourteous not to let you do so. We'll go down to the laboratory level. What kind of a network do you need, Mr Stewart?'

FIFTY-SIX

Moscow, Russian Federation
Sunday, 18 July 2017

Piotr Gavrikov was in the headquarters of the Ministry of Defence, situated on Arbatskaya Square at the junction of Znamenka Street. The 200-square-metre office on the eighth floor, the top level, was the domain of the minister, Army General Leonid Mikhail Belinsky, head of all Russian military forces, reporting directly to the Russian president. The heads of the three sections of the armed forces were sitting on the other side of a large oval table that could seat twelve. A giant screen was attached to the wall behind them and several laptops were open on the table.

Belinsky was saying, 'We are now just twelve hours away from launching the A2 attack which will shut down the infrastructures of all fourteen of our lost territories. This is a defining moment in our lives. If it succeeds, the world will witness the resurgence of the greatest socialist confederation in history and our names will become legend. However, if it fails, none of us in this room will be immune from the consequences, there will be no place to hide from the wrath of both our enemies and our friends alike. What is the final status of the programme? General Gavrikov?'

'I will attend a last demonstration of the software this afternoon, but I've seen it several times already and I cannot envisage a failure of any kind. On each occasion the deployment, the hub transfer and the efficiency of the shutdown commands were faultless, just as efficient and faultless as the new Lee-Win software we received yesterday. Based on our estimates of the proliferation of those processors in our target countries, we calculate a failure rate of above seventy per cent of all networks. They will have no option but to accept our terms.'

'What about the agent, this Chinese traitor. Is his loyalty beyond question?'

'Without any doubt. He has invested almost half a billion dollars, murdered his own family and others besides and dedicated five years of his life to this act of revenge. But just in case, I'll be with him when he sends his instructions. And he knows what awaits him if he misbehaves.'

'And his accomplice in Shanghai?'

'The same. He has been well paid and he is also aware of the consequences of failure. But don't forget the additional precautions I've personally foreseen. Nothing can prevent a successful execution of the attack.'

'Very well, Piotr, we must rely on your usual efficiency.' He turned to the man to the right. 'Stanislav, are you ready?'

Army Commander General Stanislav Dorokhin stood to attention. 'Minister, we now have more than 800,000 troops in strategic border positions from Estonia to Kazakhstan, as per the deployment plan we agreed on.' He pointed his cursor at the map on the giant screen. 'Additionally, I have positioned twelve of your *Spetnaz* Special Forces units, in close proximity to the army command positions. They can be sent in to deal with any local insurgence quietly and efficiently, without raising too much outside interest. We are ready for this historic moment and we will not fail Mother Russia.'

Admiral Bolotnikov was the next to report. Pointing at a new map, he said, 'As of last night, the whole fleet was in place as planned. The *Admiral Grigorovich* group is in the North Sea off the Swedish coast at the entrance to the Skaggerak. All of the Baltic targets, from Estonia to Belarus, are in range of their cruise missiles. With Stanislav's troops in front of them and our missiles behind, they're not in a position to argue. The same goes for the two destroyers we sent from the Crimea, they're sitting in the Black Sea, off the coast of Moldova and Georgia. The *Kuznetsov* and the *Gorshkov* are still on manoeuvres in the North Atlantic, ready to launch aircraft or missiles, if and when we so decide.'

The admiral stood proud and tall when he made his last announcement, 'We believe the deciding factor will be the threat of the *Dmitry Donskoy*. It is presently waiting quietly 450 metres under the Baltic Sea, near the island of Gotska Sandön.' He laughed deferentially. 'What you call "NATO's swimming pool", minister.' Bolotnikov was referring to the world's largest submarine, with a crew of 160, an arsenal of 200 weapons, including 20 nuclear missiles, and the capability of remaining submerged for 120 days. 'No one can argue with the *Dmitry Donskoy*.' He sat down, looking extremely pleased with himself.

'Well done, Admiral, exemplary planning, as usual. Can the same be said for your pilots, Alex?'

Colonel General Alexandr Zhigunov, Commander of the Aerospace Forces, smiled and remained sitting. 'I confirm that our pilots, our aircraft, our drones and our ground personnel throughout the area are itching to take part in this momentous event. As well as forty bases within rapid response capability on our own territory, we are on high alert at those in our strategic allies' back gardens. We have strike aircraft and bombers on standby at Khmeimim Air Base in Latakia, Syria; Gyumri in Armenia; Kant in Kyrgizstan and seven more. I believe fifty bases with 750 aircraft at our immediate disposal should provide enough support for my colleagues, if they need to call on us.'

'Thank you, Alex, nothing less than I expected. So, Piotr, the moment is almost upon us. Our military resources are, as Alexandr phrased it, "itching to take part". My overriding concern has been that the NATO members would, for once, show some concerted desire to defend their partners under attack. It's now clear to us that this won't happen. Apart from a pathetic display of US soldiers and a few battleships around the Baltic states, they have shown no interest in our movements. I think we can assume they are otherwise occupied with their domestic upheavals and will react too late and with no credible display of force.

'Everything now depends on you and your partners in crime. I suggest you go and ensure that this last due diligence demonstration is as faultless as on the previous occasions. If all goes well, we may be invited to a celebration in Red Square tonight for the rebirth of the Union of Soviet Socialist Republics. *Vsem udachi*, good luck everyone.'

Washington DC, USA

Anatoly Viktor Kopeykin, the Russian Ambassador to the United States of America, stepped out of his official limousine and entered the Harry S. Truman building, the headquarters of the US State Department, at 2201 C Street NW, a few blocks away from the White House in the Foggy Bottom neighbourhood of Washington. He was quickly escorted through the security procedures, taken up in an elevator and shown into the John Quincy Adams State Drawing Room, one of the diplomatic reception rooms on the seventh and eighth floors of the building which contain the nation's foremost museum collections of American fine and decorative arts. The incumbent secretary of state, Melvin 'Mel' Ritterbrand, was sitting on one of a matching pair of gold-coloured settees framed by exquisite furnishings from the seventeenth and eighteenth centuries. He stood up and shook hands with the Russian, inviting him to sit opposite.

After the usual small talk and accepting a coffee, Kopeykin said, 'It's always a pleasure to visit you, Mel, even at such short notice. But I don't understand what can be so urgent that you need to summon me here on a Sunday morning?'

'That's what we call a rhetorical question, Viktor. Can't you think of a logical answer? After all, it's your side that's been moving all the chess pieces, not ours.'

'You're surely not still concerned about the military exercises we're carrying out? I'm surprised at your suspicious interpretation of our purely housekeeping procedures. And don't you think your accusation is a little hypocritical? You've been moving some impressively big assets yourselves over the last few weeks.'

'You mean our North Atlantic Fleet? They roam that ocean all year long, there's nothing unusual about that. We're doing some exercises with a few thousand troops in the area, but that's all, nothing special. What is unusual is what's in these reports.' He picked up a dozen messages and waved them at the Russian. 'Let me summarise, to help your memory. Close to a million troops massed around the borders of most of the ex-USSR states, two carriers and eight battleships in the Baltic and Black Sea, and it appears from our satellite pictures that one of your subs has gone missing. We've also seen a lot of unusual activity at your southern airbases on home ground and in your ex-Soviet territories.'

'Just as we have observed at your NATO members' bases in Northern Europe, the Baltic and Balkans. Troops, aircraft, battleships. Quite a coincidence, don't you think?'

'As I just said, minor exercises, though I'm glad you noticed we're not just sitting on our hands, Viktor. Some people might think NATO's a busted flush, but there's a lot more willingness to engage than you may imagine. Anyway, I didn't ask you here to compare the size of our dicks.' He swigged back the last of his coffee. 'We've heard talk of some kind of cyber-attack being prepared by your spooks at GRU. What do you know of it?'

Kopeykin looked puzzled. 'A cyber-attack being prepared at the Main Intelligence Directorate? Against who? Where did you hear that?'

Ritterbrand had graduated *cum laude* from Harvard in psychology and psychiatry and he was good at reading people, especially when they were lying. In this case, he was certain the other man was telling the truth. *Viktor doesn't know what I'm talking about,* he told himself. In fact, neither did he. He'd been woken at six that morning by a call from a General W. R. Chillicott, whom he didn't know, at Homeland Security, with a request to invite the Russian ambassador in and ask him that question. The general had told him it was an urgent matter he was investigating personally, it was ultra-confidential and extremely urgent, 'Could you call the ambassador in this morning?' It was an unconventional approach, but Chillicott had pressed all the right buttons, and after the disastrous NATO conference the previous night, Ritterbrand had been keen to try to do something useful. Before ringing off, he'd asked the general if the cyber-attack was linked to the Russian manoeuvres, and the reply had been, 'In a worst-case scenario, yes.'

He got rid of Kopeykin as soon as he decently could and called Homeland Security. Chillicott came on the line immediately. 'Thank you, Mr Secretary. Unfortunately, that's what I expected. It's above his pay grade, and that's a very bad sign. I'll keep you informed as soon as I know something more definite.'

Ritterbrand didn't press him, he had enough on his plate and the general seemed to be on top of the situation. He couldn't know that Chilicott's only hope was a twenty-three-year-old Rwandan man named Leo Stewart.

Moscow, Russian Federation

'Shen's coming here to give me a final demo of the A2 software before we upload it tonight. I've seen it already. It's a brilliant solution, he can't be as stupid as you make out.'

'Piotr, darling, I'm glad to hear it. If it works, it will be a happy ending to the longest five years of my life. When are you coming home?' It was just four in the afternoon and Elodie Delacroix was on her third glass of champagne.

'I'm staying here until I see the trigger code successfully deployed. This is too important to risk anything going wrong. When the shit hits the fan, I should be invited to the Kremlin.

I'll call you, see if you want to come. It'll be around twelve-thirty tonight and there'll be one hell of a celebration.'

'I'll be ready waiting in my finery. *Udachi, dorogaya*, good luck, darling.'

Esther Rousseau, née Bonnard, alias Tsunami, alias Elodie Delacroix, put down her phone and took another swallow of champagne. *One more day, just one, then I'll be rid of all these bloody posturing, impotent, second-rate excuses for men.* Only the thought of the fortune she had been promised had kept her going all this time. *With that money I can start again; a new place, a new life with a new man, a real man.* No one could replace, or even come close to matching Ray d'Almeida, her Angolan lover, who had taught her lovemaking skills that drove men mad with desire, while planning and executing a brilliant plan to regain his rightful inheritance. But in 2008 his plan had somehow been foiled by Jenny Bishop, and he and his fortune had been lost to her. Since then she had been with other men, always using them to try to recover that fortune, and always seeing them fall short. *So many men, such great plans, ending in such great failures.* She poured herself another glass, thinking about the lost years of her life.

The 2010 abduction in South Africa of Jenny Bishop's nephew, Leo Stewart, had been another masterpiece of planning. Together with her shrewd partner and funder, the amoral Lord Arthur Dudley, they had succeeded in capturing the boy and blackmailing the Stewart family for a fortune. Yet, once again, the plan had failed, and she had been forced to save herself from the fallout. After the incident, Esther had kept her head down, living and working as a waitress in The Liffey Landing, a pub in Dublin, a city she loved.

Then, as the meagre capital she had managed to beg, borrow and steal began to run out, a series of lucky opportunities presented themselves and she took full advantage of them. First, she managed to capitalise on a brief romantic encounter with a UN delegate who was in Dublin for a conference and happened to visit the historic pub. Esther spoke four languages fluently and the besotted man helped her obtain a post as a translator in the Geneva headquarters.

Her life changed again for the better in March 2011, at a UN Security Council meeting, when she met Colonel-General Piotr Gavrikov, newly-appointed head of the Russian Main Intelligence Directorate, GRU. It didn't take Esther long to captivate Gavrikov and become his personal assistant, lover and many things besides. An exaggerated account of her work as a senior officer at a Swiss private bank with experience of offshore company structures convinced him she was the perfect intermediary to manage the Kremlin's international offshore activities, and Tsunami was born.

The next and most life-transforming piece of good fortune was the return, in April 2012, of a GRU undercover agent, Shen Fu Liáng, or Grigori Vedeneyev as he preferred to be known in Moscow, currently head of the Russian Trade Delegation in Washington. Liáng had come to Moscow with an incredible proposal. The seeds of a strategy that could restore the Motherland's former glory, recover its lost territories and demonstrate its power and relevance in the new world order.

Gavrikov was impressed, excited and seduced by the proposal. It could elevate him to one of the highest positions in the Soviet hierarchy. But he was deeply wary of this Chinese-Russian agent who had spent the last four years in the United States. He instructed Esther to gain Liáng's confidence, find out if he should be taken seriously. Was the plan feasible, how much would it cost, how long would it take, what were the risks of it backfiring? But most of all, was this a genuine opportunity or a clever trap, set up by the Americans? Was he really a US mole, or if not, what was his motivation for proposing such an outlandish, ambitious scheme?

Back in Washington, waiting for a response to his proposal, Shen received an invitation to a charity dinner at the Willard Intercontinental Hotel, on Pennsylvania Avenue. Sitting next to him was a highly intellectual, beautiful young woman, who introduced herself as Elodie Delacroix, a Belgian political journalist. She was writing a series of articles about Russian–US relations for *Le Point de Vue*, a French left-wing political news magazine. Her current theme was the failure of the US government to enter into meaningful talks with Russia about their rightful claims to Ukraine. When Shen checked her out online, he was duly impressed with her credentials, and the many pro-Russian articles published under her name in a wide range of newspapers and magazines that the Soviet fake news/propaganda machine had worked overtime to produce. He called her the next morning and they had lunch at Le Diplomate, a French restaurant on 14th Street, a choice she thought would impress him.

Although there was something in his character which reminded her slightly of Ray d'Almeida, Esther took an immediate dislike to the man. He seemed humourless and unfeeling, and she wasn't sure about his sexual inclinations. But within a month, she had bewitched him, moved into his apartment and learned everything about his birth and life, the reasons for his hatred of China and love of Russia, and his plan to redraw the geographical borders of his adopted country. She revealed to him her alter-ego, Tsunami, and her international activities for the Soviet regime, and convinced him he had found the right partner to help him achieve his impossible dream. Her report to Gavrikov was impressively thorough and convincing, and the A2 cyber-blackmail project was approved. Shen explained to her how Lee-Win, a leading Chinese micro-processor manufacturer with a vast global government and industrial installed base and a potentially devastating encryption-transmission innovation, was the perfect vehicle for the attack.

With a substantial budget and the shiny new Belgian passport from her Russian paymasters, she went back to Dublin as Elodie Delacroix, and rented an apartment just off Fitzwilliam Square, twenty minutes' walk from the Ha'penny Bridge over the River Liffey and near the National Concert Hall. As she was walking past it one morning, Esther suddenly thought of the enigmatic Lord Arthur Dudley, the most intriguing and complex man she'd ever known. It was he who had introduced her to music, ballet and the love of beautiful things, a love which, sadly, she'd never been able to indulge. *Until now,* she told herself, *now I can live the life Ray and I should have lived. I'm going to make the most of it.*

Shen followed her a week later, flying from Washington to Paris in his own name, then on to Dublin, as Gyeong Park, using a Korean passport he'd been given by his new sponsors at GRU. Not only was his project approved, but at Esther's suggestion General Gavrikov had prepared a list of pro-USSR multi-billionaires, the 'oligarchs', who might be interested in financing the operation. The bait was two-fold: an investment into a successful high-tech company with a potentially industry-changing innovative development, and an opportunity to cherry-pick the valuable pieces of the fourteen ex-USSR satellites when they were taken back into the Russian fold.

Over the next few months, the unlikely partners perfected their plan and began to execute the preliminary stages, starting with the acquisition of Lee-Win Micro-Technology. Chongkun Lee-Win proved to be incalcitrant in his refusal to sell the business, but it was not difficult to replace him in the transaction with his widow. His 'accident' also brought them a price reduction of twenty per cent and the oligarchs couldn't resist the combined opportunity. Esther, as Tsunami, set up the charitable trust structure hidden behind a myriad of proxy companies, and only Shen's share of the funding was required to consummate the transaction. When he revealed his murderous scheme to obtain the balance of his investment from his Chinese family inheritance, she finally understood what it was he had in common with Ray d'Almeida. He was a psychopath, prepared to do anything to fulfil his dream, to exact his revenge on the family who had thrown him out like a stray dog, to lay to rest the feeling of failure and rejection and to enjoy the taste of success and belonging, at last.

The greatest shock Esther had to cope with was when Shen mentioned that Scotty Fitzgerald, whose removal had been scrupulously planned by her, would be replaced by a brilliant young encryption programming specialist called Leo Stewart. The same Leo Stewart who had been kidnapped and then released in Johannesburg in 2010, and who now reappeared in her life at the most crucial moment of their project. But thanks to Angela da Sousa, she'd neutralised him for long enough to get the project through, and now it was too late for him to cause further problems.

She took another swig of Laurent Perrier. *I'm not going to let Jenny Bishop's family steal another fortune from me*, she told herself. *No. This time, it's going to be Esther Rousseau who wins.*

Esther had some insurance. Over the last six years, countless millions of dollars had passed through bank accounts which, as Tsunami, she controlled. By regularly siphoning off small amounts, easily hidden from the GRU accountants, she had accumulated over $300,000 in the Credit Bank of Guadeloupe in her maiden name of Esther Bonnard. It was nothing like the amount she'd been promised from the A2 attack, but she could survive for a while. She booked a BA flight to London for Wednesday morning. Piotr had promised her she'd be paid on Monday and she prayed it would be so, but she wasn't staying around in Moscow any longer. Whatever happened, it was definitely going to become the wrong place to be.

Delmas, Mpumalanga, South Africa

'I just got a text from Leo.' Abby was relaxing with her mother by the pool. She was feeling exhausted. She'd done everything she could think of to help his meeting with the Chinese, and now they had to trust him to get the job done.

'What does he have to say?'

'He thanked me, and said nice things about the hub-handover file and the time difference I pointed out. The Chinese have agreed to see his network demo and he's just received the names of the oligarchs from Ilona.'

'That sounds very positive. What do you think?'

'Sounds like he's doing what he always does, winning.'

Karen thought her daughter sounded a little jealous, but she said nothing. *It's good for her to have some competition, for a change*, she told herself.

FIFTY-SEVEN

Moscow, Russian Federation
Sunday, 18 July 2017

Shen Fu Liáng was at the headquarters of the Main Directorate
of the Russian General Chief of Staff, GRU, the foreign military
intelligence agency. The 70,000-square-metre complex on
Grizodubovoy Street had been built in 2006 at a cost of 9.5 billion
roubles to house the ever-increasing number of security personnel
working on a wide variety of 'special assignments'. GRU, together
with the FSB, the Federal Security Service, previously the KGB,
and the SVR, Foreign Intelligence Service, the principal Russian
security agencies, are engaged in every aspect of defensive and
offensive non-military warfare. These include human intelligence
and counter-intelligence through military attaches and foreign
agents, signals and imagery intelligence and surveillance from
close to two hundred SIGINT spy satellites, internal and border
security and counter-terrorism, as well as employing about 350,000
specialists engaged in a myriad of cross-border activities.

The Chinaman was in the largest of the dozens of network
centres in the vast underground labyrinth of GRU's Internet-
equipped laboratories. This was where the principal hub was housed,

the hub that was used, together with their 'Media Centre' in St Petersburg, to disseminate cyber-attacks, fake news, spying software and a vast array of other cyber tools used by the State to monitor, spy on, infiltrate and destabilise governments, essential services and businesses around the world. This was the hub that Shen would use to deploy, via Shanghai, the shutdown trigger to the A2 cells in the billions of Lee-Win processors newly upgraded with Mark VII and ACRE software, the deployment he was demonstrating to General Piotr Gavrikov for the last time before it went live that night.

He finished the demonstration, the trigger command from the first hub still maintaining the network in shutdown mode via the second, and asked, 'Are you happy with my solution?'

The general smiled grimly. 'I'll tell you tomorrow, after our targets bend the knee.'

It was during his stint in the US, in 2011, that Shen had learned about A2, the 'Analog Back Door Attack', and realised it was the ultimate cyber-weapon. Since then he had dedicated his life and his fortune to implement the technology to launch a gigantic cyber-attack that would damage China, the country that had spurned and deported him like a slave, and benefit Russia, the country that had adopted him and given him a home and a loving family. Almost by accident, he found out that Lee-Win Micro-Technology, an independent Chinese microprocessor manufacturer, had conceived ACRE, an innovative encryption-transmission technology which could be the 'Back Door' to launch his A2 attack into millions of networks around the world.

Thanks to the fortuitous meeting with Elodie, who, as Tsunami, had privileged access to Colonel-General Piotr Gavrikov, his project was approved and funded. He assumed that Elodie and Gavrikov were lovers, but he didn't care. The general believed in his project and provided the support needed to prepare it. Besides, Shen wasn't particularly interested in women, he wasn't interested in anything but his revenge. In Dublin, armed with Tsunami's offshore expertise, the oligarchs' money and avarice, and the Russian ruler's obsession to rebuild the USSR, the whole brilliant strategy was put in place. Within six months, his Chinese family had disappeared, Lee-Win was acquired, and nothing could stand in the way of the A2 attack.

Shen flew to London Heathrow on 15 November 2012 as Gyeong Park, then on to Shanghai as Shen Fu Liáng to take up his position as representative of the anonymous new owners on the governing board of Lee-Win Micro-Technology. He quickly imposed his authority and persuaded the other members to create XPC, a new subsidiary, far away from Shanghai, where he could put together the pieces of his plan without it being discovered until it was too late. The Dubai project was approved in March 2013, and by October 2014 it was fully functional and staffed by some of the cleverest brains in the industry. The ACRE encryption-transmission technology conceived by Chongkun Lee-Win was still a work-in-progress, and Shen convinced the board to transfer the development to XPC, with himself as the technical link between the two centres. Tom Connor gave a layer of normality and respectability to the new enterprise, and thanks to the brilliant minds of Scotty Fitzgerald and Sharif Kayani, carefully identified and hired by Shen, ACRE became a reality. The key to realising the five-year plan to rebuild the Union of Soviet Socialist Republics.

There had been some casualties along the way. Chongkun had refused to sell his company and a fortuitous accident was required, his own treacherous Chinese family had to be removed to provide the balance of the funds he needed, Scotty Fitzgerald had been too inquisitive, and Leo Stewart had almost ruined everything at the last moment. But he had survived all those threats and emerged victorious. At XPC, he had used Sharif's expertise to test the trigger command itself. It wasn't risky, because that was only half the solution. The upgrade had to be deployed via Lee-Win's Shanghai hub, but the obvious danger was that they would immediately stop the trigger function and the shutdown would be cancelled. A small amount of money was all it took to subvert Hoi Wei, a senior manager in the Shanghai organisation, to do his bidding and no one, not even Elodie, knew his identity. With his accomplice and some help from cyber experts at GRU, he had perfected the hub transfer software that would permit him to maintain the constant triggering until the targeted networks submitted to Russia's demands. And, most importantly, the attack would appear to come from China.

Now, at last, the night of the final act had arrived. Five years after conceiving his audacious plan for retribution, Shen Fu Liáng was about to lay the past to rest and start a new life. A new life without that bisexual nymphomaniac, Elodie Delacroix, Tsunami, or whoever she really was. Without the arrogant, amoral so-called oligarchs, and without GRU and Gavrikov or any of the people involved in his scheme. A new life with just his Russian family. Tonight, he would finally find closure.

Shanghai, People's Republic of China

'This code is not what we have deployed, so I don't see why it is relevant to anything. We can all write code that shuts down networks, but we don't upload it to our customers.'

The speaker was Han Wang Tāng, who had listened to Leo's explanations and demonstrations step-by-step, ending with the triggering of the rogue cell, Sector 470, Cell number 887,999. As always, the network had been shut down by the trigger commands. The Chinese had asked for a second demonstration, but Tāng's reaction was still one of disbelief. It was now almost ten o'clock and he had so far refrained from making any positive comment.

'Han, that cell isn't in our XPC design, but it's in your processors. It must have been placed there intentionally, for a purpose. It's not an accident that it's there, nor that we've discovered this shutdown code.'

'But that means someone has interfered with the production line here in Shanghai.'

'Dead right it does,' Leo said, relieved to hear this partial acknowledgement at last. 'Do you know a guy called Hoi Wei?'

'I know him. He's been with us for about ten years, a loyal and competent man, but not destined for greatness, if I may say. Why do you ask, how do you know his name?'

Leo produced the printout of the email, *'Expected Sunday, 12pm'*. 'We found this in the XPC server. It was encrypted, but my friends in South Africa opened it up. It was sent by Shen to hoi.wei@ sina.com.'

'What is your interpretation of the message?'

'We figure the A2 trigger code will be sent here from Moscow tonight and this man, Hoi Wei, will deploy it with the Lee-Win signature. The message doesn't say whether it's Moscow or Shanghai time, so we don't know how much time we've got to prevent it.'

'I see. That is a very serious accusation.' Han turned and spoke to his chairman. Bohai Cheong's eyes flashed and he made a voluble response, gesticulating with his hands.

Han said nothing, and Leo looked at Junjie, who translated. 'Mr Cheong cannot believe that anyone would defile the name and reputation of Lee-Win in this way. He says there must be a mistake.' The other directors nodded their heads in deference to the chairman.

'I understand Mr Cheong's doubts, it's hard to believe, but I'll prove to you there's no mistake.' Leo searched his laptop. 'Take a look at this folder. It's from the original memory stick given to Sharif Kayani in Dubai last March, by Shen Fu Liáng.' He turned the screen towards them and opened the A2 file to show the code he'd used for his demonstration, then showed the 'Properties, Details' page. 'See who the author is? Hoi Wei, the same person Shen sent that email to.' Neither of them looked convinced and he sat back in his chair, wondering what more he could say to get his message through.

Patrice, who hadn't yet spoken, came to his assistance. 'Gentlemen, Leo flew from Johannesburg and I came from Malaga to Hong Kong at a moment's notice, then Junjie joined us to fly immediately here to Shanghai. Do you think we would have taken such urgent action if we weren't convinced of this imminent global cyber-attack? Why do you think Scotty Fitzgerald was murdered and Leo was imprisoned, if not to cover up a major conspiracy? Do you remember that Shen's Chinese family was wiped out in the plane crash just before Chongkun was killed and Mme Lee-Win sold the company? We are convinced he arranged the crash, so he could inherit the fortune necessary for his share of the purchase. I'm sure you don't know this, Mr Cheong, but Shen Fu Liáng is one of the owners of your company.' At this, the Chinese directors looked stunned.

He continued, 'Why is General Chillicott, at US Homeland Security, investigating Shen and his partner, Elodie Delacroix, who we believe is a Russian agent called Tsunami, if he's not convinced of all this? These two people planned this whole conspiracy five years ago, and they are about to execute it in a few hours' time. Please, gentlemen, you must believe us and act immediately, or the world will be facing a catastrophe.'

Everyone sat in silence for a few moments, then Cheong turned to Junjie and asked, in perfect English, 'Do you know for certain who was behind the acquisition of our company from your esteemed mother?'

'I didn't know until a few hours ago. Leo, show Mr Cheong and Han the message from General Chillicott.'

Leo opened up Ilona's email with the list containing the names, photos and descriptions of Shen and his partners, and turned the laptop back to face the four directors. Next to the computer, he placed the printouts of Mme Lee-Win's BPI bank statements and Ilya Pavlychko's report, showing the payments received from the six charitable trusts, via the Moscow Trade & Kreditbank.

It took the Chinese men a few minutes to take in the evidence before them, and to register the position and wealth of the men concerned. Dumbfounded, they looked from the screen to the documents, to each other, then all started speaking at once until Cheong signalled for silence.

When his voice could be heard, Leo said, 'You must have seen the reports about Russian troops and fleet movements around the ex-Soviet satellite countries? That's what this whole five-year plan has been about. Shutting down communications across those countries until they agree to Russia's terms. Then these oligarchs can pick up the prime pieces when the USSR is reconstituted. Mr Cheong, do you want your country and your company to be held responsible for the next Cold War, or even World War?'

The chairman looked around at his colleagues, then he said sadly to Junjie, 'Did they arrange the car accident that left your mother a widow and her sons fatherless?'

'We believe it was Shen Fu Liáng and the woman. Then he took advantage of his position to build XPC in Dubai, far away from your control. We are sure you were deceived, just like my family, Shen's family, Scotty and Leo and probably many others. I hope you now believe what Leo has told you?'

Cheong stood up and bowed to his visitors. 'Thank you for coming all this way to deliver your message, gentlemen. On behalf of us all at Lee-Win, I apologise to Mr Stewart for doubting his word and to you, Junjie, I offer my sincerest regrets at what happened to your father and mother. We have been deceived for long enough, it's time to take action. What is your suggestion?'

FIFTY-EIGHT

**Shanghai, People's Republic of China
Sunday, 18 July 2017**

'And you suspect the malignant cell has been added to all our processors for several years?' Leo and the others were back in the conference room on the twentieth floor.

'Probably since you added the connectivity module. That was four years ago, right?'

'Yes. I designed it myself and it was introduced in early 2013,' Han Wang Tāng replied. 'We saw how the IoT was bringing fixed and mobile devices together, and wanted to instruct every processor to move into a mesh network environment when ACRE was perfected.'

'It was a smart move. IoT's the future. I was involved in it for a while, before XPC.'

'Did you write the interface to accomplish that remote upgrade process?'

'It was a team effort. We got it working just before they threw me into prison.'

Han appreciated the modest response. 'I would like you to know, Leo, that we've had many, many compliments from customers with all kinds of systems which automatically switched over to the ACRE mesh network without any problems at all. It was excellent work.'

'Thanks.' Leo's mind returned to the problem in hand. 'Anyway, I suppose it would have been easy for someone to add the rogue cell at the same time. Then it became part of the standard template and nobody noticed it. What does that man Hoi Wei do here? What's his function?'

Han replied, 'I hired him straight from university, ten years ago, he's only thirty-two. He did a two-year apprenticeship as a systems engineer. He's not a programmer, he works mainly on customer-facing tasks like information broadcast, updates, systems upgrades.'

'He has full access to the main hub?' Leo was trying to reconcile the A2 hub handover code with Tāng's description of Hoi. *Abby said it's pretty clever code. If he didn't write it, who did, Shen?* he wondered. *And who added the A2 cell to the template?*

'The hub room can only be accessed with a coded pass card, which is changed every day for security purposes. That hub is Lee-Win's connection to the world and it's an ultra-secure environment. Hoi is one of the few employees with authorisation to receive a pass card.'

'How do your global deployments work? I've never done one before.' Leo asked.

'Obviously we don't know where all our processors end up, but we are linked to 200 local hubs around the world, covering about eighty-five per cent of Internet-served countries. All the places we know there are some Lee-Win equipped devices. That way, we expect to hit over ninety-five per cent of them.'

'OK, I get it. You programme the main hub to make one deployment to the local hubs in the regions you want to hit, and then they retransmit the data to their specific area. And that's what Hoi does?'

'That's one of his tasks, and he has always fulfilled it very competently.'

Leo thought Han sounded too defensive, but he just said, 'If he's going to deploy the A2 code, he must be getting ready. Is he here now?'

'He shouldn't be working today. It's a Sunday and we have no deployments foreseen.'

'Where's the hub room?'

'It's on the sixtieth floor, that's right at the top of the building, near to the main aerials and transmitting and receiving equipment.'

'So, if he's up there, it's fairly certain he's the traitor.' Leo took a deep breath. *Shit! This isn't a potential threat any more, it's here and now and I'm in the middle of it.*

'I'll find out.' Han spoke on the internal telephone for a few moments. 'Sadly, it seems your assessment of the situation is correct. Hoi Wei came into the building an hour ago and asked for clearance to do some test work in the hub room. He is there alone at the moment.'

'So that's settled. What are we going to do about it?'

Patrice said, 'It's almost ten-thirty. The Moscow transmission is arriving at midnight, or later, and he can't do anything until then. If he's in there, we should neutralise him immediately, so we have time to prepare for whatever happens next.'

Junjie nodded his assent. 'I agree we should use our time efficiently, Patrice, but we are not masters in this house. Mr Cheong, Han, you are the directors of the company and we must respect your wishes. What is your decision?'

'Thank you, Junjie,' Cheong said, 'but I've never faced such a situation before. I need a few minutes to discuss the next steps with my colleagues.'

The others waited impatiently while the Lee-Win directors talked in staccato Mandarin, until Cheong announced, 'We agree that urgent action must be taken, but without causing a scandal. It would not be helpful to Lee-Win or to our country's reputation if this conspiracy became widely known. We must neutralise Wei ourselves, quickly and quietly.'

Leo frowned. 'How do you suggest we do that?'

Han replied, 'As far as we know, he is not interested in politics, so his actions must be motivated by money. That makes the problem easier to resolve. Mr Cheong and I will go up to the hub room together and negotiate a compromise with him. Any other course risks the matter getting out of control.'

'That's crazy! What if he's armed and doesn't want to listen? You'll be sitting ducks, and then he'll have hostages to strengthen his hand.'

'I don't believe he will be armed, he's not a violent man and won't expect to be disturbed. But I agree it's best to be cautious. I have my service pistol in the safe in my office, will that satisfy you? Don't worry, I was in the infantry, I know how to handle a gun.'

Fifteen minutes later, the chairman and the CEO, armed with a pass card and a NORINCO NP-42 9mm pistol, went up to the sixtieth floor, entered the hub room and closed the door behind them.

Moscow, Russian Federation

It was five-thirty, and Shen Fu Liáng *aka* Grigori Vedeneyev was enjoying afternoon tea at the Moscow Marriott Grand Hotel with his mother and sister. In the company of the two people he loved most in the world, he was relaxed and content, looking forward to his appointment with destiny at midnight. He had time to take his family home, bathe and change, maybe even have a short nap, before meeting General Piotr Gavrikov at the GRU headquarters at eleven o'clock.

He was pouring a fresh cup of tea for them all when his mobile pinged. 'Sorry. It might be important. We're finalising something tonight, so I'd better check it.' He took the phone from his pocket and an icy chill ran down his spine. The text message from Hoi Lei said only, *Timing problem. Ready now. Send instructions immediately.*

Shanghai, People's Republic of China

The phone in the conference room rang a few minutes after the chairman and MD left the room. 'It's for you, Leo,' said the Chinese director whose name he couldn't remember.

'Hello, who's this?'

'Hi, Leo. How's it going?'

'Marius! Hi. How's everything in Delmas?'

'I assume it's just fine, but right now I'm downstairs at the Lee-Win reception desk. Can you get someone to authorise me to come up?'

Five minutes later, Coetzee had met Patrice and Junjie and been introduced to the others. Leo quickly brought him up-to-date on the situation.

He immediately asked, 'How long have they been upstairs?'

'Not more than ten minutes. They went up just before you arrived.'

'And this guy, Han, he's got a pistol?'

Leo nodded, and Coetzee stood up. 'Let's go.'

'You mean to the hub room? What's the problem?'

'Leo, remember 2010? If someone's got a gun, it doesn't take ten minutes to get things sorted. Grab your laptop and let's go.'

'Why don't we get security to come?'

'You've got the CEO and the chairman in there, and you said they don't want to cause a scare. If we can sort it out quietly, so much the better. If not, there'll be time for Patrice and Junjie to get security involved.'

'OK, but we need a pass card for the hub room. How do we get one?'

'If we ask nicely, I don't think we'll need one. Time's short, come on.' Coetzee went to the door with Leo. 'Patrice, you stay here with the others. If you hear nothing in ten minutes, get security up there. OK?'

Moscow, Russian Federation

Shen Fu Liáng was in a taxi on the way to the GRU building on Grizodubovoy Street. It was only a twenty-minute ride, but it seemed to be taking hours. He was on his mobile with Piotr Gavrikov and the general wasn't happy.

'What do you mean we have to send it out immediately? Are you fucking crazy? The president fixed the time at midnight, and that's still six hours away. We can't just ignore his instructions like that, he'll have our guts for garters. What does it say exactly?'

Shen repeated the words. '*Timing problem. Ready now. Send instructions immediately.*'

'And you're sure it's from your contact? It couldn't be a fake?'

'I'm certain of it. I'll be there in ten minutes, everything's prepared, I can send it right away. I assumed you'd want to be there when I do.'

'I'm in the building now. I'll meet you at reception and we'll decide what to do. This is a fucking nightmare situation. What the hell can have gone wrong?'

'I don't know, but it doesn't change anything, just the time. I'll see you in ten minutes.'

Shanghai, People's Republic of China

'Why did you come here at short notice like that? Did something happen?'

Coetzee pressed the button for the sixtieth floor. 'It wasn't my idea.'

Leo thought for a split second. 'Aunt Jenny?'

'Right. She had one of her dreams a while ago and she was sure there'd be problems here. I should have thought of it myself. I'm sorry for putting you in harm's way without a back-up.'

'Not your fault. We should have thought more about the risks, especially when the stakes are as high as they seem to be. Anyway, you're here now, so what's the plan?'

Moscow, Russian Federation

'It's too risky to call him, it sounds like there's some kind of problem and he's not able to talk, that's why he texted. I've got to send the upload package now. If he says they're ready, it means it'll go straight out and that's what we want.' Shen was sweating freely and his hands were trembling. Five years of his life, almost half a billion dollars and closure of his hated Chinese birth right were in jeopardy, and he was stymied by a Russian general who couldn't take a decision.

General Piotr Gavrikov was in a state of panic. He had specific orders from the president of Russia and he couldn't execute them. He'd called his office, but the answer was, 'The president is unattainable for the next two hours.' The attaché he'd spoken to didn't have security clearance for the operation, so he couldn't leave a precise description of the emergency. There was no one else he could call for approval and if the deployment didn't go ahead, his career, even his life, could be suddenly over. The ball was in his backyard.

He grabbed Shen by the arm. 'Why the hell didn't you foresee something like this could go wrong? Why don't you have a fall-back plan?'

'Don't try to push the blame onto me. I've known from the beginning you had your own man in there, in case something like this happened. The message must mean both of our people are in trouble. There's only one option. Send the fucking instructions, now!'

FIFTY-NINE

Shanghai, People's Republic of China
Sunday, 18 July 2017

The sixtieth floor was deserted, and Leo and Coetzee walked along the corridor to the hub room. It was surrounded by walls of darkly frosted translucent glass, so those outside couldn't see in and those inside couldn't see out.

Leo knocked on the door. 'Han, Mr Cheong, it's Leo. Can you open up?'

A moment passed, then Cheong's voice replied, 'Everything is under control here, Leo. We'll be down in a short time, no need for you to come in.'

'Bohai, with all due respect, I've come all this way, I want to make sure the threat is eliminated. Please open the door.'

Another pause. 'Are the others with you?'

'No,' he replied truthfully. 'They're waiting downstairs.'

The door opened inwards. 'Come in then.' Bohai was holding the door, and Leo walked past him into the room. Han was sitting at a table, his hands flat on the worktop. He had a cut over his right eye and coagulated blood on his bruised cheek. Before the chairman could close the door again, Coetzee stepped forward from the side, pushed past him and slammed it shut.

'You said you were alone! Who's this man?'

'I'm Coetzee. Who're you?'

'He's Bohai Cheong, the chairman, and the other guy is Han Wang Tāng, the CEO. But I'm the guy in charge.' The voice came from a man standing at a table with a PC and screens on it at the other end of the room. Tall and dark-skinned, he was holding a pistol – Han's pistol.

Coetzee said, 'So, you're the mysterious accomplice, Hoi Wei?'

'That's him, the filthy traitor.' Bohai stared contemptuously at the man. 'I don't understand it, after all these years with our company. Why have you done this? Attacking your employer and planning this monstrous cyber-attack.'

'Money, of course,' said Coetzee. 'How much are they paying you?'

He waved the pistol at them. 'Shut your mouths and sit there with Han, all of you.'

Coetzee remained where he was and nodded to Leo to sit down. He dragged a couple of chairs over and sat alongside Han and the chairman. He said, 'You OK, Han? That's a nasty cut you've got.'

Han nodded, and Wei said, 'He's fine, I just took the gun off him. He wasn't expecting any resistance.' He laughed and waved the pistol at them.

Coetzee said, 'And you know how to handle it.'

'Shut the fuck up and sit down, I'm busy.' He turned to the computer, checked the screen and turned back to them.

'I guess that's the hub console? You're waiting for the upload from Moscow?'

'And you're Leo Stewart, the guy who tried to fuck it up. You're going to be disappointed. It's on the way, won't be long.' He pointed the pistol at Coetzee. 'I told you to sit down and shut up.'

Coetzee walked towards the Chinaman. 'Give me the gun, Hoi, before somebody gets hurt.' He reached out his hand. 'Give it here.'

Hoi aimed the pistol at his chest. 'Get back or I'll pull the trigger. Turn around and sit the fuck down.'

Leo had seen Coetzee in action before. He didn't know what he was going to do, but he sat forward on the chair, poised, ready to go to the South African's aid.

'I see you've never fired a gun. It pays to take the safety off.' Coetzee was just a metre from him.

Hoi looked down at the pistol, saw the safety catch and tried to flip it with his thumb.

Coetzee grabbed the gun out of his hand. 'Don't ever threaten to kill me, or it might backfire on you.' He slapped Hoi across the ear with the heel of his hand and he fell to the floor, grabbing Coetzee by the ankles, trying to pull him down.

Leo ran over and kicked him in the deltoid. 'Game over, Hoi.'

He screamed and fell onto his back, rubbing his upper arm. 'Fuck! You bastard, you've broken my shoulder.'

'I didn't kick hard enough for that. Just a bit of bruising in the morning.'

Coetzee pulled him to his feet and frogmarched him across the room. He pushed him onto a chair. 'Sit there and keep your mouth shut. Give me your mobile, put the password in.' Hoi didn't move. 'Do it, if you don't want Leo to kick you to shit.'

He handed him the phone and Coetzee looked at the latest messages. 'He sent a text to Shen fifteen minutes ago, telling him to send the upload immediately. Have a look at that console, Leo.'

The table was littered with files, printouts and other computer paraphernalia. There was an empty coffee mug and a plate that was being used as an ashtray. Leo pushed the mess aside to make space for his laptop. 'What's the password, Han?'

The CEO moved his chair away from Hoi and wiped a bloodied hand over his eyes. 'Thank you for saving us from this disgusting creature, Mr Coetzee, we probably owe you and Leo our lives. But I don't have the password, you'll have to get it from him.'

'What is it, Hoi?'

The man didn't answer, and Coetzee went over to him and squeezed his bruised shoulder until he winced with pain. 'If we don't have the password in five seconds, I'll break your other arm.'

'It changes every day. I stuck it on the computer screen to have it handy.'

Leo said, 'I see it, but it's in Chinese. OK, come here and explain the deployment procedure to me. It'll be faster.'

Han stood up. 'I think it's safer to keep him away from the computer, I don't trust him.' He went over to Coetzee. 'That's my army pistol, Mr Coetzee. I'll take it and guard Hoi. Mr Cheong can translate for you and Leo. Don't worry, I can handle this traitor.'

He handed him the gun. 'I've left the safety on. Can you call down and tell Junjie there's no need for security? And watch out for this slimy bastard.'

Han picked up the phone and Coetzee went to the console with Bohai.

With the chairman's help, Leo quickly found his way around the system. 'Nothing's arrived yet. I'd better get moving.' He started working on his laptop. 'How many countries are you supposed to send the upload to?'

'Why the fuck should I help you? What do I get out of it?'

Coetzee turned and stared at him. 'We'll let you live, for a start.'

Han prodded him with the pistol, 'Answer, you repulsive animal!'

'Fourteen. All the ex-USSR countries.'

'That's the hub coordinates on this list?'

Hoi nodded, and Coetzee said, 'Just for interest, how much did Shen pay you?'

'It's none of your fucking business.' Han prodded him again. 'He gave me 150,000 Euros, with another 100,000 to come. I've earned it.'

'You haven't earned it yet, and we'll make sure you don't.'

'So I suppose you'll be calling the cops now?'

Coetzee said, 'OK, listen to me. At the moment you haven't committed any crime. You're prepared to commit one, but it's still not executed. If you help us, we don't care what happens to you. It's too complicated to get the police involved and it won't change anything. If Han and Bohai agree, you're free to go as soon as we're finished here.'

'I don't see how I can help you, you're running the show now.'

Moscow, Russian Federation

'OK, they're all in agreement.' Piotr Gavrikov put the phone down with a trembling hand. It was six p.m. and he'd spoken to Generals Dorokhin and Zhigunov and Admiral Bolotnikov, who confirmed they were ready to proceed. He then called the Minister of Defence, General Belinsky, and explained the situation to him. Since the president couldn't be reached, the general had outlined the stark options for him. 'In two hours' time, if you haven't sent it and it's too late, you'll be held personally responsible. If you send it and something goes wrong, you'll still be held responsible. So you'd better send it and hope it goes according to plan.'

Shen breathed a sigh of relief. 'Thank God for that. Come on, let's go.' They raced to the elevators to take them to the underground network centres. It was almost an hour since he'd received the text. He prayed he'd be in time to fix things. If not... he didn't like to consider the alternative.

Shanghai, People's Republic of China

'Right. It's ready. You want to double-check, Marius?'

He came to the table and Leo showed him his set-up, step by step. 'Looks OK to me, but you're the expert, so we'll just cross our fingers and trust you.'

'Remind me to thank Abby. Without that last message of hers I wouldn't have known how to do this.'

'If we live that long, I'll be happy to do so.'

'Move away from the console, all of you.' Han Wan Tāng was standing behind Hoi, pointing the Norinko at them. 'Step away and sit on the floor in that corner, away from the computer. Leave your laptop there, Leo.' He tapped Hoi's shoulder with the gun. 'Make sure he hasn't interfered with your programme.'

Hoi stood up, looking round at him in confusion. 'What? What the fuck's going on, Han?'

'Never mind, just do what I told you, now.'

Coetzee laughed out loud. 'Well, well, it's the old Russian double or triple cross. Han lets Hoi take him out, so he'll stay in the clear. Behind the bad guy there's another and maybe even one more. Whose side are you on, Mr Cheong?'

The chairman was staring at Han in amazement. 'What the hell are you doing, Han? Put that gun down. Are you mad?'

'Looks like he's just protecting his investment. Right, Han? You were the back-up in case Hoi screwed up, and now you've got to take over the party.'

'I don't have time to discuss it, move away and sit down.'

Coetzee gestured to the others to stand aside as Hoi went over to the PC and interrogated the system. 'It's OK, he's created another file, but it's not connected to mine.'

'Well, we know it's Shen who's paying Hoi, but who's paying you, Han?' The South African made a hand gesture to Leo and moved closer to the table.

'What? Who's paying me? What are you talking about?' He waved the gun again. 'Get away from the console, or I'll shoot.' He took aim at Coetzee. 'I won't make the same mistake as that idiot, the safety's off this time.'

Coetzee grabbed Hoi and stood behind him, his arm around the Chinaman's throat. He snatched the plate from the desk and hurled it, frisbee-style, at Han. Leo ran forward and threw himself at him in a rugby tackle just as the plate smashed into his arm and he pulled the trigger.

The pistol exploded, and Leo cried out as he felt a burning sensation in his left thigh. 'Fuck! You've shot me, you murdering piece of shit.' He tore the gun from his hand, threw it to Coetzee then squeezed his hands around his bleeding leg.

Coetzee laid Hoi out with a rabbit punch to the head then came over and pushed Han onto a chair. He pulled Leo's jeans down and looked at his leg. By his standards the injury didn't appear to be serious, the bullet had entered and exited the flesh without breaking any bones or touching an artery. He pressed his handkerchief to the leg while Bohai brought water from the adjacent washroom, then he cleaned the wound, ripped a towel into strips and bound it tightly, remembering Karen's words at the airport, *could you try not to get shot this time?* He wished he could have taken the bullet instead of Leo.

'You OK?'

'Don't worry, I'll make it. We've still got a job to finish.'

Coetzee said to Bohai, 'No reason to start a panic. Call down again and tell Junjie everything's OK up here. We won't be too long.'

Moscow, Russian Federation

Shen Fu Liáng said, 'It's ready. Do you authorise me to send it?'

'Don't be fucking stupid. Just get on with it.'

Shen pressed *Send* and his A2 trigger and handover codes were transmitted to the Lee-Win hub address.

Shanghai, People's Republic of China

Bohai put the phone down then came over to Han, shaking his fist in his face. 'Why have you betrayed me and your friends and colleagues in this despicable way? You have brought shame on Lee-Win and everyone involved in our business, here and in Dubai. You and Shen and this man,' he gestured at Hoi Wei, now sitting on the floor, holding his head, 'working together to destroy everything we have done to ensure our place in history.'

Han turned his head away and said nothing. 'Money, of course,' Coetzee answered. 'Don't look for any other motivation, Bohai, it's always about money.'

Leo said, 'I'm not following. If Wei was paid by Shen, who was paying Han?'

'The Russians, of course,' Coetzee said. 'The truth is they were both being paid by the Russians, but neither of them knew it. It's over, Han. You realise that, don't you? Whatever happens from now on, it's me and Leo who'll be directing the traffic, not you or Hoi. You failed in your task, and I don't think Leo wants to get the local authorities involved about a minor shooting accident,' he paused and

Leo shook his head. 'Right, so if Bohai agrees, when we finish here, you and that creep over there can go and be thankful for small mercies.'

'You don't understand. The Russians will find us and kill us, both of us, perhaps our families and all of you as well. You've seen who's behind this, they're powerful men and we can't hide from them.' Han was up on his feet. 'They promised me $2 million. Two million! More than I could save in my entire lifetime. Enough to take my family away and enjoy life, instead of wasting my days and years creating brilliant inventions that other people took credit for.'

'And that's why you conspired in the death of our founder, Chongkun, the man who befriended you and treated you like a brother for so many years. You repulse me, you ungrateful, conniving murderer. You must not let him go free, Mr Coetzee, he deserves to pay for his crimes.' Cheong turned his head away, his face twisted with disgust.

'It's not true! I had nothing to do with Chongkun's death. I swear on my children's heads. Until tonight I believed he had been killed in an accident, but I see now I was naïve and stupid. When the new owners asked me to stay, I thought I would be treated with the respect I had earned, in the top job, with a proper salary, a fine car, share options and bonuses, in return for everything I had done for Lee-Win. But I was wrong. Shen Fu Liáng was appointed and replaced me as their key man, and then set up XPC, the real centre of development, out of my control.'

'It was me who invented ACRE!' he shouted at Leo. 'It took me years to develop the concept and then, before I could introduce it, the project was taken away to Dubai and you got the credit. I created the A2 cell and introduced it into the imprint. Then I wrote the trigger programme and it was kept safe in Moscow, so no one could discover it. And it was me who programmed the hub handover code to manage the shutdown from Moscow. It's all incredible technology and I invented it, me, no one else. I've been the real brain behind Lee-Win Micro-Technology for the last twenty years.'

Leo was trying to cope with these revelations. 'So, both you and Hoi were Shen's accomplices in the conspiracy?'

Han gave a derisive laugh. 'I was not Shen Fu Liáng's accomplice. I was working under the orders of General Piotr Gavrikov at the Russian Main Intelligence Directorate in Moscow. He contacted me after Shen was appointed and he told me the whole plan. He needed someone who could guarantee it would work, and I am the only person who could do that. He paid me $50,000 a year and promised me $2 million when the job was executed. Shen knew nothing about it. He was too stupid to realise it was me behind all this brilliant technology, he thought it was the work of one of their Russian cyber specialists and that man, Hoi Lei, who is not fit to tie my shoelaces. Although I was surrounded by fools, I fulfilled my task and I deserve the $2 million I was promised for it.'

He pointed his finger at Bohai. 'Do you know how much I earn? Even you are paid more than me, with your shares and bonuses. I'm the chief executive and I get $10,000 a month. $2 million was worth working for five years.' He wiped his eyes. 'But you're right, it's over now. It's all over.' He sat back on the chair, his head in his hands, a broken man.

There was silence for a long moment, then Coetzee said, 'Shen's upload might have arrived, Leo. Are you OK to check it?'

'Sure, I'm fine.' He limped over to the PC and entered the password. 'It's arrived, just two minutes ago.'

'Great, time for you to show us how smart you and Abby can be.'

Moscow, Russian Federation

'It's ten minutes since you sent it. What the fuck's he doing?' Shen Fu Liáng was waiting in General Piotr Gavrikov's office, and they had received no news from Hoi Lei.

'He's checking the upload, converting it into a Lee-Win envelope and entering the hub addresses. It can't be done in a minute. You want him to screw it up by hurrying things at this stage?' Shen answered confidently, but his heart was in his mouth. *It's now or never, please God, don't let it go wrong.*

Shanghai, People's Republic of China

'Right, it's going. I just hope he doesn't hang around.' Leo pressed *Send* and a copy of the upload received from Shen went flying off through the ether to General William R. Chillicott in Washington. It was accompanied by a summary of Leo's solution and Coetzee's recordings of Hoi Wei's and Han's confessions. They were sitting in silence next to Bohai Cheong, who had them covered with the pistol.

'I can't believe such greed and corruption. And from people whom I've known and trusted for so many years.' Bohai shook his head. 'That upload could have started a global conflict with millions of deaths, and Lee-Win would be held responsible. And all you were concerned about is money. Do you people have no shame, no morals, no respect for mankind?'

Han put his hand over his eyes while Hoi ignored the old man. 'Can I go now?' he asked Coetzee.

'Wait until we send the upload. If it's successful, and you'd better pray it is, we won't detain you.'

Leo looked at the time. 'Where's Billy? What's he doing?'

Washington DC, USA

General Chillicott was in West Potomac Park at twelve noon, watching his grandson's Sunday softball game, when his mobile pinged. He found a quiet corner and read Leo's message, looked at the upload file, then listened to Coetzee's recording. Now he had the final proof of the Russians' intentions, it was time to teach them a lesson. He typed, *Well done. Go ahead. WRC.*

Shanghai, People's Republic of China

'We have lift-off. Billy says go ahead. Do I send?'

'That's the stupidest question you've ever asked.'

Leo pressed *Send*, and his modified A2 trigger and handover codes were sent to the address he'd specified.

A minute later, an email came in from Moscow: *Confirm upload sent?*

Leo replied: *Confirm sent a moment ago.* Coetzee found the response amusing.

SIXTY

**GRU Headquarters, Moscow, Russian Federation
Sunday, 18 July 2017**

'What the hell's happened to the networks?' Andrei Ivanov, the Deputy IT Director, shouted down the phone.

'It's another system crash. We're investigating it now. You'll get a report in an hour.' Evgeny Ilyin, Head of Network Maintenance, shoved the phone in his pocket and ran down the corridor to the main network centre. The lock sensor wouldn't work with his pass card and he banged on the door until someone came and opened the dead lock. He walked into the room, an unpleasant smile on his face.

'Congratulations, Vasili, that's the third failure in a month. I suppose you have a really good explanation for me to give to the boss.'

'It's not a really good explanation, but it's the only one that makes sense. We've been hacked. The entire system, all the networks, shut down five minutes ago and nothing's working. It has to be a cyber-attack, there's no other explanation.'

'What do you mean, the entire system? That's impossible, there must be some parts of some networks working. Has there been any unusual traffic through tonight?'

'We got a minor upgrade from Lee-Win for a bug they found in their new software. But that's nothing unusual.'

'And it was downloaded without question?'

'Of course, we always do. Without Lee-Win we wouldn't have a system. And that new ACRE software is incredible. If they want to fix a bug, it's in our interests and we should be happy.'

All-Russia State Television and Radio Broadcasting Company, Moscow

'We're getting calls about a cyber-attack, from GRU headquarters. Seems all their networks are down.'

'Sounds like a newsworthy event. Shall I write it up for the morning show?'

'That's not funny, Igor, they'll just deny it. You know they don't permit publicity, especially about their fuck-ups.'

'So, we've got over two hundred TV, radio and Internet channels, and we can't broadcast a warning about a probable cyber-attack, because GRU will say it hasn't happened. I think that's pretty funny.'

GRU Headquarters, Moscow

'What do you mean it's coming and going?' General Anatole Lukyanenko, Deputy Director of the Main Intelligence Directorate, asked.

'Everything closed down for exactly two hours, then it started up again for fifteen minutes, and it's happened three times since then. At the moment it's down.' IT Director Sergei Golovkin had been called out of bed at midnight, and he wasn't feeling very happy.

'Can't our specialists discover where it's coming from and override it?'

'I've never seen anything like it. When the networks are down, nothing's working, nothing at all, so they can't even get into the system to look for the problem.'

'And when it comes up again?'

'Everything runs like a dream on the new Lee-Win transmission-encryption software. Then it just falls over again, no warnings, no errors, nothing suspicious, nothing to see. It just shuts down, as if someone flicked a switch. Somebody's in charge of our networks, and it's not us.'

'Have you informed General Gavrikov?'

'I can't find him. He's not answering any of his numbers, nor texts.'

Lukyanenko's mind went into overdrive. For the last few weeks he'd heard rumours of a cyber-attack being prepared. Nothing official, just the occasional word here and there, but it didn't appear on any of the events schedules and his boss, Gavrikov, had said nothing to him about it. It sounded like it was a clandestine plan and he didn't know who was involved. *It must be that plan, something's gone wrong and Gavrikov's gone missing.*

'Let me have a full report within the hour. I'll have to give the minister an explanation.' He was already working out how he could turn the problem to his own advantage. 'Send it to me by email.' It was easier to edit reports on the computer. This could be a defining moment in his career, he was determined to make the most of it.

Washington DC, USA
Monday, 19 July 2017

'Two days in a row. Welcome back, Viktor. Take a seat.' Mel Ritterbrand, US State Secretary, showed the ambassador to the same couch he'd vacated the previous day. 'What's so urgent you need to come here to see me so soon?' He paraphrased the Russian's question of their last meeting.

Kopeykin cleared his throat uncomfortably and sat forward on the edge of the seat. Ritterbrand noticed one of his knees trembling nervously. 'It's about our earlier discussion. I reported your comments to my superiors and they understand your concerns. This morning, instructions were given to terminate the exercises and return all troops and vessels to their homeland bases. We have no desire for our security practice sessions to be misinterpreted as belligerent activity. You can monitor these movements over the next few days to confirm my words.'

Ritterbrand said nothing. General Chillicott had called him an hour before to tell him to expect this news.

After waiting vainly for a response, the ambassador went on. 'I also checked on your reports of a cyber-attack supposedly being prepared by our Intelligence Directorate. I can confirm there's no truth in this rumour, we don't have the resources to engineer such an attack and we have no intention of trying to build such a capability. We have more important objectives to achieve, many of them working together with our international partners like yourselves.'

He sat back, trying to look more comfortable. 'As a matter of fact, my country is experiencing a wave of hacking right at this moment. The attacks are aimed at the Main Intelligence Directorate itself. Virtually every computer network in the department is affected by some kind of stop-start interference, and we can't identify the cause. Frankly, it's a national emergency which could damage the fragile stability of our global relationships. Can you interrogate your intelligence channels to assist us in our endeavours to find the cause? It would be greatly appreciated and a sign of our continually improving entente.'

'Stop-start interference, eh? Sounds tricky. I'll do what I can, Viktor. If I find anything out, I'll get straight back to you.'

'Thank you, Mel. I'll relay that encouraging news to General Lukyanenko, the new Director of the Intelligence Directorate.'

Ritterbrand's ears pricked up. 'General Gavrikov's been replaced?'

'So I was informed. It seems he suffered a fatal injury in a car accident last night. I understand he was being driven by a friend and they were both killed in the crash. Most regrettable, he was a highly capable officer.'

'That's too bad, coming on top of General Belinsky's resignation.'

'You already heard about that?'

Ritterbrand was enjoying the moment. 'Modern communications, Viktor. Shame, I hear he was a clever guy. I guess he was ready for retirement, making way for the next generation.'

London, England

It was Monday evening, and Dr Hugh Middleton was still in his office. Ilona had gone home to her flat in Bayswater. They both lived alone, he by choice and her because after being in England for almost six years, she was still looking for the right partner.

Middleton was in a melancholy mood. He was looking at the image of the woman, Tsunami, on his screen. He hadn't seen Esther Rousseau since July 2010, seven years ago. She was still just as beautiful as in his memory and he was still as much in love with her. In retrospect, he considered her last acts, to steal from him and try to blackmail him, to have been perfectly justifiable behaviour. She had expected him to deliver a result, namely a large ransom, and he had failed. Naturally, she had needed to compensate herself, and he was the obvious source of compensation; he would likely have done exactly that in similar circumstances.

But that was all water under the bridge. Since then, he had suffered the indignity of paying his debt to society, he had reorganised his life, reinvented himself and had created a successful, useful and profitable business, with an honest and dedicated partner. And now, due to a series of unpredictable and unimaginable events, everything he had rebuilt could suddenly be in jeopardy. First, Leo Stewart and Jenny Bishop, then Marius Coetzee, and now Esther had reappeared in his life. It was beyond a joke.

Fortunately, he convinced himself, *Ilona doesn't suspect anything. When this Lee-Win business settles down, it will all fade into insignificance and we can get on with our normal, banal, uneventful lives. Patience is all that's required.*

He closed his computer, switched off the lights and locked the front door. It was still bright and warm, and he decided to walk through Hyde Park on the way back to his apartment. In the darkened offices behind him, Ilona Tymoshenko's laptop received a message from Chief Inspector Lucas Meyer, head of the Antwerp SICAD.

SIXTY-ONE

**Shanghai, People's Republic of China
Tuesday, 20 July 2017**

Leo's mobile woke him at four on Tuesday morning. He and Coetzee were sleeping on camp beds in the hub room, having been alternately switching the A2 trigger programme on and off since Sunday evening. Patrice and Junjie were now comfortably ensconced in a nearby hotel. Han Wang Tāng and Hoi Lei had been expelled from the premises by the security officers under Bohai Cheong's instructions. They'd convinced the chairman that involving the police would be massively complicated and wouldn't serve any purpose. The two traitors could take their chances out in the cold. And Leo now had an interesting scar where a half-dozen stitches had closed up the wounds on his thigh.

He rubbed the sleep from his eyes and pressed the speaker button. 'Morning, Billy.'

'It's four in the afternoon here, a beautiful day, in more ways than one,' General Chillicott replied. 'How're you feeling?'

'Knackered, actually. It's been a pretty eventful couple of days.'

'But you guys delivered the goods. Congratulations guys, there's a lot of happy folk over on this side of the pond.'

Coetzee said, 'I was just a spectator, it was a one-man show, starring Mr Leo Stewart.'

'I got a call from Mel Ritterbrand at the State Department a little while ago. He'd just had a visit from the Russian ambassador. Mel told me a few interesting facts. First, they're bringing their military back home, the "exercises" have been terminated. I believe the guy, there'd be no interest in him lying when we've got GRU by the short and curlies.'

'You heard Wei's confession. He had instructions to send the upload to fourteen ex-USSR countries,' Coetzee said. 'You were right, that's what the army and navy presence was for, to persuade them to cooperate and rejoin the Soviet Club if they wanted their countries' infrastructures working again. It was a close call.'

'Too damn right it was. Anyways, he asked for my help to find the cause of a cyber-attack they're suffering at the Directorate. Can they find out where it's coming from?'

'I'm not sure,' Leo answered. 'I sent the upload back to the same hub address it came from. We figured it was GRU. It was signed as a Lee-Win minor upgrade, so they downloaded it without question. Now, we're managing their hub from here. It's a pretty neat situation, actually.'

'So you took control of the GRU hub? You outspooked the spooks? Boy oh boy, that's really neat, even for a non-techy like me.'

'It was a variation of the handover code that Abby worked out, just slightly different. I don't think there's anything they can do about it until we stop.'

'Well, even if they find anything, I guess I don't see them saying they suspect Lee-Win or China, when we've got a file three feet thick with the goods on Tsunami, Shen, the hidden Russian ownership, the A2 code and the confessions you sent me. That's a lot of shit. They're gonna want to kick this into the long grass and bury it.'

'Speaking of which,' Chillicott went on, 'I hate to be the one to break the news, but it seems your friend Shen Fu Liáng and General Piotr Gavrikov were involved in a fatal car accident last night. And the Minister of Defence has stepped down.'

Leo caught his breath and said nothing, and Coetzee replied, 'That was pretty fast work, even for the Soviets. They want to keep this whole thing quiet.'

'Right on, Marius. And Leo's gonna love this last item,' Chillicott paused dramatically. 'Remember the arm-wrestling? Well, I think I just won a round. The Russians want to cooperate with us in petitioning the UN Security Council to instigate an Internet security programme. How do you like them apples?' His uproarious laugh reverberated from the speaker, then his tone became serious. 'That Rwandan story was a timely reminder, catastrophes come in many guises. We just weren't expecting it to happen again so soon, or like this. But maybe we've learned a lesson this time around. And it was averted mainly due to you, Leo, thanks a ton. And about that job offer we discussed in San Diego, you want to chat?'

They said goodbye, and Leo was about to switch off his phone when General Chillicott added, 'By the way, you can stop the A2 triggering now. See you guys.'

Dubai, United Arab Emirates

'We just got a message from Leo Stewart. The cyber-attack has been thwarted, ACRE is an outstanding worldwide success.'

'*Wunderbar!* Finally, the news we've been waiting for, thanks and well done, Daniel. I'll call Julius right away. I'm going to ask for a telephone board meeting this morning to approve the offer. It could even be delivered today.'

'You should be thanking Leo, looks like it was him who managed to prevent the attack. It turns out that Han Wan Tāng in Shanghai was also a saboteur, what an incredible setup we got involved in. But Leo seems to have sorted it for good.'

'We certainly backed the right guy last March. We'll bear that in mind if our offer is accepted, we'll need a first-class team.'

'I hope that doesn't mean I have to stay here. I want to come back to Zurich, I'm really tired of all this good weather.'

London, England

Ilona Tymoshenko was catching up on her overnight emails. It was seven in the morning and the office was quiet. The message from General Chillicott was very satisfying. It seemed the dossier she'd sent to Leo Stewart had put paid to the Tsunami business, and he'd been able to foil the Lee-Win cyber-threat. She breathed a sigh of relief. This confirmed a report she'd received from her friend Ilya, that a hacking attack in Moscow that had disabled the GRU networks had been resolved. Ilona was sure the price had been the retreat of their forces from the borders of many countries, including her own.

No doubt Hugh will be fully informed when he comes in, she thought. *I'll wait for him to give me his own interpretation of events. Anyway, it won't be bad for our security business.*

There was also a long message from Lucas Meyer in Antwerp, with several attachments, including photographs. She went through the documents one by one, her pulse quickening with every disclosure, hardly believing what she was reading. The first revelation was that Elodie Delacroix's photograph had matched the image of a French woman called Esther Rousseau, who was wanted by Interpol. She had been on the run since 2008, when she'd been employed by a Swiss bank and was involved in a robbery with Raymundo d'Almeida, an Angolan psychopath who was killed in a shoot-out with the police in Marbella, Spain. The woman had reappeared briefly in 2010, linked to investigations into the murder of a pilot in Australia and several murders in South Africa.

The last item in Meyer's report was a *Daily Telegraph* article from six years before. The headline was, 'Peer convicted of Money Laundering'. The piece concerned a man called Lord Arthur Selwyn Savage Dudley, who had been sentenced to twelve months imprisonment for non-declaration of accounts with foreign banks. The original charges against Dudley also related to involvement in the South African murders in 2010, but these accusations were not proven and he had pleaded guilty to the lesser charges.

Meyer's notes stated that Esther Rousseau had never been found, and the police were keen to get any information that Ilona might have to open up the search. Photographs of Lord Dudley and Esther Rousseau were attached to the file. She recognised the woman's face from Ed's photo, and she also recognised Lord Arthur Dudley.

Ilona couldn't believe her eyes. She was staring at her partner, Dr Hugh Middleton.

Her mind digested these pieces of information: *Tsunami/Elodie Delacroix was Esther Rousseau, who was obviously a career criminal. As Dudley, Middleton seems to have known her. Coetzee was from South Africa, Hugh would never speak to Coetzee. He was a close friend of Leo Stewart who was born in Rwanda.* She remembered further items from the research she'd done for him: *Leo's mother wrote a book called* My Son the Hostage, *his aunt was a wealthy private equity businesswoman, Middleton-Dudley was keenly interested in Leo Stewart.* Where did all this lead?

Ilona had worked for almost twenty years in the information-gathering business. She knew that knowledge was power. The information she had received about Hugh was potentially damaging, even fatally so. It gave her power over him, great power. She sent a thank-you note to Meyer, adding that she had heard nothing further from Elodie Delacroix, but would contact him if she had any further information. Then she copied everything to the files in her personal tablet and deleted it from the office system. Hugh would never know what she knew, nor how she knew it. Not unless, or until, she decided to tell him.

An hour later, Middleton arrived at the office. 'Good morning, Hugh.' She welcomed him with a warm smile. 'Have you seen General Chillicott's report? It seems we won a great victory. Well done to your lateral thinking. I'll get you a coffee.'

'Thank you, Ilona dear, I'm delighted to hear it. Coffee would be welcome indeed.' He went into his office to read the report for himself. *She's being rather effusive with her praise,* he reflected. *I wonder what's going on in her mind.*

Shanghai, People's Republic of China
Wednesday, 21 July 2017

'Goodbye, Bohai. I'm sorry our visit wasn't exactly enjoyable.' Leo and the others were ready to leave for the airport, where they would go their separate ways, Patrice to Hong Kong to catch up on his business meetings, Junjie to Macau and Coetzee to South Africa. Leo was flying to London, then going up to Durham to spend some time with his mother.

'Wait just a moment, Leo. I have some interesting news to share. Today, we received a proposal from a Chinese hedge fund called Hai-Sat, to purchase Lee-Win and XPC. They already own MicroCentral, a Swiss processor company, and we believe it could create a very successful combination. I've spoken to our lawyers about the consequences of this conspiracy, and I intend to send them a full dossier with instructions to have the purchase of the company by that consortium of Russian criminals annulled. Not only did they commit murder to accomplish their strategy, but they broke the Chinese laws about foreign ownership.'

He turned to Junjie. 'Would you like to join me in getting back your father's company and making a transaction with this hedge fund?' He patted Leo on the shoulder. 'I have in mind a first-class CEO.'

So that's what Daniel Oberhart was doing at XPC, scouting for an acquisition! Leo laughed. 'Guys, whatever happens, our first priority is pretty clear. The A2 cell is still sitting in millions of networks all over the world. We have to find a way to neutralise it before someone else gets ideas.'

'Or,' Coetzee said, 'we could sit on it until someone decides to make the next global power play.'

Moscow, Russian Federation

Esther Rousseau was queuing at immigration control in Moscow Domodedovo International Airport. She'd seen the news on TV that morning of the death of General Piotr Gavrikov and an unknown man, and she knew exactly what it meant. Somehow, that interfering African nephew of the *putain*, Jenny Bishop, had managed to foil Shen, Piotr and the spooks at GRU. All day Monday she'd tried their mobiles, but both went unanswered and she'd feared the worst, not for them, but for herself.

Her plane to London was at eleven a.m. and there were plenty of flights from there to Dublin. The booking had been made in her maiden name of Esther Bonnard, which she had never revealed to anyone in the Russian organisation. Her French passport in that name had been renewed before she'd left for Dubai. Esther was always prepared for the worst.

Nervously, she handed the passport over, keeping her features expressionless, wondering how quickly GRU would spread out its tentacles. The immigration officer spent several moments checking it against his computer records. Finally, he stamped it and gave it back with a smile. '*Bon voyage*, Mademoiselle Bonnard,' he said.

She walked to her departure gate with mixed emotions, saying to herself, *When I left Arthur Dudley, I had only $50,000. Now, I have $300,000. I must be heading in the right direction.* Esther went to the bar next to the gate and ordered a glass of champagne. She figured she'd earned it.

EPILOGUE

Dubai, United Arab Emirates
August 2017

'Hi, Lynne, you look great.' Ed Muire helped her onto the back of Leo's Harley. She wrapped her arms around his waist as they roared along the coast road towards Club 27.

The place was quiet and they sat at the bar. Ed ordered two glasses of champagne, and the barman poured them into long-stemmed flutes.

'What are we celebrating? Something special?'

'Maybe. I had a long talk with Tom today. He was thinking of quitting, but Lee-Win have asked him to stay on. There's a big shake-up going on there after all the crap with Shen and Han. They had everyone fooled, so Tom's not getting any stick from Shanghai. The other thing is, it looks like we could be merging with MicroCentral, that's Danny Oberhart's previous company in Zurich.'

'Is that good?'

'I guess so, we'd be one of the biggest players around. Looks like a great opportunity. Tom likes the deal, that's why he's staying.'

'And what about you?'

'He offered to make me Senior VP of software development.'

'Wow! That's really cool. What did you say?'

'Told him I'd answer tomorrow.'

'What's going to change between today and tomorrow?'

'I wanted to talk to you first.'

She laughed. 'What's it got to do with me?'

'I was just wondering if you were staying for a while. If not, I wouldn't be too keen to accept.'

'So, the champagne depends on my answer?'

'You could put it like that.'

She picked up the glasses and handed one to him. 'Congratulations, Ed.' She clinked the glasses. 'And cheers, I'm willing to give it a try.'

Heathrow Airport, England

Leo was standing by the coffee bar in the arrivals hall when the young woman came through. She looked around the crowded hall, waving when she saw him walking towards her. He thought she looked beautiful.

'Hi there,' he said, kissing her on both cheeks. 'Welcome to the UK, thanks for coming.'

'Great to see you, Leo. Thanks for the invitation, it was a massive surprise.'

He picked up her two bags. 'Where are we going?' she asked.

'I booked at The Langham in Marylebone, Aunt Jenny stays there all the time. She says it's a great hotel, and it's near Regent's Park and Oxford Street with all the big department stores.'

'Sounds awesome. What's the programme?'

'I thought we could just hang out for a few days, get to know each other better under normal circumstances. What do you think?'

'I think that's a great programme. Let's do it.' She kissed him on the cheek and they walked together to the taxi rank.

London, England

Jenny Bishop was reading the proofs of the September edition of *Thinking Woman Magazine* in Dr Sue Clark's waiting room. She'd visited the doctor after returning from Spain and explained her recent symptoms of poor sleep, occasional nausea and listlessness. Sue had carried out a complete check-up, questioning her about previous health issues, illnesses and accidents, as Jenny dredged up the episodes from her memory. Then her assistant had taken blood and urine samples for testing. Now, a week later, she was ushered into the doctor's room and sat nervously, waiting for the results of the tests. Dr Clark finished consulting her dossier and looked up with a smile.

Jenny asked, 'So, what's my problem, Sue?'

'It's not a problem, Jenny, it's wonderful news. You're pregnant.'

THE END

AUTHOR'S NOTE

In 2015, when I began writing this story, there were just over 3 billion Internet users in the world. At that time, the Internet Society www.internetsociety.org, stated;

'Today we are at a defining moment in the evolution and growth of the Internet. Large-scale data breaches, uncertainties about the use of our data, cybercrime, surveillance and other online threats are eroding users' trust and affecting how they use the Internet. Eroding trust is also affecting the way governments view the Internet, and, is shaping the policy environment for the Internet around the world.

There are now, in January 2018, 3.8 billion Internet users, a 27% increase in 3 years, and the problems are increasing, not reducing. During that same period, after many years of research, two key technology components, as described in this story, were invented or discovered:

- A system of Automatic Constant Recurring Encryption, similar to ACRE, and

- The A2 Analog Back Door Attack, a physical modification to microprocessors permitting hackers to compromise a computer network.

Finally, just this month, four unrelated, independent groups of researchers have uncovered the fact that billions of chips implanted into computers and other machines since 1994, contain hackable entry points. https://www.wired.com. These attack points, named Spectre and Meltdown, are present in chips manufactured by INTEL, ARM and AMD and may take years to mitigate.

Sometimes truth really is stranger than fiction.

Christopher Lowery is a 'Geordie', born in the northeast of England, who graduated in finance and economics after reluctantly giving up career choices in professional golf and rock & roll. He is a real estate and telecoms entrepreneur and inventor and has created several successful companies around the world, including Interoute and Wyless Group. The Dark Web is based on his experience as one of the creators of The 'Internet of Things', the technology of remote equipment management. Chris also writes poetry, children's books and songs. He and his wife Marjorie live between London, Geneva and Marbella. Their daughter, Kerry-Jane, a writer/photographer, lives in London.

ACKNOWLEDGEMENTS

My thanks for their invaluable advice and assistance go to:

My nephew, Nick Street and his sidekick, Joe Baggaley, for introducing me to 'A2' and more importantly, explaining how it works. It actually exists and is a truly terrifying cyber-weapon.

My wife M and daughter K-J, proof-readers/red-liners and common sense contributors, for their patience and assistance in helping me get through Vol III and stay more or less sane.

Martin Panchaud, Mike Jeffries, Sig Ramseyer and other early readers for their honest opinions. Without readers, there is no point in writing.

And once again, especially to my publisher and good friend, Matthew Smith, for believing in my books and helping me to share them with the world.